RELATIVE TRUTHS

R. LINDSAY CARTER

ROCK AND FLOWER PRESS

First Edition Paperback

Cover design by Angelee van Allman

ISBN

Hardcover: 979-8-9859072-6-1

Paperback: 979-8-9859072-4-7

Ebook: 979-8-9859072-3-0

www.rlindsaycarter.com

CONTENTS

CHAPTER I

It is a well-known fact that the majority of domesticated cats abhor the thought of submerging themselves in water, whatever the reason may be. The same holds true for becoming completely covered in filth. An absolutely cringeworthy idea, that one.

And I, Cressida Curtain, was about to do both.

My ghastly predicament was not one I purposefully sought out but rather a misfortunate side effect of my latest job. Currently, I stood at the edge of a swamp in the middle of a forest. Up until now, I had been able to traverse through the woods with relative ease, avoiding the larger swaths of fetid water that dotted the forest. Despite the steady drizzle of rain that had started early in our journey, I had even managed to stay fairly dry, thanks to the graceful and stately evergreens that helped trap the precipitation higher up. But now, the only way forward was very wet indeed.

The trees offered less overhead protection where I now stood, the rain pattering down through the larger breaks in the overhead foliage to splatter upon what little solid ground existed, and the rest plopped rhythmically into the abundance of foul-smelling water that faced me. I could quickly feel the cold drops soaking into my fur, worming down to touch my skin. Even without the rain, this place was a dank hellhole; the plants, the tall trees swarming with bright green moss, and every piece of flotsam that lived in this stinking wetland seemed perfectly designed to ruin my day.

It was a nightmare for a cat.

And yet here I was. The reason for this was because of Grimm, my bounty hunting partner who also happened to be a huge shaggy dog. His superior nose had caught the scent of our latest quarry back in town, and Grimm had been tracking the smell on foot for miles now—taking us away from the comforts of civilization through first a vast field and then into the forest—in a relatively straight line, all things considered. But it seemed like the forest had now given way to the murky, smelly swamplands. And we weren't done with the trek yet, it seemed.

"Are you sure he came this way?" I asked my partner for the fourth time since the change from relatively dry forest to swampy hellhole.

He too stood at the edge where the forest floor turned to soup, smelling the last patch of ground. Straightening, Grimm shook his great black body, sending streams of rainwater off his shaggy fur in every direction, including onto me. I was already soaked and I'm sure I looked like a drowned rat, but I did not appreciate the added wetness from his carelessness. I flattened my ears at him. He didn't notice, but instead took one last sniff.

"For the last time, yes," he replied a little testily. "You can even see indents in the marsh where he took a few steps." Sure enough, once he pointed them out, I saw them plain as day. Clearly, the weight of our quarry and the victim he carried caused his feet to sink deeply into the muck. Grimm continued, "Are you through wasting time? It's only a little water."

"And mud, and dead, decaying things," I added, unable to keep the sourness from my tone.

It was bad enough that it had been raining steadily for the

last hour at least. It was only midmorning, but between the dense overhead trees and the heavy clouds there was a deep and oppressing gloom. Now I had to wade into this petri dish because it was too risky to skirt around the expanse of it in case Grimm lost the scent. As much as my feline sensibility screamed at me to stop, there was a murderer-turned-cannibal to find and money to collect at the end of this job. I could do this. I had to do this.

I tentatively placed a paw in the mire, pulling it out quickly and shaking it as I noticed the brown stain already soaking into my white toes. I tried again, batting the surface of the water carefully to see if it would make the going easier.

"Oh, for goodness sake," grumbled Grimm. He trotted over to me, and before I could ask him what he was doing, he planted his snout against my behind and forcefully nudged me into water until I was armpit deep. "There, now you are in. Should be easy going from here." The satisfaction was evident in his tone.

I thought I was wet before, but my submerged underside instantly soaked up the cold and putrid water. I should have turned around and clawed his eyes out, but I had been too stunned by his actions. And, if I was being honest with myself, he was right. The initial distaste was over, and I could move on now.

But I wasn't about to let him know that. "When this job is over," I stated calmly, "I am going to murder you in your sleep."

Grimm trotted right into the mire and trudged past me, staring straight ahead as if he hadn't heard me, but his tail gave a little wag, giving away a hint of glee at my words. "Hurry up. The trail is this way."

It was time to get my head back in the game, murky swamp or not. Our quarry, a young man from the nearby town, had apparently been cannibalizing his fellow townspeople on the sly for some months. Only last week, he had been caught red-handed by the locals. Unfortunately, he had given them the slip into the wilderness. But he still managed to sneak back to keep up his killing spree, often taking a solitary person in the dead of night. A bounty had been posted in Knobby Hill just yesterday, after a fifth victim had gone missing. We traveled to the town as early as we could this morning, hoping to be the first to answer the summons.

This town's genetic makeup was a bit of a hodge-podge but had a high percentage of indigenous folk. Vinland's original native population, collectively referred to as the Ancient Ones, had a fascinating background; their culture was steeped in a rich and powerful magical history, more so than any other known group of people. Among these talents were a larger-than-normal ratio of seers and world-walkers. When the first people from the old continent of Yuroba crossed the ocean and met with the Ancient Ones a thousand years ago, this country's nations as a whole decided it was time to emigrate to the next world, one they had handpicked as a sort of promised land. It was said that practically overnight, the Ancient Ones disappeared, leaving behind a few individuals from each nation to act as ambassadors to the new settlers and to carry on the traditions of their ancestors, lest they be forgotten completely. Those left behind became the Memory Keepers.

The settling newcomers had been mystified by how such a large population could just vanish overnight, and they wondered why it was done at all. But the remaining Indigenous had said it was because a powerful seer had once foretold great suffering on this world, as would happen on sister worlds, if the Ancient Ones had stayed. It was apparently enough of a warning to abandon a claim of thousands of years upon the country that would become Vinland. As it turned out, the remaining native population was well respected after the awe-inspiring display of magical talent the mass exodus had exhibited. Over the years, the population recovered, and indigenous folk could be found living in any town in Vinland. But some Memory Keepers chose to dwell together in towns that predominantly featured their rich culture. This town was apparently one such special place.

I had interviewed a couple of townsfolk before this lovely stroll Grimm had put us on. According to them, the young man had been a fine citizen until he began acting a tad strange a few months ago. Unfortunately, nobody had put his unusual behavior and the disappearance of the victims together until it was too late.

It was what his mother said that gave me the chills. She had grabbed my arm, her face drawn and ashen, her eyes shining with fear. "He has allowed the illness of the wechuge to invade his soul! My poor boy, he has always been weak of spirit. It is a sickness that has no cure, only insatiable hunger. For all our sakes, he must be put down." That was all I could get out of her before she turned, sobbing into her hands as she stumbled away and into her house.

Ick. I did not know much about wechuges, although I had heard of the phenomenon. From what I could piece together, it was akin to a magical disease that the Indigenous people of the Oracune region and surrounding areas were susceptible to. The infected became ravenous for human flesh, going to great lengths to secure their next meal, and with each victim they became more twisted and dangerous.

And now Grimm and I were tracking a possible wechuge to his murder den. What fun.

I sloshed through the water as fast as I could. The mud was cloying in some places, making the going extra slow, and my short legs were completely submerged. At some points, only my head and back showed, and I had to swim a bit with my front paws just to keep moving. Grimm had an easier time of it, considering the water usually stayed below his belly, but his increased weight did pull at him in a few spots, at times tripping him up. His efforts to regain his balance often involved a great deal of mud-flinging, often at my expense.

After what felt like hours, we reached the other side. I dragged myself out of the muck and glanced at my body.

Big mistake. My usually pristine white fur was a muddy, smelly mess. I even had mud splattered all over my back. I gave my body a shake, but the residue clung to me like glue.

"Oh, I am not going to enjoy cleaning this off," I moaned.

Grimm gave his shaggy body a shake, flinging more muck my way. "I think you may want to take an actual bath to get clean," he remarked. "It will take less time, and your tongue will thank you."

He had a good point, as much as I hated baths.

Grimm nosed the air, changing the subject. "The scent is really strong here. I think we are close. You may want to go the rest of the way on two legs." Grimm was referring to my special ability: shapeshifting from my natural cat form into a human. It was an inherited trait; only the members of my particular family line had this gift.

"Thank Freya," I muttered. This job had turned out to be more arduous than I had initially imagined, and we hadn't even reached the objective yet. "Let's do this." I took his advice, and by just concentrating, my whole body shimmered, lost form, and reshaped into a woman.

A very dirty, smelly woman with mud practically up to her neck.

"Oh, gross." I gagged as I looked at my mud-sodden trousers and boots. My cream-colored linen shirt was soaked through with spatters of muck, and my dove-gray custom vest was a mess.

Grimm let out a chuff, which brought my attention away

from my looks and back to the job at hand. Now that I was in human form, I could no longer converse with him, but he had a knack for getting his points across, language barrier or no.

"Right," I said with determination. "Lead the way!"

Grimm took me at my word and began a fast trot, searching with his nose for scent clues. I jogged after him to keep him in my sight. This went on for a few minutes before Grimm stopped, held his body rigid, and let out a short yet ferocious bark. And then he began running in earnest.

I sprinted after him, sure that our prey was just around a particular bend. I hastily snaked a hand into my vest pocket, fumbling for my silver cuffs as I increased my pace, the adrenaline pumping freely. I was so absorbed in keeping a fast pace while trying to ready myself for the arrest that I very nearly tripped over Grimm as he came to a screeching halt in front of me.

I let out a small curse as my naturally quick reflexes saved me from completely wiping out. Perhaps twenty paces directly in front of us sat what appeared to be a dilapidated shack, probably an abandoned hunting cabin based on its severely decrepit state.

"Why'd you stop?" I huffed at my partner. His only reply was to point with his canine nose. I looked in the direction his snout indicated.

The moss-covered door to the cabin banged open at that exact moment. I automatically crouched down to reach for my only weapon, which was lodged in my right boot. Hail Mary II—named thusly after the first had met its demise on a dark, crystalline world—would have stopped a criminal from doing me bodily harm, but I paused before fully extracting it. The scene before me didn't make sense. I expected to see a crazed cannibal running at us at full speed. Instead, a man appeared meekly in the doorway, his head held low and his hands hidden behind his back.

It wasn't until he began to shuffle forward very slowly that I saw what the problem was. Or, to be more specific, *who* the problem was.

"That slimy fur vomit," I seethed.

Our quarry was already handcuffed and was being guided out the door by my one and only work nemesis, Gavin St. Cloud. St. Cloud clearly had his pistol shoved against his captor's back, to produce such little fight out of the cannibal. I internally scoffed at that. Firearms were cheating in my book.

St. Cloud did not see us until he was entirely out of the cabin. When he did, his dark amber eyes grew wide for a moment as he took us in, and then he broke out in a smile, which I was loath to admit made his whole smug face quite handsome.

"Miss Curtain!" he called out with his usual charming demeanor. "Fancy running into you here. You are late to the party, however."

I scowled, seething on the inside. Of all the other bounty hunters in the world, why did it have to be St. Cloud? We had a not-so-friendly competition over hunts, and we were fairly evenly matched. I had gotten the drop on him a few times, but it still stung when he did it to me.

And apparently, this had been a doozy of a drop.

"How in Gaia's garters did you get here so fast?" I demanded, marching closer to him but staying out of distance from the wechuge. Grimm stayed right by my side, hackles slightly raised in a show of support for me.

"I took the old road that leads to this shack," St. Cloud's replied, unruffled, as he continued to guide the murderer away from the cabin. He stopped to give me a thorough once-over as soon as I was closer to him, making me recall my extremely disheveled state with much chagrin. His eyes came back to mine with a twinkle. "Did you not know about it? The locals clued me into it."

No, I had apparently not asked the right questions to be "clued into it." A huge oversight on my part. But I was not about to let the smug bastard know about it.

"We figured tracking his scent would be a more direct path," I said with as much haughtiness as I could muster while I tried to stare down my nose at him. He was taller than me, though, so the gesture fell flat.

Gavin laughed, not in a cruel way, as much as I wanted it to be. "Direct is right. Is that why you look like you rolled in the mud? You actually traversed the wetlands? Well, kudos to you. I certainly would not have been brave enough to take that route."

He started walking his captor again, away from the cabin and toward—now that I could see it—a very old and worn road through the forest. His custom black motorized carriage, or MC, was parked a few feet down the road.

"If you'll excuse me," he said conversationally, "I need to go and collect my bounty. I'd offer you a ride back to town, but, well, you are positively oozing filth, and I don't want to sully the upholstery in Scarlet."

Scarlet must have been the name he had given his MC. I had never heard him call it by name, but it was easy to deduce, given that the trim had been painted a bright red.

His comment stung. I followed after him, frowning deeply and willing myself to come back with a burning retort to put him in his place. Unfortunately, I was too dirty, too physically exhausted, too embarrassed, and too angry to let the creative juices flow at the moment. So, instead, I watched as he loaded the criminal into the back of his MC, locked it, and got behind the wheel. He closed the door and leaned out the open window toward me.

"Take care, and Miss Curtain? I do hope you are more presentable the next time we meet. Until then!" And with that last insulting remark, he started the vehicle and drove away, leaving Grimm and me behind in the proverbial and literal dust.

CHAPTER 2

Well, it wasn't our finest moment. Instead of backtracking through swamp, forest, and field, Grimm and I opted to walk the old road back to town to collect our wagon. As we trudged back, the rain ceased and the sun came out in brilliant rays, adding insult to injury. It only served to dry the muck into concrete upon my clothes and Grimm's shaggy fur, while simultaneously mocking me with its cheerful countenance. I felt anything but cheerful, and the previously moody sky had at least been an appropriate backdrop for my inner turmoil.

And to top it off, there was one more thing further souring my disposition. St. Cloud was right; I was reluctant to admit it. This way back to town *was* much faster, even without a fancy vehicle.

Once we made it to Humbert, my aging, dapple gray Percheron employee, and the wagon, I was lucky enough not to run into any of the townsfolk. I was frankly embarrassed by my hideous lack of grooming, and doubly so from being so easily outsmarted. There was no one I wanted to talk to, let alone be seen by, and with no cannibal in custody and no bounty to claim, our only option was to go home.

So, we did.

The concept of "home" was fairly new, at least for me. Grimm once had a home with a devoted owner, but that ended right before we had met, when his owner was murdered. Me? I never had a home while I was growing up. I could hardly call a rotting abandoned barn in the forest a home, even though I was born there. And after I had left its sanctuary, I was nomadic for a couple of months.

Until I ran into Fleurette. She took me in after I had been injured, and I adopted her as my human. When I decided to become a bounty hunter, she became my manager and offered to open her home to me when I wasn't on the road.

Even then, for nearly a year, I had hardly considered Fleurette's cobbled-together cottage my home. At best, it was "home base" in my mind. And even though Fleurette was my closest human friend, I still kept her at an emotional arm's length.

All that changed last summer when a particular bounty turned out to be two homeless and orphaned kids being chased by a literal bogeywoman. At a loss of what the right thing to do was, I took Fal and Wren back to the cottage, and shortly after that, I met that bogeywoman Annie Coddle myself, face to face and unsure if I would survive the encounter. I did, though, and something about that chain of events changed my thinking about homes and families.

Falcon Rambert, or Fal as he liked to be called, was a sixteen-year-old boy, and his little sister Wren was twelve. After the events of the summer, Fleurette was granted official guardianship of the orphaned siblings, and they now lived with her full time. However, due to the fact that someone out there might be looking for them for nefarious purposes, Fleurette had their names changed to keep their identities secret. Fal became short for Fallon and Wren was decided to be short for Renee, and Fleurette changed their last name from Rambert to Williams, which was her surname. The cover story was that the kids were her cousins, whom she was now in charge of raising.

Having lived by herself for years prior to all this, I had expected

Fleurette to have trouble adapting to the role of a mother figure for these two, but she excelled at it. And the kids were helpful and great to be around too, even if Fal initially had a tiny crush on me. This made things a tad awkward between us for a while, but he had quickly gotten over his schoolboy infatuation, and we now treated each other as family.

So yes, now Fleurette's home was officially mine, even if we weren't there all the time.

Sometimes our job took us far away from home, with at least a good day's worth of travel between places. The one positive aspect of this particular failed job was that the location was not terribly far away, so we made it back in just over three hours. A good thing too, considering that we had not bothered to stop and clean ourselves up before heading home.

Three hours of sitting in my disgustingly soiled clothing was enough to make my sour mood even worse. Cats do not enjoy stewing in filth, even when they have human bodies. By the time I pulled the wagon onto Rabbit Hole Road, I was more than ready to dive headfirst into the bathtub, clothing and all.

As I drove the wagon into the yard, I saw Wren outside collecting a bundle of freshly bloomed spring flowers from Fleurette's massive garden, probably for a bouquet. Fleurette's knack for plant magic meant that our property was always the first to produce blossoms, and Wren loved creating bouquets to add beauty and scent to the various rooms of the cottage.

She waved at me as she struggled to keep all of her prized stalks in her arms. She wore her favorite attire, a simple tunic over leggings, and her long, dark hair was braided down her back. The first time I had met Wren, she had been filthy, her sleek hair matted. Even now, seven months after rescuing them, my heart leapt with joy whenever I saw the kids clean and thriving, a far cry from when I first discovered them.

I gave her a halfhearted wave back as I parked the wagon in its usual spot. Wren approached me as I jumped down to tend to Humbert, who deserved to have the rest of the day off.

"Hey, Cressida! How did—" Wren stopped suddenly, a look of disgust rolling over her face. "Pee-yew! What's that smell?"

I grimaced as I tried to remove Humbert's tack. He was so tall, and I was petite, so it was sometimes a struggle. Add stiffened clothes to the mix, and I was having a hard time just lifting my arms over my head. "It's me. Oh, and Grimm too. Would you let him out of the back for me, please?"

Wren wrinkled her nose in revulsion, giving me a once-over. She ran around to the back and opened the wagon doors. Grimm jumped out and shook his body, making her audibly gag. His condition was better than mine, but he had plenty of mud flecks coating his sides and back, and his legs were thoroughly encased in dried brown muck. That, and his fur trapped the smell of rotten bog water even better than my clothing had.

"What happened to you two?" Wren wondered out loud. I said nothing, deep in roiling emotions of disappointment and despair. Instead, I concentrated on my inability to properly un-harness Humbert, which only magnified my feelings of failure.

After coming back and giving me a proper inspection, Wren declared, "You need to go get in the bath right away. I'll have Fal take care of Humbert for you. *Fal*!" This last part she yelled, making my head twitch at the shrill sound.

I sighed heavily and gave up trying to remove the tack with my grimy fingers. Wren was right.

"What about Grimm?" I asked her wearily, pushing a muddy lock of my hair behind my ear.

She shrugged. "I'll just go put these flowers in water and then hose him off outside," she decided, turning to do just that. "It's warm enough today."

She was right. March in the Oracune Region of Vinland was either rainy and miserable, or sunny and pleasant. You never knew which side of the coin each day would bring. And today happened to show both sides, as evidenced by our soggy morning.

Fal, having heard his name, had by this time come out of his bunkhouse to greet us. Since Fleurette's cabin only had two bedrooms, she had quickly transformed one of the nearer outbuildings into Fal's own living space. It worked well for the teen to have his own personal territory, yet be close to the main house and hang out with family any time he wanted to. Plus, he still had to share the only bathroom in the cabin.

Fal's black hair shone in the sun as he greeted me from afar. He had grown at least an inch since last summer, already several inches taller than my petite five-foot-three-inch frame. He stopped short, a perplexed look on his face at the sight of me.

I held up a hand in warning. "Don't. I know already. Can you please untack Humbert for me just this once? I need to do some damage control on *this*." I gestured to my disgusting body.

Fal smiled at that and nodded. "Sure thing, Cress. Don't forget the soap."

I grimaced in reply, before looking around. "Where's Fleurette? She inside?"

Fal shook his head in negation. "She went to town to run errands. Said she'd be back before dinner. I don't think she was expecting you home so soon." He gave Humbert a loving stroke on the nose, steering clear of the dirt spots I had accidentally wiped on him.

"Yeah, well, me neither," I grumbled. "Thanks for taking care of Humbert. I owe you one." I walked toward the house, passing by Wren, who had just exited sans bouquet. She held her nose theatrically as I passed by. I ignored her.

I entered the charming abode, stepping into the sitting room with its myriad plants and old furniture. I gingerly maneuvered around two chairs in the middle of the room to enter the hallway on the left-hand side. At the end of the hallway was the bathroom.

The bathroom was bright enough that I did not need to use the free energy to run the overhead light. Instead, I took a moment to scrutinize the bathtub faucet, hoping I could figure out how to make it work. I had never once had to use the facilities in this way, since any grooming I applied to myself as a cat kept my human personage and any attire I wore sparkling clean. It was a major perk of my unique heritage.

After a little trial and error, I had a steady stream of warm water coming from the showerhead. A shower sounded a bit less labor intensive than a bath, I decided on the spot. Without bothering to remove my clothes, I hopped into the tub, letting the water drench me.

I'll admit, the shower was not as bad as I was expecting. As the water rinsed the copious grime away, I was glad that I would not have to be removing it with my tongue instead.

Sometimes, things that sounded hideous to a cat turned out to be great as a human, and vice versa. I could see how a shower would be torture to my cat self. This love-hate relationship also held true for other experiences, like food. I loved mice and lizards to eat as a cat, but the thought of consuming them as a human turned my stomach. And as much as my cat self despised mint, it was pleasantly tolerable once I was human. Especially mixed with chocolate, which was also a human-only treat.

Once I felt nominally clean, I turned the shower off. I did not bother with a towel, but instead I shimmered down into cat form and gave myself a very brisk shake while the walls of the tub loomed around me. I was still quite sodden after the shake, but I figured an hour or so of grooming in the sun would take care of that. I hopped out to make my way to the front porch, leaving a trail of wet kitty prints in my wake.

That was where Fleurette found me, an hour later. I was still grooming myself, my fine fur trapping some of the leftover shower water, but I was mostly dry. Grimm had the same idea, as Wren had indeed hosed him down, and he had situated himself on the walkway in front of me. With his black fur, though, he was almost completely dry.

The first harbinger of Fleurette's impending arrival was Rupert. Out of the corner of my eye I saw the black silhouette of his body glide through the air, landing on the cottage roof with a loud caw. I ignored him. Rupert was the only family member that I did not particularly get along with. I wasn't sure why, but the crow rubbed me the wrong way. It did not help that I still didn't understand his relationship with Fleurette. Despite a difference in species, the two of them seemed to be able to communicate flawlessly, which was an enigma to me. I could understand him just fine in my cat form, but not at all as a human. The curiosity sometimes felt like it was killing me, but I refrained from asking. It was Fleurette's secret to share, and she gave no inclination she freely would.

Fleurette had ridden her bicycle to town and back. She was only seconds behind the crow in arriving home, like I had surmised she would be. As she wheeled her bicycle near the house, she stopped short with a sardonic grin at the two of us. I suppose I did look a bit funnier than usual, as my medium-length fur stuck up in some areas like overgrown cowlicks.

"Do I want to know the story?" she asked me, parking her bike. She was wearing pants, a rare occasion. Fleurette preferred billowy skirts of multicolored hues, but skirts of any color were problematic for bicycle riding.

In response, I glared at her with my bright blue eyes.

A year ago, I don't think I would have been caught in this compromising position. I had been pretending around her that I was a simple human shapeshifter, instead of the other way around. Shifters were rare, but a known thing, whereas cats with shifting abilities were basically unheard of. But my personal family line hailed from a witch's familiar, which gave us the ability to turn into humans. It was a secret that I had been told to protect with my life. As it turned out, Fleurette knew from the start exactly what I was and had been playing along to humor me. She was a member of a secret society that was dedicated to protecting my family: the Guardians of Glivver Society, or GOGS. I had told her repeatedly that the name was hokey, but considering it was five hundred years old, I didn't think they would be willing to change it.

Now, thankfully, I did not have to hide exactly what I was at home, even from Fal and Wren. They knew what I was too, and one day they would also be members of GOGS, like their late parents had been. It was rather liberating, being allowed to be who I was with my selected family.

I could have continued to groom myself and ignore my friend, but it wasn't her fault I was in such a terrible mood. So, I shifted. I glanced down at myself to see that my clothes looked a smidge rumpled and damp, but hey, at least they were clean.

"I've had a pretty terrible day, so wipe that smirk off your face," I said.

"Sorry, Cressida," Fleurette apologized, still smiling. "I just don't think I've ever seen the two of you look so bedraggled before."

Grimm, who was flat on his side soaking up the rays, lazily thumped his tail without moving another muscle. He must have agreed with her.

Fleurette continued, "How did it go?"

"How did it go?" I squinted my eyes at her. "I had to take a shower. A shower! Because Grimm and I took the stupid way through a swamp. Mud up to my eyeballs, practically! Can you imagine, Flo? And for what? Nothing, that's what. St. *Clod* beat us there and took the bounty."

At this, Fleurette turned solemn. She rushed over to hug me, stooping slightly to accommodate our difference in height and ignoring my personal humidity. Her hair, a lovely, hon-eyed-brown mass of curls and waves, swirled over me like a living cloud.

"Oh, sweetheart, I'm so sorry! I know that must sting." She knew the animosity I felt for Gavin St. Cloud.

"The worst part? It's my fault. I didn't ask the right questions and I decided to take a different approach. The wrong one. I let us down. I'm the worst bounty hunter!" All of my misery over the last few hours came crashing down over me. This was it. I'd never bounty hunt again. The dream was over. I leaked a couple tears onto Fleurette's cream-colored blouse as I clung to her.

Fleurette wasn't having it, though. She moved back, gripping my arms as she made eye contact with me. "No, no! You've been doing this for almost two years now, and you've done wonder-fully! We all make mistakes. They are learning experiences, every single one! I bet you'll never forget to ask those questions again, right? It's how we grow as people."

I sniffled. "Do you think so?"

She released me and looked down lovingly at my tear-streaked face. "I know so. Do you remember last April, when I made that custom batch of color-changing hair tonic for that one client? I thought I knew how to do the recipe from memory, but I added the wrong ingredient by mistake, and remember what happened?"

I chuckled. "Yes, I do remember that. Her hair turned green and wouldn't turn back no matter what. She had to grow her hair out and you had to give her a year's worth of the right tonic for free to make up for it."

She smiled at me, which made my heart lighter. "You see? Even your friend, who is older and wiser than you, makes mistakes. You better believe I don't try stuff like that from memory anymore!" She gave me a pat on the back and began to guide me inside. "Now, this will improve your spirits. I know how much you hate going into the Guild Headquarters, so I went today to pick up your mail for you. How does that go for cheering you up?"

"A long way!"

I belonged to the bounty hunters' guild, but only because it was a requisite to hunt legally. It was a boy's club, through and through. While I was slowly making headway in earning my fellow hunters' respect, I still hated having to go inside the building to check my cubby for mail every once in a while. Misogyny in the workplace was still very much a thing there, especially considering I was the only female guild member.

Fleurette laughed and fanned a single envelope at me before placing it on the side table in the living room. "Just one thing today. Don't forget to read it. Help me with some dinner?"

At the word "dinner," my stomach grumbled. Fleurette sure knew how to cheer me up.

After dinner had been made and consumed, Fleurette put Wren and Fal to work in the kitchen for cleanup and dragged me out behind the cottage into her greenhouse for what she called "practice." What did practice entail? Mostly frustration on my end.

"Try again," Fleurette encouraged.

Last summer, as I was rescuing the Ramberts, I had a spell placed on me by Annie Coddle that severely jeopardized my life while I was in cat form. At the same time, my shifting abilities developed an odd stickiness—for lack of a better term—which made it more difficult for me to shift. When my life was nearly snuffed out by Annie in person, I was able to use this stickiness to stay in my shimmer form and defeat her enough to escape with my life. And the stickiness went away directly after that.

I had since come to embrace a theory about that episode: the difficulty to shift was a defense mechanism that enabled me to stay as what was basically an amorphous being of energy—a form that best mimicked that of a true familiar's. During that particular encounter, I had stayed in this state for a matter of minutes, which was orders of magnitude longer than the fraction of a second I usually had.

While retelling this part of my story to Fleurette after my harrowing encounter, she had mulled it over and come to the conclusion that staying in energy form for an extended period not only saved my life at the time, but it could come in handy for the future and I must learn how to do it on command.

And thus, practice.

Shifting quickly was as natural to me as breathing, as it was imperative that nobody saw my transformation. Present company excluded, of course. Shifting slowly was unnatural and extremely difficult to do, as it turned out. But Fleurette would not be deterred.

I took a deep breath and focused on shifting from my human body to my cat body. As I felt the change begin, I tried to hold off fully transforming. My vision and hearing shorted out, but then became all-encompassing as my physical body converted to pure energy. As soon as that happened, though, I lost my grasp. My senses bounded back, and I looked at the world through feline eyes.

"Good!" Fleurette exclaimed. "That was better! You held it for two seconds!"

Shimmering back up to be able to communicate better, I groaned. "Flo, I've been doing this for almost seven months, and all I've achieved is a lousy two seconds? When are we going to call this a waste of time and end my torment?"

Fleurette pursed her lips at my defeatist attitude—not to mention my use of her nickname, which she knew I only uttered when I was annoyed with her. "I know that's the crummy day talking, because two seconds is a vast improvement over a tenth of a second. You should be rejoicing in your accomplishments! I want you to keep working. Every day. Even when you are out on a job."

I rolled my shoulders, feeling drained. "Fine," I reluctantly agreed. "Can we be done for today, though? I need some rest."

She pursed her lips at me. "In the spirit of ending your hard day, sure. But," she held up a finger at me, "don't think this is over. We don't know if your stickiness will return if you are ever in danger again. We can't leave that up to fate. You must do everything you can to stay safe."

"Yes, Mother," I agreed sardonically. She gave me a look, to which I replied with a grin to cushion the sarcasm. As much as I was feeling salty toward Fleurette for pushing me when I was not in the mood, I knew deep down she was right.

Probably.

She gave me her classic eye roll at my sass. "I forgot to mention earlier," she said, ultimately ignoring my mood. "I spoke with Lawrence today via crystal. He'd been looking into Gregory

Elkins for us."

"And?"

Elkins had been the man who first posed as Fal and Wren's great-uncle, and then posted Fal's bounty when his first tactic failed. He was the main reason why the kids were in hiding, with their names changed. We had failed to dig up anything about him ourselves, so Fleurette had turned to GOGS for help. Lawrence had been instrumental in making Fleurette their guardian.

"Nothing concrete. The man keeps an incredibly low profile, which is surprising. Lawrence did ask another GOG to do some research on dreamwalking, though, since we suspected Elkins may be the same man who lured Wren to Annie's dimension. It turns out it's very rare and not well documented, but dreamwalking into people's dreams is a form of mind magic, and most scholars agree that it is related to the magical subcategory of somnification."

"Somnification?"

"It's the ability to put someone to sleep," Fleurette clarified.

"That's it? That's all the info they were able to dig up?"

She shrugged. "What can I say? It's almost as if the guy hasn't existed for very long. And we can only guess that he might be the dreamwalker. For now, we'll keep feelers out for new information as it comes. Be patient."

A disgruntled noise escaped my throat. "I hate that word. Patient."

She smirked. "I'm well aware."

"Welp, I think I'll turn in early. It's been a day." I wasn't exactly tired, but the stress of the failed job, and now this disappointing lack of news about Elkins had pushed me over the edge.

A knowing nod was Fleurette's reply. As I left the greenhouse, I couldn't help but think it would be nice to have someone use somnification on me, just for the night.

I was over this day.

I stood in the cavernous crystalline room, back in Annie Coddle's prison dimension, unsure of how I got there. Lightning reflected off every surface, and it poured into my body as quickly as I flung it back out, the electric arcs dancing into the far reaches of the room. I witnessed through my all-seeing eyes every standing person being hit with the electrical force, flinging them back until they were all motionless. The last of the lightning spent, I resumed my human form and turned in a circle, staring at the destruction around me. Sure, some of the prone bodies were the enemy guards and Annie herself, but I also spotted Wren and Fal and Fleurette amongst the body count.

No, that can't be. Fal and Fleurette weren't there!

There was another prostrate person there too, a man I did not recognize but at the same time seemed so familiar to me. I cried out as I realized all of my loved ones had been hurt because of me. I took a step toward the man ...

"*I curse you, descendant of Glivver!*" Annie's booming yell echoed through the room and through my mind, stopping me in my tracks as a deep and crushing ache started up in my chest. The pain grew, like an entity carving space out within my soul, making me crumple as I clawed at the spot, needing to see the hole that now resided within me ...

"Cressida!"

I came out of the nightmare with a start, claws out as I sat upright haphazardly. One of my errant claws hooked into Grimm's lip, and he let out a tiny noise of pain. This helped cement me in the real world, chasing away the cobwebs of the dream. The ache in my chest persisted, however. That pain was very real, a wound upon my very soul that refused to heal.

My curse.

"I'm sorry." I breathed, trying to steady my racing heart and dull the ache. "Are you okay?"

Grimm nuzzled me affectionately. "I'm fine," he assured me. "You just poked me, but didn't break the skin. Are *you* okay?"

The ache in my chest began to die away. "Just a nightmare."

If only that were all it was. In truth, having Annie's curse thrust upon me was a very big deal, and one that had dire consequences. Glivver's prophecy, spoken five hundred years ago when she used her last earthly magic to banish the witch from this dimension, promised that as long as our lineage continued, Annie could never return. Annie's curse, however, made it impossible for me to find my one true love, and therefore made it impossible to have a child of my own, thanks to the highly meticulous biological rules our lineage placed upon us. With no child to replace me, the curse effectively ended Glivver's line once I died, allowing Annie to come back to our dimension to do what she pleased.

It was almost funny, in a macabre way. Up until being cursed, I could not have cared less about finding love. I wanted to live my life my own way, and only later on worry about passing on the legacy. I barely gave it a thought. Now that the choice had been stripped from me, my mind continued to dwell upon the lost opportunity. I regretted losing the one thing I had taken for granted.

Very few people knew about the curse, since Fleurette did not want to panic anyone. She was determined to break the curse before drawing attention to it. It was a secret kept by myself, Grimm, Fleurette, and the children. No one else knew.

Especially not my mother. I'd never hear the end of it. And

that was not something I needed on top of everything else.

I stood up and stretched my spine upward. Grimm took the opportunity to reposition himself on the sofa that had become our new sleeping spot ever since Wren had taken the spare bedroom for herself. Not that she wasn't prone to occasionally sharing—with me, at least. She claimed Grimm was too big and took up too much of the bed.

Speaking of Wren ...

"Wren is crying again," Grimm murmured. Sure enough, I could hear the quiet sounds of a child weeping. It was too low for a human to hear, but Grimm and I had superior ears.

I yawned as I stepped over Grimm's legs to jump to the floor. "'Night, partner," I told him as I shimmered up and tiptoed to Wren's door.

I knocked quietly, letting her know I was there, before cracking the door open. "Wren?" I softly said.

She snuffled in response, further proof of her crying. "I had a nightmare," she said with a wavering voice.

I sighed and walked into the room, shutting the door behind me. "Me too," I admitted.

It may have seemed like a coincidence, but Wren and I had nightmares for different reasons. Mine stemmed from almost dying and being cursed. Wren's nightmares involved her deepest fear: that in spite of us telling her she had not been in control of her body at the time, she had been the reason her parents were murdered.

I sat on the bed, reaching out a hand which she grasped strongly. Wren had adjusted surprisingly well to her new life, but this one emotional scar that she was able to hide in the daytime refused to heal at night. I knew how she felt, because as much as I put on a brave face, sometimes after an emotionally trying day my mask slipped and revealed the inner demons I normally kept so well hidden.

There was only one thing that could help to heal the two of us. Time.

Well, that, and cuddles.

"Can I stay?" I asked her. She nodded, knowing I could see the motion in the dark. Instantly, I morphed into my cat form, crawling into the crook made by her arm and body. Nestled in, I started purring as Wren stroked my fur in a pleasing manner.

This was our secret ritual that helped keep the nightmares at bay. We did not need this every night, but bad episodes still happened more frequently than I would have liked. I normally would never willingly lie in a human's lap and allow my fur to be touched, but Wren's hands were always gentle and soothing.

Soon enough, her hand drooped, and I became too sleepy to continue purring. We both drifted off to a deep sleep devoid of dreams, good or bad.

CHAPTER 3

The next evening, I chose to relax in my favorite spot, the loveseat in the sitting room, for a post-meal grooming session. I had taken the day off from everything to clear my mind from the horrible previous day. Still, vestiges of defeat occasionally wafted in and out of my psyche. I tried to ignore the sour mood that continued to hound me. Being extra clean was the right way to get my mind on track, though, and I was pleased to feel the silky softness of my pristine fur under my tongue. Finishing up, I sighed with contentment and settled in for a pre-bedtime nap.

From the kitchen, Fleurette called out to me, "Cressida, did you ever check that mail?"

No, I hadn't. I had blissfully forgotten that blasted envelope's existence. I turned my ears away, annoyed at the interruption, but made no other move. That envelope came from the guild, and right now I wished to pretend that I did not have a job with that guild at all. My profession was a problem for tomorrow. Or the next day.

Fal was next to me on the loveseat, working on a bit of schoolwork. Wren sat across from me in the old wingback chair, sitting sideways with her feet dangling over one of the arms. She read from a small book in her lap. This would have been a normal everyday scene if not for her unusual gift. Wren was a projectionist, meaning she could cast images at her will, including changing her own appearance and even projecting herself and others into different dimensions. She enjoyed creating living embodiments of the stories as she read, so at the moment our sitting room was slowly transforming into a lush rainforest, complete with vines hanging from the ceiling and exotic butterflies flitting through the air. As fantastic as all this sounded, we were so used to it that none of us batted an eye, even when a tropical bird landed on Fal's shoulder to inspect his homework.

Fleurette's voice must have cut through Wren's reading fugue, and she noticed I did nothing to respond to the mistress of the house. "Cress, did you hear Fleurette?"

Bless her, she was still learning cat body language. I ignored her too, although I did add a slight tail flick for her interruption.

Grimm, who was just below me on the floor and intently watching an imaginary tapir wander into the hallway, raised his head. "What are they saying, CC?"

As much as I wished to ignore him too, it was clear I would not be getting a moment's peace until I answered him. I cracked an eye open to see his sunflower gaze on me.

"Fleurette picked up a piece of mail from the guild yesterday," I responded with flat emotion.

Grimm snorted air out of his nose. Actual mail was fairly uncommon. Usually, our jobs came from the notice board outside of the courtyard, and on occasion we were personally asked for via my enchanted message mirror.

"Are you going to see what it is?"

I closed my eye, dismissing the subject. "I can't possibly see why I should at this moment."

I heard Grimm hoist himself fully to his feet. What I did not expect was his great snout nudging into my side. I flattened my ears as my eyes went wide. My claws came out to anchor myself into my seat. "Hey, cut it out!"

He play-growled at me softly. "I know you want to pretend you don't have a job right now, but we haven't checked the mail in a couple of weeks. What if it's an important bounty?"

I stretched, flashing my claws as I spread my toes. "Fiiiine," I muttered to him. "But if it's nothing at all I'm going on hiatus for a couple of days. And I'm taking a nap in peace!"

I shimmered up into my human form, tucking an errant strand of black hair behind an ear. Glaring at the large dog and waving away some butterflies, I moved over to the side table and picked up the envelope.

"ATTENTION: CRESSIDA CURTAIN," it read on the outside in bold letters, "CONTENTS TIME SENSITIVE. OPEN IMMEDIATELY." It was dated a week ago.

Muttering under my breath, I tore the envelope open and removed a single piece of paper from within.

To the Recipient of this letter,

The client I represent is in need of special assistance in locating a specific criminal. If you have received this letter, it means that you have been acknowledged as one of the best in your field, and this letter is for your eyes only. There is a very significant reward for anyone who takes on this case. There will be a briefing on Wednesday, March 10th at 6:30 p.m., location Knobby Hill Courthouse, Room 145, Knobby Hill, O.R. If you are located outside of the Knobby Hill jurisdiction, your travel fees will be compensated upon arrival. All questions will be answered at this meeting. Attendance is mandatory for participation in this bounty. Please bring this letter with you, otherwise you will not be admitted. Do not be late!

Respectfully,

T.A. Babcock, Esq.

Babcock, Brothers, and Hoterson

I reread the letter as my brain hadn't quite clicked on yet. I was considered one of the best in my field? My heart made a squeal of delight at the massive compliment. I had only been a bounty hunter for about two years now, and, since I was young, petite, and female I had to work much harder than my colleagues to get any recognition. To receive the chance at this bounty reaffirmed my love of this job. To hell with Gavin St. Cloud for making me feel worthless.

Did I want to pursue this bounty? As ambiguous as the letter was, yes. Yes, I did.

I kept reading to find the details on when the meeting was taking place. March 10th. Why did that date sound so familiar? A feeling of dread settled in my stomach.

"Fleurette," I called out, my eyes still glued to the letter. "What's the date today?"

From the kitchen, she replied, "It's the 10th! Why?"

"Freya's furs!" I muttered as I hastily withdrew my pocket watch. It felt like an eternity before I had the object in my hand, and I nearly dropped it as I fumbled to open the face, my revived heart working double time.

The watch face read 6:13.

"*Grimm!*" I screeched, causing Wren to let out a small squeal as the rainforest vanished, Fleurette to rush into the room with sopping wet hands, and Grimm to jump into the air with a slight bark. I ran a hand through my hair, flustered beyond words.

"What on earth is it, Cressida?" Fleurette asked with only a pinch of her usual calm demeanor. She dried her sudsy hands on her skirt, alarm filling her beautiful brown eyes.

I raised the letter in my hand. "Big bounty. Important meeting. Starts in fifteen minutes. Can't be late." I spoke disjointedly as I waved the paper in the air. Grimm trotted to my side, his ears pricked forward with curiosity and concern at my behavior.

My friend snatched the letter from my wild hand and gave it a quick once-over. "I see," she said, returning to her tranquil state. She looked me in the eye. "Right. There's time. Borrow my bike. It will go faster than cat legs."

My mind flashed to Fleurette's bicycle. She was much taller than me, with lovely long legs, which meant one thing. "Your bike is too tall! I can't stay upright on it!" I stammered, gesturing to her vertical advantage over me.

Wren piped up encouragingly, "You can borrow mine!"

I glanced at her. She was still shorter than me, but only by a bit. I had ridden her bicycle a few times before, mainly because Fleurette insisted I learn in case of emergency. Bless Fleurette and her smart foresight.

Fleurette nodded. "Yes, do that."

Without another word, I sprinted toward the door, ready to hit the road.

"For Hecate's sake!" Fleurette ran after me. "Don't lose your head, Cress! You'll want this!" She thrust the letter back at me. I grabbed it and stuffed it in my vest pocket. She clutched me by the shoulders and looked me deep in the eyes. "Breathe," she softly commanded.

I nodded, perhaps a little tersely, but did as I was told. Once I had sufficiently calmed down, she let go of my shoulders. "Go. But be careful!"

Without another word I sprinted out the door to locate Wren's bicycle, Grimm hot on my heels.

Our cottage resided about two miles down Rabbit Hole Road, which meant it usually took about ten minutes to get to town via bicycle.

I made it in eight.

Granted, I very nearly killed myself on a pothole that I somehow did not see until it was too late to avoid it, and it was highly possible I may have bent something on the frame. I would have to pay to get that fixed, since Wren relied on her bicycle for transportation to and from school. But, by the time I pulled up to the stately courthouse that was the crown jewel of Knobby Hill, I was in one piece and still on time.

I hastily parked Wren's bike on the lawn and fleetingly hoped no one would steal it. Racing up to the courthouse doors, I flung them open and ushered myself and Grimm inside. A guard stood within the foyer, a smooth rounded crystal in his hand. I was a regular within these walls, and I knew the drill, despite wishing to speed through protocol. Nevertheless, I bent and removed Hail Mary II from my boot and placed it in a tray on the table while the guard approached to frisk me for any dangerous weapons I hadn't revealed.

He went slowly, waving the clear orb up and down my body. I tapped my foot impatiently and pursed my lips. When he straightened and nodded, I didn't even stop to thank him, but bolted down the corridor that led to the meeting rooms.

"No running in the courthouse!" he yelled after me. Grimm and I ignored him.

We rounded a bend in the hallway and kept going straight. I was not as familiar with this section of the building and had to keep checking the door numbers as we went. Finally, at the end of the hall, I spied two rather large men stationed outside of a door. This must be the right place.

I halted in front of them, panting heavily. One man stood in front of the closed door—as I suspected, it had ROOM 145 in golden letters directly above it—and the other was slightly ahead of it, blocking my way with a stony face. He had a clipboard in his meaty hand.

This living wall of muscle stared at me impassively, apparently unimpressed by my entrance.

"Did I make it in time?" I asked between breaths, hoping

some levity would soften his features and make him appear more human.

His slight scowl did not waver. "Name," he grunted, ignoring my question.

I straightened, trying to control my breathing. "Curtain. Cressida."

Stone-face glanced at his clipboard. He clicked a pen in his hand to make a notation on the paper attached. Still staring at the item in his hand with a small scowl on his heavy brow, he made another one-word demand. "Invitation."

"Oh, right ..." I patted at my vest pockets, a momentary blinding panic overtaking me at the thought that the invitation might have slipped out in my mad dash to get here in time. But no, I finally felt the crisp edges within one of my pockets. I pulled it out with a flourish, brandishing it in front of Stone-face's nose.

He took it, flipping it open to check its authenticity. Time was still ticking down and I had yet to learn if I could go in. My whole body buzzed with anticipation. Finally, he made a low grunt. "Go on in."

Relief flooded me. I breathed a thank you as I sauntered past, Grimm matching my pace as soon as I started to move. But Big Guy #2 didn't budge as I approached him. Instead, he glanced at Grimm with a frown.

"No dogs allowed."

I huffed a breath. "But he's my partner!" I countered.

Big Guy #2 raised his eyebrows in a mocking sort of disbelief. "Is his name on the list, Huck?"

"Nope." That was from Stone-face. "Just C. Curtain. No dog."

The door blocker turned his attention back to me. "If he isn't on the list, he isn't getting in. That's the rule."

"Please?" I tried nicely, just short of batting my eyelashes.

Big Guy #2 actually rolled his eyes. "Look, lady," he said firmly. "The meeting starts in just a few minutes. Either you go through this door alone, without your dog, or you both go back through the big doors at the front of the building and get out of my hair. I don't really care which choice you take. But it's now or never to make that decision. So, what's it going to be?"

"Oh, well, when you put it so nicely," I spat out. I turned to Grimm. He had been following along with the conversation as best he could, although I knew he was not understanding the nuances. "Sorry, partner," I told him. He let out a very faint whine, his three-quarter pricked ears flopping down dejectedly. I sighed. "Go wait in the lobby. I'll fill you in after."

Grimm's golden eyes held mine for a couple of seconds before he turned quickly and padded down the hall and out of sight. I caught the two men sharing a "look-at-the-crazy-lady-talking-to-her-dog" expression before the door blocker moved to the side and opened the door for me.

"Thank you," I said with a hint of snideness as I breezed past him and entered the room. In response, he closed the door without a word.

Now that I was finally inside, I could take a breath of relief, although I did miss having Grimm by my side. I quickly surveyed the room. It had a classroom feel to it, with a table at the front and off to the side, and a chalkboard front and center. Two columns of tables faced the blackboard, each column containing three tables, and each table big enough for two people to sit side by side. It looked like twelve bounty hunters had been invited to this shindig, and it would appear I was the last to arrive. In fact, all of the tables were full, except for one empty seat off to my left at the middle table. Before I moved forward, I took a look at who I was sharing a table with.

And then I groaned audibly.

"Miss Curtain," Gavin St. Cloud called out to me amiably. "I saved you a seat!"

CHAPTER 4

W hat had I done to anger the gods?

St. Cloud gave me a rather over-the-top smile as our eyes met. I was positive my dismay only made him happier. He patted the chair next to him.

I did a quick scan of the room again. As much as I hoped an empty chair had magically appeared since my last perusal, there truly were no other available seats. I gritted my teeth and scowled as I trudged over to the middle table. I stood before him, taking an oddly perverse pleasure in the fact that for once *he* would have to look up to *me*. Before I could think of anything to say, however, a small door to the left-hand side of the room near the blackboard opened and a portly, balding man wearing glasses and a suit trudged out. He was followed by a second man, whom I gave a cursory glance at. I noted a bald head and muscles before bringing my attention back to the first man, who plopped down a stack of folders on the front table. To the room in general, he called out, "Alright, everyone, take a seat. The meeting will soon start."

I was the only person standing, so I suppose that comment was directed at me. Not wanting to draw even more attention to myself than I already had, I sat facing forward and purposefully not looking at St. Cloud. I refused to give him the pleasure.

But as the bespectacled man took some time to arrange his papers and prepare for the meeting, I asked in a low voice as I kept my head forward, "How did you know I'd be here?"

Gavin huffed a breath of amusement. "Logic. Seeing as how *I* got an invitation, it made sense for you to get one too, since you are just a step lower than me."

I whipped my head around at him, fire brimming in my eyes. So much for not looking at him. "Excuse me?" I hissed.

He smirked at my anger, which only maddened me further.

I had to set the record straight. "If I recall correctly, there's been eight jobs we've competed for, and I've beaten you to the punch on four of those. That makes us even."

"Nine. Did you forget about yesterday?"

I wrinkled my nose in distaste.

St. Cloud nodded. "That means I'm one up, which makes me the better hunter."

"Oh please." I focused my attention back to the front of the room. It looked like the meeting was about to start, considering that the man was nearly finished neatly stacking his folders. The second person had dragged a chair over next to the blackboard and sat down. I scrutinized him in more detail. He was certainly a bigger man than the first, both in height and build. He wore a simple black tee that showed off impressive arm muscles. His head was completely bald, and it gleamed under the overhead lights. His face was hard, and there was something about his countenance that made me uneasy. No longer wishing to watch this man, I turned my attention back to Gavin, who had dug something out of his pocket and placed it on the table in front of him.

Once his hand moved away I could see what it was. "What's with the pocket watch?" I asked him under my breath.

He smiled fondly at it in response as he positioned it in front of him to sit open on the table. "It was a birthday present to myself. Do you like it?"

I shrugged. It looked old; the brass enclosure was worn away in spots and the face was old-fashioned in appearance. "It's okay, I guess."

Before I could add anything more, the man in the suit strode to the front of the blackboard. It was time for the meeting.

"Thank you, gentlemen," he paused as he made eye contact with me, which made me squirm a little, "and lady, for attending this evening.." I hated when it was pointed out that I was the only female bounty hunter in the area. The man continued, "Especially those of you who had to travel from out of town. We appreciate the Northwest Bounty Hunter Guild for providing accommodations for all of you who needed it. My name is Thomas Babcock, and I represent Mr. Lightfoot of Lightfoot Shipping Industries. My client is a very important man, and he wishes for this particular incident to stay out of the knowledge of the public eye. Hence the purpose of this meeting and your assistance in the matter."

Mr. Babcock opened a folder he held before continuing. "To get to the point, my client hired an accountant last year in September. In November, it was brought to Lightfoot's attention by other employees that funds were going astray. By last month, February, it was clear that somebody was embezzling, and just as Lightfoot was about to confront the new accountant, he disappeared. He took with him a little over half a million dollars."

St. Cloud whistled low at the number.

I frowned. "All this for an embezzlement case?" I said under my breath. Sure, that was a lot of money, but it still did not add up in my mind.

Mr. Babcock continued, "Not only did he steal a small fortune from Lightfoot Shipping, but he also started a fire in his office building to cover up his crime. Unfortunately, the blaze was out of control and the fire ended up killing three other office workers."

Oh, well, this made more sense now. An arsonist who killed people would warrant a bigger investigation.

"Naturally, we made inquiries on our own to discern his whereabouts, but the guilty party has done a very good job of covering his tracks since the fire. He has gone to ground, and his whereabouts are completely unknown."

Babcock cleared his throat. "This is where you come in. My client did not want to publicly post a bounty due to his desire to keep all of this quiet. And he only wants to hire the best on this assignment. The guild was kind enough to send my firm a list of twelve of the absolute first-rate hunters in all of Oracune Region. They made this list based on percentage of successful bounties, as well as average time per bounty and range of skills. Gentle-men"—again, he looked at me while I slightly died inside—"and lady, you are it. This is a huge honor, as this case is for your eyes only."

As Babcock paused, a small murmur went through the room.

"We're number one, we're number one," St. Cloud softly chanted beside me.

I smirked, although I tried to hide it. No sense in letting the clod know he amused me slightly.

"And so," the lawyer continued as the murmurs died down, "here is the case. My client is hiring you to track down the guilty party, apprehend him, and deliver him to Lightfoot's associate, Mr. Hobbs here." Babcock flourished an arm toward the bald muscle man sitting next to the blackboard. Hobbs tipped his head slightly at his acknowledgement.

Babcock continued, "Mr. Hobbs will then take it from there and bring the guilty party ultimately to justice. He must be *alive* and in good health, or your contract will be void. Any deviations will also render payment for your job void.

"I must warn you, though. The guilty party is non-magical, but he is to be considered dangerous."

I heard a very faint buzzing sound, like a tiny bee trapped in a glass. It was so weak that normal human ears would not have picked up on it. I looked around briefly before finding the source: St. Cloud's pocket watch. I stared at it for a second, noticing that not only was the time off by a few minutes, but the hands seemed to have stopped working altogether, before starting up again.

I smiled to myself, amused that Gavin would purchase such a worthless piece of junk as a present.

I dragged my attention back to the lawyer, who continued speaking, "Because of this and the requisite that he be delivered alive, my client is preparing to pay a sum that goes above and beyond your normal bounty reward." Babcock paused with a small smile on his lips.

One of the hunters in the front row took the bait. "How much?"

Babcock held up a finger. "Before I say the amount, there are a couple of caveats. First, this payment will only be given to the hunter who brings our quarry in safely. We will only be paying this amount once, so if you decide to team up you will have to split the bounty. Having said that, for anyone who signs the contract tonight, we will also be giving you a travel stipend of $1,000. This will be used to pay for any expenses you may run across during the job, including food and lodging if you need it."

The susurrations in the room grew loud.

"$1,000 just for accepting the job?" I muttered, mostly to myself, but St. Cloud heard, as he turned to look at me. That amount alone was worth more than many of the bounties I had acquired in the past. "If that's the signing bonus, what could the bounty possibly be?”

To answer my question, Babcock spoke again. “Now that we have that out of the way, the hunter who collects the bounty shall receive $15,000.”

The room exploded with masculine voices filled with disbelief and joy. Me? I was struck dumb by the amount being offered. I had never heard of a single bounty being worth that much.

Babcock held up his hand to quiet the room. “Now is the time to decide. If you choose not to accept the job, I will ask you to sign a nondisclosure agreement. The agreement will have a small charm placed on it, ensuring that you will forget all of the details of the bounty, including my client’s name, the details of the criminal and incident, and the sum. I will pay for any travel expenses you incurred to get to this meeting, but nothing more, and you walk away after that. If you would like to accept the job, I will have you sign a normal contract and you can get started right away. The last thing I have for you is a folder with all the information we have on the guilty party. This is all the help you will be getting from either me or my client, so use this information to the best of your ability. Be aware, everyone, that there will be fierce competition and I cannot guarantee that you will be the hunter to finish the job. Also remember that this may be a dangerous operation. Babcock, Brothers, and Hoterson, and Lightfoot Shipping Industries, shall not be held liable for any injuries or death on the job. Funeral expenses will not be paid by either company, so make sure your insurance is up to date with the guild if you choose this mission. Please weigh the pros and cons carefully before you make a decision. I will be at this table with NDAs and contracts to sign. Please come see me when you are ready to make a decision. You won’t be able to leave this room until you do.” With that, Babcock turned back to the table and grabbed the stack of folders. He passed half of the stack to the table in front of us with instructions to take one per person and pass the rest behind them, before heading over to the other side of the room. After passing the folders out, he sat at the table, neatly stacking his documents into two piles. Hobbs rose from his chair to drag it over nearer to Babcock.

St. Cloud let out a breath. "Well, that was certainly an uninformative briefing."

I was inclined to agree, seeing as we were given just the basic information and not much else to go by. I was still reeling at the dollar signs, however. And I wasn't about to admit I shared an opinion with my nemesis.

"I suppose that means you'll be passing it up, then," I commented. "Shame."

"On the contrary, I'm more intrigued than ever! He must be a highly dangerous man to justify such a significant reward," Gavin declared, although his brows crinkled into a tiny frown as he stared at his pocket watch. Perhaps he'd noticed that it wasn't working properly.

The folders made their way back to us. St. Cloud grabbed one and handed another to me before passing the last two behind us. He opened his folder right away. "He certainly looks harmless enough," he commented as he scanned the first page. I looked at the folder in my hands. The word CLASSIFIED was stamped on the outside. I opened it.

The first page was a blown-up copy of a speculograph—a picture produced with magic—of a man from the chest up. It lacked the usual crispness of a well-made speculograph, the black and white quality being grainy. I inspected the picture. The man it showed appeared to be in his mid to late forties, with thinning hair, a longish, tired face, and small, rectangular glasses. He was smiling, but the smile looked fake. Based on the pose and the forced smile, I surmised this was a picture taken for work.

He looked like any other mundy who worked for a living. I certainly couldn't see anything dangerous based on his appearance. But if anyone was aware of the old adage that looks can sometimes be deceiving, it was me. I could count on my fingers the number of people who actually knew what my true shape was.

I flipped the spec over, finding the back side blank. I trained my eyes on the next sheet, which looked to be the official dossier for the bounty.

"WANTED FOR EMBEZZLEMENT AND MURDER," the paper read, "ROGER CURTAIN."

CHAPTER 5

I never knew my father. My mother, Belinda, left him after she was stuck in cat form while pregnant with me. She was very tightlipped about my father anytime I asked about him when I was a curious kitten. I had eventually stopped asking questions.

So, the only pieces of information I had about my father were the following: he was a mundy, he was an accountant, and his name was Roger Curtain.

I stared at my father's name on the report for much too long, not moving. I think I was a bit in shock.

"Problem, Miss Curtain?" St. Cloud's voice cut through my shellshock.

Still looking at the paper in my hands, I let out a faint, "Hmm?"

"Your face matches your hair," he mused. "At least the white bits of it. Are you well?"

That dragged me from my stupor. I grasped a chunk of my platinum hair to inspect, ignoring the streak of black in the front. "My hair isn't white," I muttered at him.

"Still, you're paler than usual. This man isn't a relation of yours, is he?" Gavin grinned at me. He now held his pocket watch in his hand.

I scoffed, perhaps a bit too forcefully. "Of course not. Why would you think that?"

He gave me the look one reserves for lying children and idiots. "The last name, perhaps?"

I waved my hand dismissively. "There must be several Curtains out there. It has to be a common surname."

It was his turn to scoff, but he did it with a grin on his face as he peered at his watch.

I shook my head. "What is your fascination with that thing?" I asked him.

He shrugged. "It's my newest acquisition and I enjoy looking at it. So tell me, Miss Curtain, are you planning on taking the job? I would so very much enjoy getting ahead of you by two bounties instead of one."

I took a moment before answering. The bounty had to be my father. It had to be. Even if Curtain was a common surname (which it wasn't; I was sure of that), I doubted there were many Roger Curtains running around in this vicinity, or anywhere else in the world, for that matter. This begged the question: was he guilty of the crimes this dossier stated he committed? I would have liked to think that my mom's true love was a more decent person than this.

I studied his face once more. There was something about the shape of his eyes and his mouth that seemed slightly familiar. It was not strong, but yes, I could tell there was some family resemblance. In my gut, I needed more answers. What was he like? How did he get himself into this predicament? Well, there was one way of getting answers. I couldn't go forth and look for him on my own; I would forget everything I learned about tonight because of the NDA. But if I took the case I could answer some of these burning questions, and get to the bottom of this predicament. That decided it for me.

"Yes, I think I will," I answered, my tone smug. "I need to even up the score again."

St. Cloud smiled at me, and once again I was reminded of why I had become so tongue-tied around him the first time we met. Then he opened his mouth and destroyed the illusion. "Excellent! Yesterday was fun, but this will be even better!"

At the reminder of how yesterday went down, I frowned at him. He did not seem to notice but stood up and held out his hands to usher me toward the lawyer. "Ladies first," he said magnanimously.

Narrowing my eyes at him, I vacated my seat. Turning my back to my obnoxious nemesis, I stepped up to the table just as a bounty hunter in front of me finished signing his contract.

Babcock glanced up as I approached. He plastered on a fake smile for my benefit. "Ah, yes, the lady of the group! Tell me, Miss ..." he glanced at the clipboard to find my name, "... Curtain, what will your answer be?"

I affirmed my desire to take the job. Mr. Babcock produced the contract for me to sign. I read it over carefully. There was nothing unusual that I could place on the paper before me; it seemed to be a well-crafted agreement written by the lawyer himself. Taking a second to breathe deeply, I signed it. As he pulled the contract away from me, he mused aloud, "Curtain, Curtain, it's not a name you hear every day, is it? This isn't your uncle or something, is he?"

I shook my head. "No, sir," I lied. "It's just an amazing coincidence."

"Well, do be careful out there, young lady," he admonished unnecessarily. I gritted my teeth but did not reply. I was used to well-meaning older men looking out for me, as unwelcome as it was. I merely nodded and walked away.

I glanced around the room. St. Cloud, the only man I knew here, still had to sign the contract. But he was chatting with another hunter off in the corner. Nobody else bothered to approach me for camaraderie, and I wasn't keen to exchange small talk with strangers anyway, so I decided it was time to make my exit. Better to get an early start, after all.

As I was leaving, though, St. Cloud called out to me from across the room: "Oh, Miss Curtain! It was lovely to see you again. You did a wonderful job removing all of that mud from your person. Brava!" All eyes turned to me at the comment. I imagined a sudden spotlight pinning me in place. I could feel my face heating up at the unwanted attention St. Cloud had brought my way. *On purpose.* I either needed to leave the room or punch the smarmy ass in the face for the thinly veiled insult and ensuing scrutiny. Seeing as how I might be arrested for causing a violent scene, I opted to make a hasty exit instead, my face burning with angry embarrassment.

Grimm met me outside the courthouse. He had been keeping an eye on Wren's bicycle, since I had haphazardly abandoned it on the lawn to get to the meeting. He wagged his tail at my appearance but tucked his ears back upon seeing the look on my face.

"I swear to Freya, Grimm," I muttered at him as I angrily stalked over to the bicycle. "I'm going to do some sort of violence on St. *Clod* if he keeps this up."

I continued to fume and mutter under my breath as I picked up Wren's bike and began to walk it down the street toward Rabbit Hole Road. Grimm stayed by my side, listening to every word I said but unable to respond. I would have loved to have shifted down to fill Grimm in properly, but that would have to wait until we were back home, since I needed my human form to maneuver the bicycle.

As I walked the bike and continued to seethe, I espied an MC parked by the side of the road. It was black with red trim, and its cargo hold had been modified to fit an incarcerated person within it. I instantly recognized it: St. Cloud's ride.

Something clicked in my brain. He dared mess with me? I'd mess with him. Revenge.

Scurrying over to it, I took a good look around me to make sure no one else could see us. It was quite dark by now, so I felt confident that we were alone and unobserved. Setting the bike down carefully, I went to the passenger side door of St. Cloud's precious MC and tried the handle. The door opened with a small click.

Grimm whined, as if to ask me what I was doing.

"Shh," I cautioned him as I opened the door just a fraction wider. "Keep a lookout, will you?"

With the door open, I crawled inside and crouched down, hiding my larger human body from any possible eyes. Once I felt secure, I shimmered into my cat form. Now that I was much smaller, I could easily move about the interior. I positioned myself on the passenger seat and took a good look. The fabric, soft and pliant, was made of a cloth that snagged slightly when I carefully put a claw into it. It reasoned that other things might get caught up in the weave as well. And to really make my day, the color was jet black. This was becoming too perfect.

I gave myself a good scratch with my back claws to help loosen up some of my white fur, and then I flopped over on the seat, briskly rubbing my body all over the surface, making sure to stretch up the back rest to leave no area unscathed. Once I was satisfied with the result, I repeated my actions on the other seat. Then I surveyed my handiwork.

Both black fabric seats were now covered in a thin coat of my fine white cat hairs, which contrasted nicely with dark fabric. Some fur rested on the surface, but many more were trapped by the fibers of the cloth, and I knew from experience that those would be a major pain to remove.

Best of all? I had made sure to rub my scent glands all over that interior. St. Cloud would not be able to smell anything with his puny human nose, but to any animal that happened to get a whiff of his darling MC, that baby was *mine*.

It was the little things that tickled me.

Wasting no more time, I resumed my human form, stealthily extracted myself from the carriage, and carefully shut the door. Picking up the bicycle, I motioned for Grimm to hurry along with me, leaving the scene of the crime with the quick gait of a guilty person, but, more importantly, with a much more cheerful demeanor.

CHAPTER 6

R egained cheerfulness aside, it was time to get down to business.

After the mental excitement of the previous night, I had a terrible time sleeping, even more so than usual. My annoying brain swirled with the ramifications of this job. By the time the sky was just starting to turn from purple to dove gray, I had decided enough was enough and that I needed to talk to the one being that would know some nitty gritty facts that might help my case. Specifically, my mother, Belinda Curtain.

She lived just down the road from me, on Lyle Williams' farm. Lyle was Fleurette's father as well as the local veterinarian, and he also happened to be a member of GOGS, despite not having any magical talent himself. That meant he was privy to the secrets my mom and I kept about ourselves. He graciously allowed Belinda to live on his property, the big barn being her usual haunt of choice. It made finding her an easy task.

She was not on board with me accosting her before the sun was up, however. Apparently, she enjoyed sleep just a bit more than me.

"What are you on about, Cressida?"

I huffed a breath and tried to keep my ears forward in a neutral expression. This conversation was taking place in cat form, since Mom rarely donned her human mantle these days. She claimed she was in retirement and chose to live out her life as a cat, despite the fact that this choice would age her faster. It was harder for me to hide my agitation that so often occurred around her, however, when I was in feline form. But I had to try. No sense in antagonizing her right away, despite my natural inclination to do so.

"I need to know everything about my father. Your husband. I ... kind of took a case involving him."

Mom stared at me, her green eyes assessing. Her ears were already held to the sides of her head in a look of annoyance, despite my best efforts. I'm not sure why I thought this would go well, considering the hour and the fact that she had never once opened up to me about him in my three years of life.

"Cressida," she began slowly, my name a chastisement all by itself, "whatever case you took, un-take it. That part of my life is over. End of story."

A tiny growl sounded in my throat before I could stop it. "It doesn't work that way, Mother. Besides, something doesn't add up. I need to know what kind of man my father is. I need you to be open with me."

Mom's ears swiveled backward just a bit more, edging from annoyed to angry. "I'm warning you, Cress, drop it. You are my priority now, not your father."

My blood boiled. I knew without a doubt she still loved my father, if only for the fact that part of our family legacy was to only fall in love with one man, the fated true love. True love could not just be turned off like a light switch because one left their spouse. Mom was denying her feelings, and for what purpose?

"How can you say that? You love him!"

"Why must you carry on this way, Cressida? I have cared for you and done everything for you since the day you were born! Your father is not a part of your life. This is the cat's way. Leave it be."

"I can't. It's too late to back out now," I countered, adding a tail lash.

She sighed and closed her eyes, a low growl escaping her.

I waited for her to open her eyes again before I continued, "I was hired to arrest Roger Curtain. I'm taking this opportunity to investigate the situation to possibly clear his name instead, if he turns out to be innocent. I'd like your help on this, Mom. I don't know what his fate will be if one of the other hunters gets to him instead. I would like to think that you wouldn't want your husband, the father of your only child, to be falsely arrested for a crime he didn't commit. It will be easier for me to do this if I have a leg up and you help me, but I'm doing this with or without your help." I stared flatly at her, my tail twitching aggressively behind me.

She stared back, mirroring my slightly combative body stance. It was a good thing I had left Grimm at Fleurette's house, considering this sort of tension between mother and daughter made him uncomfortable and he had a penchant for inserting his rather big body between us to break it. I didn't want to break the pressure this time; my mother needed to see that I was serious. I was willing to physically fight her for this information.

After a moment of mutual angry staring and tail lashing, my mother deflated. Her shoulders drooped and she broke eye contact. "I don't like this, Cressida," she stated. "I'd rather you didn't get involved. There's a reason I left your father, despite my love for him. But I know you, and you are as stubborn as they come."

My heart gave a hopeful leap. Was she really going to help me?

"I'm only going to tell you the bare basics," she warned me with a small tail thrash. "You know that it took me a long time to find my true love. I was seven years old by the time I met your father. And he was already in his late thirties. We were married for many years before I became pregnant with you."

She was not telling me anything useful, and in fact this was the same trickle of information I had already been fed by her before. But I stood still and listened to her, not wanting to scare her off from continuing.

"We lived together in Dogwood. The big city?" She waited until I acknowledged that I knew where Dogwood was. It was the closest metropolis to Knobby Hill, about five hours north and to the west, as the wagon traveled, at least. She continued, "We had a lovely little apartment on Beech Street—that's beech like the tree, not the ocean—which was at the southern end of the city where buildings weren't packed quite so densely. Southwind Commons was the name. It had a communal garden out back filled with lots of trees for privacy. That part was a must for me, as you can imagine. I always left the kitchen window open, even in the dead of winter, just in case I needed to get out of the apartment in cat form. Roger thought the window thing was a funny quirk of mine."

"So he didn't know?" I interjected, becoming fascinated with this slice of life she never divulged to me.

"No." She paused to lick her foreleg. "Roger didn't have a magical bone in his body, and he was the mundiest of mundies. By keeping our heritage a secret from him, I followed the path of many of our ancestors, including Glivver, I might add. I didn't think he would understand what I was."

I thought about that. I kept what exactly I was a secret because my mother had always warned me that there might be people out there who would want to break the prophecy of Glivver by eradicating our line. I was used to pretending to be an ordinary human out in public, but would it be worth it pretending in front of someone I was sharing a life with?

At the thought of having a spouse, my chest gave a small but painful pang. The curse was reminding me that Annie Coddle had made it impossible for me to find my true love. Best not think about it then and there. The ache in my fractured soul throbbed for a moment before settling down again.

Luckily, Mom didn't notice my wince of pain. She thought for a moment, her tiny pink tongue barely peeking out of her mouth as she paused her grooming. "He did see me from time to time as a cat," she mused, almost to herself. "He would go to work, and I would have the whole day to myself, to sleep as a cat, since I couldn't sleep as myself at night. Or to prowl in the garden. Our neighbors always assumed I was a friendly stray. But on occasion Roger would get home earlier than I expected and catch me off guard. He often loved to sit outside on a bench after work when the weather was nice. I would approach him, and he would always pet me so nicely. Then, I would disappear back into the garden where no one could see me and transform back into my human self. I always told him I had been out either shopping or hanging out with friends. He did not know I didn't actually have any friends."

I had no words for this sad admission. It sounded like a lonely life in a self-made cage.

Mom got back to her story. "The hardest part of all of this was waiting for you to happen. I knew I needed to have a child in order to pass along the legacy and fulfill my bargain with the prophecy, but it took five long years before you came along. It was long enough for me to begin to doubt that I had married the right man. I had already decided I would need to leave Roger before your birth. I even wrote a letter that I kept in a secure space, and I had plans to leave it out for him when the time came."

I tried to keep my body language neutral as I thought of how callous it was to preplan leaving the love of your life, with nothing but a note explaining (mostly incorrectly) your sudden and permanent absence. Perhaps my mother's actions three years ago were enough to drive the man to a life of crime out of grief and desperation. It was a thought worth exploring at least.

"So, that's all I know about your father. I left him as soon as I couldn't change back into a human and set out for the barn I had pre-chosen years before, where you were then born. And the rest is history."

I mulled it over. "So, you think he is still in Dogwood?"

She yawned widely, showing off her teeth. "Could be. But it's been three years since I last knew of his whereabouts. I purposefully lost touch, you know."

"Is there anyone who would know where he might be? A close friend of his?"

She gave me another unblinking stare, taking a few seconds to respond. "We weren't exactly socialites. Roger worked long hours and I puttered about, much like what I do now. Hmm. There was one person who you might be able to track down."

"Who?" I asked eagerly.

"Roger's secretary. Or old secretary, since I'm sure she no longer works for him. Monica ..." Mom trailed off.

I needed more than a first name in a big city. "Monica ...?" I nudged.

"It started with a G," she continued, somewhat unhelpfully. "Gray? Graves? Greeves! That was it, Monica Greeves."

"So, go to Dogwood and find a Monica Greeves. Got it." It wasn't much to go by, but I bet it was more than the other hunters had. They still did not have a destination, let alone the name of an old associate. "Mom, thank you. I think I'll get a head start on this business and leave today. Say hi to Lyle when you see him."

Mom put a paw on my shoulder to stop me from leaving, her claws out just enough to snag my fur. "Cressida, you need to be careful," she admonished again. "I won't be losing my only daughter because she was curious about her father. Cats normally don't have anything to do with their fathers."

"Cats normally don't have human fathers either," I countered. "This is more than blatant curiosity, Mom. I have a feeling there is more to this than meets the eye."

I turned to leave, jumping off the hay bale where we had had our meeting. As I walked away, I heard my mother say something so softly, I almost did not hear it. I would guarantee my whiskers I was not meant to hear it. But heard it I did.

"If only you knew how right you are."

CHAPTER 7

As I've mentioned before, I was born in that abandoned barn, which had been swallowed by forestland miles south of the big city, and raised there alone by my mother. After I was mostly grown up, I explored the world around me, but stuck to small communities that bordered my forest. And once I met Fleurette on one of my ramblings, I pretty much adopted Knobby Hill as my official town.

As such, I had never stepped foot in Dogwood, despite being conceived there.

Sure, there had been the occasional bounty posting for Dogwood, but I specialized in the supernatural cases, like werewolves, vampires, and the recent wechuge. Supernatural things tended to stick to the country, where it was easier to hide. I left the city cases to the mundy hunters.

No, I was a country girl through and through. Which meant that I was just a tad nervous to venture into the urban jungle.

We started out at eight in the morning, after I had filled Grimm in on what my mother had shared with me. The slight delay in departure also allowed me to catch up with Fleurette, whom I had relayed information to the previous night. She knew I was new to city life. Having ventured into Dogwood just a handful of times over the years, she wanted to help me get my bearings.

"Hold on, I have a map somewhere," she told me. After a quick search in a filing cabinet, she located her map, a battered and dog-eared sheet of thick paper. Together, we took it to the dining room table and unfolded it.

The map encompassed all of the metropolis and a halo of the surrounding area. I had studied maps of our nearby rural communities, and I marveled at the difference between those maps and this one. The sheer scale of the city, along with densely packed squares of the city blocks, contrasted sharply with the small and open nature of the average tiny town.

The good news was that everything was nicely labeled, from the highways leading to Dogwood to the tiny streets in the heart of the city, and it included a few landmarks within the city as well. Fleurette pointed to a road connecting to the southern part of Dogwood, like a string tied to an irregularly shaped balloon. "This is Highway 24," she said, running her finger up the green line. "It will lead you straight into Dogwood. Do you know how to connect to 24 from here?"

I thought for a moment, bringing up a mental map in my mind. "I believe so. Just jump on Cobbler Road north of Knobby Hill and follow it to Harving, then connect to West 60, which will take me to 24, correct?"

She nodded. "And don't forget, you'll want to take the Highway ramp going north. From there, it's a straight shot to Dogwood because the highway goes through the city." She began to fold the map back up. "One last thing I wanted to, well, warn you about: it's not as common anymore to see horses within the city. The last time I was there, they had a separate lane for horses and horse-drawn vehicles because they move at a slower pace than MCs. I would not be surprised if horses are altogether banned in parts of the city."

"Why?" I asked, aghast at the idea.

She shrugged. "Horses take up more resources, such as food and water, and make messes in the streets that need to be cleaned up. Plus MCs take less space to park. It's all in the name of progress."

I pursed my lips. All valid points, for sure, but I personally hated MCs. Besides, I *had* to take Humbert, because without him, the journey would take much too long, and time was of the essence.

At least Fleurette hadn't said anything about dogs not being welcome in the city.

And so, here we were, making our way to an urban environment that tested the boundaries of my comfort level. I told myself it would be worth it in the end.

About an hour into our journey, we moseyed through Harving, a sleepy town even smaller than Knobby Hill, making sure to take a left when the sign indicated. That left took us to West 60, which became a smooth, paved road, different from the hard-packed dirt roads I had become accustomed to on many of my travels. As our journey continued, I noticed an uptick in traffic; a cyclist here, a saddled horse and rider there. And the closer we got to Highway 24, the more everyone seemed to be in a rush. I was swept along with the notion, urging poor Humbert to go just a bit faster with each passing mile.

It all came to a frenzied head as we turned off West 60 onto Highway 24, where we suddenly encountered two lanes of traffic going north, and many of the vehicles on the road were motorized. Despite their fairly quiet engines, MCs still emitted an artificial hum that grated on my heightened senses. It was no wonder I enjoyed country life better, considering rural folks took longer to modernize. For now, though, I would have to get used to the annoying frequency; my wagon currently seemed to be one of the only non-mechanized vehicles on this stretch of road.

As the highway continued for what seemed like endless miles of uniformity, I let my mind wander a bit, allowing Humbert to slow marginally from his slightly frantic gait as I tried not to jump every time an MC passed me on the left. This was certainly a slice of life I had never witnessed. I thought back to what my mom had told me about living in the city and having to adapt to the crush of humanity surrounding her at all times. I shuddered. Certainly, that life would not do for me. How did my mother manage for five years while she was married? It was no wonder she enjoyed peace and solitude so much now.

At last, after about five hours of total travel, Dogwood loomed up like a behemoth in the distance. I stayed to the right—the designated horse lane that allowed the swifter MCs to pass us with ease—as the buildings slowly multiplied and swallowed us up. Soon enough, I was immersed in the city, suddenly feeling very small and trying not to get lost in the incredible culture shock.

Now that I was in the heart of the leviathan metropolis, it was time to turn off the main road. My first goal was to find Miss Greeves, a veritable needle in a haystack, and I wouldn't be able to accomplish this task by staying on the main artery, as much as I was reluctant to veer away from it. As I had been lost for ideas about how to go about finding Monica, Fleurette and I had discussed it at length. I had argued that finding a single person in a large city would be practically impossible, but Fleurette had a different opinion.

"Because there are so many people all living together, they make sure to keep better track of them. It's the people living in the country that can get lost in the shuffle."

So, using the map, she had tracked a route to a business that was sure to help me: Information.

"Cressida, city life is different in many ways," Fleurette had said. "One of the biggest differences is the magical technology. There is a huge market for crystals there."

"What's so special about crystals?" I asked.

"Anything can be enchanted, but some items are more difficult than others. Crystals are among the easiest and cheapest items to enchant. Enchanters tend to flock to the metropolitan areas, where they can easily find jobs and sell their wares. Life is faster there, so there is a larger market for such technology as communication crystals and the like. Ergo, it is easier to find a person in the city by means of businesses such as Information."

Information was on West Reed Avenue, according to the map, which turned out to be a decently wide street perpendicular to the highway in an older section of the downtown area. The avenue was divided between eastbound and westbound traffic by a row of stately deciduous trees. Buildings as tall as ten stories graced either side, with a generous sidewalk for pedestrians and the occasional stand selling wares.

Within minutes I located a building with a giant sign proclaiming this to be Information. Now the trick was parking.

There was no room to park my wagon on this main street. I kept moving forward, but once I was three blocks away and still without a parking spot, I started to get nervous. I was caught up in a fast-moving stream, without an eddy in sight to break away from the current. The farther away from Information I traveled, the more my chest tightened. I had to tell myself to loosen the iron grip on the reins as well; Humbert would soon be able to sense my anxiety, which would not do either one of us any favors. I needed a solution to this problem, and fast.

A red light ahead of me urged me to halt Humbert. As the cross traffic took their turn to move, I glanced around. My eye caught on a large flash of bright orange to my left, and I zeroed in on the gaudy color. It was the vehicle waiting at the light next to me, a two-seated phaeton, with the word TAXI declared in big black letters along the top. I moved my eyes from the phaeton and over to the bicycle it was attached to, upon which sat a young woman, her black hair liberally streaked with violet and pulled back into a high ponytail. Her bike was stopped slightly ahead of where I perched in my seat, but I saw her attention drawn to Humbert next to her, and she slowly swiveled her head back until we made brief eye contact.

I made a hasty assumption that she knew more about this city than I did, and an equally hasty decision to use that to my benefit.

"Excuse me," I called out.

She had just started to turn her head back to the intersection, but she swiveled it again at my voice. "Yeah?" she called back, craning her head up a little to see me fully.

"I'm new in town and need to park my wagon. Do you know where I can legally do so?"

She thought for a second or two and nodded. "Your best bet is to go to the horse lot on 78th. It's cheapest to do all-day parking and leave your wagon there. Taking a taxi is way easier if you need to go places in the city."

I nodded knowingly, even though I hadn't a clue where 78th might be. "Do you think you could show me how to get there?"

The young woman pursed her lips, then shrugged. "I don't have a fare right now, so if you want to pay me, I'll show you the way. How does $10 sound?"

I swiftly agreed, and as the light changed to green, she cut in front of me. She deftly led me down the road, then right, and finally turned left into a large, paved area with a tall fence. All across the concrete yard stood a variety of carriages and wagons, all without horses. A tall stable with wide double doors stood the back of the lot. Just ahead of that sat a small square building with a large window facing forward. I surmised it to be the office for this whole affair.

The taxi driver led me through the open gate and stopped just inside. She grinned up at me. "This here is the best parking lot for wagons," she told me, her tone smug. "Albert is the manager, and he has the fairest prices."

I nodded in understanding and climbed down from my seat. I fished a $10 note from my vest pocket and walked it over to where she was resting on the seat of her bicycle. Plucking it from my hand, she tipped her head at me. "Thank you. Do you happen to have a mirror on you?"

She was referring to an enchanted message mirror, which was a common form of long-distance communication. I did happen to have one, as Fleurette insisted on having some way of contacting me. It was not foolproof, however, because while I was in cat form, my mirror resided in my interdimensional pocket along with my clothes and was quite unreachable.

I nodded, and she gestured for me to take it out and hand it to her. Once I did as she beckoned, she produced a crystal stylus from her pants pocket. With a deft, olive-toned hand, she drew a symbol on the mirror surface and then handed it back. "The name's Rosa," she informed me. "If you have need of a ride while you're in Dogwood, just tap my name and send me your closest cross streets. I'll come find you."

"Thank you," I replied sincerely. I was glad to have a connection in case I needed to travel around the city. Clearly, driving my wagon here was not an ideal situation.

Rosa shrugged but grinned. "Enjoy your stay in Dogwood," she called as she mounted her bicycle and pedaled away.

An older man, slightly overweight and heavily tanned from years in the sun, approached. This must have been Albert. Sure enough, he guided me to park my wagon in a designated spot. Once I had done so to his satisfaction, we talked about the price.

I agreed to pay for a whole day, which included stabling Humbert, as it was cheaper than paying per hour. Once I had paid, a younger man came and began to unharness my horse employee. Albert went back into his tiny office, leaving me to my own devices.

I stretched, allowing circulation back into my rear after sitting on the hard bench for five hours. I then made my way around to the back of my wooden wagon, opening the double doors and crawling inside.

Shutting them firmly behind me, I took a moment to fish a key out of my pocket to lock the doors from the inside for maximum privacy. With so many bodies milling about in the same area, I was extra cautious of my secret.

There was a sharp contrast between the daylight brightness outside and the relative dimness of the lantern in the windowless interior. I gave my eyes a moment to adjust before surveying the inside of the wagon. Directly ahead of me, lying on our roll-out mattress, was Grimm. He gave me a hearty tail wag, the force making a heavy thumping sound against the mattress. I smiled at him and then shimmered.

"I think your ride was much more comfortable than mine," I commented, giving my legs an extra stretch as I arched my back to work out the kinks.

His tongue lolled out of his mouth for a moment, reminding me that while Grimm was usually a serious dog, he did have a goofy side to him as well. "I slept through most of it," he admitted. "I only woke up when I heard your voice yelling something. That high-pitched sound can cut through glass."

"I wasn't yelling," I replied with a haughty sniff. "I was making myself heard over the noise of the street. This place is wild. I can't believe anyone would purposefully live this way."

"So, we made it, I assume?"

I nodded, a very human thing to do, but sometimes my other nature's mannerisms slipped out. "Now we need to go find Monica. I found the information building, but I had to keep driving away from it. Fleurette was right; they are definitely phasing out allowing horses in the city. I had to use a specific parking lot designed for the few horses around. I even had to pay extra for a groom to take care of Humbert for the day. It's outrageous!"

Grimm humphed. Concepts such as money held little interest to him, which is why I was always in charge of the finances. "Well, didn't you say we were being paid regardless of our success at this job?"

"Yes, that's true," I admitted. The $1,000 I'd been given upfront for traveling expenses meant whoever was footing this bill had some serious dough.

"Well, anyway," I continued, "we're a good few blocks away from the Information building. I paid for Humbert to be taken care of all day, so if we need to travel about the city, we'll have to either walk or ride in a taxi."

"What's a taxi?"

Grimm had been born on a mountain, raised from early puppyhood by his mother and a monk who bred Lycanhunds. After he was purchased by his late master, he lived for just a few short years in a town even smaller and more isolated than Knobby Hill. Just like me, he had never been to a metropolis before.

"That, my uneducated country dog, is a vehicle that drives around the city and gives people—like us—rides for money."

"You needn't speak as if you are this worldly thing," Grimm gruffed at me. "You've never stepped foot in a city this big either."

"Yep, which is precisely why I'm terrified out of my mind. C'mon, let's get a move on. Time's a-wasting."

As if to prove my point, a loud bang resonated on the back doors, scaring me half to death and causing Grimm to issue a low growl in his throat.

"Hey, in there!" came the voice of Albert. "We don't allow folks to sleep here!"

Apparently, we had dallied long enough to arouse the suspicion of the manager. As soon as my heart stopped leaping for my throat, I changed back into human form and unlocked the door. Crawling out, I gave the surly man my sweetest forced smile. "Sorry about that. I was just collecting my dog before I left."

On cue, Grimm jumped down from the wagon. His head nearly came up to my chest, and with his shaggy black hair and piercing yellow eyes, he was intimidating, to say the least. The man's face went slightly pale at his appearance.

"What is that thing?" he asked with a quiver in his voice.

I smirked. "This is my dog. He's perfectly harmless so long as I tell him to be." I stroked Grimm's ears affectionately. He looked up at me in adoration.

"If you say so, lady. Looks to me like a hellhound, if I say so myself. Sorry to have bothered you, miss."

With a head nod, I walked toward the lot entrance, Grimm at my side. Once we were out of earshot, I told him, "Don't worry, you're much cuter than a hellhound."

Grimm wagged his tail and perked his ears at my words, pleased with the compliment.

CHAPTER 8

I thought I was used to people giving me and Grimm funny looks. We made for an unusual pair, after all. But I was not prepared for our welcome in the big city.

The sidewalks were packed with pedestrians going about their busy lives. As we walked toward Information, I had time to notice an interesting aspect of human psychology. If a person saw me first, they either stared too long or smiled as soon as I made eye contact, but either way, there was a ninety percent chance that they were not going to stop their trajectory and would sooner run into me than move aside for me. I had to dodge bodies since I did not want to collide with a stranger.

On the flip side, if a pedestrian caught sight of Grimm, they would immediately give us a wide berth. And if I happened to catch their eye after they looked at Grimm, there were no stares or smiles, but rather a nasty glower in my direction. I hadn't the foggiest what that was about.

It wasn't until an older woman with a shrill voice yelled at me about "leashing my beast" that it dawned on me: the sight of an unleashed dog struck fear into the hearts of the city dwellers for reasons that escaped me. After all, Grimm was an angel, placidly trotting by my side. So, as it turned out, dogs weren't much more welcome in Dogwood than horses, unless they were lap-sized and leashed. The dog prejudice was certainly true for businesses as well, since once we reached Information, I spied a sign that proclaimed dogs were not welcome inside. Grimm had to wait outside as I conducted my business. At least the weather was pleasant for his outdoor interlude.

The lobby of Information was satisfyingly large, with a circular desk in the center operated by four different people. One of the employees was busy with a client, but an affable-looking man with the name tag ADAM beckoned me over to his station right away.

I approached with a small smile on my face, hoping to appear as amiable as possible. I neither had an inkling of how this business worked, nor did I have any clue what I was doing, but I didn't want to come off as an idiot.

"Love the hair," Adam said to me once I stood before him. My smile got wider. Not once had I ever heard that before. Usually, I just got stares, but then again, no one surmised that the black streaks at my temple were natural, not dyed. The man continued without waiting for a response from me, "How can I help you today?"

I leaned closer to the pleasant man. "I'm looking for someone ..."

"Aren't we all?" he interjected with a smile on his face.

I took it in stride. "Her name is Monica Greeves."

He took out a notepad. "Spelling?"

I gave it to him with the addendum that I wasn't fully sure the spelling was correct. He wrote it down on a notepad. "Let me see what I can find."

A large, rounded chunk of glass sat on the desk to his left. No, not glass. A crystal. Adam stared intently at it and murmured words before placing his left hand on the smooth dome and grabbing a pen with the other. He closed his eyes and bent his head. My brow furrowed as I looked on in befuddlement over his actions. As I watched, a yellow glow appeared from under his fingers where they contacted the surface; it spread through the crystal. Adam seemed to be concentrating heavily, and then immediately began writing on a piece of paper under the pen, not opening his eyes the entire time.

Three minutes later, he stopped writing, straightened his head, and opened his eyes. Grabbing the piece of paper, he gave it a once-over before stating, "All right, miss, I found three Monica Greeves with the spelling you gave me, one Monika Greeves with a K, two Monicas with the last name spelled G-R-E-A-V-E-S, and three more Monica Graves, just in case."

I stared at him. "How did you do that?"

He looked momentarily puzzled. "Do what?"

I gestured a hand at the crystal. "How does it work?"

"Oh, that. You must be new around here." He gave a small but friendly chuckle. "I have a special affinity for krystallomancy, as we all do here at Information. That means I can easily tap into enchanted crystals and utilize their magic," he added when he saw my look of confusion at the word. I appreciated his explanation and nodded with understanding. He continued, "These are special enchanted crystals that are all connected to a database. I simply do my thing to extract the information."

"Neat." Fleurette wasn't joking about the heavy use of crystals here in Dogwood.

Adam tapped on the paper he had written on, bringing me back to the task at hand. "So, with this information, what would you like to do?"

Oh yeah. His list. That was a lot of different women to search through. I frowned and bit my lower lip, at a loss. This suddenly became a lot tougher.

He nodded knowingly at my silent freakout. "Do you have any other information to help narrow it down? Address? Spouse name?"

"Hmm, she used to work for a Roger Curtain," I added.

"I can cross-check the place of work, if you know it."

I shook my head. "All I know is that he's an accountant. But he no longer works at the same place."

Adam shrugged. "Fair enough. I will just delve a little deeper to check for job histories. I can't guarantee we'll find her that way, though. Just give me a few more minutes. This is deeper work."

He touched the crystal again, eyes closed and head bent. His head twitched to the side every once in a while, as if he were reading through files in his mind. For all I knew, that was exactly what he was doing. I watched with interest as he frowned on occasion or quirked his lips.

Finally, he wrote something down and then lifted his hand, breaking his connection with the crystal. "I searched each name, and only one has ever worked in an accounting firm, Harrison and Harvey. No Curtain, but it's the strongest lead I've got. It's the second Monica Greeves, spelled the way you gave me."

"That must be her," I conceded with some uncertainty.

"Now that we've found your person, what would you like to do with this information?" Adam asked.

Without pausing, I responded, "I need to get in touch with her."

"Do you have a communication crystal? It looks like she has one, based on her file."

I shook my head. Communication crystals were expensive, and most rural people did not use them. They required a complicated bit of magic to create, and very few witches out there were advanced enough to have the proper magic. My mirror was good enough for long-distance communication, usually.

"Well, I'll let you borrow mine then." Adam pulled an amethyst-colored crystal of about four inches in length and about an inch in diameter from his pocket and held it in his hand. He breathed on it and then mumbled a few words over it. The crystal began to glow a soft white color. He handed it to me. "Just say, 'Monica Greeves,' and think of the person you want to connect to in your mind."

The crystal was oddly warm in my hand. I said the name, and, even though I didn't know what Monica looked like, I focused on what little knowledge I did have of her in my mind. The crystal glowed brighter and let out some soft pings.

A few seconds later, a quiet, tinny, feminine voice sounded from the crystal. "Hello?"

I was astounded for a brief second and then gathered my wits. "Hello, Monica Greeves? You don't know me, but I am working an important case, and I was hoping you could answer some questions for me."

The voice was silent for a beat. "Who is this? What is this in regard to?"

"My name is Cressida Cur ..." I froze, realizing I couldn't give my last name, as it was too coincidental. "... tis. Curtis. I'm investigating a case concerning Roger Curtain."

Another pause, this one longer. "Do you have my address?" Her tone was brusque.

"No, I do not. Just your crystal energy."

"Good. Let's keep it that way." She seemed to think. "I can meet you at Bell and Nectar at 7:30 tomorrow morning. Will that do?"

"Bell and Nectar?" I repeated.

"Yes. It's a tea shop. Do you need the address?"

"I can find it. Thank you, Miss Greeves."

She huffed. "I can't guarantee I'll be helpful."

"I understand. I'll see you tomorrow."

She must have done something on her end to stop communication because the crystal made a small ping, and the light dimmed to nothingness. I handed the crystal back to Adam.

"Thank you," I said. After a pause, I added, "Can I get the address for Bell and Nectar?"

Once I had that information, I thanked him again, before looking sheepish. "Do I ... pay?" I asked with a small amount of trepidation. This was a new service to me, and I had no idea how the system worked.

Adam smiled kindly. "No, ma'am. Information is a government-run business, and it's free for public use."

After a third round of me expressing my appreciation, I made my way to the exit. I walked out of the glass doors, deep in thought. I had managed to secure a meeting with Monica, but for tomorrow. That meant I needed to sleep here somewhere. Which, in turn, meant I needed to make sure I could keep parking my wagon at the lot.

Grimm let out a bark as I left the building, breaking me from my thoughts. I glanced at him. He had been waiting patiently outside for me, and I wondered if it had agitated him to the point that he was needlessly making noise. If so, that was unlike Grimm. Normally, he was very concise with his communications, only barking when needed. I gave him a puzzled look, and he pointed his nose behind me. Ah, the bark had meant something, after all. I turned in the direction he had pointed.

Gavin St. Cloud was leaning up against the building, grinning at me. I had been so distracted by my thoughts that I hadn't noticed my surroundings. I mentally chided myself. As a small animal, I knew how dangerous it was not to pay attention, especially in an unfamiliar environment. I blamed the distractions of the city.

I frowned in Gavin's direction. He merely smiled wider.

"Well, well, well, what a coincidence!" he greeted, casually pulling his watch out of his pocket and flipping it open.

"What are you doing here?" I asked, a scowl instantly forming on my face

"I imagine I'm here for a similar reason," he responded. "I tried to pet your dog, but he growled at me."

"He's not my dog," I replied automatically. "And he doesn't like you."

Gavin only smirked. "Animals usually love me. Did you teach him that?"

I shook my head levelly. "He just naturally happens to have good taste."

He widened his grin, clearly finding amusement in my words. "Were you successful in your query with Information?" he asked.

"I don't think that's any of your business. Why are you in Dogwood?"

He gave me a look like I was an idiot. "It's the obvious place to start looking, given the fact that Curtain was living here for years before he disappeared. Surely you must have come to the same conclusion since you are here as well?"

"Of course," I replied.

Gavin checked the time and gave a little frown. He looked back at me. "Did you have other information that led you here?"

He was clearly fishing for answers. "I'm not saying," I said smoothly. "And if you think I'm giving you any help in this case, you're delusional."

"That remains to be seen." Gavin snapped the watch shut again and tucked it back into his pocket. "Well, Miss Curtain, as thrilling as it is to run into you, I must get back to the hunt. There's $15,000 waiting for me." With that, he tipped his head and walked into Information.

I glanced at Grimm, who still looked agitated. "Don't say anything," I warned him. My dander was up.

Grimm only sneezed in response.

I had only one other tidbit of information to go by, and since it was only about two in the afternoon and I had until tomorrow morning to kill, I figured I might as well do a little more digging, even if this part was more for personal reasons and less to do with the case. Motioning for Grimm to follow, I began walking down the street, even farther away from the parking lot where Humbert was temporarily housed. I'd deal with that after this mini-expedition.

Once I was a few blocks away from Information—and away from the prying eyes of St. Cloud—I took my mirror out and tapped out my cross-streets for Rosa to find me. A few seconds later, she sent a confirmation message with an ETA of ten minutes.

True to her word, Rosa pulled up in her bicycle taxi with not a minute to spare. I had been sitting against the building with Grimm cuddled up next to me. We both stood up in unison, and Rosa stared at him, her eyes widening.

"I guess I forgot to ask, are dogs allowed in your taxi?" I inquired politely.

"Does that thing qualify as a dog or as a pony?"

I shrugged. "He's a Lycanhund, bred to take down werewolves. They need to be big to do that."

"No kidding? I've read about them but never thought I'd see one. Well, I normally don't have a problem with dogs in my taxi, although I'm still not sure he counts as one. More like a person in his own right, if you ask me. Hop in."

I liked her way of thinking. We did as we were told, Grimm going first, and then me squeezing myself in after him and shutting the small door.

In front of us, Rosa asked, "Where to?"

I thought back to what my mother had told me. "The Southwind Commons apartments, on Beech Street, please."

Beech Street ended up being fairly far south. I watched with each passing block as the building density lessened, and more houses with tiny yards and businesses with green belts took the place of high rises. Rosa pedaled right up to a lovely brick building three stories high, painted a creamy white with navy blue trim on all of the windows. For what it was, it looked inviting.

I got out of the taxi, allowing Grimm out as well. "Do you mind waiting here? I should only be a few minutes," I asked Rosa.

She swiveled her leg over to my side of the bike with a smile. "As long as I keep the meter running, I'll stay here all day."

"Great." I glanced down at Grimm. "Um, would you feel comfortable hanging out with Grimm? I don't think dogs are allowed inside."

"This handsome beast is named Grimm? Fine by me if it's fine by him."

I looked at my partner, who perked his ears forward and wagged his tail. I knew deep down he would rather have stayed by my side, but he was intelligent enough to know why I wasn't bringing him. "He's fine with it," I replied with a smile.

I walked through the double doors that marked the entrance to the apartment building. Directly to one side of the hallway a large window showed off a small room, a sign above the door marking it as the leasing office. An older gentleman with thinning silver hair and glasses in the shape of half-moons adorning his face could be seen. He sat at a desk that faced the window, but he hadn't seen me enter the building because he was immersed in a book.

I knocked on the door to his office before turning the handle and walking in. The man looked up from his book and gave me a friendly smile as I made my way to the front of his desk.

"Hello, dear. If you're here about 3A, I'm afraid I've already leased it this morning."

"Oh, um, I actually was hoping you could help me with something else," I inelegantly countered.

He placed his book down to give me his full attention. "Is that so? Go on." His voice was pleasant, and he pushed up his spectacles on his nose.

"I was hoping to contact someone who used to live here. He rented here about three years ago, but unfortunately, I lost touch with him before he moved."

"Oh? Perhaps he left a forwarding address. What was his name?"

"Roger Curtain."

"Oh, Roger!" the gentleman clapped his hands together. "He and his wife lived here a good many years. Wonderful tenants. Never a peep from them. Always paid on time. Yes, I remember Roger."

"That certainly sounds like them," I bluffed.

The man stood up, turning to the filing cabinets behind him. "I'll just take a look-see at his file for a forwarding address, Miss …"

"Curtis," I supplied untruthfully. I supposed I could have passed myself off as a long-lost relative, but that hit a little too close to home for my comfort.

"Arthur Demp. Pleased to make your acquaintance." The older man opened a drawer and rifled through for a few seconds before pulling a file out. "Here we are," he said with exuberance. "Let's see … yes, yes, they moved out … three years ago this May."

"They?" I was slightly taken aback by the verbiage. I was born in February, which means my mother must have left him in December.

"Yes, Roger and his wife. What was her name? Melinda?"

"Belinda," I provided for him.

He snapped his fingers. "Yes, that's it! I'm normally better with names, but I hardly saw her. She must have been a bit of a homebody. Anyway, they both moved out that May. They dropped the keys in the lockbox and left early in the morning, so I never got a chance to say goodbye. Shame, really. Such wonderful tenants."

I relaxed. My mother did leave much earlier, but my father stuck around for another half a year and apparently did not tell anyone at the apartments that his wife had left him. Interesting.

The landlord continued to scan the file in front of him. "It appears Roger did not leave a forwarding address. He had me send the deposit check to his business address. Sorry, my dear."

I waved a hand in dismissal. "It was worth a try," I said kindly. "Thank you for taking the time to look it up for me. Can I ask just one more favor from you?"

He smiled indulgently and nodded. I continued, "Roger had spoken of your shared garden space out back. He said it was a modern marvel. Would it be possible for me to take a quick peek?"

Arthur thought for a second. "Well, I suppose it wouldn't hurt, as long as it's a short visit. I don't want to disturb my tenants."

"I wouldn't dream of it. Just a couple of minutes," I promised earnestly.

"Very well, Miss Curtis, come this way." He got up from his desk and shuffled to the door, opening it and ushering me through. Once we were back in the hallway, he led the way to the back of the building, where a green door stood. Taking a key from his pocket, he unlocked the door and held it wide for me. "There you are, my dear."

Giving my thanks, I walked outside into a beautiful outdoor

space. Stately willow trees, hedges, flowers, and even a small pond feature created a modest glimpse of nature for these city dwellers. Everything was the fresh, bright green of the start of spring.

I sauntered to a wrought iron bench and sat down, taking in the scenery. I imagined this was the very same bench my father had sat in while he absentmindedly stroked a stray calico cat that was actually his wife. Sitting here, I could conceptualize the life my parents shared together in this place, be it for a short while.

I wondered if I would ever break the curse and share a life with someone.

It was no wonder my mother chose this apartment as her home, considering that it was an oasis of peace amid the busy city. What a life. No wonder she was so happy living on Lyle's farm, catching rats for a living. It must be a dream compared to this lifestyle.

I sighed and stood, taking in my surroundings one last time, memorizing a life I had never lived. Perhaps it was for the best that my mother didn't stay here and raise me in this environment. I'd have become a completely different person, I'm sure.

I made my way back to the door and let myself in. After stopping to thank Arthur for his help and kindness, I exited the apartment building, and in my mind, I closed that chapter of my parents' life.

Outside, I found Rosa sitting on the sidewalk next to her taxi, with Grimm's great head in her lap and his feet in the air. His tongue lolled out of his mouth as she scratched his furry belly.

I chuckled. "I see you two are getting along."

Rosa grinned as I walked over. "You know, this dude is just a giant softy," she cooed.

I guffawed. "Don't tell that to the criminals," I chided. Looking at Grimm, I said, "C'mon, big guy, let's not damage your reputation any farther."

Grimm stood and shook himself, sending long black hairs into the air around him. Rosa stood too, brushing off her pants. "I can't help myself," she said. "I just love dogs, even the big man-eating types."

"Oh, you don't have to worry about Grimm eating you," I teased. "You're not his type."

"That's because I'm not a man," Rosa replied with a wink.

CHAPTER 9

I made it to Dogwood. I found Monica. I even squeezed in a sightseeing tour to my parents' love nest. Check, check, check. I mentally patted myself on the back for doing all of this within twenty-four hours of knowing about this job.

Now all I had to do was kill time until the following morning's appointment with Monica. First up: food. Rosa had dropped us off close to Information, as it was a good central hub for any of our needs, according to her. Seeing as I was a lost kitten in a big city, I took her for her word. And she was right. I found a glut of restaurants within a three-block radius. Grimm and I chose one based on the smells alone, and I wasted little time in ordering takeout dinner for the both of us. With food in hand, we discovered a small but lovely park just another two blocks away and had a scrumptious picnic on the lawn. We had lucked out with glorious spring weather for our first day in Dogwood, but now it was getting colder with the sun hanging lower. Time to turn in.

It was mostly dark by the time we walked into the parking lot. Albert was still at his station, eating a large sandwich that kept slopping condiments onto his hands as he bit into it. I knocked on the door since his attention was on his meal, and he hadn't noticed my return.

"Excuse me, sir. Do you have an overnight rate?" I kept my

tone polite.

Albert hastily wiped his hands on a towel beside him. "Yes, I do," he told me promptly. "Are you interested in continuing your stay here?"

I nodded. "I need to stay in town for at least another day. Can I go ahead and prepay for that as well?"

Albert looked gleeful at the thought. He quickly summarized the added costs and billed me for them. As I handed over the payment, I added, "Oh, I was able to procure a hotel room for myself, but dogs aren't allowed. Would it be okay if my dog slept in my wagon overnight? You wouldn't have to take care of him; he's quite used to being in there for sleeping."

It was a lie to say I had a hotel room, of course, but Albert had already made it clear that humans at least were not to sleep on the premises.

He mulled it over before consenting, but not until I promised to come back directly at opening time to take care of him. It worked out, as the lot opened at seven in the morning, and we needed to be at the coffee shop by 7:30.

Aware that Albert could see us from his vantage point, I made a show of unlocking the wagon's doors and ushering Grimm inside. I similarly made a point to inspect my wagon from front to back, deliberately leaving the small hatch behind the driving bench open a cat's head width. Lastly, I loudly said goodnight to my partner and strode resolutely out of the lot and down the street.

I kept walking until I was far from eyesight, then stopped. I spied a small alleyway between buildings just to my left. Ducking down the alley, I kept all of my senses on high alert. I hid behind a dumpster, ignoring the putrid smell of rotting food. Satisfied that no one could see me, I shimmered into my natural cat form, relishing the returning feeling of relief after a long day of being a human.

My feline senses were quite sharp compared to my human ones. Case in point: as a human, I thought I was alone in the alley, but now that I was a cat, I was instantly aware of my mistake. I turned quickly, just as a small gray streak rushed towards me, like silver lightning. I jumped to the side, narrowly missing being pounced upon by a fellow cat. I arched my back, my fur sticking up to make myself look larger, and backed up to give myself more maneuvering room.

The other cat shook itself and then mirrored my stance. I had enough time to note that it was a short-haired silver tabby before it growled menacingly. "This is *my* territory."

I took a quick smell, scenting the other cat. It was difficult from this distance, but I detected a slight scent of altered female hormones. I carefully took a closer look at her, noting that while she was skinny and scrappy, she had an extended belly. This queen was pregnant and only a couple of weeks away from delivery, if I had to guess.

Taking a chance, I assured her, "I'm not a threat. I'm just passing through, I promise."

The other cat relaxed slightly, still on alert for any tricks. Her nostrils flared. "I've never smelled you before. You have an odd scent."

She was smelling my magic. Despite being born a cat, my heritage would forever mark me as different from mundane cats. If I wanted to have any friendly relationships outside of my immediate family, it would most likely have to be with humans, or other magically-blooded creatures, like Grimm. My scent marked me as too peculiar for amiable association with most other felines.

When I didn't reply to her comment, she lashed her tail at me, her ears still flat against her head. "Get a move on, then. I don't like you. But I will say this, from one cat to another: be careful out there. We are being hunted. Stay in hiding if you don't want to get caught."

"Get caught?" I asked, hoping for clarification. She was clearly tired of allowing me into her turf, though, because she let out a scream of rage and lunged at me again. Not wanting to get into a catfight, I turned and ran.

I sprinted back to the parking lot, carefully avoiding pedestrians and any and all vehicles. I made it back to the lot much faster than I had left it and carefully slunk through the open gates. To the average human eye, I was just a stray coming to check the place for prey. I imagined Albert would not mind having some help in the barn with rodent control, so hopefully, if I was spotted, no one would raise an alarm.

Sure enough, I made it safely to my wagon without a peep from any humans that might still be wandering about. With practiced ease, I jumped onto the bench seat and then up to the hatch, squeezing my small body through the gap I had left open.

Being inside the confines of the dark wagon felt like coming home to a warm and cozy den. All day today, I had been on edge due to the complete unfamiliarity of this environment. For the first time since arriving in Dogwood, I could fully relax and acknowledge I was safe from danger. It certainly helped that there was a large, shaggy, and familiar dog already here, waiting for me.

"What a day!" I groaned as I padded over to Grimm. He had already sprawled out on the mattress, which I hadn't bothered rerolling. I settled into the crook made by his front legs and his chest, not bothering to groom myself. I'd wake up in a few hours to do a thorough washing.

Grimm heaved a sigh, which pushed upon my back. "I thought it was pretty boring."

"That's because you didn't get to come with me inside buildings. I wonder why dogs are so unwelcome?"

Grimm huffed. "That taxi driver certainly made me feel welcome."

A strange pang of emotion coursed through me for just a second. I mentally shook it off. "I'm glad I ran into Rosa. She's shaping up to be a handy ally. It must be nice to find another human who isn't afraid of you, hmm?"

"Sure." He rolled onto his belly, completely dislodging me from my cozy space. I tucked my ears back in agitation and licked my paw to wash my face to quell it. Grimm nosed me in the neck affectionately, which helped settle me. His next words did a bit to unsettle me again, however. "I wouldn't bank on the human part, though. At least, not fully."

"What do you mean?"

He sighed through his nose as he flopped his chin between his front legs. "Her smell. It's not mundane. But I've never smelled anything like it. It's similar to yours, but ... not."

I flopped over into his side again, adjusting my body for maximum comfort. "Interesting. Well, whatever she is, I'm happy to have made the connection. I imagine there are all sorts of magic users living together here."

Grimm snorted in agreement. Changing the subject, he asked, "What's the plan for tomorrow?"

"I have a meeting with Monica first thing in the morning, and hopefully she'll give us more information to find my father. I'd love to wrap this up tomorrow so that we can get out of this city, one way or another. I don't like it here."

A yelling match between two angry-sounding men started up on the street just outside of the parking lot. Grimm and I were not used to such noisy assaults on our ears, on top of what we had encountered in the city all day. This place seemed to thrive on such exuberant energy. It was frankly exhausting.

He groaned. "Ditto."

I slept poorly all night, partly due to the never-ending noise that occurred—MCs traveling the road, people talking, dogs barking in the background, and all the other foreign noises that went along with city life—and partly due to nervous anticipation over the morning's meeting. By the time the sky began to lighten, I was more than ready to get the show on the road. At quarter till seven, I sprang up and out of the wagon, cautiously making my way back to the alley. I made sure to inspect it thoroughly this time, but the gray tabby must have been out hunting, luckily for me. As a human, I strolled back out and was patiently waiting at the locked gates when the first attendant arrived for his shift.

From there, it was only a matter of collecting Grimm and making our way to Bell and Nectar. Thankfully, the shop was within walking distance, as I had discovered yesterday after looking it up on the map. We arrived fifteen minutes early, much to my pleasure. This gave me an opportunity to scrutinize the location. The exterior was quaint: a three-story brick building with roses growing in the boxes of two wide windows that flanked the red front door. From the look of it, the building was mixed-use, with apartments above the ground-floor shop. Off to the left-hand side was a small patio for outdoor seating, which suited me perfectly. The shop windows were currently steamy, indicating it was much warmer on the inside than it was standing on the sidewalk. As to be expected, dogs were not allowed within, so I left Grimm at the door and went in to order.

Bell and Nectar was a cozy tea shop filled with wonderful smells of oolong, jasmine, sugar, and pastries. I was delighted to see a selection of baked goods in a glass case next to the cash register. My stomach growled just looking at them.

I had a small wait, as the place was busy, but the line moved quickly. A young man who looked like he hadn't quite woken up yet took my order. He handed me a number on an upright little pole, instructing me to place it on my table.

"Can I sit outside?" I asked him as I took my change and my number.

"Go for it," he replied.

Back outside, I claimed a table near the front door, which had two chairs adorning its sides and enough room for my goodies. Placing my number on the table, I waited with Grimm at my side.

The lovely March weather still held, with sunshine peeking over the buildings and chasing away the night's dampness and chill, but off in the distance, I saw some rather ominous clouds, and the air smelled damp, a harbinger of rain to come. It was just our luck that the nice weather seemed to be turning.

I turned my eyes away from the sky and surveyed the scene. This part of town seemed to be more upscale, with the tea shop being flanked by a boutique on one side and a crystal gallery on the other. Across the way, I spied an apothecary and a small convenience store. Only the latter was open at this time.

As could be expected, Bell and Nectar was popular with the morning crowd. In between my perusal of my surroundings, I people-watched, keeping an eye out for any woman who might be Monica. Two men entered the tea shop, as did an elderly lady. I didn't have a clue what age Monica was, but I doubted she was old.

At twenty-seven past the hour, my order arrived: a pot of breakfast blend tea and two giant bagels with a generous helping of cream cheese. I thanked the server and slipped one of the bagels to Grimm, who gulped it down before I could finish pouring my tea. I took a bite of mine, relishing the tangy creaminess of the cheese spread. I was just adding a healthy splash of cream to my cup when I realized someone had stopped in front of my table.

"Miss Curtis?" the woman who stood before me asked.

So much for being prepared. I hastily wiped the cream cheese off my upper lip, making sure to fully swallow the bite of bagel. Monica Greeves was a woman in her late thirties, with volumized honey-blonde hair styled immaculately at shoulder length. She wore a smart gray skirt suit over a bright pink blouse, the cut neatly tailored. Her makeup was flawless, giving her skin a healthy glow and accentuating her blue eyes. She looked grave and wary as she stared at me.

"Miss Greeves," I replied with a smile, hoping to put her at ease. I motioned for her to take a seat. "How did you know who I am?"

Monica shrugged. "Just a guess," she replied without any emotion. She added, "You're much younger than I was expecting."

"Oh?" I wasn't sure what to say to that, so I did not engage further with the comment at hand. "Would you like a cup of tea?"

She shook her head. Before I could say anything else, she reached into an oversized purse by her side and took something out. She placed the object in the middle of the table.

"This is a truth crystal," she stated. "I must insist that you use it while you speak to me. If you refuse, I get up and walk away. If you lie to me in any way, we're done. Is that clear?"

I stared at her for a moment. "You came prepared."

She continued to watch me without blinking. "Please touch the crystal. Or I walk."

I chewed on my lip for just a second. I needed to be careful. It wasn't as if I enjoyed lying to people, but I had secrets I needed to protect. However, I also needed Monica's cooperation, or I risked a major dead end in my investigation. And a major dead end could mean a major dead dad, possibly.

I reached out and placed my fingertips on the crystal.

Monica nodded approvingly. "Do you have any intention of harming Roger Curtain?"

Perhaps this would be easier than I thought. "Absolutely not," I replied immediately.

The crystal under my fingertips glowed a soft purple at my words. Monica nodded again, this time with a mien of relief on her face. "Thank you," she said. "I have to be very careful. What *is* your intention with Roger? I won't just give out information."

"I'm working a case."

"What kind of case?" She kept her eyes on the crystal.

"I was hired to find him, as he is implicated in an arson case, along with embezzlement and manslaughter. But," I held up a finger on my other hand while keeping touch with the crystal, which still glowed a truthful color, "I suspect Mr. Curtain is innocent."

Monica breathed deeply and leaned back in her chair after seeing the crystal's response to my words. "I knew it was something bad by the way he acted."

"So you *are* in contact with him?"

She glanced around, as if looking for anyone who might be listening. She then focused on me, leaning in conspiratorially. I leaned in too. "Roger came to me a month ago, looking terrified. He said he was in trouble and needed to disappear. He wouldn't give me any details, though. He said he didn't want to implicate me."

"Go on," I urged.

She sat back again. "That's it," she said with a little head shake. "I've been there for Roger through it all: his marriage, his so-called divorce, his new job. I had never seen him quite this shaken up.”

“So-called divorce?” I asked, my attention diverted by those words.

“Yeah, I guess technically he and his wife never got a divorce. But Roger never told anyone but me that she had left him.” She had a look on her face, almost like a longing.

Her expression raised my hackles. I was perturbed just thinking about what this woman might have meant to my father. “What exactly *is* your relationship with Roger Curtain?” I let the question slip before I could think it through.

My questioning seemed to catch her off guard. Perhaps it was the sudden scowl on my face that accompanied my words. “I was his secretary, professionally,” she stated stiltedly. “But his confidant, his *only* confidant, when he needed one the most.”

That did not necessarily clear things up for me. “Are you his lover?” The words felt bitter as they left my mouth. I hated to think that my father would have abandoned his wedding vows for this woman.

“Who exactly sent you?” Monica retorted, her words even more acerbic than mine had been. “Are you working for that woman?”

“What woman?”

“His *wife*.” She spat the word out as if it were poisoned. “I won’t have anything to do with you if you are. That woman has caused enough harm to Roger.”

Her accusations aimed at my mother slapped me in the process. I needed to turn this around, fast, but at the same time, my curiosity was piqued. Against my better judgment, I decided to allow this train to run a little further to see where it headed. “I promise you; I am not working for her.” I paused, choosing my words carefully so as not to set off the crystal. “But I am aware of her existence. If you think she might be pertinent to the problem at hand, I would love to hear about your perspective."

The crystal was appeased. Monica was too. "I had never seen Roger so ... happy, I guess, as he was when he was married. For five long years, he was his own man, at peace. And then one day, that bitch left him, high and dry. There one day, gone the next. No reason, no explanation."

"No note?" I couldn't help asking. Mom had told me she had left a note for him when she left. I had no clue exactly what it said, but I had spent my entire life with the understanding that she had given him some sort of explanation for her departure. To hear otherwise rocked me to the core.

Monica waved a dismissive hand. "Sure, there was a note," she said. I internally relaxed. "But who leaves their doting husband with just a note? I never understood what Roger saw in her. She was a little plain, if I'm being honest, and closed off to other people. She spurned any attempts I made to be her friend."

I bristled at the harsh words directed at my mother but kept my ire to myself. Before I could come up with a response, Monica continued, "And to answer your rather personal question, Miss Curtis, no, we are not lovers, although not for lack of trying on my part. That woman messed up Roger so badly I think it turned him off from all other women."

Another relieved but silent sigh from me. I wasn't sure why it bothered me so much to think of my father being intimate with other women. Not that I wanted to think about him with my mother either. Ew. But to hear he had remained faithful after everything she put him through? It was like a balm on my soul.

"Anyway, the bottom line is that I saw Roger about a month ago, and he asked me for help. I haven't seen him since."

My balm evaporated. "So you don't know where he is?"

Monica gave a sardonic grin at my fallen face. "I didn't say that."

My heart quickened. "Can you tell me where he is?"

Monica shook her perfectly coiffed head. "Here's the thing: how do I know telling you will be the best thing for Roger? What if I'm luring him into a trap by giving you my secrets?"

"That's an excellent point," I said, mulling it over. I stared at her, trying to show her I was earnest through my eyes. "Truthfully? I don't know if telling me won't put Mr. Curtain in more danger than he already is. But here's what I do know. At this moment, there are multiple bounty hunters searching for him. And these hired hunters? They're good, Miss Greeves. Like, the best of the best good. And out of that bunch, I am the only one who believes Mr. Curtain has been framed, and I'm the only one who is looking for him in order to help him, to warn him. These other guys? They'll eventually sniff him out with or without you helping me. The problem is, they will probably get to him first. Unless, I have a leg up on them. This man you profess to care for, he's in need of my help. The only question that remains is, are you going to help me help him? Will you be my leg up?"

Admittedly, it was a little heavy-handed, but the crystal held its pretty purple color throughout the whole speech, and Monica seemed to soften a bit when she realized I had spoken the truth.

"Okay, Miss Curtis. You've put me in a spot, for sure. I don't like it, but you're right." She dug into her purse, pulling out a business card and a pen. "Here's the address. My father owns the building, so we were able to sneak him in. Roger even paid for a full year's worth of rent."

"Where did he get the money for that?" I asked on impulse. From the sounds of it, my father should not have been rife with cash.

Monica shrugged as she wrote on the back of the card. "Heaven knows; he wouldn't tell me. He doesn't have a communication crystal, so you'll have to go in person. There. He goes by an alias too, as you can see." She pointed with her pen as she slid the card over to me. I picked it up.

"Ron Carraway?"

She nodded. "He picked it out. Said it would be easier to remember if he kept the initials the same. Now then," she stood briskly and held out her hand for the crystal I still had my fingers resting upon. I handed it to her. "I hope I've been of help. That's my card you have. I work in a beauty shop now. No more secretarial work after Roger. I have my contact info on there, so please let me know if Roger is safe. And Miss Curtis?" She gave me a pitying look as she hoisted her bag onto one shoulder. I met her gaze. "Fire your hairdresser. Whoever put those black streaks in your hair hasn't done you any favors, honey."

With that last parting shot, she walked down the sidewalk, leaving me at the table with a growing smile on my face.

CHAPTER 10

I continued with my breakfast, although the tea had turned cold and the cream cheese now cloyed in my mouth. Plus, a knot had formed in my stomach that seemed to want to push the food back up my esophagus with every swallow.

I knew where my father was.

This was huge. I couldn't contain this information alone. I needed to talk to someone. I needed Grimm.

He was, of course, still at my feet, curled placidly around my ankles in a very large black dog ball. I was surprised Monica hadn't made some comment about him, but then I realized he had stayed very still during the exchange and, from her vantage point, rather looked like a large black fur coat that I had shucked under the table.

I nudged him gently. He looked up at me.

"Grimm, I need to talk. Go scope out the back area. I need to pee."

He rose to his feet instantly, alertness in his body posture. As he trotted past the shop front to find the alley, I walked resolutely into the tea shop. At the back, there was a small door marked RESTROOM. It was unoccupied, much to my relief. Inside, there was a single toilet and a sink, all in shades of powder blue. And, thankfully, there was a small window that was slightly ajar to allow a hint of spring breeze to waft through. I opened it all the way, turning the trickle of airflow into a sudden blast. The window would have been too small for a human to fit through, as well as too high to climb through easily. That wouldn't be a problem for me, however.

I had learned something about myself long ago: I abhorred using the bathroom in my human form. It felt completely unnatural to me. So, I had toilet-trained myself in cat form. All it took was a little coordination as I perched on the rim of the toilet bowl to do my business. I still had the urge to cover my waste, but I had also taught myself to flush the toilet, which took care of that little problem too.

Having done my business, I leapt up to the opened window. There *was* an alley back here, as I had surmised, filled with empty boxes and trash. Oh, and a rather large black dog who was eyeing me with curiosity.

"What's going on, Cress?" he asked, his three-quarter pricked ears almost fully alert.

"Monica knows where my father is."

"Great. What's the story?"

I sniffed the windowsill in feigned nonchalance. "He came to her, asking to be hidden. She put him up in her father's apartment building. Or rather, he put himself up. He seems to have money. Don't you find that strange?"

He shook himself. "You have money," he pointed out.

I huffed. "I have some, but not *that* much."

"I don't understand the difference."

I flattened my ears. "You just don't have a good grasp on what having money means. There's a difference between carrying $1,000 on oneself versus paying for an apartment for a full year in one sitting. I'm guessing a magnitude of ten, at least."

"Is that a lot?"

No matter how smart the dog, mathematics would always

be incomprehensible. Canine brains simply didn't function that way. I shook my head.

Grimm yawned, flashing his substantial teeth at me. "Is there a reason you are wasting time on this moronic conversation? Why are you stalling?"

"I'm not stalling."

"Oh yes, you are." He stretched his front legs out with a groan. "Are you nervous to meet him?"

I paused in my answer. I had an opportunity to meet the man that had sired me, the human that was my mother's true love. A complete enigma to me. What if he was a horrible human? What if there was a good reason why my mother left him?

"No," I lied.

"Liar."

Before I could retort, a knock sounded on the bathroom door. Startled, I nearly fell out of the window. Once I had regained my perch, with a few added scratches in the woodwork's paint, I hissed, "We'll go now." I jumped off the sill and transformed back to a human, exiting the bathroom and relinquishing it to the next patron in line.

The address Monica had given me was too far away to walk, according to my map, so I messaged for Rosa to give us a ride. Again, she was game to chauffeur us to our destination. As we climbed into her phaeton, I thought about what Grimm had told me last night. I was curious to know what she might be, but ultimately, I didn't say anything. After all, I had major secrets I kept, so she must too. Besides, how could I explain that my dog had told me she did not smell fully human? I would have had to answer too many follow-up questions for that one.

Secretive cabbie aside, I was tense the entire trip there. But why wouldn't I be? After all, I was only going to meet my father for the very first time. A man who didn't even know I existed. And Freya only knew how he felt about my mother after she abandoned him three years ago.

Grimm was tense beside me in the taxi because I was tense. His motto was misery loves company. I could not even speak to him to loosen him up because Rosa might have heard me, and I knew that most people had a weird hang-up over individuals who talked to animals conversationally.

To add to the mental discomfort I was already feeling, the sky decided to open up and start raining. The smell of petrichor filled the air as a light drizzle started, staining the streets around us dark grey and blotting out any residual sunshine. Rosa's taxi was covered, but the doors had no glass in the windows, so there was no escaping the sudden humidity.

Rosa, who had no canopy overhead and was completely exposed to the elements, did not complain, however, and steadily pedaled her way to our destination. She seemed cheerful at the change in the weather, humming a little ditty under her breath and jauntily moving her body to the machinations of her bicycle.

She pulled up to a high rise close to the heart of the residential downtown area of Dogwood. I got out of the cab, my heart pumping harder than usual, and the tight knot rooted in my belly. I looked up at the building before me. Unlike the cozy ambiance of the apartment complex my parents had shared, this building was indistinguishable from the other high rises, and it had a foreboding feel to me.

Or maybe that was just my unease clouding my senses.

I turned to Rosa and handed her a stack of bills. "I'd love for you to stick around, but I don't know how long I'll be." Or, for that matter, what my ultimate goal was. Was I there just to warn Roger? Convince him to come with me? At this point, I was truly winging it, because my brain refused to come up with a better plan. I gave my head a little shake to get back on track.

Rosa took my seemingly scattered self in stride, however. "No problem," she assured me, "I'll stick around for a bit. Unless I get a fare I can't refuse. Besides, I enjoy hanging out with Grimm."

I smiled at her, although inside, I felt a tiny pang. It was an ugly feeling, even though I couldn't pin down the sensation. I shook it off. "I'm sure he'd appreciate that. I usually take him with me, but Dogwood hasn't exactly been dog friendly."

I bent down to be eye-level with my partner. "Wish me luck," I whispered to him. I was sure he could see the uncertainty warring within my eyes. He thumped his tail on the wet sidewalk and gave me a quick lick on the chin, his nonverbal way of bolstering my courage. I patted his head as I turned to walk into the building.

Out of the rain—which had increased in volume considerably since it had started—I fished Monica's card out of my pocket and checked the apartment number. 302. That meant the third floor. I stared ahead, seeing closed metallic doors before me, with a button to the side. An elevator, presumably.

I had never seen an elevator in real life, but I had heard of them and had an idea of how they worked. I strode forward and pressed the button on the wall. Sure enough, the doors opened before me, inviting me into the tiny box they had hidden from view just a moment before. Steeling myself, I walked into the box. Once inside, I found more buttons, now labeled with numbers from one to five. I pressed the button labeled "3", and after a few seconds, the doors closed. A brief lurch made my stomach jump unpleasantly, and it was followed by the sensation of movement, which was equally unpleasant.

Luckily, it was over quickly. The elevator stopped, and the

doors opened, freeing me once again. I jumped out without preamble. Perhaps I'd take the stairs back down.

My new surroundings appeared to be a hallway branching both left and right. A small plaque told me apartments 300 through 305 were to the left, and 306 through 310 were on the right. I took the left path.

As I counted down the numbers, my heartrate ratcheted up. By the time I was standing in front of 302, I felt almost light-headed, as if I were in a dreamlike trance. I closed my eyes, breathing deeply and willing my pulse to calm down.

I'll knock on the door, and he'll let me in, and I'll warn him of the danger. And together we'll absolve him of this crime. Easy peasy.

I knocked on the door.

A second passed, and nothing happened. My heart rate sped up again. What if he wasn't home? I hadn't thought of that.

Before I could fully panic, however, I heard footsteps approaching the door from the other side. Now my heart was beating so quickly it was almost painful.

The door clicked as the lock disengaged, and it swung open just enough for me to see most of the face of the man behind it.

"Can I help you?" he asked.

I stared. This was him. In the flesh.

Roger was not a terribly tall man, perhaps only five inches taller than me, around the same height as Fleurette. He was of lanky build, no excess fat from what I could see through the sliver of the door. His sandy-blonde hair was thin, graying, and a bit unkempt, and he had the high widow's peak of a balding man. Wire frame glasses partially hid his eyes, which were blue. Not the unnaturally vibrant blue of mine, but a gray, faded version. And his nose, while more masculine, was very much like mine.

He cleared his throat, and at that moment, I realized I had

been staring without answering his question. Not wanting him to close the door in my face, I blurted, "Are you Ron Carraway?"

He paused for a moment but nodded. "That's me."

"I'm Cressida Curtis."

He raised his eyebrows as if to ask me to continue. This was horribly awkward. I needed to get inside to talk to him. Surely, we couldn't carry this conversation out in the hallway for anyone to hear. I improvised. "I've been sent by Mr. Greeves to check pipes." Well, that wasn't my smoothest lie.

He frowned. "I haven't submitted a repair request." He seemed poised to close the door. I needed to turn this around.

"Oh, it's just a routine inspection. It won't take but a few moments of your time."

Roger seemed to straighten and make up his mind. "I'm sorry, Miss Curtis, but I don't have the time for that. Besides, you don't seem to have any tools with you. If Mr. Greeves takes issue, jus—"

"I need to speak with you!" I blurted, interrupting him.

"Good day!" he stated, and began to shut the door.

"It's about Roger Curtain!" I nearly yelled in desperation.

The door stopped its trajectory. It paused with only a tiny crack left open. And then it opened enough to see one of Roger's eyes, which was wide. "What did you just say?"

I took a breath. "Please, this is really important, *Mr. Carraway,*" I said in a low tone, emphasizing his false name.

He looked at me through the slit. He sighed heavily. And he opened the door. "Come in," he said, resigned.

I wasted little time following his order. Behind the door was a tiny hallway that opened into a modest living room with a view of the city. I stopped just a few feet in, waiting for my father to close the door and direct me which way to go.

Roger guided me into the living room, motioning for me to take a seat in a chair facing a loveseat, in which he sat. I smoothed

my hands down my trousers, my nerves back on display now that
I had succeeded in one small task.

"So, Miss Curtis," he said matter-of-factly, "what exactly do
you know?"

CHAPTER 11

I looked over at the man who was obviously my father, based on our comparable colorations and the shape of his nose. He seemed oblivious to any similarities between us, and I was more than fine with keeping him in the dark. The last thing I wanted to do was surprise him with his paternity, mainly because he would ask questions that could not be answered mundanely.

"What exactly do you know?" he asked me.

"I know that Ron Carraway doesn't actually exist," I answered his question slowly, "but Roger Curtain does."

"Who are you?" he asked. I detected a hint of anger in his voice, but when I met his eyes, all I saw were splashes of fear, resignation, and a deep well of exhaustion.

I was treading on thin ice here. "I told you; my name is Cressida. I'm going to be fully honest with you. I am a bounty hunter, and your previous workplace hired me to find you. What you need to understand, though, is that I have no intention of arresting you."

He let out a ghost of a chuckle. "Trust is a commodity I can no longer afford."

I nodded. "I understand that. But at this moment, all I want to do is talk. I swear."

He splayed out his hands. "By all means, let's talk."

"Did you do it?"

He blinked at the very blunt question. "Did I steal from the company and then burn the office to cover my tracks? No. But why take my word for it?"

I shrugged. "From the minute I was offered this case, something felt off. You don't seem like the type of person to do those things."

"How would you know?" He squinted at me, pushing his glasses up his nose. "Have we met before?"

"No, no," I answered hastily.

"Hmm. You seem slightly familiar. But I can't place why."

I gave a little nervous laugh. "Just one of those faces, I guess." I silently willed him to stop scrutinizing me. "Tell me, Roger—can I call you Roger? You can call me Cressida—why did you go into hiding? Why not come forward and clear your name?"

"Let me tell you a little story, Cressida." Roger shifted on the loveseat, propping one leg over the other as he seemed to settle in. "I was down on my luck. My wife left me, my workplace was floundering; it was a huge mess. Out of the blue, I was offered a job with a huge jump in salary. As far as I could tell, they specifically headhunted me for the position. So, of course I took the job. Now, I'm good at accounting, but I'm nothing special. On top of a pay bump over my last job, I started receiving huge bonuses on a regular basis. My boss didn't seem to know much about them, other than telling me that I was a hard worker and deserved to be rewarded. I added them all up in the end, and they totaled about \$200,000. This went on for a few months, during which I became increasingly ... suspicious, for lack of a better term. Nobody else is receiving bonuses like I am. On top of that, I started to hear rumors around the office that the books weren't adding up correctly. But my books were adding up just fine."

He stopped to take a deep breath. "Finally, come February, I was jumped in my own office."

"What happened?" I was now on the edge of my seat, quite literally.

He moved his head from side to side slowly. "There's a master ledger somewhere, where Lightfoot himself claimed to keep track of all expenses in the business. I started getting to work early to try and look for it while most people weren't around. That day, before I could enter my office, I had decided to look in one of the other offices, which was vacant at the time. A coworker ran into me in the hallway. He had a question for me. I told him to go ahead into my office and wait for me. As he entered my office, he was attacked. The attacker thought it was me."

"Who was the attacker?"

He shrugged. "I couldn't see well, since my office was dark, but it was some big hulking guy from the little I did see. As he knocked around my innocent co-worker, he made some mention about how that's what embezzlers deserve and how he was going to kill me. I only knew I was the target because he said my name a couple of times. Once I realized they were after me, I fled the building."

"They said you committed arson to cover your tracks. Three people died."

He shook his head, looking like a sad hound dog. "More like to cover *their* tracks. I smelled the smoke once I was far enough away, but there has been no mention of the fire or the deaths in any news source beyond a quick blurb in a paper that said it was a small kitchen fire in the building that was quickly put out."

He assessed me again. "How did you find me?"

I was caught off guard by this sudden change of topic. "Oh, uh, Monica told me."

His eyebrows raised. "She trusted you with that information?"

I shrugged. "We had a conversation over a truth crystal. It was the only way she would have given me that info."

He pursed his lips. "I've been very grateful to her and her family. I don't know what you coming here means for me. I've been trying to do some investigation into all this to somehow clear my name, but there's not much I can do. I'm forced to live in the shadows. I hardly leave the apartment for fear of being seen."

"I'm here to help you," I stated with a small smile. "Let me help clear your name."

"Why do you care? Weren't you hired to apprehend me?"

I chuckled. "Yes, I was, but I'm in the habit of helping wronged folk, even if it's less lucrative for me."

"I can't be sure I trust you." Roger gave me a sad smile.

"I don't blame you. It sounds like your piece of seemingly good luck turned to rubbish rather quickly. I'm going to try to prove myself to you with actions, though. So, what can I do first?"

He considered my words. Finally, he answered, "The master ledger. If we had that, it would prove they legitimately paid me at least some of the money they are claiming I embezzled. I have a theory on where the ledger is."

"What's that?" I asked, leaning forward.

Roger opened his mouth to speak, but he was interrupted by a loud knock on the door. The sound made me jump. Roger frowned.

"Excuse me for a moment," he said, getting up from his seat.

I was half inclined to tell him not to answer the door, but before I could, he was already opening it. "Yes?" he said to the open door.

From my seat, all I could see was the back of my father as he blocked my view beyond the door. But there was no mistaking that smooth masculine voice that answered.

"Hello, sir, do you happen to be Ron Carraway?" asked Gavin St. Cloud in his most pleasant voice.

CHAPTER 12

Oh no. No, no, *no*. I had just had Roger opening up to me, almost trusting me, and now this? How had St. Cloud found him so quickly? This was a nightmare.

The horror that washed over me deafened my ears to my father's reply.

St. Cloud's next words increased the icy hand gripping my throat. "Are you alone at the moment? I'm looking for my partner, Cressida Cur—"

"*No!*" I shouted as I leapt up from my seat. I couldn't allow the idiot to say my last name in front of Roger. I raced down the hallway, silently apologizing as I nudged Roger out of the way to take his place at the open door, and tried to close it in St. Cloud's face. Unfortunately, he had a grip on the door, and he was stronger than me. "We are *not* partners!" I hissed at St. Cloud, loud enough for my father's benefit.

Roger backed up from the door, allowing me control.

St. Cloud's face broke into a smile upon seeing me. "Why, Miss Cur—"

"—tis," I said as quietly as I dared, interrupting him.

He had the gall to wink at me. "Miss Curtis," he amended cheerily. "There you are! What *have* you been up to?"

"What are you doing here?" I spat.

From behind me, Roger called out in an almost bewildered tone, "I'm just going to go make some tea." The sound of his footsteps receded behind me while I kept my attention on the menace at the door.

St. Cloud smirked knowingly at me, disarmingly charming as usual.

"How did you find this place?" I demanded. I still held the door just wide enough for him to see only me. An odd protectiveness had arisen in me, and I didn't want him laying eyes on my father's place.

"It was surprisingly simple, really." He ran a hand through his dark brown locks. "Did you know that Information is a government-run business? That means that the employees are on a government salary. They are paid well, but it could always be better."

"So?" I couldn't understand what he was getting at.

"Well, I had a lovely discussion with one of them. Adam, was his name? Anyway, it turns out that Adam is saving up for his wedding."

I had a slight sinking feeling as St. Cloud continued in an upbeat fashion.

"He has been trying hard to make a nest egg so that he and his intended, James, can go on a lovely honeymoon together. Naturally, he was very pleased when I offered him some money under the table to help facilitate that."

"He what?" I mumbled half-heartedly.

"Oh yes. In exchange, he gave me a piece of paper with some of his scribblings from the last person he talked to."

Me. I was the last person he had talked to. "You bastard!" I hissed under my breath.

St. Cloud ignored my verbal abuse. "I wondered why you would be so interested in a Monica Greeves, so I decided to do a little research. From what I gathered, Monica worked for Mr. Curtain once upon a time. Some further digging discovered that her family is well-to-do. As a matter of fact, her father owns this very building."

From the kitchen, a kettle started whistling.

Gavin smiled again, probably metaphorically patting his back over his cleverness. "Once I learned that little fact, I simply got a list of all the current tenants and how long they've been here. The name Ron Carraway piqued my interest because the initials matched up to Roger Curtain. He also began renting only a month ago. It seemed suspicious enough to warrant a meeting with him, at the very least."

The kettle began whistling furiously.

"And lo and behold, when I pulled up to the building, there was a big black dog off to the side, being loved on by some woman. So I figured you were here. And look at that, I got it right."

I clapped my hands sarcastically. "Great," I deadpanned. "Now beat it."

"The question is, Miss *Curtis*, what exactly are you *doing* here? It certainly doesn't seem like you are arresting the man." Gavin frowned. "And speaking of, where is the man in question?"

I realized the kettle was still screaming in the background. It should have been taken off the heat by now.

Oh no.

Ignoring St. Cloud, I raced into the kitchen, and I screeched to a halt. There, frantically whistling from the stovetop, was the teakettle at the far wall. And there sat an open window, the rainy breeze puffing out the white curtain covering it.

But Roger was gone.

I stopped the screaming of the kettle first, then turning off the burner and moving the shrill contraption off the heat. Then, I bounded to the other side of the room and yanked the filmy kitchen curtain to the side, taking a face full of rainwater in the process. Ignoring the wetness, I stuck my head out.

Right outside the window, there was a fire escape. It was empty.

Of course. Curse my luck.

"Is he out there?"

I started, nearly knocking the top of my head on the window frame. Straightening back up, I turned to glower at Gavin St. Cloud, who had snuck up behind me. "No sign of him."

St. Cloud turned without another word, striding purposefully out of the kitchen and toward the apartment door. I followed after, not daring to let him out of my sight.

We took the elevator back down together, neither of us speaking. And together, we strode out of the building. As soon as I cleared the double doors, I saw Grimm, quite wet and with a perplexed look to his eyes, sitting patiently in front of me.

Alone.

Rosa was gone.

Being an intelligent animal, I connected the dots easily. "He took my cab."

St. Cloud swore. "Can your mutt track him?"

I glared at my nemesis. "He's not a mutt, and his name is Grimm. And I doubt it. If Curtain were on foot, yes, but he can't easily track a scent of a moving vehicle, and if he could, he'd be too slow to catch up. Not to mention the rain makes it all the more difficult. Plus the other vehicles ..."

He held out his palm. "Stop, I get it." Rain pelted us in earnest now, the day having taken a complete turn from the early sun of this morning. Much like my outlook on how this day would turn out: optimistically sunny earlier, and now pessimistically moody.

How could everything have turned upside down so quickly? My father was *right there*. There was only one person to blame for this mess.

"You just had to go barging in up there!" I yelled at St. Cloud, who seemed deep in thought. "I had things under control!"

He looked up at my words, an angry frown on his features. "I beg your pardon! I'd like to know exactly what you 'had under control!'" he used air quotes as he mocked my words. "Because it sure didn't seem like you were arresting the guy!"

I had never seen Gavin St. Cloud so ... angry. He usually kept a cloak of smugness wrapped around himself, which irritated me to no end. To see him this animated, even to my detriment, was incredibly satisfying.

But I realized yelling at each other on the sidewalk in the rain was perhaps not the smartest endeavor. "Look, can we go back up? I'm freezing out here, and I need to search for clues as to where he might be going next." I shivered theatrically to prove my point.

St. Cloud huffed. "Yes, but I'm looking for clues too, Miss Curtain. Or should I call you Miss *Curtis*?"

I ignored his verbal barb, instead motioning for Grimm to follow me. It was incredibly wet out here, and he deserved to be by my side for this, dog laws be damned.

St. Cloud followed the two of us. "What are you doing?"

I shoved the doors open, not bothering to turn my attention to St. Cloud. "I'm going up. Like we just discussed."

"Yes, but what about the dog?"

"I'm letting my partner work the case." I swiveled around quickly, nearly causing my nemesis to bump into me. "My actual partner."

I turned and continued walking to the elevator. Gavin caught up, his smug cloak fully back in place, as was the twinkle in his velvety amber eyes. "Oh please, it was just a little lie to get me in the door. I can't begin to imagine what lie you told him to be let inside."

The doors shut, and the elevator lurched as we ascended. I turned my head to look at him. He had his damn pocket watch out again.

"I do not lie!" I countered.

"No?" He smirked as he checked the time. "I beg to differ, Miss Curt*is*."

"Ugh. I didn't want to freak him out by having the same last name. Big deal. It's not the same, and you know it."

"And why would that freak him out? It's not as if you two are related." He continued to check the time.

"Would you stop that?" I scowled as the elevator came to a stop, "That thing doesn't even keep the right time!"

Gavin only smiled widely before exiting the elevator and striding back to 302. I hurried to keep up, with a confused Grimm bringing up the rear, all three of us leaving a trail of water in our wake.

Back inside the apartment, I slammed the door a little too forcefully. "Fine," I conceded with a smidge of anger. "You want to know what I was doing? The man is innocent. I was trying to help him."

Gavin, who had been putting his watch away, suddenly flipped it back out, opening the face in one smooth motion. "The hell he is."

"It's true."

His eyebrows shot up as he glanced at the watch. He took a moment before answering, "But that's your belief. It doesn't make it true; it only means you believe it to be true."

It was almost as if he was talking to himself, convincing himself of this. I let out a heavy sigh, flipping wet blonde-and-black hair out of my face. "Look at the facts, St. Cloud. He's never so much as gotten a ticket in all of his forty-five years. All of the so-called evidence we have is hearsay from the very company that hired us! What if they're framing him?"

He shook his head, still glancing from his watch to me over and over. He finally gave me his full attention. "Why do you care, though? We were hired to arrest him, not investigate. It's not our job to discern who's guilty and who's innocent."

"Maybe it should be!" I paced the living room. "Doesn't it bother you in the slightest that we might be arresting a man who isn't guilty? That we would hand him over to a company that isn't going through the proper channels but is rather acting as judge, jury, and executioner?"

"No."

I stopped to gawk at the man, but he was frowning at his watch again. He looked up, slightly frazzled. "I mean, if these things bother you, maybe you're in the wrong business."

"Maybe I am." First the Ramberts, and now my dad. I was beginning to see that the world was not as black and white as I once thought it to be. The older I got, the more shades of gray appeared. I shook my head. "Look, if he were truly guilty, I'd be the first to hand him over to collect the bounty. But I can't do it. Not after what I've learned. Can't you just take a moment to hear me out? Please?"

I had crossed the room during this speech, and I grabbed Gavin by the arms. I had never touched him before, not even to pass him a mint, and now I was reduced to pleading with my competition. Oh, the shame. But this was how desperate I was to make St. Cloud see the truth.

He looked down at where my hands rested on his arms: first the left and then the right. He considered for a moment. Finally, he nodded.

Relief rushed through me. I released my desperate grasp. "Thank you."

"But on one condition."

Oh, here it was, the dropping of the other shoe. I looked him in the eye, waiting for him to continue.

"If you can convince me that he *might* be innocent, then you will agree to investigate this case together. If at any time hereafter I find evidence that in fact soundly links him to this crime, you will forfeit any bounty from this case to me, and I will continue to search for him, with or without your help."

I took a moment to digest this condition. "You want to work this case together?" I asked, perplexed. "Why?"

He smirked again, in that disarming way that had me looking like an idiot the first time we met. "I have my reasons. One, to keep an eye on you. I don't necessarily like you going off-script like this. Two, we seem to be evenly matched, so it makes sense that pairing up will get the job done faster. And three, I think it will be fun."

"Fun?" I sounded highly skeptical.

"Of course! It's highly amusing when you lie to my face constantly."

"I don't ..." I took a breath. Technically, I did lie to his face quite a lot, but he couldn't possibly know that. Except he apparently did.

Was my father worth working alongside my enemy? I glanced at Grimm, who had stayed quiet yet attentive this entire time, watching us argue back and forth. He was not going to like this.

Not one bit.

I took one more deep breath and sealed my fate. "You've got a deal."

CHAPTER 13

Okay, so I had just agreed to partner up with my arch-nemesis to clear my father's name. Not so bad, right?

Grimm did not see it that way.

"What do you mean, you made a deal with St. Cloud?" he growled at me. We had only a few short minutes to speak, as the man in question had decided to run down to his MC to grab something, leaving Grimm and me in temporary privacy. I tried to break it to my canine partner as succinctly as possible, but Grimm wasn't having it. "This is the man that has belittled you and stolen bounties from you for the past two years! What on earth possessed you to think that teaming up with him would be a good idea?"

I arched my feline back a bit at his angry posture. "It wasn't my first choice, believe me. But he backed me into a corner, Grimm. I could have either said forget it and let him walk away, letting him believe the best course of action was to arrest my father, or agree to his demands. As much as I enjoy insulting his intelligence, he's actually incredibly smart, and I was worried he would find my dad without me and turn him in for the bounty! I need to crack this puzzle before anyone else gets his hands on him. You saw how quickly St. Cloud found Roger. Even with our leg up, we barely beat him here." Of course, that was St. Cloud using *my* clues to find him, but I dared not tell Grimm that. "Speaking of Roger, did you see what happened to him?"

Grimm shook his body, his fur still damp with rain. "I was hanging out with Rosa. She gives the best ear rubs."

"Better than me?" I shot back before I thought it through.

Grimm assessed me with his yellow eyes. "I suppose not. Anyway, a man came running around the corner like a demon was after him, saw the cab, saw Rosa, and started talking quickly. Too quickly for me to understand. Then he thrust money at Rosa, and she got on her bicycle and he got in the taxi, and off they went. And then you and the clod came bursting out of the front doors just a little bit later. I had no idea the mystery man was your father, otherwise I would have tried to stop him."

I heaved a sigh. "Did you at least get his scent before they left?"

Grimm considered. "I think so. It all happened so quickly, but I'm fairly sure I could pick up the scent, given the chance."

"Let's hope so."

Footsteps echoed in the hallway, signaling our alone time was done. "But this is happening, partner," I warned quickly. "So be nice. No biting!"

I shimmered, becoming my human form just seconds before the door opened, and Gavin walked in. Grimm only let out a small growl at the sight of him. I frowned at Grimm. "What did I just say?"

He only stared at me, his sunflower eyes boring into mine. No ear droop, no tail wag. He was sending me a clear message: *I'm not a bit sorry*.

"We'll discuss this later," I reprimanded him.

St. Cloud chuckled and shook his head. "You know, you'd get a lot more respect if you didn't hold conversations with your dog."

"He's not my dog," I automatically retorted. "And who says I want respect from people with closed minds about animals?"

Gavin only brushed my words aside with another little head

shake. "Let's begin our search. Where do we start?" he said instead.

I scrunched my lips. "The bedroom?"

His eyes lit up. "Ooh, getting straight down to business! Perhaps I'm not that kind of guy?"

I stared at him in utter confusion for a second too long before I caught the innuendo. "Oh please, St. *Clod*. I prefer not to feel nauseous while I work."

He chuckled as we made our way to the bedroom. Inside, there was a single bed, neatly made, a dresser with an unassuming sock hanging out of it, and a desk that looked uncharacteristically messy. A huge stack of papers took up one half and a ledger the other.

"This seems like as good a place as any to start," I said.

St. Cloud immediately went to the stack of papers and started perusing each one individually. I squeezed over to his left to try to see what was on them. He was going through them awfully fast, however.

"Well, this is interesting," he murmured.

"What is it?"

He held up a receipt. "A grocer's bill, paid in full."

I frowned. "What's so interesting about that?"

"Nothing. This whole stack is useless drivel." St. Cloud slammed it down on the desk. "If anything, this all points to Curtain being loaded. All of these receipts to grocers? And this apartment that has been paid in full with cash? That's a lot of money. Where could he have gotten it from? Oh, wait ..."

I ignored the sarcasm. "I told you, some of the money that he supposedly stole had all been gifted to him legally." I had filled St. Cloud in on what my father had told me after making the deal to work with him.

"So he says. It sounds like something a thief would say to cover his tracks."

"Which is why we need to find that master ledger." Where could it be? Roger had said he couldn't find it at work. Could it be at someone's place of residence?

Speaking of ledgers, I decided to look at the one on the desk. I opened it to the first page, and something fell out, landing at my feet. I picked it up, noting that it was a piece of paper, creased and wrinkled from time and countless handlings, from the looks of it. I opened it to its full length and read the first couple of lines.

"Dear Roger,

This is the hardest thing to write, but I must. You should know that my time with you has been some of my happiest years, but circumstances change ..."

It was my mother's letter to my father. My heart stuttered at the revelation. But now was not the time to dwell on this. I discreetly folded the letter back up and tucked it into my vest pocket, saving that extremely personal detail for later when I wasn't with my nemesis.

I turned my attention back to the ledger, surveying the first page. Instead of numbers lining the pages, however, there were small, neat handwritten notes in a combination of blue, black, and red ink, depending on the line.

"Hey, look at this," I quietly called to Gavin. He leaned over me to see what I had found. I squinted to read it.

Feb 8th: Ledger not in office, am certain. Must be kept at some-one's home. But who?

Feb 9th: Need to remember who else had access to funds at LFS. Lightfoot, silent partner, attorneys?

Feb. 10th: Library trip. Scared to be caught. No name for silent partner. He exists!!

The writing continued, each ledger line a single thought my father had jotted down. I flipped the page, scanning the contents.

"It's his diary, of sorts," I commented. "It looks like he was trying to clear his name."

"He's done a bang-up job so far," St. Cloud muttered.

This page was much the same as the first, continuing into this month. Some lines were crossed out, where others were starred with a red pen. One starred entry caught my attention, as it was in capital letters.

*EQUINOX BALL

There was no date associated with it, but the previous line was from two days ago.

"What's an Equinox ball?" I asked.

I pointed to the line in question. Gavin leaned in closer, crowding my personal bubble. I fought the urge to step away, not because I did not like him there but because his nearness wasn't unpleasant, and that confused me.

"Surely you've heard of the Spring Equinox," he said to me.

I rolled my eyes. "Of course." The Equinox was a popular holiday, especially for magical folk. Fleurette always had a small celebration at her home, taking the time to cleanse the cottage of bad energy and welcome in new beginnings and light for the upcoming longer days.

"Well, if you're rich, the Equinox is a popular time to hold balls. You know, large parties with dancing? It's not enough to celebrate with the family. One must prove they are above others in order to let in the seeds of transformation the Equinox supposedly provides." There was an unusual tone of bitterness to his words. I frowned at this unexpected mood, so different from his usual bluster. He didn't notice my expression, but his acerbic tone vanished as quickly as it had arrived. "I think there was something about a ball in this stack, come to think of it. Let me look."

He again picked up the pile of random papers and began

systematically looking at each one. "Here it is! This is a flyer from Lightfoot Shipping Industries."

I snatched the flier from his hands. "The Fifth Annual Spring Equinox Ball, hosted by Orson Lightfoot ... to be held on Saturday, March 20th, at 8 p.m. ... location TBA ... Mark your calendars! All employees will be entered into a raffle on March 1st. Four names will be drawn, good for yourself plus one guest."

"So generous of him to invite four of his employees, with their plus ones," Gavin stated dryly.

I agreed with him. "Is this supposed to be a great prize? It must be a fancy affair."

"It is." He pointed to the bottom. "Formal attire required."

"Okay, Roger seems to think the ball is important. Is it because he thinks the location at which it's being held is the same location as the ledger? How would he know where that is, though?"

St. Cloud seemed to think. "Perhaps before he ... left the company, they had updated the location? Look, this flyer is dated back to January."

"Good idea!" I gushed, and then looked at him. He was smiling. I was immediately on guard. "What?"

"Oh, it's just us, getting along, working a case together. It's rather refreshing, isn't it?"

I humphed. "Don't get used to it. I had a momentary lapse of judgment."

He smiled disarmingly at me again. "So you say, so you say."

I decided to ignore him. "So, what's our plan? It seems like this is a good lead, but we need to figure out the address first. If it turns out it's being held at a rec center, I doubt the ledger will be there."

"I doubt it will be held at a rec center," St. Cloud scoffed. "Balls are for the elite, which means they are usually held at someone's estate so that some rich snob can show off their obscene amount of wealth in front of their peers."

There was that acidity again. It sounded like he spoke from experience. I snorted. "You aren't jaded at all."

He shrugged, smiling, although the smile seemed forced. "Just calling it how I see it."

"Well, it's best to check before we get our hopes up anyway."

"Before *you* get your hopes up. I'm still of the mind that Curtain is guilty."

I frowned. "Whatever. I might have an idea about how to find the address. But I'm going to need to do this alone."

St. Cloud shook his head. "Miss Curtain, I am not allowing you to give me the slip like that."

"Oh, please. I could have given you the slip three times over if that was my plan. You can stay here with Grimm. If anything, you'll give *me* the slip and go looking for Roger to collect that bounty."

He clutched at his chest in mock shock. "I give you my word; I would never do that!"

"And I gave you mine!" I shot back.

"What exactly is it that you would plan to do by yourself?"

I paused. "I can't tell you. It may not be legal, and I don't need you snitching on me." Plus, it involved my cat form, which he would never find out about if I could help it.

"Fine." St. Cloud once again drew out his pocket watch. I rolled my eyes.

"What are you doing?" I asked as he slipped it open.

He looked at me. "Checking the time. Give me your word that you will come back and continue this investigation with me and that you will tell me everything you learn while you were gone."

I pursed my lips. That ornery feeling I often encountered in St. Cloud's presence was back, but if this was the only way to do this one thing alone, I'd have to play nice. "I promise, I will *not* give you the slip, and I will come straight back here, where you will be with Grimm, and I will tell you all I learned while I was gone, or may I be struck down by a mechanical carriage."

St. Cloud watched every word I said and then glanced at the watch for just a second before putting it away. I narrowed my eyes. There was something fishy about that. But he beamed at me and said, "Wonderful! Have fun!"

CHAPTER 14

I hated leaving Grimm alone with St. Cloud. My partner had the gall to raise one side of his lips to flash a canine tooth at me when I told him to stay behind, a sure sign of his displeasure. And I was certain I'd get an earful from him once we were together again. But I had no choice in the matter. He would not have been very helpful on this mission, considering I needed to go for small and stealthy, not large and menacing.

I had messaged for Rosa to come back to pick me up, but she did not return my mirror messages. Frankly, I wasn't surprised by this turn of events, seeing as how Roger had absconded in her taxi. No doubt he had told her all sorts of terrible things about me, and she decided to wash her hands of our acquaintanceship. I couldn't really blame her, even if the things I imagined my father saying about me were untrue.

Instead, I had to hail a different taxi to get to my destination: Lightfoot Shipping Industries Headquarters, where my father used to work.

I had the taxi driver drop me off a block away, and I made sure that he drove off before I did much of anything else. Once he was out of sight, I casually made my way to a small alley near the building and ducked behind the dumpster to change into a cat. After that, I sauntered back out onto the sidewalk, mindful of the larger humans walking about.

Despite the fact that it felt like the longest day ever, in reality, it was only half past noon. The rain that had drenched me just a couple of hours ago had once again tapered off to a light drizzle. There were more than a few people exiting the building in front of me, taking advantage of the break in the weather to go on their lunch. This was what I needed to get inside the front door.

Said door had a doorman. I watched from a safe distance away, hidden behind a large potted plant at the edge of an awning, to survey him. As I observed him, he opened the door for a man going out to lunch ("Have a good lunch, Hal!", he briskly greeted), and stopped a woman from entering with a brief conversation, handing her a visitor's pass before allowing her through the door. It was just as I had suspected; he would not have let me enter as a human if I did not have a reason to be there.

I bided my time, watching him and my surroundings, until smartly dressed businesspeople began to make their way back from their lunch breaks. Each of these persons had a lanyard they flashed at the doorman before being graciously swept back into the building.

Time to act.

I chose one such person, a petite woman in a white blouse with a long, swishing, dove-gray skirt. She held an umbrella over her head, despite the lightness of the current precipitation. As she walked with dainty steps toward the building, I darted out and took position near her skirts to the left side, hidden from the doorman's view.

She also flashed her lanyard, earning a smile from the doorman. "Miss Kemp," he greeted with a head nod, opening the door for her as she closed her umbrella. Having done that, she strode into the building, with me acting as her small, white shadow.

Once inside, I stopped following Miss Kemp as soon as we

were out of the doorman's line of sight, in order to get my bearings. I stared at a sign before me, which I assumed stated where each company was located within the building. I made sure to keep my ears trained behind me to pick up any sounds of possible employees heading my way. And then I got to reading.

As a human, reading came quite naturally once I'd learned. But as a cat, it took extra concentration to make out the words, lest the letters jump and jumble. It was as if my cat brain simply was not equipped to read, but because I had that magical twist in my genes, I was just able to force it to work when others would surely fail.

It took more seconds than I liked to admit, but eventually, I figured out that Lightfoot Shipping was on the second floor, suite A. It was time to find the stairs.

After a bit of slinking, I found the stairwell tucked off to the left of the elevator. I ducked into an alcove to change back into a human in order to open the heavy door leading to the stairs. While I was at it, I stayed a human to traverse them, seeing as it was much easier and faster to do so. Finally, I peeked my head out of the second-story door. No one was around.

I soon found out why. There was a hint of smoke in the air, and once I rounded the bend and found Suite A, there was a large sign posted to the door that informed me that due to fire damage, Lightfoot Shipping Industries had been temporarily relocated to Third Floor, Suite F. Back to the stairs I went.

The third floor had a bit more human activity to it. Once again, it felt prudent to revert to cat form for maximum sneakiness. I had been lucky enough not to be spotted yet, but I had a feeling my luck would run out soon. Sure enough, as I skulked down the hall to the proper suite, a young man came up from behind me. There was no place to hide.

"Oh, hello," he said, raising the timbre of his voice to sound friendlier. He must have seen me jump at his appearance.

I had two options: go on the defense or play sweet. Despite my natural inclination to act aloof and run away or to arch my back and hiss, I figured those would not work well in this situation. This man seemed amiable enough; maybe I could play with his heartstrings a bit. So, at the sound of his greeting, I turned, lifted my fluffy tail straight up in the air, and trilled, ending in a question: "Prrrt?"

As I suspected, the man metaphorically melted. "Aww," he cooed, as he reached down to pet me.

Here's the truth: I had never allowed a human to so much as touch me until about eight months ago, when I bonded with Wren after our near-death experience at the hands of Annie Coddle. Since then, I'd allowed Wren, Fleurette, and even Fal to get the occasional pet in, although always on my terms. They respected that about me.

A stranger, though? No telling what their true intentions would be. But I knew being friendly would work in my favor. I fought the urge to shy away from his hand.

My trust was rewarded. He gave me a decent ear scratch, followed by a full-body stroke. It wasn't bad, honestly. I played it up by turning and rubbing against his pant leg, purring audibly. He reacted accordingly, going for another pet before straightening. "Sorry, kitty, I have to get to work now. I don't know how you got in here, but best run along, okay?"

He turned to stride down the hall, toward Suite F. This was my chance. I scampered behind him, sneaking into the suite as he opened the door. I could hear him give a half-hearted protest, but I simply ignored him and kept running deeper into the office suite, stopping to get my bearings only when I had lost him. Now it was time to do a little snooping.

Honestly, I wasn't sure exactly how to go about this. I needed to find out where the ball was being held. I assumed there would be a room in the office with this sort of information in it. Perhaps a human resource office?

As I slunk about, I had to hide to avoid human interaction. It was irksome and made this mission feel ten times harder than it should be. I mentally chided myself over this clumsy oversight. I should have waited until evening to break in, but time was of the essence in this case. However, investigating might take a while, and the longer I stayed here, the likelier I'd get caught.

This may have been a major issue if I hadn't overheard a conversation through an open door. I poked my feline head in to hear better. Two women were standing by a sink in what I assumed to be the breakroom, each holding a mug. "I can't believe Rona gets to go to the ball," one woman said, her tone catty. "I wonder what she'll wear."

The other smirked. "Aw, jealous much, Whit? Maybe if you ask nicely, she'll take you as her plus one."

The other woman laughed. "I doubt that. You know she's sweet on Alex."

"The new guy? Roger's replacement?"

My ears perked.

Whit nodded. "That's the one. Alex is nice to look at, but I miss Roger. He was so sweet."

The other lady nodded in agreement. "I cried like a baby at the memorial. Those poor people. They didn't deserve to die in a freak accident like that."

"It's a little spooky to think that just below us, four people died."

I wasn't sure I heard right. Four people? I had been told three.

"What if they're ghosts? Can you imagine walking into the breakroom, and there's Roger, getting himself a cup of coffee like nothing ever happened, but he's partially see-through!"

They both chortled and then looked sad again. These ladies might have had the most inane conversation ever, but my mind was reeling from what they said. They thought Roger was dead? And they didn't know about the arson?

But, as Roger had pointed out, no arson was covered in any of the newspapers. So perhaps there wasn't any. Clearly, there had been a fire. My nose did not lie about that sort of thing. But perhaps it truly was just an inconvenient kitchen fire.

This was a lot to handle.

The two gossips took this moment to exit the room, and I took my opportunity to go inside. As I sprinted around the door frame and hid behind a trash can, I overheard one of the women say, "Did you see something? It looked like a cat!"

"Maybe it was a ghost!" the other answered teasingly.

Luckily, neither decided to investigate. I came out of hiding and did a quick visual sweep of the room. Chairs, a table, countertop with various accoutrements ...

Aha! There, a bulletin board, directly in the line of sight where the two ladies had been gossiping. And upon closer inspection, I saw a large piece of paper attached to it.

I transformed in order to read it more quickly. At first glance, I saw a note of congratulations to the winners of the Equinox Ball raffle, followed by a list of names, and—

Voices in the hall interrupted me. I quickly snatched the paper off the board, tearing one of the corners as I did, and stuffed it into my vest pocket before turning back into a cat.

Not a second later, a small group of men came through the door, talking and laughing together. One spied me, frozen with indecision on the floor before him, and yelled rather loudly, "Hey, look! There's a cat!"

The last thing I needed was to be grabbed by one of these ham-fisted gentlemen, so I broke my paralysis and sprinted between their legs to freedom. I had exactly what I had come here for, and now it was time to get out.

I had become severely turned around, however, and had no clue how to find the door back to the main hallway. To make matters worse, two of the men were now chasing me and yelling about it to anyone who poked their heads out of their respective offices.

I normally did not give in to panic, but having a horde of humans trying to wrangle me had me in a tizzy, and I simply could not make my brain work rationally. After two trips around the main areas of the office space, enough people had blocked certain ways and corralled me to what I recognized as the main entrance. No one was angry, but rather confused, much like myself, and many of them made wheedling noises and uttered words in placating tones, such as, "Here, kitty kitty!" or, "Puss puss, it's okay!" to get me to calm down.

But under these circumstances, there was no calming me down. I felt more trapped by these well-meaning office workers than I had when I was literally imprisoned by Annie Coddle herself. All I needed to do was shift to be able to open the door and walk to freedom, but of course, that wasn't an option. I simply cowered against the door and let out a frightened growl.

This terrifying standoff came to an abrupt end when the same man I had met in the hallway pushed his way to the front. "Hey, everyone, back up! You're scaring it!" This saint of a man simply opened the door, allowing me to escape. I did so promptly.

As I raced toward the stairs on four swift legs, I could hear someone questioning how a cat got into the office to begin with. I turned the corner, seeing the heavy door that led to the stairs. As quickly as possible, I shimmered up, opened it, and fled down the stairs in human form. Once on the main floor and out of the stairwell, I transformed back to feline and sprinted out of the door, not caring who saw me. I was done with subterfuge; now was the time for pure escape.

CHAPTER 15

G avin St. Cloud opened the door to let me into my father's apartment. "Ah, you're back! Uh—is there something the matter? You're looking a bit peaked."

I had spent some time directly after my escape simply walking about the city in the hopes that I could calm myself down after the events of the office building. Calming myself would facilitate my being able to think properly again. Focusing on placing one foot in front of the other did the trick, and soon I was contemplating why exactly being cornered in that office had scared me so much.

Normally, I was able to stay as cool as a cucumber while getting out of tight corners. Even when things seemed fairly bleak last summer in the abandoned school, I kept a level head. This allowed me to sneak Wren out from right under the nose of St. Cloud himself.

But then again, the difference between that adventure and this one was the fact that I hadn't truly been cornered in the school. If I dug deeper into that particular harrowing week, there was an even worse misadventure that very nearly killed me. I *had* been rather trapped in front of Annie Coddle, with no seeming way to escape. It was only my special shimmer that saved me that time. Perhaps that episode had left more scars on my psyche than I had wanted to admit. I'd have to watch myself to make sure I was truly okay.

Once I had rationally reached some deep-seated conclusions about my mental health, I decided to take a taxi to the parking lot to pay for another overnight fee. I conceded that I would be staying at least through part of tomorrow, and so I needed to make sure Humbert was still being taken care of. After that, it was another simple taxi ride (but still not from Rosa, regrettably) back to the apartment building to spend time with my partner and my nemesis.

"I'm fine," I lied as I stalked into the apartment. Gavin shut the door behind me, and I could feel him frowning at my back. I went directly to the loveseat, flopping into it with a sigh. Grimm approached and nuzzled my arm with affection and a hint of concern. I scratched his ears absentmindedly.

St. Cloud sat in the armchair, facing me. "Well?" he asked expectantly.

I sighed again, completely slumped over in the most unladylike fashion. I dug into my pocket and pulled out the rather crumpled piece of paper that I had snagged from the office. "I got something, but I didn't get a good chance to look at it. But I did learn a couple more things of interest as well."

"Go on."

"I happened to eavesdrop on a couple of office workers. Based on the conversation, they were led to believe that the fire was accidental, not arson. And they attended a memorial service held by the company. It was for four deceased people, not three."

"Who was the fourth person killed?"

"Roger." I grinned at the look of confusion that blossomed on St. Cloud's face. "Exactly. They think Roger's dead. Neither were they told it was arson, nor were they told he did it. He was a victim, same as the other three."

"But Curtain's not dead," he pointed out unhelpfully.

"Of course he's not. You and I saw he's clearly alive. Even the lawyers and the owner of Lightfoot Shipping know that. So why was the arson covered up? Why make all of his co-workers think the guy's dead?"

"I don't know." He slouched back in his seat, perplexed. "Whoever covered this up basically made him a ghost. If he's dead to the company, is he dead to the world? Did they file a death certificate on him?"

"I don't know. And I don't know the why of it either. I assumed the company would have pointed the blame at Roger, since that's why we were hired in the first place. It makes me wonder what exactly they had to cover up, and why they implicated him to us but at the same time martyred him to the office."

"It's certainly strange. What else did you find there?" St. Cloud pointed to the rumpled paper in my hand.

I smoothed it out and read it over properly for the first time.

CONGRATULATIONS TO THE WINNERS OF THE LIGHTFOOT SPRING EQUINOX BALL TICKETS!

Geoff Mathers
Rona Hilliard
Riku Shimada
William Croft

Your special invitations will be mailed to you by March 10th. Please bring your invitation with you to the Ball for admittance. All other information will be given on the invitation, including address, as this is a private residence.

**This is a formal event! Dress accordingly!*

"Well," I said grudgingly, "we still don't know where the ball is being held."

Gavin mused. "No, but now we know who has invitations."

"What are you thinking?"

He grinned at me. "I'm thinking I could pass as a 'Riku Shimada,' given that I'm half Tyonoshimese. What do you think?"

I frowned a tiny bit. "Huh?"

He shook his head at my ineptitude. "Listen, after hearing what you had to say, I'm beginning to think there's more to this story than what we were told. Curtain himself seemed to make a connection to this ball as a place of interest. I think we need to go and see for ourselves."

I stared at him. "Are you serious?"

Gavin seemed taken aback. "Wasn't it your idea to go to the ball in the first place?"

I threw up my hands. "Yes, but not as guests! I figured we'd sneak in and check things out."

He shook his head at me with mock disapproval. "Tut, tut, Miss Curtain. Sneaking in would be wrong."

"And impersonating invited guests wouldn't be? What if we get caught?"

He had the audacity to laugh at me. "You really are something! I'm fairly certain the chances of us getting caught 'sneaking in' are much higher than going as invited guests, especially if we have an invitation to be there."

He had a point, damn his handsome, annoying face. "Fine," I conceded. "But how do you propose we get said invitation? Steal it?"

"Is that really how your mind works? Leave it to me, my little cat burglar. You'd be surprised how well talking to somebody can work."

While I wasn't necessarily a burglar, his little moniker hit too close to home for my taste. I was sure it was a complete coincidence. "Fine by me. But today is, what, the twelfth? That means we have about a week until the ball. Time's ticking."

St. Cloud tipped his fingers from an imaginary hat brim and pulled his watch out to check the time. Again. "Oh, don't you worry about it, Miss Curtain. I'll go now and see what I can do. Promise me you'll stay here until I get back?"

"Of course," I responded with an eye roll. He nodded at my words, tucked his watch back into his pocket, and strode purposefully out the door.

"Alone at last," I sighed dreamily, fully back in my cat form and happily licking my chest.

Grimm had been lounging by my side while St. Cloud was here. He placed his head on his paws and blew a loud breath through his nose.

I looked at him with half-lidded eyes and my tongue peeking out from mid-groom. "Why so glum, chum?" I asked him.

He straightened his head, coming into a sphynx-like pose. "You have to ask?"

I shook my head briskly, tucking my tongue firmly back in my mouth at the seriousness of my partner's energy. "Well, yeah. What's up?"

He stared, those yellow eyes boring into me. "You left me behind. With *him*."

"I had to." I stretched my body toward him, reaching out toward his paws with my front legs. Pulling myself forward, I tried to rub my head against his jawline, but he moved it to the side at the last second. "I needed to get answers, but I needed to get them stealthily and small, not large and menacingly. You understand that, right?"

He flopped over on his side, heaving a great sigh. "I do, but honestly? This whole trip has been one big disappointment for me. I can't go inside buildings, I can barely talk to you, and I even let your dad take our cab and get away. On top of that, I wasn't able to track his scent after that blunder! I'm feeling a bit worthless, and to make that thorn of worthlessness dig deeper, you've decided to partner up with the *clod*. I've been replaced."

My heart broke at that speech. While I was out risking myself, Grimm had been stuck doing ... nothing. Hearing him say it from his point of view made me realize how one-sided this whole trip had been.

"No way. You are not being replaced, Grimm. I was forced to partner up with St. Cloud; otherwise he would have continued to relentlessly pursue Roger. I couldn't chance him finding my father first and collecting the bounty. Trust me, I'm about as happy with the arrangement as you are." I invaded Grimm's personal space, rubbing my cheek against his as he lay prone on the floor. Grimm grumbled a bit in his throat but otherwise did not move as I showed him my appreciation for his presence.

"I still don't like it," he muttered as I curled up against his neck and purred placatingly.

"You don't have to like it," I assured him, "but can you at least tolerate it for a bit longer? Our next order of business is breaking into a ball to try to find a ledger that may clear Roger's name. I doubt I can take you along with me for that either."

"What?" Grimm sat up, completely dislodging me.

I licked my back to soothe myself. "It's next week. We just need to get that affirmation of Roger's innocence."

"And then what?"

I paused mid-lick and turned back to Grimm. "What do you mean?"

He huffed. "Say you prove beyond a measure of doubt he's innocent. What happens next? Do you go to the people who framed him and say, 'Hey, person who hired me to catch this guy for you, I decided to investigate further, and it turns out you're wrong, so you need to let him go free?' How do you think they'll take that news, Cress? Do you think they'll say, 'Oops, my mistake,' and walk away?"

I stared off into the distance, completely at a loss for words. I suppose I hadn't given all of this much thought beyond proving my father had been framed. But Grimm was right. If the company who hired me was indeed framing him, proving his innocence was not going to be the end-all.

"I don't know," I finally admitted. "I guess I need to figure out why he was framed in the first place."

"It's a start."

"After all, why him?" I added, getting on a roll. "You saw him. He's small and unassuming."

"Yes, well, you certainly take after him in the small category, if not the unassuming category."

"Shut up. I'm serious; I overheard his coworkers gush about how sweet and shy he was. Is. He's not dead, despite what they think. Why single him out?"

Grimm sighed again. "I can't begin to understand why. Perhaps there's something in his past that makes him the perfect scapegoat. Or maybe it's because he's so shy and sweet. Maybe they figured everyone would think it's the one you least suspect."

"See? This is why I need you. You always get me thinking about other angles. I do need you, partner. I always will. You are never worthless to me."

"Thanks, CC. I think I needed to hear that. Just don't go liking your partnership with St. Cloud over me, do you hear?"

I snorted. "Never. He is a means to an end, nothing more."

With the solid warmth comforting me, Grimm and I fell into an easy nap while we had this scant alone time in this alien environment.

A knock on the door jerked me awake instantly, sending my heart fluttering momentarily. I was discombobulated, having fallen into a deeper sleep than I had meant to, and for a second, I had no clue where I was. But Grimm murmured, "The clod is back," which righted my world again.

Shifting back to human quickly, I strode over to the door, unlocking it and opening it for Gavin. It must have started raining again because he looked a bit wet, his hair disheveled in a dashing way, and his bronzed complexion glistening as if it had been dew-kissed ...

"Are you going to let me in, or shall I just let you ogle me in the doorway some more?"

His words dashed against me like water in the face, snapping me out of whatever sleep-induced lapse of judgment I had been suffering under. I moved to the side instantly. "Please," I snapped. "I don't ogle. I just woke up from a nap, and I'm still a little groggy. You look like a drowned rat."

He walked in, smiling devilishly at me as he did. I looked away, embarrassed that I had been caught in the act.

"It's raining again," he simply replied as he made to sit on the chair.

I followed him into the room. Grimm had sat up and fixed his wolfish eyes on St. Cloud. A small rumble sounded in his throat as they made eye contact. I frowned at my partner, giving him a slight head shake.

St. Cloud cleared his throat. "What did I do this time?"

I shrugged. "Exist? Seriously, my partner isn't a fan of yours."

He chuckled, murmuring the word "partner" under his breath

in amusement. I pretended not to hear. It was an argument I frankly didn't need at the moment.

"So, are you going to tell me how it went?" I demanded.

St. Cloud leaned back, dripping water all over the chair. "Swimmingly, actually," he told me with a wink. I ignored the wink, fixing him with a stare. He continued, "I tracked Riku Shimada down via Information. He is indeed from Tyonoshima, although he's been here in the O.R. since he was a young child. He's fairly introverted, which surprised me to learn after he had agreed to meet with me. He does have a fiancée, Marilyn Croft, who is apparently much more outgoing than he is, based on what he said. We had a great chat, and I offered to buy his ball invitation for the sum of $300. He readily agreed because he wasn't too keen to go in the first place, and he could use the extra money for his wedding. He said the only reason he was planning on attending was that Marilyn had been excited to go."

"Did you give him a reason for why you wanted to go in his stead?"

He smiled. "I gave him mostly truths, unlike some people I know. I just explained that I was a bounty hunter and I needed access to the ball for a case I was working on. He didn't seem to think it would be an issue for me to impersonate him because he didn't think anybody going would know who he is anyway. He seems to keep a low profile at work."

"Hold on, back up," I interjected with a raised finger. "What are you implying, 'unlike some people I know?' Do you mean me?"

He shrugged and smirked. "If the shoe fits."

This really shouldn't have bothered me as much as it did. After all, I did need to lie on a regular basis to preserve my giant secret. But there was something about St. Cloud calling me out on it, as if he took it personally, that made my blood boil. I huffed, "Why do you insist I lie all the time? I'll have you know that just this morning, I held an interview over a truth crystal and passed with flying colors."

As the words left my mouth, something in my brain clicked. Truth crystal ... basically an object enchanted by a magical person. Fleurette had told me that crystals were the easiest items to enchant, which was why they were so common, but any object could be enchanted, given that the enchanter was powerful enough.

Any object ... like a pocket watch?

"You son of a bitch," I hissed. St. Cloud looked startled at my curse. "It's the watch, isn't it? You've been using that damn thing on me every chance you get. No wonder you've been 'checking the time' so frequently!"

St. Cloud's shock gave way to amusement that he tried to hide from me. It just made me even angrier to see his mirth at my obvious wrath. He held up his hands in mock surrender. "Okay, I'll admit it," he said all too pleasantly. "But you should know it was never anything personal."

"Nothing personal?" I repeated, outraged. "When you've used the damn watch on me without my knowledge and then accuse me of lying over and over again, it's nothing personal?"

"Keep your voice down!" He looked around the room, as if expecting someone to pop out of a hiding place. "These walls tend to be thin, and we don't want a neighbor reporting us to the management. We aren't exactly supposed to be here." He took a breath, trying to diffuse my volatile mood. "Look, I mean, it's nothing personal because I purchased the watch to help with my bounty hunting. People lie all the time when it comes to protecting people they care for. This helps me suss out small details that otherwise may get overlooked, even if it can't discern absolute truths from relative truths. You just happened to be collateral. And I admit, I didn't tell you because I thought it was initially rather funny to discover just how much you lie."

"Oh, I'm so glad I amuse you," I deadpanned.

"Anyway, I promise I won't use it on you without your knowledge, deal? Can we get on with the issue at hand now?"

I glared at him. "This"— I pointed at my serious expression—"is my 'this isn't over, it's on hold' face. But seeing as how I'm an adult, I accept your apology."

"I don't recall actually apologizing to you."

"I'm cataloging that for a future date as well." I pursed my lips, still angry, but cooling off. He gave me a sheepish smile.

"Very well," he agreed.

"So, back to the matter at hand. What's the plan? Did you get the invitation or not?" I asked curtly.

He fished into his inside vest pocket, drawing out an envelope, which had not been waterlogged or creased somehow. "Right here. I had to follow Mr. Shimada back to his apartment to get it. I met Marylin too. She happens to be a blonde, as luck would have it, although she doesn't dye parts of hers with black streaks."

I took a moment to compose myself before I inadvertently strangled the man. "Can I see how your watch works?"

That threw him off guard. "I suppose," he finally replied, reaching into his pocket to retrieve it. He opened it and handed it to me. "When the watch senses a lie in the general vicinity, the hands will immediately stop for five seconds. It also vibrates very softly if the face is closed or if the lie is big enough. The only kink is it can't discern absolute truths from relative truths, which is why I don't fully believe Curtain is innocent, even if you say otherwise."

Well, that was actually very clever. No wonder his watch never seemed to keep the correct time. I looked at the face, watching to make sure the second hand was still working properly, before turning it around to show St. Cloud that it was moving. As soon as he focused on the watch, I stated loudly, "*I have never dyed my hair.*"

I didn't need to see the watch face to know that the hands still ticked merrily away. Gavin, on the other hand, raised his eyebrows at the truthful admission. I snapped the watch closed with force enough to make a loud click, and then I tossed it at his lap. He caught it, fumbling slightly since he was unprepared.

"Ah, that's how it naturally grows, then?" he stammered. I nodded without blinking. Sheepishly, he ran his fingers through his dark umber hair. "You can't blame me for thinking otherwise, it's so ..."

"Unique?" I supplied. He nodded. "Yeah, I get that a lot. Which is why I needed to prove to at least one person that it's real. It gets old after a while."

"Understandable. Well, shall we look at the invitation? I only glanced at it to make sure it was real before leaving Shimada's."

He got up and sat on the sofa, patting the seat next to him. Not waiting for me, he opened the envelope and removed a cream-colored folded paper. Allowing myself to forgive him temporarily, I sidled over to see the invitation, sitting close enough that our legs brushed together for a brief second. I quickly moved my leg to remedy the situation.

Gavin unfolded the paper, revealing a fancy script in dark gold ink.

Riku Shimada and guest,
You are cordially invited to
The Lightfoot Spring Equinox Ball
An evening of dancing, refreshments, and celebrating the changing of the season
Hosted by
Orson Lightfoot of Lightfoot Shipping Industries

"Deerhorn Manor. There it is," I murmured.

"Have you heard of it?" St. Cloud asked curiously.

I shook my head, still examining the invitation. "Kousa is the town just south of here, right?"

"Mm-hm. We passed it on the way to Dogwood from Knobby Hill. A lot of rich businessmen own property there, since it's an easy commute to the city." Gavin folded the invitation back up and went to put it back in the envelope. "Well, my tux is back in Knobby Hill, so I'll need to go back there before next Saturday anyway."

"You own a tuxedo?" I blurted before I could think about it. He was debonair, all right, in a smarmy kind of way, but bounty hunters weren't normally the type of people to have enough need of a tux to justify owning one. Besides that, he didn't even have his own place. He rented a room from the guild.

"I do. It comes in handy on occasion, even for a bounty hunter. Do you own a dress?" he looked me up and down, probably thinking that he'd only ever seen me in one set of clothes throughout the last year and a half.

He wasn't far off, either. I never changed my clothes, except to don my short sleeve linen shirt in the summer months and back to my long sleeve when the weather turned cold again. Otherwise, I always had on the same trousers, vest, and boots. Grooming myself as a cat always kept them in pristine condition. So no, I definitely did not own a dress.

"I'll get one here before I head back home." I reached into my vest pocket, touching the hard edge of the business card Monica had given me this morning. I decided she would most likely be of help in figuring out how to dress myself for a formal occasion. Luckily, I still had money to burn from the stipend.

Gavin nodded and stood. "Well, that's settled. I'll probably head out of here in the next couple of days. I want to make sure we aren't overlooking anything obvious. I'll be in touch on Thursday or Friday to check in with you. Deal?"

I nodded.

He nodded back. An awkward silence filled the room. He looked like he wanted to say something else but stopped. Finally, he said, "Well, see you around, Miss Curtain." He tipped his head at me with a small smile and walked out of the door.

As soon as the door shut firmly, I heaved a big sigh. I shook my head. He was gone and out of my hair for at least most of the next week. I should have felt glad to finally shake the menace off. So why did I feel like there was a small void in me now that he was gone?

CHAPTER 16

The next morning, I checked my message mirror, as was my habit after being a cat. I normally did not receive many messages overnight, but since it was so thoroughly silenced when it was tucked away in my interdimensional pocket, I felt it prudent to check. This time, there was a single message awaiting me. From Rosa.

My heart skipped. I opened the message.

"I AM SAFE. ROSA SAID TO TRUST YOU. SORRY FOR LEAVING. REGARDS, RC."

Not from Rosa then, but from Roger, via Rosa's mirror. I nearly welled up after reading the message, and despite its simplicity, I read it multiple more times, reveling in the unexpected feeling of gladness the three short sentences brought. Even the unnecessary "regards" at the end made me giddy.

And most importantly, Roger was still safe. Now, I could focus on the next task at hand without being distracted by worry over his happenstance.

I traveled to Monica's place of work to speak with her. I told her what had happened with my meeting with Roger. While she was slightly annoyed that he was spooked enough to run again, she was glad to hear that I was progressing with the case and that I was on the right track to clearing his name. I was even magnanimous enough to show her the message from him, which did wonders to assuage her thunderous mood.

I explained my need for a dress and that I had no fashion sense beyond my usual wardrobe. After a small quip said under her breath about a lack of fashion sense even with my usual wardrobe—I'm fairly certain I was not meant to hear it—she directed me to an upscale boutique, which she assured me would be helpful in finding the perfect dress for the occasion.

She did not make any more mentions of my hair.

The boutique was indeed helpful, although I'm convinced I blocked out most of the memories due to sheer sensory overload. I only slightly recall being measured, trying on some gowns, being fawned over by multiple salesladies, and leaving with a dress in a zip-up bag ("Be sure to hang it up the minute you get home to avoid wrinkles, dear!") and matching shoes after paying an exorbitant price for it all. Who knew fashion was so expensive?

After that, I decided enough was enough, and it was time to leave Dogwood. I had kept my father's ledger-turned-journal and locked his apartment. Together, Grimm and I made our way back to the parking lot, had Humbert hitched up, and left Dogwood. For forever, I added mentally, but only time would tell.

Now, I was taking a much-needed breather in an empty cottage. Wren had private lessons on Saturdays with a GOGS member to learn about her rare form of magic and how to better use it. Her teacher, while not a projectionist himself, was considered an enthusiast, as he had studied the history of people like Wren extensively. Fleurette had also whisked Fal away for his apprenticeship under her tutelage, since they both shared an affinity for herbal magic, but Fal also had the potential for greater magic. All three were gone when I arrived home, so I had some blissful time to unwind after the extremely stressful events in Dogwood.

All too soon, though, my family returned. They each expressed joy in their various ways upon seeing Grimm and me in the sitting room.

"Cress, did you know that some projectionists go on to become dimension travelers as a job? I think I might want to do that when I grow up," Wren told me enthusiastically about ten seconds after walking through the door.

Fal, who was busy petting Grimm around the ears, looked at his sister. "You did some of that already and nearly died because of it. Do you think that's the wisest thing to do?"

Wren scowled at her protective older brother. "That's because I didn't know what I was doing. I'd have to practice and be prepared to make it safe. That's what Maurice said."

Maurice was her teacher, and it was obvious to all of us that in Wren's mind, he hung the moon. She was twelve now, after all, and certain feelings were beginning to awaken within her.

Fal rolled his eyes at his mention. "I don't like it. I want you to stay in this dimension where I can keep an eye on you."

The siblings fell into bickering, with choice words such as "overbearing" and "reckless" being thrown about. I gave Fleurette a look from across the room. She smirked, clapped her hands to get their attention, and sent them off to prepare dinner. Fal and Wren went to do her bidding, still whispering words at each other, although it was plain to see that it had simmered into playful ribbing.

Fleurette looked at me, assessing. "I can't wait to catch up."

We went out into the greenhouse, where Fleurette had all manner of baby plants growing, getting ready for farmers markets where she would sell her starts. It also made an excellent private space, with the amount of foliage covering the windows and the soundproofing of the glass.

I told her everything, even the fact that I was working with my nemesis. Fleurette utilized her special plant magic as she listened, running her fingertips along wilted or discolored leaves to help them instantly perk up or turn a more vivid shade of green. She listened patiently, as she usually did, without interrupting much. Once I had her all caught up, she took a moment to digest all of this information.

"Cressida, dear, are you sure this is the right move? Going to Lightfoot's ball? There's certainly something off about this whole scenario."

"I'm sure, Fleurette. I even bought a dress. I need to find that ledger to prove at least to myself and to Gavin, that my father is not guilty of anything."

"Gavin?" Fleurette quirked an eyebrow at me.

I froze, thinking over the words that had tumbled so thoughtlessly from my mouth just seconds before. "Well, yes, St. Cloud. You know."

She smiled. "You've never once called him by his first name. Are you feeling alright?"

I quickly shook my head with a chagrined smile. "Just tired. And apparently spending too much time in his company."

"Very well." She thankfully dropped the subject. "Beyond the ledger business, what else are you planning to do?"

"I'm not sure. Honestly, I have no clue why they are targeting my father. It's a giant puzzle piece that I just can't find. I can't help but feel that if I knew *why* he was being framed, I could do more to exonerate him."

Fleurette became silent. Finally, with some hesitation, she said, "Have you been to talk with your mother since you got back? I think she may know more than she is letting on."

"What do you mean?" I asked.

Fleurette pursed her lips. "It really isn't my place to say anything. But here's food for thought. Has your mom ever talked about why you have never met your grandmother? Or your mother's grandmother? What if your family is being targeted?

And Roger just happens to be the next target?"

I shook my head. "Nobody knows I am the descendant. How can they?"

"Somebody knows you are the descendant."

"Who?" I asked, completely drawing a blank. The only people who knew my secret were Fleurette, her father, and the siblings. And GOGS, of course.

She looked me in the eye. "Annie Coddle."

My blood ran cold at the name.

CHAPTER 17

F leurette was right. I needed more answers. I needed to talk to my mother again.

I walked the one-and-a-half miles down the road, this time with Grimm by my side. He had been so sidelined during this whole episode that I felt it was only right for him to be a part of this one small act. I still wasn't sure it would be fruitful. But Fleurette had hit a particularly large nail on the head. Namely, why hadn't I ever met my grandmother?

My mother was almost fifteen years old, which sounded old for a normal cat, but my family lived much longer than that. Even if my grandmother was twenty, she should definitely still be alive. Even my great-grandmother could easily still be kicking.

As a younger cat, I always believed my grandmother was not in the picture because, at some point, Mom had had a falling out with her. Hell, I sometimes wanted to have a falling out with my own mother, so it didn't seem very far-fetched to me. But I suppose I never actually asked.

Well, now was my chance.

Mom was in Lyle's barn, in her cat form as usual. Her green eyes widened to see me alongside Grimm, who was apparently in business mode: head low, tail straight, and eyes penetrating.

"To what do I owe this pleasure?" she asked sardonically.

I walked up to her. "Mom, we found Roger. We found him.

He was framed, and he's back on the run, but he knows I'm trying to help him."

Mom looked slightly twitchy. "You found him? And he's alright? That's good, but don't you think you ought to drop it now, Cressida?"

I stared at her, my tail starting to thrash from side to side. "You didn't want me to help him in the first place. You don't want me to continue the investigation. What is it that you don't want me to know? What are you hiding?"

She looked at me and then at Grimm, her own tail lashing and her ears held back slightly. Finally, they came forward as she melted into herself a bit. "I just wanted to keep you safe," she admitted.

"Why would I not be safe?" I asked.

"Because ... because ..." she floundered.

"Belinda," Grimm growled. She arched her back on reflex before settling back down submissively.

"Because your grandmother went missing!" she finally blurted out.

I shared a look with Grimm. Pointing my nose at her, I asked, "Care to explain?"

She huffed. "When I was a kitten, my mother, Charlotte, told me that her mother, Serena, disappeared one day when my mother was about a year old. Because of this, my mother moved farther west almost immediately, to distance herself from the general area. Somewhere along the way, she met my father, but she did not stay with him long, it seems. Then she had me. We moved around a lot, never staying too long in one area. When we stopped near Dogwood, that's when I finally met your father and found my true love."

This was a story I had never heard before.

"Roger and I married a year after we met, just a small civil ceremony, since I only had my mother and he had very few friends. His parents were already deceased by that time. We settled in the Southwind Commons, as I told you before. My mom decided to stick around the outskirts, living in a very small shanty of a place. She came to visit us once a week to check in.

"About a year before I became pregnant, she became a bit ... well, unhinged in a way. She insisted she had been investigating certain people, and claimed they were a part of a super-secret organization calling themselves the Annie Coddle Fanclub, or ACF for short."

"What is it with these people picking terrible names for their secret organizations?" I interjected.

"Well, I'm not sure about that, Cressida. Truth be told, I didn't believe my mother initially. It sounded incredibly far-fetched. But to appease her, I listened, and I discovered the perfect place to hide if and when I needed to leave Roger. I squirreled things away in that old barn for about six months before I became pregnant. Just in case. But I didn't *want* to leave your father."

"So what happened?" I asked.

She let out a little sigh through her nose. "My mother went missing around October of that year. She never missed a check-in with me, and then, suddenly, she was gone. It panicked me, to be honest. I thought about going into hiding then and there, but I simply couldn't leave Roger. And I couldn't tell him what was going on, either, because then I'd have to tell him the truth about everything."

I let out a little growl. "And what would have been so terrible about that?"

She narrowed her eyes. "I told you, Cressida, your father wasn't magical. He didn't know any magical people. We had been married for years at this point, and I figured if he knew, he wouldn't be able to accept it. He would have left me."

"So you left him first?" I argued, anger lacing my words. "Best to get that old proactive strike in before he did, eh, Mother?"

"How dare you!" She spat like a snake. "I left your father the minute I learned I was pregnant to protect myself, to protect you, but most importantly, to protect him! I thought if I was gone, they'd trace my trail and leave him be!"

"You left him heartbroken and alone!" I cried out. I imagined the old and creased letter, read by Roger a thousand times. I had read it that first night after Gavin had left. The letter was complete hogwash, placing no blame upon Roger per se, but also not giving a clear and concise reason for her sudden departure. It had made my blood boil to read it and imagine Roger holding on to this last remnant of his wife, of the life he had known. It made me angry all over again just thinking about it. My ire at my mother caused me to lunge forward, claws extended. Mom returned the gesture with a lunge of her own, her ears pinned tight against her head and her teeth bared. I swiped out at her, barely missing her face. We both yowled in mutual displeasure as we struck our battle poses.

"Ladies!" Grimm roared, literally sticking his snout between us. He nudged me away from Mom, confident that I wouldn't lash out at him accidentally. Both Mom and I took a few minutes to do some mutual angry grooming, cooling off the heated atmosphere.

After I had sufficiently regained my temper, I looked Mom in the eye. "As you were."

"Well, as I was saying, as soon as I was pregnant and stuck in cat form, I knew I had to leave, not because I didn't love him. It was the hardest thing I've ever had to do. If you had a true love, you'd understand."

That remark hurt more than a swipe to my face would have. I hunched my shoulders to shield myself from the pain. But I couldn't let it go. The dam burst.

"Yes, well, I guess I'll never know, will I?"

Mom cocked her head. "What do you mean, Cressida?"

I had not told my mother before about the curse. I hadn't wanted to worry her. But I had let the proverbial cat out of the bag now. "When I faced Annie Coddle last summer, she ... cursed me."

Mom looked stricken. "What?"

I refused to say the words that were etched into my soul. "I can't fall in love, Mom. So forgive me if this callous take on your happy marriage leaves me with feelings of resentment."

"Oh, Cressida," Mom approached with a look of concern. I shied away, but instead of attacking me, she began grooming the top of my head. I closed my eyes at the ministrations, trying to let go of these unhappy feelings this conversation had dredged up.

"Fleurette seems to think the curse can be broken. Please, just forget I ever said anything. I didn't mean to tell you."

"I wish you had told me sooner, Cressida. I suppose this whole fiasco with your father makes more sense now. You were looking for something you think you've lost. Well, I may have cut ties with the love of my life, but I did it for a noble reason. I suppose you can take comfort in that."

I opened my eyes. "Yes, how noble of you to destroy the one thing that made you happy."

The glare was back in her expression. "You can mock my words all you want, my child, but you are my biggest priority, Cressida. No matter what, the line of Glivver must go on, curse or no curse. So I'm glad I left your father. I'm glad I hid you in that barn. Nobody found us while we were there. I would have stayed in that barn for the rest of my life had you not forced me to live here."

"Oh, please. I didn't force you to do anything. You act as if this place is a hellhole."

"No, no, don't get me wrong. I'm glad I'm here. I can stay as a cat, and I have the protection of Lyle and the rest of the GOGS. But I think staying for the year at the barn kept us safe. Even Fleurette said GOGS couldn't find us while we were there. It was my hope that our time away took the scent off of us."

"But now you're worried about me? Because of Roger?"

She paused before answering. "Frankly, yes. What if they made the connection? You are my top priority, Cressida. If it means I have to sacrifice the love of my life to keep safe the other love of my life, then so be it."

I shook my head, a bad habit I picked up from being human. "I appreciate your honesty, Mom," I told her. "Even if it was at such a late date. You've made your bed. Fine. But I'm an adult now. And I can't let a good man be sacrificed for my wellbeing. You raised me to have too strong a conscience for that."

I walked over to her, butting my head against hers. "I love you, Mom. But this is something I need to do."

She didn't say anything to me as I turned around and departed the barn without looking back.

Once we were back at the cottage, I explained everything to Fleurette. She was surprised to hear the new information my mother had divulged.

"Your mother is right about one thing; she did a fantastic job of disappearing before she had you," she mused. "GOGS completely lost track of her after she left your father. Which means you didn't even exist to us until you waltzed out of the forest."

Fleurette had told me previously that every new cat of Glivver's line was being monitored in one way or another. I was the first cat to learn of the society's existence and become friends with some of the members. And it was only through happenstance that I wandered into Fleurette's territory and came back on their radar.

"Did you know about my grandmother and great-grandmother's disappearance?" I asked her.

She shook her head. "That was a bit before my time. I only became a full-fledged guardian about five years ago, and there were others dedicated to watching over your other family members. If you hadn't happened across this area of the country, I doubt I would have been assigned to you. I should mention too, that once the newest in line is born, we generally don't follow the past generations much, since they've already done their part for the prophecy. But I'm going to submit a request to learn more about your grandmother and see if anyone else has heard of this ACF."

"Thank you, Fleurette."

She gave me a pat on the shoulder. "I know you hate fighting with your mom. I think I would, too."

She looked sad for a moment, thinking about her own mother. A powerful witch, Fleurette's mom had left her family very suddenly when Fleurette was just eight years old. It had apparently gutted Lyle, and it took them many years to heal. It must be still painful, given they never knew why or what happened to her.

Just like the pain I was sure my father felt, never knowing why his wife left him.

Fleurette waved off her momentary sadness. "If it's any consolation, I think you are doing the right thing, helping your father. Perhaps in the future, we should start checking in on not just past cats, but past husbands as well."

"Well, in order to do that, I still have to get a husband, remember?"

She scrunched up her face at me. "Are you still worried about that silly curse? I told you, have faith. We'll get around it somehow. Curses are not infallible."

It was easy for her to say. She didn't feel a gaping hole in her chest every time she thought about a future spouse. But I only nodded in response.

"Now, I'll contact GOGS first thing tomorrow about all of this. You've already harassed your mom enough about this business. Is there anyone else you can think of who might have some information that would be useful to you before Saturday?"

I thought for a moment, then something popped into my head. "You know something? There just might be."

Glivver sat before me, her silver fur long and sleek, shining in the effusive white light. It was no small feat to finally fall asleep while concentrating on contacting my ancestor, who existed as a sentient memory that I could access while dreaming.

"Hello, Granddaughter."

I stretched my body forward, marveling at how light I felt here. "Hello, Glivver. How have you been?"

"Until you came along, I do not have much recollection. So I will say that I am well, for the sake of propriety," she answered cheekily.

"Right. Well, here I am. I might be in a bit of a pickle, to be honest."

"Yes, I know." While Glivver did not necessarily spy on me, she was all knowing when she was in her incorporeal familiar state.

"Do you know what happened to my grandmother and

great-grandmother?"

"I'm afraid I do not. Remember, I can only help the newest descendant. The rest fade into the background, although I *can* feel previous generations' energies while they are still alive."

"And? Do you feel their energies?"

She paused for a moment, staring into space with her brilliant blue eyes. Finally, she fixed them on me. "Your grandmother, no. But I sense a very faint energy from your great-grandmother."

My heart lurched. My grandmother was dead? But her mother still lived? "Can you tell me where she is?" I asked.

Glivver flicked her silky tail. "I'm afraid not. I can only sense her energy, not pinpoint where it is."

I slumped, feeling defeated. "Of course, it couldn't be easy."

"Life generally isn't," Glivver pointed out wisely.

"What about my father?" I asked suddenly, as the thought hit me. "Do you know where he is?"

Her slow blink was answer enough. "I simply cannot sense or see anything to do with the mortal realm of humans. I see our family and nothing more."

"No, I understand. I'm just frustrated, Glivver. I'm frustrated that I can't do much to help Roger, who is in a mess through no fault of his own, I assume. I'm frustrated by my curse, because I'm having all these feelings dredged up by asking my mom questions and by learning about my father, and it gets me thinking about my future with finding my true love and having a kitten, but then I remember I don't have that future. But if I did, you'd better believe I wouldn't leave him."

"Who says you'd have to leave him?" she asked, sounding genuinely curious.

I stared at her. "Well, it's the thing to do, generally. Mom left my dad because she didn't feel he could handle the truth. Many of my ancestors left their husbands when they had a child. Even you did."

She widened her eyes at me. "I did not leave my husband."

"Come again?"

She flicked her tail again, this time a bit harder. "I did not leave my husband. This is a lie that has been passed down through the generations, probably to justify your ancestors leaving their spouses for more selfish reasons."

My ears pricked forward. From the time I was a young kitten, I had been told repeatedly by my mother that most of my ancestors had chosen to leave their husbands upon learning they were expecting, due to the fact that we have to go through pregnancy as a cat. And Mom told me the story of my original ancestor, Glivver herself, who set that precedent.

"Did you know that true love means that the person will love you no matter what? It means if you are truthful with your partner always, they will always be there for you. Before I was married, I knew with all my heart that my Jonathan would understand *who* I was, everything I was. And so I told him the entire story before marriage. Do you know what happened?"

"What?" I asked, mesmerized.

"He believed me. He was curious, he asked questions, and in the end, he accepted me for who I was. Now, granted, I did not know the part about the feline pregnancy. I approached him while he was chopping wood and meowed to get his attention. Jonathan was confused as to why I wouldn't turn back into his wife. But he did not abandon me. Not intentionally, anyway."

She seemed sad suddenly. "What happened?" I asked.

She breathed deeply. "He was attacked by bandits and killed by the very ax with which he was chopping wood. I could do nothing to help since I was still expecting. I had to raise my daughter Arabella on my own. But she too told her true love when it was her time. He also accepted her and stood by her.

And she got the joy of raising her child with her husband. It was only long after I had left the mortal realm that my descendants began the so-called tradition of hiding their true selves from their spouses and leaving them at that critical time."

I didn't know what to say. What Glivver told me was tragic. It may have happened five hundred years ago, but the wound of losing her husband so young clearly still pained her. I bent forward and nuzzled up against her, purring to comfort her. She leaned into me, purring back.

"Thank you, Granddaughter. You should go—get some true rest. But remember what I have said. Your true love is still out there, curse or not. And he will be there for you, no matter what. Love is a powerful thing. Don't squander it like so many of your ancestors have done."

"I won't," I swore, and I meant it.

CHAPTER 18

The next few days passed in a blur. Wren was delighted by the prospect of me going to a ball, despite the pretense that took me there. She wanted to help me get ready for it, to which I readily agreed, considering she knew more about formal affairs than me. And Fleurette had me help around the cottage, preparing for their own little family celebration of the upcoming holiday. I was only sorry to miss the casual festivities with the people that mattered most in my life.

On Thursday, I received a message on my mirror from St. Cloud.

"MEET ME AT GUILD FOR PREP 5PM TODAY," it read. "DON'T BRING DOG."

I rolled my eyes.

At 5 p.m. sharp, I arrived at the guild headquarters in Knobby Hill, with Grimm by my side. St. Cloud was waiting in the lobby, near the mail cubbies. Leaning against a large wooden support column, he smiled when he saw me, and his grin grew even wider when he saw Grimm.

"Your reading skills leave a lot to be desired," he teased without malice.

For once, his taunting didn't rub me the wrong way. "I can read just fine. It's your critical thinking skills that need work." I kept the usual snideness out of my voice.

Grimm looked at me, his head cocked to the side for a second in confusion. I shook my head, a subtle communication that I did not know why he was confused, and then brought my attention back to St. Cloud. He straightened, holding out an arm in a sweeping gesture. "This way, madame."

He led me through the lobby and into a hallway that I knew contained the rented rooms for the hunters who used the guild as their home base. It was quiet at the moment, but as we walked down the hallway, a door to my right opened suddenly. Startled, I gave a little jump back, only to see a familiar face in the doorway.

"Baby Bounty Hunter?" the man asked with a note of confusion.

"Oh, hey Allen," I greeted stiltedly. Allen was another hunter with whom I was familiar. He was somewhat nicer to me than the other resident hunters, but he still lorded over me with a superiority complex.

That, and last summer he had made me very uncomfortable by insisting I get a drink with him because I owed him for an information exchange.

He seemed like he was about to ask me why I was here in the guild dormitory, but two things happened. First, Grimm barged his way to my side, an obvious reminder that Allen should mind his manners, and second, St. Cloud stopped walking to come back to my side.

Allen gaped. "St. Cloud?"

Gavin smiled politely and nodded in acknowledgement. "Miss Curtain, just this way," he said to me, placing all of his attention in my general direction.

I nodded at him and began walking again. "See ya, Allen!" I called over my shoulder. Allen didn't say anything, but I could sense him staring after us.

Gavin stopped in front of a door with the number 19 painted

at the top. He unlocked it and opened it wide, ushering Grimm and me in before entering himself and shutting the door behind him.

I took a moment to look around. It was surprisingly roomy and clean, with a small bed, neatly made and pushed against one wall, a tall dresser by the door, and a chest on the other wall. Heavy light green linen curtains covered the only window, making the room rather dark. St. Cloud turned on a lamp that rested on the dresser, filling the room with a soft glow. He strode over and sat on the bed.

"Welcome to my room," he said cheerfully.

Grimm sniffed around, finally coming to sit on a small, braided rug in the middle of the wood floor. I looked around for a chair, but none were to be seen. I did not want to sit on the bed with St. Cloud; a move like that felt too casual and awkward to me. He motioned to the chest, so I perched on it.

Outside the room in the hallway, I heard a male voice talk in hushed tones, "Hey, Colton! You'll never guess who St. Cloud has in his room!"

Another masculine voice, also trying to be quiet, answered, "A girl, I wager."

The first voice, presumably Allen, replied, "Not just any girl! Baby Bounty Hunter herself!"

"Ah, go on!"

"It's the truth; I saw them myself!"

A low whistle sounded. "But don't they hate each other?"

"Sure didn't look like it to me."

"No fooling! Hey, Mathers! Get a load of this!"

I heard every clandestine word clear as a bell, thanks to my superior magical senses. I doubted Gavin could understand the banter as well as I could, but given the rising commotion outside his door, and the blush encompassing my face, he could understand the gist of what was happening.

"Don't pay them any mind," he told me. "The men who rent from the dorms are hard up for entertainment, and they're worse than a bunch of hens when it comes to gossip."

I looked away, embarrassed to be the topic of said gossip. "Freya's furs," I muttered to myself.

"Hey, you're a hot topic around here. There was a pool going around a while ago to bet which of us would get you alone in his room first. Looks like I won."

I looked up sharply, just to see his usual smug grin resting on his face. "St. Cloud, I swear if this is the only reason I'm here..." I stood up to leave.

He stopped smirking and motioned for me to sit again. "Calm down; I was teasing. Mostly. I really do need to discuss this ball with you. Winning a pot was just an added bonus." This last sentence was delivered with a twinkle in his light-brown eyes.

I stayed standing. "I don't appreciate being treated this way by the guild. Like a ... bucket of swill presented to a bunch of pigs."

St. Cloud stared at me, assessing. "It's just a bit of fun. Are you really this much of a man-hater, Miss Curtain?"

"I don't hate men." It was true. I had a deep respect for many of the men in my life. Lyle acted like a surrogate father to me with his kindness and guidance, and Fal was growing up to be an incredibly decent human being.

"Oh really? Sorry if I find that hard to believe, with the amount of complaining you do towards the other bounty hunters."

"No, really. It's not men I dislike; it's the attitude that I can't stand, that I'm somehow inferior because of my gender. Not all men hold this particular view, but somehow bounty hunting seems to attract that certain special group. So no, St. Cloud, I don't disapprove of someone just because they have a penis.

I disapprove based on their actions and how they treat other humans. If women constantly berated me and told me I wasn't qualified for my job based solely on what's between my legs, I'd hate them too. I just want the respect I deserve."

He frowned. "I respect you."

I raised an eyebrow.

He held out his hands in surrender. "Okay, I know it may seem like I don't, based on this scenario, but I really do. You are incredibly good at your job. I wouldn't have insisted we work together otherwise. You're right—we shouldn't have objectified you like this. I got caught up in the moment and didn't stop to think about how it might make you feel. Please, don't leave. I'm sorry I engaged with the other meatheads in this wager."

I stayed still, calculating. His apology had loosened up some of the anger that bit at my chest. I narrowed my eyes at him. "Split the pot with me, and I'll stay."

"Deal." He held out his hand. I shook it and then settled back down on the chest.

"So, what's the plan?" I asked, trying my best to ignore the muted hubbub in the hallway.

"Have you got a dress?"

"Yes," I answered evenly.

He did not look convinced. "A nice one?"

"Yes!" I raised my voice. "Is that all you wanted to ask me? I have other things to do."

"I'm just double-checking, for goodness sake. Marilyn would have been decked out for this. I'd hate to see you show up in some frowsy getup. It would ruin the illusion."

"What else do you have to talk about?" I questioned tiredly.

He grinned again, and despite his smug appearance, he looked quite handsome at the same time. "I looked up the address. It's swank city, Deerhorn Manor. Lightfoot must be loaded. It's on the outskirts of Kousa, set in the country a bit and on a great parcel of land."

"Okay, and?"

"And so if we're caught, we won't be getting away very easily, is all. I just wanted you to know beforehand." He ran his fingers through his hair, a sure sign that he was becoming bothered.

"Well, fine then. Good to know. So, I'll be meeting you there?"

He stopped messing with his hair to stare at me. "No, Miss Curtain, we'll need to arrive together."

"Why?"

"Because you're my fiancée, remember? Couples always arrive together for these sorts of things. And before you say anything else ridiculous, my plan is to pick you up from your place, because we are taking Scarlet. You are absolutely not allowed anywhere near your dilapidated wagon while you are wearing formalwear." He gave me a look as if he was waiting for me to argue with him.

I did start to open my mouth, but I thought it through. Of course, it made sense that I couldn't drive myself over in my wagon. It functioned perfectly, but it would never win any beauty awards. St. Cloud's sleek and modern MC fit the scenario so much better. "Fine."

"Just like that?" he asked, perplexed that I didn't argue.

"Do you want me to raise a fuss?" I asked him with a threatening tone.

He laughed. "No, I suppose not. Very well, what is your home address?"

I balked. "Don't you have it?" I asked. I knew he didn't.

"I tried looking it up, but you have all your mail sent here. I even asked some of the boys, but no one knows where you live. I need to know *now*, Cressida."

His use of my first name threw me for a moment. I was always

Miss Curtain, or very infrequently, Cressida Curtain. Never just Cressida.

He sensed my reluctance. "Please remember, we are on the same team for this one. Here," he fished into his pocket, drawing out the dreaded watch. He showed the face to me. "I promise I won't tell anyone where you live." The second hand did not falter as it raced around the face.

I met his eyes, touched that he would show proof of his honesty in this matter. "Very well," I finally gave in. "Do you know Rabbit Hole Road?" He nodded. I continued, "It's down that way, about two miles. Last cottage before the road turns to country. The official road number is 100, but you won't find a marking of it on the property."

"Excellent! It's a date, then." Gavin said with a wink. "I'll be there to pick you up no later than 7:15. Please be ready by then. Shall I escort you out?"

There was still commotion out in the hall. "I think I'm good," I told him. I figured both of us showing up together again would only fuel the rumor mill.

St. Cloud tilted his head to acknowledge my decision. "Until Saturday, then," he said, smiling.

I walked over to the door, Grimm by my side. Flinging it open, I counted no less than eight grown men gawking in the hallway. I stopped to meet each one in the eye, despite my discomfort. "Gentlemen," I greeted coolly before heading down the hall to make my escape. As much as I wanted to run, I walked evenly, keeping my head high while avoiding the whispers, until I was back outside.

Nobody followed me, thankfully, but once I was out of the town's borders, I changed into my feline self and ran like the devil was chasing me.

"I don't want you to go."

I looked over at my partner, meeting his gaze. It was Friday morning, and he hadn't voiced any concerns since our meeting with Gavin. His sudden statement was completely unexpected. I perked my ears forward, ready to listen to whatever he had to say.

"Grimm, we've been over this. I have to go," I told him.

He gave his head a shake. "I've been thinking about this a lot ever since we left the guild," he said. "Something doesn't sit right with me."

"What is it?"

"It's the way you've been acting around him."

"Excuse me?" Of all the things that I thought Grimm would say about the upcoming mission, something so personal did not make the list.

He huffed. "I don't like how *nice* you've been to him. You always used to go into a defensive posture around him, as if guarding yourself with an invisible shield. Now, you're dropping your guard. You're ... receptive to him."

"Grimm, I think you are reading way too far into things. Sure, I've been a bit more friendly with him, but that's only because we are working a case together. You know, to find my father and exonerate him? Maybe I decided it would be better to play nice rather than push the guy away."

My tail began lashing back and forth as I spoke, clear evidence of my growing frustration. Grimm made it worse by adding, "I just don't like the idea of you spending time with him without me. Especially in a setting that promotes closeness, like a dance."

"Oh, for Freya's sake," I grumbled. "Are you jealous?"

He said nothing.

"You are, aren't you?" I stood up, my tail fully thrashing now. "What are you jealous of?"

He stood too, towering over me. "It should be you and me looking out for your dad, not you and *him*."

I flattened my ears at his threatening body stance. "It would be nice if it was, but it's not. That's the way it is. But Grimm, I have news for you. You don't own me. I get to make my own choices about who I associate with. And listen to this, buster: one day I'm going to have to find my husband, and when I do, are you going to be jealous of him as well?"

Grimm, who had been looming over me with his ears pinned back, suddenly dropped them and took a step back, looking confused. And strangely hurt, which made my heart ache.

"I never really thought of it before," he admitted sheepishly.

"You know I love being your partner, Grimm, and I'm happy you are part of my family. But when it comes to my personal life, you need to allow me to make my own decisions."

"I know, I know. I'm ... sorry. I just ... when I see St. Cloud, I really want to bite him. I know you used to feel the same way, and we were a united front. But now, you don't seem to hate him anymore. And I still do. It's just very confusing for me." He slumped down, resting his head on his front legs and looking forlorn.

"Hey," I replied, coming over to lick his cheek, "People change. I'm not bosom buddies with St. Cloud, despite what you think. The guy still rankles me. But maybe I'm starting to see him in a slightly different light. You can still hate him, but please understand, I need to go with him to the ball. It's the best option for finding out what's going on with Roger. Okay?"

Grimm lifted his head to nose my small body affectionately. "Okay."

CHAPTER 19

I t was finally Saturday, the day of the ball. I woke up nervous, which honestly surprised me. It wasn't like we were actual attendees, but I still felt an unexpected thrill over the prospect of going. Perhaps there was a little girly girl in me after all.

I spent the majority of the day as a cat, soaking up as much normalcy as possible. After all, who knew how long I would have to stay in human form to get through this task.

At around 4 p.m., I groomed myself as thoroughly as possible—my face, my ears, my back, my chest. I cleaned between my toes and my nether regions. I even groomed my tail, despite the fact that part of my anatomy wouldn't even translate into a human part. By the time I was done, it was about 5:30.

I assumed a little under two hours would be plenty of time to get ready, but Fleurette and Wren seemed to think this was blasphemy. Fal, I noticed, was conspicuously absent.

Since I had never once gotten fancy before, Fleurette took charge. She dragged me into the bathroom, where she wet my hair with a comb, despite it being freshly cleaned from my ministrations. While she turned away to grab something, I looked at myself in the mirror. My damp hair hung down to just past my shoulders, limp and bedraggled. I looked like a drowned cat. I couldn't possibly imagine how she would make me look fit for a ball. But Fleurette had just gotten started. She took out a small bottle from a nearby shelf and pulled off the cap.

"What's that?" I asked, eyeing it.

"Oh, this is one of my hair tonics. It will keep your hair looking silky smooth, give it shine, and make it easier to wear up. I added some incantations to help keep those slippery hairs of yours from falling out of the coiffure I intend to do. Plus, smell—" she shoved the bottle in my face. A hint of vanilla and an unidentified floral scent invaded my nostrils. I admit, it smelled divine. "All the ladies will be wearing perfume, trust me. This will be a good scent for you."

She poured a dollop out of the bottle, rubbed her hands together, and ran them through my damp hair, twisting and fingering until all of my fine strands were coated.

Her boar bristle brush then made an appearance, and she spent a few minutes brushing my hair until I could see a visible silky shine.

After that, she spent the next forty minutes creating an elegant updo, braiding part of my hair and sticking countless pins into the rest of it to create a low-swept sleek bun. Upon completion, she turned to Wren, who was watching the whole process with a look of rapture.

"Makeup?" Fleurette asked her.

"Oh yes," she agreed, clapping her hands together.

I was dubious. I had never once seen Fleurette wear makeup, and we had all agreed that Wren was still too young. I certainly never wore it. Would I end up looking like a clown?

Yet again, I should have trusted my friend.

"I used to wear makeup when I was younger. I still remember how to apply it. And Wren here has been studying the latest trends and applications. Don't worry, Cress dear, you'll look amazing."

Another half hour of makeup application followed. Fleurette

and Wren agreed that a subtle palette would be perfect and chose some soft browns with a hint of gold to go on my eyes.

As she applied the shimmering powder, Fleurette murmured, "With hair as light as yours, how on earth did you end up with such dark lashes? I hardly need mascara for them."

I smiled and spoke carefully so as not to jostle my face. "Simple. Have you never noticed that my cat eyes are rimmed with a darker skin color?"

Wren piped up, "Oh, I have! It looks like you're wearing subtle eyeliner. It really makes your eyes pop."

"Exactly. And thank you for the compliment, Wren. Many cats have this. Apparently, this dark ring around my eyes translates to dark eyelashes and eyebrows when I'm human. Just a fun magical genetic quirk, I guess."

Even with my lovely, naturally dark lashes, Fleurette did end up applying a coat of mascara. It was the worst part of the entire makeup ordeal.

And lastly, for my lips, Fleurette applied a peachy-red gloss that wasn't too bright, but just a few shades darker than my natural lips.

The witches that they were, they would not allow me to see my makeup or hair until I was fully ready. There was one last thing to do: don the dress.

Said dress had been hanging from a hook in its garment bag in Fleurette's bedroom all week. Fleurette had glanced at it earlier to make sure it was wrinkle free, and then zipped up the bag. I hadn't looked at it at all since arriving back home.

Now, Fleurette directed me to take my clothes off. Luckily, she had had the foresight to have me remove my shirt and replace it with a button-up before doing my hair and makeup, so that I did not need to take anything off over my head. I promptly unbuttoned it and removed it, along with my boots and trousers.

I was left standing in my underwear.

Human taboos held little sway over me. I suppose I should have been self-conscious being near-naked in front of other people. But Fleurette was more like a sister to me, and she had made it clear that I was not her type. Plus, being a cat, I did not have a strong sense of shame when it came to the human body. After all, I was always naked when I was in my natural form. I even almost dressed down in front of poor Fal last summer, quite by accident.

And Fleurette did not have me stay naked for long. First came the corset, which she laced up deftly, followed by the shift and finally, the dress. She zipped up the back, smoothed out the planes of my torso, and stepped back.

"Oh my, Cressida," she breathed.

"Is it that bad?" I turned around, finding the mirror in the corner.

A stranger stared back at me.

My hair, usually worn loose or in a hasty ponytail, was done up sleek and smooth in a low knot, with one side braided from my crown to the bottom and incorporated into the elegant bun. My makeup simply highlighted my eye structure and cheekbones, with a slight shimmer making my face flawless. And the dress ...

I had small breasts. I did not even wear a bra under my loose clothing. But the corset pushed what boobs I did have up and out, creating a small amount of cleavage that barely peeked out of the neckline. The top of the dress also had folds of fabric at the bust in a cowl-neck fashion, creating the illusion of more substance. Spaghetti straps held up the cowl neck top, but there were also off-shoulder sleeves a couple of inches thick gracing the sides of my arms. The dress stopped being loose directly below the bust, perfectly fitting my body down my torso and then flaring slightly at the knee. It showed off my toned form and gave it the illusion of feminine curves that were always hidden behind the normally shapeless clothes I wore. The entire dress was a rich light blue, like the color of morning glories, but with a minor metallic sheen that made the color shift slightly to incorporate more silver or more violet, depending on the light.

The color also brought out the intense blue of my eyes.

I was taken by this image of me. I looked stunning.

"There's just one small problem," I murmured. I pointed to the two black streaks in my hair, which were interwoven into the updo. It did not look bad, per se, but ... "If I'm to blend in, I can't have my black streaks. Nobody else has these. They'll give me away." I should have thought of this sooner.

Before I could go too far down the rabbit hole of self-pity at the thought of ruining my lovely hairstyle, Wren, who had come back into the room, chimed in, "Oh, we already thought of that. Come sit on the bed for a second."

Intrigued, I glided over to the bed and sat primly, aware of my posture for the first time. Corsets were a wonder for straight spines.

Wren came over, grinning. "I've been practicing a new trick," she said. She raised her hands and held them on either side of my head. Concentrating deeply, to the point that her eyes nearly bugged out of her head, she tensed her hands for a few seconds. Then her whole body relaxed. "There."

I felt nothing. She motioned for me to look in the mirror again. I turned around and, to my surprise, my hair was one uniform color like cornsilk.

I turned back to her. "How did you do that?"

She grinned proudly. "I projected onto you."

I raised my hand to touch my hair but thought better of it. "You can do that? How long will it last?"

She seemed a bit tired as she answered. "It's something I just learned I could do. I can't do large things yet, but if I keep practicing, I'll get better. It won't last a super long time, but I'll bet it will at least last until midnight."

"Just like Cinderella?" I joked.

"Funny you should mention that," she replied. "Did you know historians believe the 'fairy godmother' in the story was actually a projectionist? That's how she was able to transform everything, but since it was a lot of projectioning, she could only hold it until midnight. Still, to be able to project an entire outfit *plus* a coach and horses, she must have been crazy powerful."

"Are you having to intentionally hold this illusion?" I asked her, just a tad concerned that a twelve-year-old was in charge of my hair color.

She shook her head. "No, now that it's on there, it will stay until I run out of energy. It's like a slow drain on a battery. I've been practicing with similar-sized projects, which is why I'm confident it will last through the entire ball."

"Wren, you're incredible!" I gushed. She blushed at the compliment.

"Oh, one last thing," she said suddenly, "I don't think the projection will hold if you change into a cat."

"Duly noted. No transforming at the ball." It was a slight inconvenience, but I didn't think being in cat form would be incredibly helpful for this event anyway.

Fal came barreling into the room just then, stopping short at seeing the three of us clustered by the bed. He sheepishly said, "Uh, sorry for the interruption, but I just saw an MC pull up to the house. Cressida, I think your date is here."

I stood up. Wren must have been blocking his view of me before because Fal blinked, a stunned expression crossing his face. "Woah. You look amazing."

I smiled at him. "Thanks, Fal. It's a different look, isn't it?"

Before he could reply, Fleurette butted in. "Fal, will you please greet our guest and let him in? Cress dear, there's just a couple of finishing touches you need before you go."

Fal dutifully left. Fleurette handed me the matching shoes to put on. The salesladies had initially wanted me to don two-inch heels, but I had declined, given the fact that I had never worn heels in my life, and I was certain I'd break an ankle in them. The compromise was what they called "kitten heels," a name that internally cracked me up. These were just half an inch tall, and much more manageable.

I stood just as a knock sounded on the front door. The cottage was small, so I could hear well no matter where I was in the house. I heard Fal open the door.

St. Cloud's voice spoke from the doorway, "Hello. I'm here to escort Miss Curtain to the Spring Equinox Ball."

"That's my cue," I said. Fleurette put a hand out to stop me from leaving the room.

"One last thing," she said, picking up something from her bureau. She held it up, and I saw it was a necklace. It was made of three parts: two long, thin filigree pieces with a small pendant in the middle. The pendant sparkled with a diamond inlaid within it, the facets shaped like a teardrop. A small amount of fine chain was connected to the other end of the filigree pieces. The entire piece was made of gleaming silver.

"Fleurette, it's beautiful. Where did it come from?"

She smiled with a hint of sadness. "It was my mother's," she told me as she walked behind me to clasp it around my neck.

I turned to the mirror one last time. The necklace fit perfectly with the dress. The filigrees graced my exposed collarbones, with the pendant falling perfectly into my decolletage. It completed my look perfectly, but I had reservations.

"Are you sure I should wear it?" I asked my friend. The fact that it was a remnant of her mother weighed on me.

She nodded, looking proudly at me. "It's perfect for you."

I wanted to hug Fleurette, but I worried about ruining my look. She understood, though, and only clasped my bare arms affectionately. "Time to go," she whispered.

Nervously, I exited her room and walked down the dark hallway and into the sitting room. Fal seemed to be glowering at St. Cloud, standing near the front door. I stopped short when I turned my attention to my faux date.

Gavin was wearing his tuxedo, a black affair that hugged his body, showing off the shape of his muscular chest and arms. His crisp white button-up shirt contrasted beautifully with the black ensemble. Normally he sported some stubble when I saw him on the job, but this time he was freshly shaved, highlighting his square jaw. His dark hair had been slicked back stylishly.

I had always harbored a physical attraction to Gavin St. Cloud, as much as I was loath to admit it to anyone. Seeing him now in this state sent the attraction into overdrive.

He hadn't seen me yet, since he was busy studying the surly teenager in his midst. I cleared my throat.

He turned in my direction. "Ah, there ... you ... are ..." he trailed off as he got a good look at me. I walked forward, coming into the light of the sitting room. St. Cloud gawked unashamedly. "My gods, Miss Curtain, you look stunning."

His compliment made my heart swell. This was the man who had tormented me every chance he got for the last year and a half. To see in his eyes that he thought I was beautiful should have been a vindication, a chance to rub it in his face, but instead, immense happiness bloomed within me at his words.

Fleurette had followed behind me. She now draped something soft and warm over my shoulders. "For the ride," she said. I smiled at her and continued walking over to Gavin. Gavin dragged his attention begrudgingly from me to survey the room.

He landed on Fleurette, who was the oldest person present and therefore a source of authority. He held out a hand. "Gavin St. Cloud," he introduced himself politely, but with a hint of his usual swagger.

Fleurette shook his hand. "I know who you are, Mr. St. Cloud," she said, not unkindly. "I'm Cressida's manager, Fleurette Williams."

I saw a twinkle in his eye as he took that tidbit of information in. "I'll be sure to have her back tonight," he assured her.

Fal butted in, "Keep her safe!"

St. Cloud turned to Fal with exaggerated confusion. "I'm sorry, who are you? Are you her father?"

Fal scowled at the absurdity of Gavin's question. "No, but she's family. And you'd better take care of her."

St. Cloud flashed one of his self-confident grins, clearly amused by Fal's antics. "Or what?"

"Or else we know where to find you!" piped up Wren from behind Fleurette.

Grimm, who had been lounging on the loveseat, got down and growled at St. Cloud, adding his two cents to the mix.

Gavin's grin vanished, replaced with a look of concern as the entire room seemingly ganged up on him.

Fleurette once again took charge. "Alright, everyone! Let's settle. Mr. St. Cloud, as you can see, Cressida means a great deal to us, so we would be most appreciative if you were to return her in one piece tonight, especially given her proclivity for getting into trouble."

"Hey!" I retorted, but without any real protest.

Fleurette smiled at me and tugged the warm shawl up my arms further. "You two be safe tonight. Good luck finding the answers you need."

"Thank you." I smiled gratefully at my friend before walking over to Gavin's side. "Shall we, Mr. St. Cloud?"

"We shall, Miss Curtain." His self-assured air had returned. We left the cottage, carefully making our way to the MC. Gavin even held the vehicle's door open for me, like a true gentleman.

As he started the motor and turned on the headlamps, he said with some levity in his voice, "What is up with your family?"

"What do you mean? They're just protective."

Gavin chuckled as he navigated the MC out onto the road. "That's putting it mildly. So, you live with your 'manager?'"

I could hear the quotes he put around the word. I wasn't sure what he was implying. "As a matter of fact, I do. Is there a problem with that?"

"No, but it may explain why my charms don't work on you."

His implications clicked in my brain. "Your charms don't work on me because you *have* no charms, St. Cloud. Fleurette is my friend, nothing more."

"Ah, well, that's good then. Nothing wrong with having friends. I must say, your living conditions aren't at all what I pictured you'd have."

"Should I be offended by what you're about to say?"

"You're awfully fired up, aren't you? I only meant I wasn't expecting a room full of people giving me the stink eye. You seem like a bit of a loner to me."

I thought about that. I admitted, "I *was* a loner, but my chosen family is amazing, and they really care about me." I suddenly realized something, and my heart sank. "I forgot to say goodbye to Grimm," I moaned.

"So?"

"So," I uttered loudly, "he already didn't want me to go. Now he's going to think I forgot about him. He's already put out about not getting to go tonight."

St. Cloud was silent for a moment. "You do know he's a dog,

right?"

I didn't respond. There was no point in trying to explain the relationship I had with Grimm to the man. Instead, I changed topics. "This is the first time I've ridden in an MC." It was fairly smooth, I had to say, although it felt weird being stuck inside a box with windows, rather than out in the open like when I sat in the wagon's seat. Plus, now that we were on the road, we were going faster than I ever had before in a vehicle. It was rather terrifying, yet exhilarating, at the same time.

St. Cloud perked up. "Scarlet is top of the line," he stated, pride evident in his tone. "She'll get us there in about half an hour's drive."

That was actually impressive. I had done the math earlier. It would have been around a three-hour drive if I had taken the wagon. Still, I felt the need to take St. Cloud's hubris down a notch.

"Oh, what's this white hair?" I asked innocently, glancing over at my nemesis.

He gripped the wheel tightly, his gorgeous jaw flexing. "I thought I had gotten it all cleaned up. Some animal got in here and made a mess about a week ago. Took me forever to get all of those white hairs out. Must have missed a couple."

"Oh dear, that sounds terrible," I lied gleefully.

I must have let a little too much cheerfulness slip into my voice because Gavin looked over at me with a frown. I simply smiled innocently at him until he gave his attention back to the darkened road.

"So," he said, clearing his throat, "let's take this opportunity to go over our characters. You know, just in case there's anybody there that knows of Riku and Marilyn."

"Sounds like a solid plan," I agreed, fiddling with my wrap.

"Okay, then," he said, pulling out of Knobby Hill onto the

faster road. He kicked up the speed, making a thrill race through me. I tried to pretend I wasn't affected. "My name is Riku Shimada. I immigrated to Vinland with my family when I was three years old, and I work in the customer service department, overseeing individual accounts for overseas shipping. I enjoy reading and hiking on my days off."

Without looking in my direction, he pointed at me. "You are Marilyn Croft. We met at an art gallery because you like to dabble in painting. We've been engaged for two months, and we haven't set a date for the wedding yet."

I looked at my hand. "And where's my ring?"

Gavin pursed his lips. "It's in the shop being repaired because the setting was loose, and we were worried about losing the diamond. You were upset by the timing of the problem, because of course, you wanted to show off your ring, but that's life sometimes."

"Fast thinking," I remarked appreciatively.

"You're not the only one who can lie on their feet." He glanced at me, noting the look of displeasure I was giving him. "Too soon?"

"Yep."

He cleared his throat. "The important thing to remember is that we, Riku and Marilyn, are deeply in love. We need to sell that. You can't be looking at me like you are doing right now."

"How am I looking at you?" I asked out of curiosity.

"Like you're a tiger waiting to pounce. Not in the good way, either. So take that passion and turn it into a different emotion. Can you handle that?"

I smiled widely. "Of course, *darling*."

"That's the spirit."

We fell into silence. I could see him sneaking glances at me every half second or so. Finally, he broke the silence. "I must say,

Cressida, you clean up well. Who knew?"

Why did I feel a tiny thrill when he used my first name? But as soon as the rest of his comment entered my brain, I squashed that little sensation like a bug.

"What are you insinuating?" I asked, insulted.

"Don't get snippy again. You literally only wear formless clothes. I didn't even know you had a figure under them. It's nice to see you looking like a woman for once."

I wanted to pinch the bridge of my nose, but I didn't dare for fear of ruining my makeup. It was true that my standard attire was worn for the sake of comfort and functionality and not necessarily for style points. But I took pride in my looks, no matter what form I was in, and I knew for a fact that I looked damn good in my usual trousers, linen blouse, and dove-gray vest. I'd hardly qualify them as "formless," even if they weren't tight-fitting.

"For your information, St. *Clod*, I always look like a woman. Because I am a woman. Just because I usually don't fit your typical, misogynistic standards of a dress and makeup doesn't make me any less of a woman."

"There she is." He smirked as he stared at the road. "I was beginning to think your demeanor had changed along with your look, but I see you're still the same prickly thorn with a sharp tongue you've always been."

"I ought to punch that smirk off your face."

"And risk bruising me right before the ball? Do you remember what's at stake? Your *Roger*, a man you insist on calling by his first name, of whom you are no relation, despite my watch telling me otherwise. Ring any bells?"

I took a deep breath. "You really do enjoy gnawing at old bones, don't you?"

He quirked his head to the side in acknowledgement. "It

would be nice to know all the facts since I'm risking my neck *and* my reputation for you."

He had a point, damn him. I warred with myself for a moment, trying to decide which plan of action to take: double down on the lies I had told or take a giant leap of faith and confide in my nemesis? Common sense won out. Because there was a lot at stake here, and he deserved to know at least part of the story.

"Fine," I said. "Do you want to know the truth? I'll tell you. But you have to keep this between us, or I'll come after your testicles with a rusty knife."

He squirmed visibly at the visual. "Deal."

"The reason I want to help Roger Curtain is because he's my long-lost father."

He guffawed. "You're having me on!"

"I am not. Get out your precious watch if you must. I'd bet my right hand you have it on you tonight."

"You'd be right," he declared. "Very well, it's in my vest pocket. Fish it out for me, will you?"

I paused for a moment before leaning over and sticking my hand underneath his tux jacket, fumbling for a pocket. As I leaned closer in my search, a spicy-sweet musk rolled over my nostrils. I wanted to breathe deeply, but I took that moment to look at St. Cloud's face. He was grinning much too widely.

I jumped back to my side. "You sneak! You just wanted me to feel you up! Get it yourself."

His grin cracked even wider, but he did as I demanded. He held the watch out to me. "You'll have to open it. Say what you said again."

I repeated my statement. St. Cloud took a moment to glance at the watch face, his eyebrows shooting up in surprise. "So, you were in on it all along?"

"What? No!" I hastily replied. "I'd never met my father before.

I only recognized the name at the meeting. And you can't say anything to him about me either. He doesn't know I exist."

"He has no idea you're his daughter?"

"None," I reiterated. "And for now, I'd like to keep it that way. That's why I told him my last name is Curtis. Please promise you won't give me away."

"Of course," he said. "My, my, what a sordid little family reunion I've stumbled into. How exciting!"

"I'm glad one of us is amused," I said sourly.

He just smiled.

CHAPTER 20

We reached our destination shortly after. I still marveled over the quickness of our trip; perhaps MCs weren't completely mechanized evil. But now that we were there, my nerves got the best of me, and I almost wished the ride had taken longer as Gavin drove through the lavish open gate.

He pulled into a long driveway leading up to an enormous, stately house. There was already a line of vehicles—mostly MCs but also some fancy horse-drawn carriages—ahead of us. We waited for our turn with nervous energy.

Then it was his turn to park in front of the opulent entrance, replete with columns and a grand double door. The entire walkway up to the front was lit with a multitude of bulbs. Gavin got out and hurried to my side, opening the door for me and holding out a hand for assistance. I nearly ignored it but remembered that I was playing a character, so I graciously let him pull me up. Once I was out, a valet came running up to park Scarlet.

Gavin offered me his arm, which I looped with mine, and we walked sedately up to the entrance together. I sneaked a glance at the man by my side. Gavin held an air of confidence; clearly, this was an environment he had some familiarity with. In contrast, the closer we sauntered toward the grand doorway, the more timid I felt. I decided it was prudent for Gavin to take the lead in this venture, at least initially. I had to suppress the urge to bolt and run.

At the open door, a servant stood austerely, a clipboard resting on a high stool by his side. He held out his hand upon our arrival to accept our invitation. Gavin fished in his pocket to procure it.

"Names, please," the servant drawled as Gavin slid the invitation into his waiting hand.

"Riku Shimada and my plus one, Marilyn Croft," Gavin replied. The servant took the invitation, opened it, checked our fake names off a list on the clipboard, and then beckoned us to enter.

We were in.

I couldn't help but gawk at the opulence on display. The grand foyer we now stood in was absolutely cavernous. The ceiling stretched up for at least three stories, with a wide marble staircase sweeping up from the left of the room and over to the right against the wall. Lavish paintings dotted the walls, evenly spaced.

Already a great many people milled about inside, dwarfed by the grand scale of the room. They chatted in small groups or simply did what I was doing, taking it all in with awed looks on their faces. Others filtered into a room off to the left of the foyer. But the constant stream of guests entering from the outside swiftly replaced those who exited the immediate vicinity.

The sea of bodies, and the crush of opulence quickly took over my senses. My heartrate picked up and I shrank into myself. My animal instinct was to run and hide, preferably to some dark corner. I fought the urge, reminding myself that humans did not often run screaming from rooms, not without a good reason, at least. I needed to stay focused. I could do this.

A servant approached us, seemingly indifferent to my discomfiture. "Madam, may I take your wrap?"

"Oh, yes, please." I pulled it off, not needing the extra warmth as I could already tell it would be stifling in here.

He reverently placed it over his arm and then swept the other out in a gesture. "This way, please."

We followed him straight through the grand hall to underneath a stairwell, where a set of double doors stood open. A cloakroom resided directly inside, where my wrap was deposited, and then the way opened up into a giant domed room, where gilded framework encased an abundance of intricate murals featuring what I assumed to be Hellastic gods and goddesses—Zeus, Hera, Aphrodite, Apollo and the like—frolicking.

A small orchestra played in one corner on a small stage, and in another corner stood an impressive bar display, managed by more servants. Other well-dressed servers carried hors d'oeuvre platters through the growing throngs of guests.

Speaking of the guests, I felt like I had been thrust into a fantastic menagerie of birds in this gilded cage of a ballroom. The ladies were bedecked in dresses of all the colors of the rainbow, with glittering jewels gracing throats and hair. The men were no less resplendent despite their more monochromatic attire. With their fitted tuxedos, I imagined them as penguins escorting their birds of paradise about the room.

I, normally so self-assured, grasped onto Gavin's arm as if to prevent myself from drowning in this visual and audio cacophony. He glanced over at me and gave me a surprisingly thoughtful and reassuring pat on the arm.

"Marilyn, my love, are you well?"

The name threw me for a second, but I regained my senses. "I'll be okay. It's just a lot to take in. Give me a moment to acclimate to this zoo."

"Fighting werewolves gives you a spine of steel, but a gaggle of rich folk throws you off your game? Who knew?"

I hated his observation, as precise as it was. I jabbed his side with my elbow. "I'm in my element with werewolves. Besides,

Grimm does most of the work."

He chuckled. "Perhaps a dance would help you settle in?"

Before I could give him a resounding no, he had pulled me to the middle of the floor, where other couples spun in swirling circles. He turned toward me, grasping my right hand in his left, and placed his other hand on my waist. Instinctively, I threw my free hand on his shoulder, as the other ladies had with their dance partners.

In a moment of panic, I realized I had never asked anyone to show me how to dance. A huge oversight when one agrees to attend a ball with dancing, I lamented. I decided to follow St. Cloud's lead and hope for the best.

As he twirled me around to the music, I wondered what I should be doing with my eyes. Was I supposed to take this time to watch the other couples? Or was I supposed to meet my dance partner's gaze? I opted to do both, starting with looking around first and then turning my attention back to Gavin.

"Wow," he murmured as our eyes met.

"What?" I asked rather breathlessly. My heart gave a funny turn.

"You are terrible at dancing."

I shallowly whacked him on the shoulder I was holding. He grinned at me, then continued, "You're so graceful in your movements normally; I figured you'd be better at this. I'm pretty sure you've stepped on my feet more than on the dance floor."

"Shut it! I've never danced before," I hissed, my face growing hot.

"Oh, well, for your first time? You're still terrible," he teased, clearly enjoying my obvious discomfort. "Why don't you stop overthinking everything and just move with me and the music?"

Until he said that, I had no clue I was even overthinking. Instead of trying to mimic what he was doing with his feet and thinking about what to do with my eyes, I let go and just danced in his arms, letting the music flow through and guide me.

"Better," he commented. I let out a small smile, allowing myself the freedom to simply have fun instead of worrying if I was doing it right.

"You really think I'm graceful?" I asked, seeking some sort of placation.

He nodded. "Normally, yes. You move so fluidly, like a panther stalking its prey."

Well, that was a fair assessment, but I was not going to tell him that. "Thank you."

He glanced at my hair with interest as we moved across the floor. "By the way, where did your black streaks go?"

I raised my eyes as if I could see my own hairline. Making eye contact again, I smirked. "Magic."

He raised his brows, impressed. "Yours?"

I shook my head instantly. "Oh, no. A friend. I figured it would help us blend in a bit more if I didn't have unusual hair."

"No doubt it would. Well, Miss ... Marilyn, what is our plan of attack? We need to figure out where the ledger might be, if it's here."

I pondered that. "If I was the owner of the ledger, I'd have it in my home office."

"Those are often called studies in large places like this."

"Fine, in my study. So, if we know where the study is, we can search there."

He cocked his head around to look at the ballroom. "How do you propose we discover its whereabouts?"

"Do you think any of the guests might know? Surely some of these people are Lightfoot's personal friends."

He looked rueful. "I'm not sure anybody who has this much wealth actually *has* friends. More like colleagues and would-be moochers."

I glanced at him askew. "There's that pessimistic view of rich people again."

"Hmm?" he hummed, although I'm fairly certain he heard me. I let it drop. He finally acknowledged, "It's as good a place to start as any. Shall we mingle?"

My anxious side screamed no in my head, but my logical side won. "We shall."

Unfortunately, it wasn't as easy as I had anticipated.

"So, Miss Croft, are you related to a Daniel Croft, by any chance?"

My face was starting to hurt with all of the forced smiling I was doing. I was getting tired of this. "No, I'm not, I'm afraid. Say, this house is fantastic! Have you ever had a tour?"

The older woman in the bright red ballgown with rubies on her ears simpered. "Oh no, this is my first time here."

Another dead end. St. Cloud and I had gone together to talk to people in the hopes of getting a feel for the layout of this mansion. But after striking out together a few times, we decided to split up to cover more of the crowd. I was beginning to lose track of the number of people with whom I had already approached to strike up banal conversations before moving on after learning nothing.

A distinguished-looking gentleman with only a fringe of hair stood off to the side. I decided he'd be my next victim. I politely excused myself from the ruby woman, who easily turned to a different willing conversationalist. I approached the bald man casually, smiling when we made eye contact. "How do you do?

I'm Marilyn Croft."

He looked at my outstretched hand with little interest, giving it an extremely limp shake. "Donald Chesterfield," he told me with a bored mien.

"Mr. Chesterfield, how do you know our host?"

He barely glanced at me. "We go to the gentlemen's club together."

Well, that seemed a bit more promising. "Oh? Have you had the honor of an invitation to Mr. Lightfoot's estate before?"

He nodded, staring out into the distance. "On many occasions."

My heart rate picked up. "I'm just extremely fascinated by grand old houses! Tell me, what sort of rooms does his house have? A library, perhaps? An in-home office?"

Mr. Chesterfield nodded absently. "Yes, yes, he has those things. And an indoor pool as well. But no ballroom."

My brain stuttered. "Isn't this a ballroom?"

He nodded again. "Yes, a rather nice one at that. My apologies, Miss Coff, I must go speak to someone else now." With that clear dismissal, he left me standing there, trying to wrap my head around his words.

"Crab puff, miss?" a voice asked from behind me. It was one of the servers offering appetizers.

"No, thank you," I said woodenly, still trying to figure out the confusing conclusion to my last conversation.

"Are you quite certain you don't want one, Miss Curtis?"

It took a moment to realize that the surname he used was not the same false name as the one I was using here at the ball. I whipped around to confront the waiter. I was met by a middle-aged man just a couple of inches taller than myself, with glasses and thick black hair that neither matched his pallid skin tone, nor looked exactly real.

It was a wig.

The wig-wearer was my father.

"How—" I began.

He smiled, offering the tray to me again. "It's lovely to see you, Miss Curtis. I almost didn't recognize you."

"What are you doing here?" I hissed.

He looked around. "Oh dear, I seem to be out of the special crab cakes you requested. If you'd just follow me to the kitchen, I can accommodate you," he said, loudly.

He turned and made for a side door I hadn't noticed earlier. I followed demurely, although internally, I was thrown into a turmoil of emotions.

The door opened into a narrow hallway. Straight ahead, the banging sounds of pots and pans met my ears, and delicious smells wafted down the corridor before us. I surmised this particular hallway led directly to the kitchen. Roger quickly turned to a door to the left, however, and entered it after making sure the coast was clear. I followed and shut the door behind me, blanketing us in darkness.

The darkness did not last long, however. Roger pulled a chain in the center of the tiny room, illuminating that we were in a supply closet.

Before I could help myself, I flung my arms around my father. "Roger, I'm so glad you're safe!" I whispered.

He seemed taken aback by my sudden display of affection but awkwardly patted my back until I let go of him. Belatedly, I realized he still held the tray of crab puffs, but Roger's balancing skills were on par, for not a single piece had dropped. He set the tray down on an empty shelf.

"Miss Curtis, I see you found my ledger."

"Cressida, please," I urged him to call me. "I did indeed. I did not expect to find *you* here though!" I thought for a moment.

"How did you get in here?"

He looked amused. "I'll admit I had outside help getting to the manor. From there, I merely timed my arrival with the waitstaff hired for the event, and I've been passing myself off as a waiter ever since."

I wondered if the "outside help" was our mutual acquaintance, Rosa. "As glad as I am to see you, you can't be here, Roger. They're still looking for you."

He nodded. "But I need to find the ledger first. It was a risk I was willing to take to clear my name."

"So you haven't found it?" I asked, my hopes dashed.

Shaking his head, he added, "But I was able to search the whole of the first floor. Most places like this have their studies on the ground floor. Mr. Lightfoot does not. My assumption is that it's on the second floor. I simply haven't had the time to search further."

A thought occurred to me. "Does this place have an indoor pool?"

He frowned in confusion. "I don't believe so. Why?"

"I don't think this is Lightfoot's house."

"No? Well, I still believe this is the best bet for the location of the ledger. I just need to sneak upstairs to continue my search."

I pondered this for a moment. "Roger, I am here with ... a partner, of sorts. Not my, er, romantic partner, you see, but a different partner—"

"Miss Curtis?" I shot him a look at the formal name. "Cressida? You're rambling."

"Right. Anyway, we are here undercover to find the ledger. You need to get out of here before you are discovered. Can you slip out easily?"

He mulled it over. "I suppose so. My friend is still waiting for me outside. Although I'd much rather look for it with you."

I shook my head emphatically. "Nope. We have this covered. Listen, you need to get yourself someplace safe. Do you have any paper on you?"

He patted down his uniform, procuring a small scrap of paper and a pencil. I snatched both and scribbled quickly. "This is a safe place in Knobby Hill. It's a little cottage about two miles down Rabbit Hole Road. The lady who owns the place is Fleurette. Tell her I sent you, and she'll help you."

He nodded, grateful, as he read the address. He looked at me, his eyes shining. "Thank you, Cressida, for helping me. I'm not sure why I deserved to have a guardian angel such as yourself." He paused, studying me. "You look so familiar. I had that same thought the first time I saw you too. Are you sure we've never met before?"

"Quite sure," I said firmly, not wishing to delve into why I seemed so familiar to him at this moment in time. "Now, please, go as soon as you have the chance! St. Cloud and I will take it from here."

He nodded his affirmation to do just that. He made to leave but stopped abruptly, making me want to tear my hair out at his inaction. Grabbing the hors d'oeuvre platter from the shelf, he gave me a kind smile and said, almost to himself, "Cressida. It's such an old-fashioned name." He held my hand and squeezed it with some small affection. "You know, my grandmother's name was Cressida. It's nice to hear it's still being used on the younger generation."

I nearly gaped with an open mouth at this tiny tidbit, but Roger did not wait for any reply. He dropped my hand, crept to the door, and, after cautiously opening it and peering out, he slipped through the opening and out of my sight. I waited a beat more before also exiting and joining the party.

My mind reeled at the innocent revelation my father had given me. I was named after my great-grandmother! Mom had never given any reason as to why she chose my name. Lost as I was to this pondering, I didn't pay close enough attention to my surroundings. As I went through the door leading into the ballroom, I bumped into the back of a portly man. "Goodness, I'm so sorry!" I spluttered at his backside. The man turned around to address me.

I recognized him immediately, and my stomach dropped.

CHAPTER 21

Mr. Babcock, the lawyer who hired me to hunt Roger Curtain, stood before me, assessing who had just rudely bumped into his backside. Despite my fraying nerves, I had the wherewithal to drop my face and do a little curtsy in order to try to hide my features.

"My apologies," I mumbled. I risked a glance at him. He seemed not to recognize me.

"Quite alright, my dear," he replied before turning back around.

I took the opportunity and my apparent luck and sped away from the lawyer as quickly as my dress and kitten heels would allow. The last thing I wanted to do was tempt him to study me further and connect the dots.

I was now armed with the knowledge that first, my father was still okay and would soon be well hidden by Fleurette, and second, searching the first floor would be a waste of time, and we needed to search the second floor. Now I just needed to find Gavin.

I did a visual sweep of the ballroom but did not see any obvious signs of him. I began to head toward the center, but I saw Mr. Babcock again, and this time he was heading my way. Panicked, I swerved back in another direction, ending up staring at the bar.

A young lady behind the bar smiled at me. I did not return it, seeing as Babcock had stopped near the bar and I was trapped.

"Would you like some champagne, miss?" the bartender asked me politely, holding an already poured flute in my direction.

Without thinking, I took the glass. I held it up to my nose. Fruity, astringent bubbles popped beneath my nostrils. It smelled like cat deterrent of the highest level. I twisted my face in distaste and handed the glass back to her. "Ugh, no thank you."

She took my action in stride, setting the rejected flute off to the side. "Perhaps something else? Wine?"

I knew wine was basically fermented grapes. Yuck. I shook my head.

"Spiced cider?"

I considered that option. I liked spices in general, and of all the fruits, apples were the least repulsive. "Okay."

She turned to get the cider for me, and I glanced over my shoulder to see that I was still penned in by the lawyer. Just my luck.

"Here you are, miss." She handed over a tall, glass mug filled with a cloudy amber liquid. I accepted it graciously.

It smelled of apples and cinnamon, and something else I couldn't place; it bit at my nose slightly but not unpleasantly. I took a sip. The heady aroma accosted my tastebuds with a spicy sweetness, and a fiery warmth slid down my throat and into my belly when I swallowed.

The warmth surprised me, especially given the fact that it did not hurt at all but simply spread outward and enveloped me like a warm hug. I'd had cider to drink at home before, but I'd never had a reaction like that to the spices. I wondered what mix of flavors they used to produce the effect. I took another sip.

After half of the cider went down easily, I decided to take another glance behind me. To my relief, Babcock had moved on. Taking my mug with me, I started back across the floor to search for Gavin again.

The music played in the background, and I was suddenly taken with the idea of swaying to the notes as I crossed the floor. I took another drink from my mug, marveling at the continued spreading warmth that was now starting to take away the heaviness of all of my limbs. I stopped walking for a moment to savor the new sensation.

"There you are." The familiar voice cut through the music. I opened my eyes, which until this moment, I hadn't realized I'd closed. Gavin swam into my vision.

I smiled at him. "There *you* are," I replied.

Gavin looked quizzical at my exuberance. "Marilyn, my love, let me introduce you to some new friends." He led me over to two women, both of a matronly age and bedecked with enough frills to create a whole new outfit. They both looked expectantly at our arrival.

I clung tightly to Gavin's bicep with my free hand. It felt remarkably firm under my grasp. He put a supporting arm around my waist, and I found myself leaning into him.

"Marilyn, love, may I introduce Farrah and Harriet Cornwell? This is my fiancée, Marilyn."

I tilted my head in their general direction as they did the same. The motion nearly unbalanced me, and I tightened my grip on Gavin. I also took another tiny swig of my cider.

The woman on the right, dressed in a royal purple gown, said, "Riku was just telling us about your upcoming nuptials. Congratulations."

The other woman, in a jade green ensemble, added, "Just look at them, Farrah. You can see how much in love they are."

The floaty feeling was getting more intense the longer I stood there. "We are indeed. Right snookums?" I tilted my chin up to Gavin's face. He seemed slightly flustered. I turned my attention back to the ladies. "And how long have you two been married?"

Their mouths dropped open as they stared at me like I had lost my head. Perhaps I had; it would account for the strange detachment I was experiencing.

Gavin cleared his throat. "Dearest, Farrah and Harriet are *sisters*."

Oops. I let out a small chortle at my mistake.

Before they could respond, Gavin cut in, "Apologies, ladies. Might I excuse myself and my lovely wife-to-be? I think we need some air." He ushered me away.

"Where are we going?" I tilted my mug to take another drink, only to realize I had finished my cider sometime during that awkward conversation.

He stopped once we were out of sight of the Cornwell sisters. He looked at the mug suspiciously. "What are you drinking there?"

"Would you like some?" I asked, holding the mug out only to realize that I had just finished the contents moments before. I giggled at my forgetfulness.

He narrowed his eyes at me. "Are you drunk?"

I shook my head, but the movement made me dizzy. "Of course not! I never drink."

He took the cup away from me and smelled it. Straight-faced, he asked, "Did you have a spiced cider?"

"Ding-ding-ding!" I replied cheerfully.

He fought to keep a smile off his face. "Do you know what's in a spiced cider?"

"Cider and spices, duh." My head was swimming much more now. While I still relished the floaty feeling, I was also starting to feel a bit queer in the stomach.

"And rum," he added.

"Rum?" I repeated in a small voice.

He nodded. "A lot of rum, actually. Come on; we need to fix this."

Gavin took my wrist gently and led me out of the ballroom, setting the mug down on a table before taking me into a private room on the other side of the great hall. He stopped abruptly, causing me to run into him from behind. That action reminded me of something important I had to tell him. What was it again?

"Here," Gavin said, distracting me from my faulty memory. He had a tiny vial in his hand that he now unstopped and held out to me.

I was immediately suspicious. "What is it?"

"It's a drunk-me-not potion. I brought it just in case."

I pushed his proffered hand away. "I don't want it. Knowing you, it's poison."

He looked askance. "It's not poison. I would never poison you."

"You might if it meant you'd be the best bounty hunter." I was very sad at this notion. Why did he have to be so cruel?

He shook his head. "Even then, I wouldn't."

"Would so." I sniffled, feeling suddenly miserable. "You want to murder me in this little room and be done with me once and for all. What did I do to deserve this fate? Why don't you like me?"

"I like you just fine."

"Liar. You hate me. You tried to poison me."

He looked exasperated. "Look, I'll take a little first, okay?" He let a few drops fall on his tongue.

He didn't die after a few seconds, so I decided to trust him. I tilted my head back and let the drops fall into my open mouth. It was bitter and sour at the same time, and I nearly spat it back out. But then my limbs stopped floating, and my head cleared.

Within seconds I felt very, very foolish.

"Better?" Gavin asked.

I nodded, not able to look him in the eye just yet. "I've never had a drink before in my life."

"Never?" He seemed dubious. "What made you start now?"

I scowled at him. "It was an accident! They should have named that drink 'spiced rum with cider.' It certainly would have cleared up any confusion."

"Well, now you know. And I have to say; I think drunk Cressida is rather cute."

I glared at him, but not with my usual menace. "Thanks. For, you know, looking out for me. Not for the backhanded compliment."

He shrugged. "I told your manager I would look out for you. I had a feeling the potion would come in handy. We need a straight head to finish the mission. Speaking of, I have a bit of news."

"So do I!" I interjected, remembering everything that had transpired before my little drunken mishap. "I ran into Roger."

"He's here?" Gavin seemed thoroughly surprised.

"Yes, but I sent him away. He told me that he searched the first floor, and he believes the study is on the second floor."

"It is. And I know another staircase we can take to find it."

I brightened. "Excellent. How did you get that little nugget of information?"

He scratched his chin. "I only had to talk to about two dozen different people before I ran across someone who knew anything. Somebody named Mr. Hoterson, I believe?"

That name seemed vaguely familiar, but I couldn't place it. I shrugged it off. "Nice work. Oh, I also saw Babcock."

"Who?"

"The lawyer who hired us. I sort of bumped into him. I don't think he recognized me, though. It figures he'd be here at Lightfoot's party."

We both took in the implications of having the lawyer here with us. If he recognized either of us, it could put a serious damper on any further investigations into this matter.

Gavin spoke up first. "We'll just have to do our best to avoid him, then. I figure we can sneak upstairs at ten when the entertainment is happening to keep everyone preoccupied at the ball."

"How soon is that?" I was getting impatient with having to hang around and not get down to business. Plus, my feet were starting to hurt in these shoes. I missed my soft, flat-heeled leather boots.

He took out his pocket watch. I rolled my eyes. "You know that thing doesn't keep the correct time, right?"

He only grinned and pressed a tiny button on the side of it before showing me the face. "It does if you use the reset button here," he explained. "It's about a quarter til."

"Thank Freya," I moaned with relief. As much as I enjoyed how I looked all dolled up, I was not enjoying the discomfort that went along with it.

"What shall we do until then? I think it would be prudent to be seen back in the ballroom so as not to arouse suspicion. Shall we have another turn on the dance floor?" He shot me a cheeky wink.

I narrowed my eyes at him. "I'd rather be tortured at this point." He smiled at my dramatic statement. "But you're right, let's head back to the ballroom. Appearances and all."

Arm in arm to keep up with said appearances, we casually strolled back to the massive ballroom. A good number of people danced in the center, and even more strolled about, drinking beverages or engaging in conversation.

One such couple, who we had met and talked to earlier in the evening, approached us. They were an older pair, perhaps in their late fifties if I had to take a guess. I could not for the life of me remember their names.

"Ah, Miss Croft and Mr. Shimada!" the lady greeted us, "Where did you two go off to?" she added with a suggestive tone.

"Now, now, my dear, let the young lovers be," her husband admonished lightly. "Just because we are too past our prime to go sneaking off for a little alone time."

The wife smiled knowingly. "Ah, to be young again. When did you say the wedding date was?"

I was having a hard time keeping up with the tone of the conversation. Did they really think we had gone off somewhere to kiss? It seemed like a bold assumption to make. St. Cloud took it in stride, though. "We haven't quite set a date yet. I was hoping for August, but Marilyn thinks it's too soon."

I had very little knowledge of the ins and outs of human engagement. But I took a chance. "That's right. After all, I was hoping to convince my sister to be my maid of honor, but she won't be back in the country until at least October. So many hungry children to feed in Opherica, you know."

"Oh, but darling, you know I can't wait that long," murmured Gavin. He took hold of my hand with fake adoration. I looked down, my face heating at seeing our hands linked together.

I quickly gathered my wits. "Well, you're just going to have to try," I said sweetly, gazing at him with mock adoration.

The wife interjected, "Ah, I can see just how much you love each other."

We turned to her, smiling. I could barely hold back a burst of laughter over the ridiculousness of it all.

Before they could say anything more, the music stopped. "Ladies and gentlemen, may I have your attention please," boomed a voice from the small stage.

"That's our cue," I whispered to St. Cloud. He squeezed my hand in reply.

We made our excuses to the couple talking to us ("Off to sneak in a bit more alone time!" I heard the woman say as we walked away), and Gavin led me slowly to the edge of the room, where another closed door was hidden in the corner. As the speaker introduced Orson Lightfoot to the stage, I turned to get a look at the man who had ultimately hired us.

If I had expected Lightfoot to be an imposing figure, someone who would ruin the life of a man such as my father, I would be rather disappointed. He was of average build, middle aged, with a thick head of brown hair and a beard to match, and glasses perched on his nose. From this distance he looked neither calculating nor cruel. No villainy was present in his countenance, no matter how hard I strained my eyes.

Gavin allowed me this moment of perusal before tugging on my arm. "Come on," he whispered in my ear. "No time to waste."

I turned without a moment of hesitancy and exited through the door after him.

CHAPTER 22

The stairs we climbed were narrow and drab, indicating they were servant access only. After the inundation of opulence from the ball, I didn't mind a little modesty in decor.

"Okay, which door is it?" I asked Gavin once we reached the second floor. Luck appeared to be on our side, as we hadn't run into anyone yet. Unfortunately, this particular staircase led us smack dab in the middle of a wide, green-carpeted hallway that ran the length of the house on either end, with numerous doorways on either side of the corridor.

He shook his head. "I don't know. I assume we'll have to open a few rooms to find it."

"Peachy," I muttered. "How did this Horsten fellow know the layout of this particular place, anyway?"

"I imagine by being an acquaintance of Lightfoot." St. Cloud opened a door on the right. It was a lavish linen closet.

"I don't believe it's Lightfoot's house," I said, trailing after him as he went for the next door.

He paused. "What makes you say that?"

I rehashed the confusing conversation I had with the last man I'd interrogated. St. Cloud snorted.

I hardly think that proves anything," he said dismissively. I tensed. St. Cloud switched to the left side of the hall, opening a door. "Library," he reported, ignoring my clear irritation.

I was about to retort, but voices sounded from behind us, in the stairway. I pushed St. Cloud into the library, quickly following him and shutting the door behind me.

"What was that about?" he asked just a touch too loudly.

"Shh!" I admonished, aware that my superior hearing had alerted me much sooner than it would have alerted him. I pressed my ear up against the door, listening. Gavin seemed to get wise, and he too leaned near me.

"... sure it was her?" came a masculine voice from the stairs, getting louder as the speaker approached.

"He couldn't say for sure, but he did remember the hair color. He said something was missing, but it was fairly coincidental." This came from another male voice, a deep baritone.

I stopped breathing. Could they be talking about me?

They stopped just outside of the library. I debated whether or not to flee or continue listening. I chose the latter, as risky as it was. "He's searching now, of course, but it's difficult with so many people in the crowd," said the baritone.

Footsteps led away from our door, thankfully. They stopped again, further away, but I could still plainly hear the voices. "Fine, just do what needs to be done."

"Of course, sir."

A lock clicked, and the footsteps went inside a room. It seemed to be the room adjacent to the library. "Quick, over here!" I whispered to Gavin, spotting the white shape of a connecting door in the semidarkness.

Silently dashing over to the door, I once again commenced eavesdropping. "Joseph got another cartful for us to ship, sir. Fresh from Dogwood," Baritone said.

A sigh escaped the other. "I was rather hoping not to deal with that tonight. Didn't you tell him I was hosting a ball?"

I glanced at Gavin. Was that Lightfoot with him? I assumed

his speech would have lent us a bit more time. Gavin only shook his head in confusion.

"Yes sir, but you did tell him to unload them as soon as he had caught enough. He's waiting out back for you. I told him it might be a while."

"Very well. Might as well sleep them now while we have a few moments. I'd like to know when we can stop these special shipments, but I don't dare until I hear from Mother. I do wish she would get back to me. It's been months. I can't imagine what's keeping her."

Their footsteps left the room and faded away, taking their voices with them. When it was apparent they were truly gone, I let out the breath I had been holding.

"Did that make an ounce of sense to you?" St. Cloud asked me in a hushed voice.

I thought it over. A shipment ... of what? Something alive, I assumed, since the first man had said something about putting them to sleep. I shook my head. "I hope it's not me they are after."

"Why would it be?" Gavin once again dismissed me. I scrunched up my mouth in frustration but did not talk back. Instead, I tried the handle of the door. It swung open.

"Now this looks like an office to me," I said with satisfaction. We walked into the lit room, with framed art and multiple deer antlers mounted on the walls. An ornate heavy desk stood in the center of the room.

I made a beeline for it.

Each drawer I opened was a disappointment: nothing but stationery and pens, each monogrammed with a GE. I rifled through them anyway, but ... nothing. I sighed, and then gave it some thought. Perhaps the ledger was in a safe. And perhaps the safe was behind a piece of art.

I turned my attention to the walls. I scanned the various paintings hung on the first wall, looking for something that could hide a wall safe.

"Man, whoever this guy is, he sure has a thing for deer," I muttered. That thought struck a vague memory, but what was it? I couldn't tell.

From across the room, Gavin replied, "Well, it *is* Deerhorn Manor."

My eye caught on a good-sized framed map of the Oracune Region, complete with geographical terrain and the names of the various cities and towns. It was just the right size, but also it was at an odd height, almost too low. My hope rose. I grasped the lower corners, raising the frame away from the wall. To my relief, I spotted smooth metal peeking out underneath, instead of the white paint of the room.

"Here!" I cried out, perhaps a bit too loudly in my exuberance. Gavin rushed over to help me remove the map fully from the wall. He placed it underneath the safe on the floor, leaning it carefully.

"Well done!" he praised, making me smile with pride for a second.

I was rather stymied, however.

"How can we guess the combination?" I asked, looking at the safe's number pad. Gavin only shook his head, also at a loss.

I looked down at the map and crouched to study it. I had noticed upon my first brief inspection that a handful of town names had been written in bold. Intrigued, I bent down onto my knees to get a closer look, ignoring the awkwardness the dress presented in doing so. I peered at the first name, noticing a tiny number 3 next to it. Upon further inspection, the bold towns of Dogwood, Branford on the southwestern coast, Addelboro in the middle of the region, and Kousa all had the numbers 1 through 4 appearing next to their respective names.

But how did these towns relate to numbers on a keypad? Perhaps a geographical location? Maybe if I imagined the map as a keypad, the towns could become numbers.

"Try 2, 7, 5, 2," I told Gavin as I superimposed the keypad over the map in my head. He punched the numbers in.

Nothing happened.

Of course it wasn't that. I studied the map a second time. I noticed some letters going along the top of the map, from A on the left to G on the right. Searching the perimeter of the map, I spotted the numbers 1 through 5 going down the left-hand margin. Of course! A gridwork to determine location. Perhaps the combination relied on the grid numbers?

"Okay, try 2, 5, 4, 2," I instructed, running my finger to the left to find the corresponding number for each town in the order they were given.

This time when St. Cloud pulled the lever, the door swung open with a clunk. "I must say," he said with a hint of awe in his voice, "that was a stroke of genius."

I waved the compliment away, eager to see what was inside the safe. I got to my feet and sidled up to Gavin to look inside.

A large book, its pages slightly wrinkled, was stored within. A ledger.

I think I squealed upon seeing it.

"Here, place it on the desk," I instructed Gavin, as he removed the ledger from its hiding space.

St. Cloud placed it down and opened it to a random page. "What exactly are we looking for?"

I stood by his side, contemplating. "Babcock said the thefts started in November, correct? That's about the same time Roger began to receive his bonuses too. I say let's start there."

He nodded his agreement, flipping forward in the book to find the start of November.

"There!" I exclaimed, seeing the name R. Curtain written next to the expense column. I leaned over to get a better look.

"I'll be damned," Gavin breathed, reading the same thing, "you were right after all."

I glanced at him. "You don't need to sound so shocked," I said. I turned my attention back to the ledger. A few lines below that, something caught my eye.

"DONATION: Addelboro Correctional Facility, $10,000," I read aloud.

"What's the date on that one?" St. Cloud asked.

I squinted at the fine print. "November twelfth of last year. Why?"

He rubbed his chin in thought. "Well, I could be wrong, but I used to live out that way when I was younger, and I'm fairly certain that the Addelboro facility was shut down years ago."

"Maybe they recently reopened it?" I suggested.

He cocked his head to one side. He did not look convinced. "Maybe. I try to stay abreast of prisons, since my job is to find the criminals who may reside in said places. I think I would have heard if the facility was operational again."

"Well, let's keep looking for other oddities in the other months leading up to February," I pressed, turning the page.

Another large bonus for RC (a further shortened version of my father's name, I presumed) graced the top of December's expense list. And just below that, I saw an entry that made me suck in a surprised breath: a donation to ACF for $20,000.

"ACF," I said shakily, pointing to the entry. My mother's warning flashed in my mind. "Annie Coddle Fanclub."

"What?" Gavin said, puzzled. "ACF stands for Addelboro Correctional Facility."

"But what if it doesn't?" I asked, turning to him. I must have had a maniacal glint in my eye, because he gave me an odd look.

"What if it's a cover for the real meaning of the acronym?"

"What are you going on about?"

I huffed. "ACF stands for a secret society, the Annie Coddle Fanclub. It's too much of a coincidence that the letters match up with a defunct prison. It's a front. And Roger is taking the blame for this money that is clearly being donated to the society."

"Miss Curtain, what ... who?" he pinched the bridge of his nose. "I don't understand. "Who is Annie Coddle? Why is there a secret fan club for her?"

"She's ..." I trailed off, trying to think of a way I could explain this without giving too much away. "She was a very powerful witch from about five hundred years ago. She tried to rule the world and was banished by her cat familiar."

"A fairy tale." St. Cloud's dismissal of my words rankled me. I scowled at him.

"No, not a fairy tale. Why does everyone say that? She's still out there, and clearly there are people who want to see her come back."

He shook his head. "And you would know this, how? I'm sorry, Miss Curtain, but you seem to be prone to illusions of grandeur if you believe this stuff."

"Gavin!" I snapped. He looked at me, his expression almost shocked. "I would know because my family was heavily involved in her banishment. And I've met the witch myself!" He hadn't interjected, but he still stared at me with a look of astonishment on his face. I became self-conscious. "What?"

"That's the first time you've ever called me by my first name," he said softly, taking a step toward me. I stayed still, astonished that such a small thing would have such a big impact upon him. I didn't have much time to ponder, however, because once again there were voices in the hallway, right outside the door.

We had no time to run for it, for the doorknob was already

turning. In one large step, Gavin was in front of me. He reached out and wrapped his arms around my torso, drawing me flush with his body. "Wha—" I started to say.

"Don't hit me for this," he whispered as two things simultaneously happened. The first was the door opening. The second was Gavin St. Cloud holding me tightly, tipping me backwards in his arms, and planting his lips upon mine.

I was too shocked to struggle or hit him. Instead, my brain shorted out and all I could do was let him kiss me while my heart thundered and my breathing ceased. Instinctively, I wrapped my arms around his neck, drawing us closer together.

While my mind and body struggled with sudden turmoil, the voices at the door became much louder. "That was the largest shipment of cats yet. We'll move them out at midnight," one man said. The other seemed about to reply, but both men stopped short once they realized they weren't alone in the room. The first man instead exclaimed, "What in the hell?"

Gavin and I sprung apart, allowing me to catch a bit of a breath. I took a shy glance at Gavin, who looked chagrined at the interlopers. He said, "Sorry, sirs, my lady and I were looking for a quiet room for some quality time together. We didn't know we were intruding."

His actions finally made sense. He hadn't kissed me because he wanted to. It was an act for the sake of these men that now stared at us.

The first man was thin, yet solidly built, and appeared to be in his early sixties. His silver hair and beard were perfectly manicured, and he wore a tuxedo of finest quality. He stood ramrod straight with a frown upon his face. The second man was unfortunately very familiar, with a bald head and heavily muscled arms. Just like at the meeting from less than two weeks ago, he wore a tight black tee and a perpetual frown on his face. He was the man we were supposed to report to when we apprehended Roger. Hobbs, I believe was the name we were given.

The first man studied us, noticing the heavy breathing I was doing. "Young man, I suggest you and your young lady get back downstairs where you belong. It's horribly rude of you two to go traipsing through another man's house, especially for something so banal as a makeout session."

We both mumbled apologies and started to head for the open door. This man must have been the owner of the house, and it seemed like a bad idea to loiter anymore. Besides, we had seen with our own eyes that my father was indeed innocent. I was all too happy to go.

"Wait," the silver-haired man commanded. His tone brooked no arguments and we both froze in place. I looked at where his gaze fell. It was the ledger, which was still open upon the desk, and not in the wall safe where it should have been. He glanced sharply at us. "What are you playing at?" he demanded.

Well, the jig was up, it seemed. I went on the defensive, hoping that perhaps if I explained a little of this situation, I could win this man over. "Sir, are you aware that Lightfoot wrongly accused a man of embezzlement?"

He laughed then, an unpleasant sound given the circumstances. "My, my, my," he said, amused, "you must be one of the bounty hunters I hired."

"*You* hired? Are you Lightfoot?" I asked, unsure of this man's identity.

He chuckled. His teeth were white and straight as he leered at us. "His silent partner. The bumbling oaf has no clue that Curtain is still alive. He was led to believe he died in the fire."

Now I was really confused. "But didn't he hire us to bring him in?"

"Us?" the man turned his attention to Gavin. I kicked myself for accidentally implicating him along with me. "A pair of rogue hunters. How interesting."

"Not really," I drawled. "When it's very obvious the party being hunted is not guilty, it doesn't take much more than a moral compass to switch allegiances."

"Ah, young lady, but you're a bounty hunter. Surely you of all people know that hunters aren't supposed to be burdened with such a thing as morality. It makes the job more difficult."

"So I've learned," I said, looking over at Gavin and remembering him saying something similar to me. "Perhaps I'm in the wrong field, then."

He studied me shrewdly. "Well, It's no matter now. The fact is that you went and stuck your noses in a business that wasn't yours. This renders your contract with me void, and renders your lives forfeit." He turned to the large man and spoke to him. "Add these two to the shipment. I'll need just a moment to recharge. We'll need to find out what they know."

"Yes, boss." The large man moved to grab ahold of me, as I was closest to him. If he surmised I'd be easy to catch, he was gravely mistaken. I jumped back behind Gavin and quickly stepped out of my shoes. The dress still hindered my full range of motion, but I could at least scamper about more easily bare-footed.

Hobbs instead turned to Gavin, who instantly crouched into a defensive position. As the large man approached him, Gavin swung out with a fist, connecting with Hobbs' chin. He may have well been a mouse swatting at a tiger for all the good it did, however. The large man barely flinched, smiling at the attempt.

"Cressida, run!" Gavin demanded.

I glanced at the library door, calculating our chances. "Not without you," I told him. I grabbed his forearm and tugged him backward. He must have seen that a fight with this man would be futile, because he quickly turned and, grabbing my hand, we both made a run for the side door.

I was just about to grab the handle when Gavin's hand fell limp and tugged out of my grasp. I turned in confusion. Gavin lay in a heap at my feet, not moving. My heart leapt in fear for him. Had he been shot?

I should have left him and made my escape, but he was in this mess because of me. I crouched down to examine him, finding no wounds. I was thankful to see that he was breathing normally.

He seemed to be simply sleeping.

"There we go," the suave man said satisfactorily. "One down, one to go. I must inquire, is it Cressida Curtain? Babcock thought he had recognized you downstairs, although he wasn't certain." I stayed silent, glowering at him as I crouched next to Gavin. He continued, "Curtain ... that's not a very common name, is it? Might it be possible that you are related to Roger Curtain?"

"Why should I tell you anything?" I sneered at him.

He only smiled at my vehemence. "Perhaps you'd care if you knew who I was," he replied cryptically.

"And who are you?" Curiosity got the better of me.

He gave me a mocking bow. "Gregory Elkins, my dear."

Before I had time to respond, he held up a palm toward me. I saw a hint of bluish light flash from it.

I instantly lost consciousness.

CHAPTER 23

I came to slowly. The first feeling that registered in my struggling consciousness was a rhythmic rocking sensation, from side to side. This in turn made me realize I was lying face down on an irregularly-shaped object. My face was pressed against a surface that was hard but yielding, and along with the slight side-to-side motion, the surface also rose and fell in a different pattern. I groaned as I opened my eyes, allowing them to get used to the red-tinted darkness they now beheld.

"Awake at last, are we?"

"Gah!" I jumped at the voice that came from a location all too close to my head, pushing my lower body upward. This movement was stymied, however, by an extremely low ceiling. I bashed the top of my head upon it and fell back onto the irregular object I was still sprawled upon.

The object was Gavin, I realized as my eyes adjusted to the low light levels and my heart stopped trying to pound its way out of my ribcage. I had been sleeping with my head resting upon his chest, and my legs sprawled over his. He was on his back, staring at me with a small amount of amusement despite our predicament. Speaking of said predicament, I took a moment to survey our surroundings. There wasn't much to see, because it appeared we were in a coffin-sized wooden box, wide enough for Gavin to lie down with a tiny amount of room on either side, long enough that we both could fully stretch out, and, as I had demonstrated, not tall enough to sit up. There were a few empty knotholes in the wood, and that was where the red light was able to filter in and lend us a tiny bit of visibility.

Based on the way I had just awakened on top of him, I gathered that we had been thrown unceremoniously into the box; first Gavin, and then myself. I suppose I should be lucky to be the one on top, given my smaller frame.

I took a deep breath to further steady my pulse. I could feel the edge of panic within me upon finding ourselves in a new predicament, but it dissipated quicker than I would have imagined possible. Then again, this was not the worst spot of trouble I had found myself in recently.

I rubbed the back of my head where it had hit the lid. "Where are we?"

He gave his shoulders a small shrug. "I just woke up a few minutes ago. All I can surmise is we seem to be trapped in a wooden box, and that happens to be in a train's boxcar."

That would explain the rocking motion, along with the rhythmic chugging sound I now had allowed to filter into my brain. I wiped my mouth, feeling a bit of dried drool trailing down my chin. "Just fantastic."

I thought back to what I had learned just before passing out. The suave man, the man who owned that enormous house, was Gregory Elkins. He was the same man who had posed as Fal's and Wren's great-uncle, and when that failed, put a bounty out on Fal to try to collect him. We never did find out why he wanted the Ramberts so badly. Luckily, it had seemed like he'd given up his hunt for them.

And now he was after my father. Why, though?

"What do you know of Gregory Elkins?" I asked.

Gavin rolled his head from side to side. "I think I've heard the name in passing, but I don't know anything about him. Why?"

"Because that's the man that we just met. He ... put us to sleep somehow."

"What exactly have you gotten us into, Cressida?"

"Me? As I recall, you came along willingly enough. I never asked for your help."

He guffawed. "As I recall, you begged me to not go after your father. That's practically the same thing as asking for my help."

"It is not!" I retorted angrily. "I merely asked for you to stop the hunt, not team up with me. That's on you."

"Well, perhaps if I had known a few facts ahead of time I would have made different choices. Like, for instance, the fact that Roger Curtain was your father."

"Oh please," I rolled my eyes, scooting up Gavin's body a bit to hover over him so he didn't have to strain his neck to see me. "I have my reasons for keeping some things to myself, believe me. Besides, I'm pretty sure you knew he was at least related to me from the get-go."

He smirked. "Thanks to my trusty pocket watch, yes, I had an inkling."

"Peachy," I said. "So, we are in a box. On a train. Going somewhere. Put here by a man named Elkins. What else am I missing?"

"Elkins was the man who put out the bounty on Curtain. Not Lightfoot, as we were led to believe," Gavin pointed out.

"Ah yes, Lightfoot thinks Roger is dead, apparently. But does he also think Roger stole the money?"

"He must. But that money went as a donation to the correctional facility, which means it was never stolen in the first place."

"Right, but I still think it's a cover for something else," I said.

"A cover for an ancient witch?" St. Cloud still sounded skeptical about my claim.

"No. A cover for a secret organization filled with people who want to bring the witch back to this world. For whatever reasons fail me. She's pretty terrible."

"Mm-hm."

I decided to let it go for now. My mind was reeling over the implications that Gregory Elkins had a possibly big link to Annie Coddle. "The big question remains, why does Elkins want my father in the first place?"

I thought back to the conversation I heard from behind closed doors. Something about a fresh shipment from Dogwood. Elkins having to sleep "them," whoever they were. Sleep …

"Elkins put us to sleep magically. He also did the same to whatever the mysterious shipment is," I deduced.

Gavin chewed on his lip. "That explains the passing out, certainly."

Another thought occurred to me. Wren had once described a man with silvery hair, perfect posture, and straight teeth. This man was in her dreams and led her to explore Annie Coddle's dimension, which in turn allowed Annie to use Wren as her personal puppet. Wren's description perfectly matched Elkins. That was the connection! Now I was convinced ACF stood for the secret organization, not the facility.

I sighed at the implication. "If I'm not mistaken, he's also a dreamwalker."

Gavin laughed. "How do you figure?"

I groaned. More secrets that were not mine to tell. "I know someone he was manipulating through dreams. At least, her description matched the guy we just met. And if he has the power of somnification, it's not too far-fetched to assume he has other powers related to sleep, right?"

"No, I suppose not," Gavin admitted, although I could tell he remained unconvinced. "If there are others in this box car that have been put to sleep, perhaps they too are awake now. Should we risk calling out to them?"

I agreed. I could see through one of the knotholes that there were other boxes in the space like ours, even if we didn't know the contents within. Both Gavin and I called out, but the boxcar stayed silent.

"Whatever the shipment is, it must still be asleep," I concluded. "So why are we awake?"

"I have two theories," Gavin supplied helpfully. "One, Elkins had just used his power to put to sleep a lot of 'somethings' before he hit us with his power. I seem to recall that he said something about needing to recharge. So he might not have fully juiced us."

"And what's the other theory?"

He breathed deeply. "We had just taken the drunk-me-not potion not long beforehand. That stuff is potent enough to counteract not only intoxication, but some magical maladies as well. It makes sense that it would perk us up faster than Elkins intended."

"Well, in that case, it's a good thing I got drunk, isn't it?" I teased. "I'd hate to still be asleep."

"Speaking of sleep, did you drool on me?" he asked. He lifted his head to look at his chest.

"No." I swept a hand over the place where my head had rested, feeling a damp spot. "Yes. Sorry about that."

"Forgiven." He rested his head back down, sighing. "This may be it for this tux. Drool or not." He glanced back up at me. He maneuvered a hand in front of my face, stroking a piece of my hair in an intimate gesture. I froze, unsure of what he was doing. "Your streaks are back," he murmured soothingly.

"Are they?" My immaculate hairstyle had fallen in some areas, revealing that yes, I did indeed have my two black streaks back. That meant it was at least after midnight, as Wren could only guarantee she could hold the illusion that long.

"Yep. I'm glad. I rather missed them, you know."

I scoffed. "Missed making fun of them, perhaps."

He grinned. "No, no, they may be unusual, but they suit you. They are bold, in-your-face, and weird."

"St. Cloud, I swear if you are trying to rile me up ..."

His face fell. "Aw, are we back to formalities? Which I've deduced means you are currently mad at me."

I smirked. "It's my standard emotion toward you. No, I take that back. Irritation is more like it."

"I beg to differ. I see many other emotions in you. You just don't want to admit it. You're an incredibly stubborn woman."

"See, this right here is what I'm saying!" I exclaimed heatedly. "You push my buttons past the point of agreeable, and then pretend like you don't hate me! And then you wonder why I act the way I do around you."

"Hate you!" He scoffed, denying my accusation. Then, he grew serious. "Do you hate me?" He asked quietly.

I paused, taken aback. Did I? "I ... think I used to," I admitted quietly, looking at his face from above him as I still sprawled on his body. "After all, you started it."

"Started what?" he asked sincerely.

"The ... the ... competition between us," I answered, searching for words. "Did you know I was actually excited to meet some fellow bounty hunters when I first started out? I was eager to learn from the best. And then when I met you, I was so tongue-tied that I came off as some imbecile, and you painted a giant target on my back, and you've had it out for me ever since."

"Is that how you see me?"

"Yes!" I brushed some fallen strands of hair out of my down-turned face. "You demean and belittle me every chance you get, and lord it over me when you beat me to the punch. How could

I not think that you hate me?"

"I don't, though," he said. "I thought this was just a friendly competition we had going."

"Friendly, after the way you've treated me at times?" I retorted.

"Yes, Cressida. And let's not pretend it's been one sided, either. You've thrown enough mud in my eye, not to mention all the lies. You aren't perfect either. You can be a right pain in the ass." His words became a touch heated.

"*I'm* a pain in the ass?" I repeated snarkily. His hands fell upon my waist from behind. I didn't shrug it off. "Gee, Gavin, it's about time the gloves finally came off. Why don't you show me how you really feel about me?"

He frowned. "Fine, I will." And he lifted his head up and kissed me.

I did nothing for a second as he moved one of his hands up to cradle the back of my head, pushing my face closer to his. I froze, not comprehending that for a second time in one night, Gavin was kissing me. But unlike our last kiss which had been a motionless ruse on his part, this one had gravity behind it, and after just a small second, I found myself reacting to it with great favor. The heat of the argument gave way to a different sort of warmth, one that coursed through me and made butterflies dance in my stomach. An unfamiliar tingle took hold of my body. As he moved his lips against mine, I found myself kissing him back with just as much fervor.

He deepened the kiss, opening his mouth and drawing me in. With my lack of experience, I mirrored him, eliciting a small groan from his throat that only served to ignite me further. He clenched my hair, holding me fast, while the other hand at my waist gripped me closer to his body. I in turn fisted his tux at his chest, further rumpling his nice clothes. I was beyond caring, though.

A fire had ignited within me, causing all sense of logic to flee. I only wanted more of this sensation. Gavin answered this insatiable call, flicking his tongue out and into my mouth and lowering his hand to cup my rear instead of my waist.

I broke the kiss to take a labored breath, and Gavin wasted little time in nibbling his way down my jawline to my neck. I gasped at the sensation, enthralled, before moving my head back to claim his mouth like the heedless animal I had become.

As we made out, I became aware of a hardening against my thigh, which mentally gave me pause as I tried to figure out what it was. I may have been innocent in the ways of coupling, but I knew the mechanics on an academic level. It only took me a few seconds to realize that this was Gavin's arousal. The realization set another thrill through me, and I deepened the kiss as he unsuccessfully pawed at my clothing to get to my bare legs.

The moment the thought of sex truly entered my consciousness, however, something unbidden happened. A different kind of sensation coursed through my chest, an unpleasant, deep ache that chased out all the passion. Pounding words echoed within my skull:

"I curse you, Descendant of Glivver, that from this day forward, and for the rest of your life, you will never fall in love with a man. Without true love, the line of Glivver will die with you!"

Those words reverberated in my mind, and the effect was akin to being drenched in cold water. Immediately my libido shriveled and fled. I gasped and broke the kiss, raising my upper half as high as I could away from Gavin's searching mouth. "Wait, wait, stop!"

He looked at me with hooded eyes. "What is it?" he asked.

I shook my head, frazzled. "I—I can't. I can't do this!"

He huffed a breath, half laughing. "Why not?"

I tried to lift my weight off Gavin; it wasn't fair to be having this conversation with him while I inadvertently egged him on by lying on top of him. After all, it was still apparent that he was aroused. "I can't make out with you. I can't have sex with you."

This time he took me seriously, letting go of my butt and the back of my head. "Okay," he said slowly. "Whyever not?"

I took a moment before answering, listening to what my heart was telling me. "Because I don't love you." The curse and my whole body were telling me this, and because of my special heritage, it had shut down the desire to kiss anybody other than my true love once I had allowed rational thought back into my brain.

He paused, stunned, before letting out a chuckle, which rankled me. "What does that have to do with anything? I'm sorry to say I don't love you either, Miss Curtain, but I'm fairly certain we were both enjoying that."

I grimaced at his words. "It may not mean anything to you, but it's complicated for me."

"Complicated? No. It's just two adults having a bit of fun. No strings. No declarations of love. Why would that need to be factored in?" His face changed. "Unless ... Miss Curtain, are you a virgin?"

By this point I had extracted myself from St. Cloud, finding purchase with my knees on either side of one of his legs, and my body hunched over to avoid banging my head. He too removed himself slightly, leaning up against the back of the box as much as he could. I could only glare at him from the small distance allotted to me in this box. "I don't see how that's any of your business," I replied as haughtily as I could.

He deduced the hidden answer easily enough. "By gum, you are!" He studied me, as if seeing me in a whole new light. "How is that possible? I never would have expected that from you."

I bristled. "What are you implying by that?"

He held up his hands placatingly. "Nothing bad, I assure you.

You are just so self-assured. You exude a natural sexuality that fills the room and makes every man notice. You're a predator. A sexy panther."

I had to laugh at his choice of words.

"It's just surprising that you have this natural allure and yet you are so inexperienced," he continued. He stopped, his eyes widening as he thought of something. "Oh no. Don't tell me you've never kissed before either."

I stayed silent, chagrined that he was sussing out all my little secrets.

He took that to be a yes. "Oh gods, I'm so sorry. If I had known, I might not have tried that little tactic back in the study."

"But you still might have?" I asked, amused at his discomfort.

He grinned. "Maybe. It's something I've wanted to do for a while, and it seemed like a good idea at the time." He became serious again. "But honestly, Cressida, how can you be your age and still be a virgin? And not have kissed anybody? Did you grow up on the moon?"

I frowned at my knees. "I told you, it's complicated. I—my family, really—there's rules to follow." He frowned, clearly perplexed by my lackluster statement. I didn't blame him, as my reasoning sounded abysmal even to me. "Let's just chalk it up to the fact that I need to love someone in order to *be* with him."

He didn't look convinced.

I huffed. "Where's you damn watch?"

He fished into his vest pocket and handed it to me. I opened it, turning it to face him. "I know you think I lie to you to vex you," I said, "and maybe that was true in the beginning. You can be a very annoying man," I let out a little laugh as I said this. "But that's not the reason for most of my lies. I do it because if the truth got out, I would be in danger."

"Danger," he repeated.

I nodded. "Yes. There are things about me that I have to keep a secret, for not only the sake of me and my family, but for the sake of the world. This is bigger than you and me, Gavin. So, if I lie to you, please don't take it to heart. It's not about you, it's about protecting myself."

I looked him in the eye the entire time I spoke, and not once did he look at his watch. Instead, he slipped it out of my hand and snapped the face shut. "I believe you," he said plainly.

Tears sprung to my eyes. "So, you won't badger me anymore about it?" I asked in a small voice.

"C'mere," he said, stuffing his watch into his jacket pocket. He scooted back down and rolled to his side, creating enough room next to him for me to do the same. I slid forward, turning to my side so that we faced each other with a small pocket of space between us. He propped his head up with a hand. "I won't badger you anymore," he responded. He reached out and tucked a bit of hair behind my ear. "Can we start over? I'm really not a bad guy. I think you short-circuited my brain the first time we met, and it caused me to try to put you in your place. It was wrong of me; I see that now. I'd like to be friends. Can we do that?"

I wiped my eyes, smearing whatever makeup remained there. After all this time, I was finally seeing the real Gavin. He had made a mistake in being a jerk to me when we first met, an egregious error on his part. But I hadn't helped anything by returning the animosity with such fervor. "I think so," I responded.

"Friends who occasionally make out?" He waggled his eyebrows.

I laughed. "Definitely not."

"Can't blame a guy for trying. That was insanely hot, you have to admit."

I nodded. "It was fine."

"Fine? Ouch." He clapped a hand to his heart. "You sure know how to wound a guy."

I decided to ignore his attempts at another makeout session. After all, I could admit to myself that it was amazing, but the curse had to go and ruin it. I was left with zero desire after that little reminder. "How about friends who have a healthy competition in their given field that causes them to give each other a hard time, but not in a soul-crushing way?" I countered.

He pretended to consider before smiling. "Deal."

"Go easy on me, though. Considering how much I loathed you for the last couple of years, I might take a readjustment period. I hope you've learned a valuable lesson in how not to strike up an acquaintance with women you find attractive."

"I know, I know. I never loathed you, but I'll admit it's been a rocky relationship, no thanks to me. But I'm glad to hear you no longer hate me."

"I can't say the same for Grimm, though," I said, remembering my true partner with a pinch of longing. If it were him inside this box with me, I wouldn't have shared a passionate kiss with my nemesis, and I could have spent this time in the comfort of cat form, at least. The corset in my dress was starting to dig into my ribs painfully.

I missed him. I hoped he wouldn't flip when I wasn't home when I said I would be.

"I have to ask, what is it with that dog?"

Gavin's question may have been fairly innocent, but the fact that he'd always looked down his nose at my relationship with Grimm left a sour taste in my mouth. This was one subject that I think would always be of contention. "It's one of those things I can't be fully truthful about," I said. "The only thing I can tell you is that I saved his life, and he saved mine. That sort of thing leaves a bond that traverses species."

"Hmm, fair enough. So, what can I do to at least stay on your good side?"

I thought about it. "I know literally nothing about you. Tell me about yourself. Something non-huntery."

"Well, how about how I used to be a scared little boy?"

My interest was piqued. "Go on."

"I mentioned before that I am half-Tyonoshimese. My mother was from Tyonoshima. My father," he said this word with a hint of disdain, "traveled there when he was in his forties to seal a trade deal. He met my mother and, as the story goes, had nothing but eyes for her. My father often sets his sights on something and won't budge until he gets his way. It was no different with my mother. He wanted her, and even though she was already betrothed to someone else, he got his way and took her back to Vinland as his bride. I was the result, not a year later."

He scratched his nose. "I loved my mother very much. Because she had been forced away from her homeland, she put all her energy into educating me about our shared culture. It was filled with stories of demons and ghosts, and she regularly shared these with me from a young age, because she wanted me to have an interest in my heritage as well. Unfortunately, I had a very vivid imagination as a child, which made these stories feel just a tad too real for my taste. Did you know there is such a thing as a bathroom demon? It licks up the filth that accumulates in bathrooms. It's said to be harmless, but when I was five years old, I couldn't go in our bathroom for a month because of that story."

"Did you ever see one?" I asked, intrigued.

"No, they don't live here. Only in Tyonoshima. I have no idea why those islands are such a hotspot for creatures, but they certainly have them in droves there."

"Have you ever traveled there?"

He shook his head. "My father refused to return to Tyonoshima after taking my mother home. She was heartbroken, because she had family there, a sister who had a baby before she left. But my father was a stubborn man, and he ruled our household with an iron fist. So my mother relied on me to learn as much about her way of life as possible. Father hated it, though. He hated that I was prone to nightmares and needed extra cuddles from my mother. He wanted me to be tough and brave, a masculine man like himself."

"That's funny, considering my mom wishes I was less tough and brave."

"But you're a woman," he pointed out.

"So what? Bravery isn't a masculine or feminine quality. Anyone can be brave, just like anyone can be pigheaded or stupid. But I digress. Please continue with your story."

He watched me, waiting for more hooded insults to come forth, but I just smiled sweetly. He finally continued, "He took me under his wing and started teaching me the 'manly arts;' you know, boxing, shooting, and the like, when I was twelve. I started to become less afraid of my mother's stories around that time too. I still had nightmares, though."

"I know what that's like," I murmured. "But if you were so sensitive to stories of creatures, why go into bounty hunting? Especially since you specialize in the supernaturals, like I do."

"Well, when I was close to graduating from school, my family's house was broken into. My father is repulsively rich, and it was just too much of a temptation, I suppose. Unfortunately, my mother was home at the time."

"Oh no." I covered my mouth with my hand, knowing where this was going.

He nodded solemnly. "The robbers killed her. And they got away."

"Oh Gavin, I'm so sorry."

He fought back some emotion for a moment. "It ... changed me. I was filled with rage. It didn't help that my father, while sad, didn't do a thing to find them. I think his love for her had worn away long before her death. So, I swore then and there that I'd find them. I joined the guild shortly after, and I've been a hunter ever since."

"Were they supernaturals?" I asked.

"No," he answered. "Just regular scumbags. They were actually caught a couple of years back. Not by me, but I felt relieved that justice had been done. No, I like the supes because they remind me of my mother and her stories, even though they are completely different monsters. And it reminds me that I'm no longer that scared little boy hiding in his closet."

"Don't you think that scared little boy is still inside of you? Just buried deep?"

He chewed on his lip. "Maybe. Maybe that's why I reacted the way I did to you the first time we met. Maybe you reminded me of some of my mother's creatures, and it scared me enough to put up a false front with you to scare you off."

I mock-gasped. "Surely not the bathroom licker!"

He laughed. "No, there are plenty of monsters that are sensual, or cunning. Like a kitsune. Or a jorogumo."

"I have no idea what either of those are, but I'll take your word for it," I said.

We settled into a companionable silence. I should not have felt as comfortable with Gavin St. Cloud as I did, considering our past. But my animal side craved affection on my own terms. Grimm always fulfilled that craving when we slept together at night, especially in the den-like atmosphere of my wagon. This box only served as a very small den, and Gavin's warm body next to mine soothed me.

It wasn't long before Gavin drifted off, lulled by the warmth of our shared body heat and the gentle rocking of the train. I was too uncomfortable to follow suit in my current form, but I let my mind drift, content to replay the many revelations this odd journey had brought me.

CHAPTER 24

I t was another two hours before the train came to a lurching halt. I had gone into a semi-doze during the remainder of the ride. but Gavin had fallen completely asleep, and the forward momentum awakened him rather abruptly.

"I think we've arrived," I commented unnecessarily.

"The only question is where. And what fresh hell awaits us," Gavin added. He looked at me in the red hue of light. "Say, you don't happen to have a weapon on you, do you?"

"Oh, sure, I tucked it down in my cleavage," I replied sarcastically. Gavin's eyes dropped to my chest. I smacked his arm. "Of course I don't have a weapon on me! Where could I possibly hide it?"

He bit his lip in thought. "It's too bad. I didn't bring my pistol either. It was too obvious with the tux."

That was the same reason I didn't bother with Hail Mary II; strapping it to my leg would have been too noticeable. "I guess we overestimated our abilities, huh?"

He grimaced. "This definitely wasn't part of my plan."

I looked around the box unhelpfully. My mind kept going back to my family. I had told them I'd be home by two in the morning. Within the darkness of the boxcar, I had no way of knowing what time it actually was. Still, I figured it was later than that.

"Fleurette is going to be so worried. Grimm too," I said, mostly to myself.

"Well, at least someone knows where we were and that we didn't make it back. Silver lining?" Gavin commented.

The car door opened with a jarring clank. The red glow was replaced by early dawn dimness, followed by yellow lamps.

"Here, Hank, let's get these unloaded!" a deep masculine voice called from outside the train. "Aw, holy hell, there's six boxes this time!"

I peered through one of the knotholes; two men lifted themselves into the compartment. The glow of the lamps illuminated the other boxes, all roughly the same size as ours. One of the men let out a low whistle after a quick perusal of the contents of the boxcar. "The hell are they doing over in Dogwood?" he hissed to his companion. "Are there any cats left at all?"

"Cats?" Gavin whispered to me. I pondered that, remembering a fragment of Elkins' conversation before he had discovered us. He had mentioned cats as well. And didn't that stray cat I ran into back in Dogwood say something about being hunted, and not to get caught? Perhaps this was where the cats were going.

But if the other boxes held a shipment of actual cats, what was the purpose?

Together the two laborers maneuvered the first box to the open door, whereupon two more men on the ground took the box from them. Once the men in the car had passed off that box, they started on another closer to us. One of the men grunted as he lifted, "This is a bit heavier than normal."

"Lift with your knees, dummy," the other man huffed as he picked up his side of the box.

"You think it's a special shipment?" the first said in an oddly cheerful demeanor. They struggled to the edge, cautioning the two men on the ground that the box was unusually heavy. Then they turned to our box.

"What do we do?" I hissed, debating between staying silent to see what would happen or letting the men know we were in here.

Gavin took the decision out of my hands. "Hey, let us out of here!" he yelled loudly.

"Yo, this lot's awake!" one of the men shouted. "How's that happen?"

"Dunno, maybe the boss was low on juice. I wouldn't worry too much. Shut up in there!" This last line was delivered with a furious kick at our box.

Gavin actually laughed. "Ouch, you really hurt our box's feelings!" Even I had a small chuckle.

The men ignored us after that but soon found out that the two of them alone could not lift our box. "Jim, Gaff, get in here!" the box-kicker ordered. With the four of them, they were able to unload our box, although none too carefully. We dropped to the ground rather thoughtlessly, jarring my body and rattling the wood. One of the men chastised the rest, cautioning against weakening the integrity of the box.

"Maybe we can break out now," I whispered to Gavin. He nodded.

"Oh, there you are, Hobbs," one of the four said. The rest murmured their greetings.

"Hobbs?" Gavin asked me in a low voice.

I nodded. "Lightfoot's 'associate,'" I said. "The beefy bald man back at the mansion."

"Oh yeah."

Hobbs must have taken the train along with us, although I imagined his accommodations were much more comfortable.

I peered out of my spy hole but couldn't see him, although his voice came from close by. "Alright, men, take this lot to the cattery and this one to questioning directly. This one," I sensed he was standing next to us, "is going to the dungeons. I'll help with that one."

He was met with an assortment of agreements, and once again our box was shuffled about. I could no longer see out of my knot hole, because a man stood directly in front of it, so all I could do was enjoy the rather long and jolting ride.

Eventually, our box was placed down, surprisingly gently compared to the first time. I heard the men walk away and the clang of a heavy metal door being closed.

"Don't move," Hobbs said gruffly. I assumed he was talking to us, but I couldn't exactly tell.

A tremendous *WUMPH* resounded and our box rattled with a severe impact. The lid blew off, letting in a smell of charcoal.

I shrieked and clasped my hands over my head, but no debris hit me. Instead, the burnt smell was replaced by a cool, damp, and musty air. I lifted my head, taking in my surroundings.

A chorus of laughter filled my ears as I lifted my head timidly. A group of four men, with Hobbs at the forefront appeared amused at my apparent fright. As soon as I made eye contact, though, they dispersed, Hobbs leaving last with a leer that gave me chills. And then we were alone.

Still crouched within the box, I took in our new surroundings. We had been placed inside a square prison cell, one side featuring all bars and the other three made of solid concrete. I glanced at each wall to check for windows, but none existed. The only light came from a single tiny bulb well above our heads.

"Can I get out now?"

I started at Gavin's voice from below me. After a second of paralysis, I hastened to move off him, awkwardly stepping out of the box that had been our cage for so many hours. He got out stiffly, taking in our new digs as he stretched.

"Oh, shit," he muttered.

"What?" I asked.

"I know where we are."

I did not like the resignation in his voice. Before I could ask him to clarify, however, he finished the thought. "We are in the Addelboro Correctional Facility."

I shivered, not just at the implication of where we now were, but also because it was damn cold in this prison cell. The box had kept me sane while we traveled on the train to our unknown destination because it had reminded me of a safe and cozy den. But it also had the added benefit of being warm, thanks to its confined space with a significant lack of airflow. Our combined body heat had made it feel decadent temperature-wise, and now that I had been stripped of my safe box, I realized I was only wearing a rather skimpy gown with no real sleeves and no shoes. I hugged myself to try to keep warm.

Gavin noticed my discomfort immediately. "Here," he said, shrugging off his tuxedo jacket and passing it to me. I hesitated, a combination of the old resentment of not wanting him to help me and a new concern for his wellbeing, but upon seeing he still had on a long sleeve shirt under the jacket, I decided I needed the extra layer more than him.

I slipped on the jacket, marveling at the borrowed body heat it gave off. "Thanks," I said appreciatively. Now that I was warming back up, I could focus on my surroundings a bit more. "Addelboro, huh? How exactly do you know that?"

He moved along one of the concrete walls, checking our surroundings thoroughly. Over his shoulder, he said, "I told you; I grew up on this side of the mountains. I thought this building was neat when I was a kid because it was built on a lake. See this?" He pointed to the ceiling above us. "It's basically a bunker. We are actually under the water here."

"What? Why?"

He shrugged. "The main portion is built above ground, on a small island, which they connected to the mainland by a stone bridge. I took a tour once, right after the facility closed. The above-ground portions were used for the usual stuff: robbery, manslaughter, petty crimes. But they built these, well, dungeon portions, if you will, for the really bad stuff. And it wasn't public knowledge either."

"What the public didn't know they couldn't condemn," I mused.

"Exactly. I recall hearing about torture being committed here in the guise of interrogation or day-to-day punishment. The worst of the worst came down here, and most of them never saw the light of day again. I'm talking murderers, serial rapists, the type of people you never want to see rehabilitated. Still, it wasn't exactly the right way to treat prisoners, so when the news did finally break, that's what got the facility shut down in a hurry." He glanced at me. "I'm surprised you didn't already know about it. It was all over the news about ten years ago."

I internally chuckled. I hadn't even been born ten years ago, and my history lessons from my mother had been spotty at best. It was no wonder this particular event had slipped through the cracks. "I didn't pay much attention to stuff like this," I admitted for his benefit.

He nodded as if that made sense, thankfully. "I took a tour of the place shortly after it closed. The subterranean portion of the tour was incredibly short—just a quick walk down the stairs and a peek into the first room we came across. But I remember the feel of this place, and the ceilings look the same everywhere down here." He shuddered. "And within a year, the place was bought by a private company, and the tours stopped. It's been empty ever since." Gavin scratched his chin. "At least, that's been the story. I suppose it's not empty after all."

"No, it would appear it's not." I sighed, looking at the barren concrete walls. "Why do I always end up in a dungeon cell?" I said to myself.

"What was that?" Apparently, I hadn't said it as quietly as I thought.

"Nothing," I hastily amended.

Gavin drew a hand down his face. "So, what now?"

"I'd say escaping would be a top-notch idea."

"From this place? Not likely. From what I remember, prison breaks didn't happen here. Not only are the bars reinforced, but even if one happened to get out, they'd get lost down here. It's a maze. It'd be more productive to pray to the gods."

I snorted. "Tried that before, didn't work."

Gavin side-eyed me. "Oh yeah? Which god? I'm fond of Susanoo or Amaterasu, but I don't think they'd be much help in this situation."

I had never heard of them; I wasn't about to show my ignorance, however. "My patron god of choice is Freya."

"Freya?" Gavin sounded incredulous. "What on earth made you pick her?"

I rubbed my arm and didn't meet his eyes. "She's a battle goddess, in charge of love and fertility, and ... she likes cats."

I shouldn't have added that last part.

"Cats!" Gavin practically shouted the word. "What's with them coming up in every conversation? What's so special about cats?"

I frowned. "What's wrong with them?"

He pinned me with a stare. "Don't tell me you, of all people, like cats."

"I'm rather fond of them." My tone was heated.

"I'd peg you as more of a dog person."

"No, just Grimm. I'm not a fan of most dogs." I looked at

him. "You really don't like cats?" I was beginning to regret my passionate kissing session with him.

Gavin shook his head. "I don't think much of them. Little demons, mostly." He held out his right arm, unbuttoning his cuff to expose his wrist. I peered at the skin, noticing four thin, white scars marring the surface of his wrist in perfect parallels to each other. "Remember that abandoned school from last summer? You warned me it was haunted. I thought you were just having me on, but something very weird happened in there. I was accosted multiple times by a white cat. I figured it was a vengeful spirit until it clawed me deep enough to leave these scars."

I did indeed remember that school. It was where I had found Fal and Wren hiding and where I took them under my wing. And *I* was the white cat that had tormented Gavin in order to sneak Wren out from under his nose.

Gavin continued his tirade: "So when you ask me if I like cats, Cressida, I can only say that I'm not very fond of them. They haven't given me a reason to be."

"Fair enough." A tangle of emotions twisted inside of me that took a bit of sorting out. As I picked through them, I recognized anger, embarrassment, and guilt. The anger and embarrassment were clearly because Gavin was inadvertently unapproving of an integral aspect of my very existence. Not liking my species was tantamount to not liking me, even if he didn't realize this. But the guilt? That was over the fact that I'd had an active role in his dislike of felines. "Sorry," I apologized to help assuage my shame.

He merely shrugged before responding, "It's quite alright, Cressida. Perhaps one day, I'll change my view on the creatures. I somehow doubt they'll redeem themselves in my eyes, but stranger things have happened. Until then, to each his own."

Redemption: now, there was a thought. If I could get us out of here, I could at least make up for the scar I had given him. I dragged my attention to the bars. They were solid looking, but the gap between each one looked to be about four inches. I had an idea.

"Gavin, I need you to turn around and not turn back until I say so."

He looked at me funny.

I sighed. "Please?"

He raised an eyebrow but did as I asked, not without an exaggerated huff for the request. Once I was certain he was going to keep his back to me, I shimmered.

I wanted to bask in the glorious relief that came with having my natural body back after prolonged exposure to my human form, but time was of the essence. Carefully, I measured my head against the width of the nearest bar gap. It was tight, but my whiskers told me I would fit. Wasting no time, I squeezed through.

Once on the other side, I transformed again. The whole event took only seconds. I brushed down my gown as I called out to Gavin, "You can turn around now."

He turned immediately. I could tell he had a smarmy retort ready on his lips, but one glance at my new location made the sass on his face morph into utter incredulity. He rushed over to the bars, examining them. "How ...?"

I smiled at his dumbfounded expression. "Trade secrets," I replied.

He pursed his lips at me and shook his head at my response. "I assumed you wanted to strip naked with that request. I had half a mind to peek. This, though, is not what I expected." His half-smile dried up with a somber look. "Can you get me out?"

I regretfully shook my head. "Sorry, no. I would if I could. But I'll scout out and see if I can find a set of keys or something. I'll come back for you; I promise."

Gavin's brow creased. "I can't say I like hearing that you'll be traipsing about on your own. That man Hobbs is dangerous. If you get caught ..."

I placed a hand on Gavin's own, which was clutching at the bars. He quieted down. "Don't worry about me," I soothed. "I know how to be sneaky. I have some tricks up my sleeves."

"Obviously," he snorted, gesturing at my seemingly miraculous escape from the cell. I smiled, stepping backward on bare feet, before turning away from him and walking around the corner and out of his sight.

Once I was free from a human gaze, I reverted to cat form. Exploring this depressing maze as my true self would help speed things up, I reckoned. I had a feeling Gavin and I were in some serious trouble. I needed to get us out of here as quickly as possible.

CHAPTER 25

Gavin had said we were currently situated under the lake. In order to escape, we needed to not be under the lake. Therefore, my first order of business was to find some stairs.

I slinked along the wall, ignoring the damp mustiness of the air that seemed to cling to my fur, weighing me down. After turning two corners, I hit a fork in the hallway. Both ways looked the same at first glance: dark, with an occasional closed door. I crouched by the wall to the right, pondering my choices.

Gavin was correct: this place was a maze.

As I sat in complete silence, my left ear picked up the faintest sound, a pattering shuffle that my cat brain instantly recognized. I crouched in anticipation, my pupils expanding to blot out my blue irises and let in as much light as possible. Within seconds, the pattering grew louder, and a tiny mouse rounded the corner.

I pounced before the rodent could even contemplate its danger. One of my paws landed on its tail, and the other squashed its body flat to the ground, although I made sure not to put too much weight upon it. I may have been hunting, but my goal was not to maim.

The mouse let out a terrified squeak, and it bravely tried to turn its head to bite my toes. Luckily for me, I was positioned in a way that I was safe from its teeth. Rodent bites were not for the faint of heart.

"Stop it!" I admonished. Cats rarely speak to their prey, preferring instead to be silent killers. My communication seemed to stun the tiny creature into submission. I pressed on. "I don't want to eat you, understand? I need help figuring out this dungeon. Do you know your way around?"

The mouse stayed perfectly still under my paws, the only sign of life being a slight vibration from its quick breaths and frantic heart rate. It did not answer my question in any way.

I was afraid of this. Just as cats rarely tried to communicate with prey animals, prey animals hardly spoke to the things trying to eat them. I had never heard more than a word or two from the creatures I ate, and usually those small communications were directed at fellow small critters. This mouse was simply not going to talk to me.

"Okay, you don't have to use words," I said as soothingly as possible. "I'm going to let you up, and you are going to stay to answer some easy questions. If you run, I *will* catch you and end you."

I gingerly lifted the paw that was holding the mouse down. My other paw stayed on its tail as a failsafe. The mouse crouched on the floor and shivered but stayed put.

"Good mouse," I told it. "Here's the deal. I need some information. If I ask you a question and your answer is yes, rise up on your back legs. If it's no, flatten to the floor. Do you understand?"

The mouse hesitated before pushing off the ground and standing tall on its back legs. I let out a small sigh of relief.

"Good. Now, do you know your way around this place?"

The mouse stayed standing and stretched its body upwards just a fraction more. I assumed this would be the answer, considering that this mouse was quite small, probably fresh from its nursery nest and not old enough to travel away from the prison.

"I need you to be my guide. In exchange, I promise not to eat you, and to keep you safe from any other beings we may run into. Can you do that, little mouse?"

The mouse faltered, falling back to its front feet. I despaired at the thought of having to kill this tiny creature after all. This was the most positive rapport I'd ever had with a possible meal. But after a few seconds, the mouse made up its mind and once again rose up.

"You have my gratitude, mouse," I told it, removing my paw from its tail and flattening myself to the ground. "Climb up onto my neck. I may walk faster than you. You can touch my ear tips to guide me."

The mouse's eyes bugged out even more than the beady orbs usually did. But, after just a second of hesitation, it did as I bade and jumped up onto the back of my neck. I could feel it squirm about up there until it seemed to have a good grasp near the back of my head, tiny needle claws gripping my skin through my fur. The sensation was odd, part creepy, part soothing, like I was getting a mini massage.

I stood up. "Right, the first place I want to go is up, to where there are windows with natural light. Can you take me there?"

The mouse let out a faint squeak, which sounded like a positive affirmation to me. He touched his nose to my right ear, signaling me to take a right at the fork. I began walking.

Whoever designed this place must have purposefully made it labyrinthine. I supposed it made sense in order to confuse possible escapees and make it easier to catch them. I gave myself a mental pat on the back for my quick thinking in turning a mouse into my guide. It was working like a charm. At each new turn and fork, my diminutive companion would brush against one of my ears to tell me which way to go.

Left.

Right.

Another right.

Finally, I was faced with a set of stairs. Relief flooded me. With the mouse still on my neck, I carefully climbed, keeping flush with the right-hand side of the staircase. At the top, I was met by a solid door.

"Of course, there would be a door," I said mostly to myself, but perhaps also for the sake of the listening rodent. At my words, the mouse squeaked excitedly just once and then leapt off my neck. I turned quickly in the direction he had jumped. An unusually large part of me was sad that he had abandoned me so easily, considering how useful he had been in showing me the way to freedom. But deep down, I did not blame the little fella for ditching a predator at the first possible chance.

To my surprise, the mouse hadn't run away after all. He had only scampered over to a duct off to the left of the stairwell. The cover had seen better days and was only half hanging on, leaving a hole big enough for a cat to slide past.

The mouse stood on his hind legs, watching me expectantly with his dark beady eyes. I strolled over to him. "Clever mouse," I praised.

In response, he made a mighty leap at me, startling me in the process. His aim was his spot behind my head, however. As soon as he was settled, I squeezed into the duct.

I walked cautiously forward, noting that this duct was yet another maze, with branches to the right and left every few feet. The mouse seemed to know this hidden tunnel system well; he led me straight to the last branch and motioned for me to turn right. After just another couple of feet, we came to the end of the duct.

This cover was also corroded, especially at the back. Even in my small cat form, I was able to easily tear some of the rusted slats away and squeeze myself out to freedom.

I found myself in another jail cell, but this one was somehow nicer than the one that Gavin and I had been put into. The biggest difference was the window high up on the wall to my left. A window that was open to the elements but with bars to prevent a human from escaping. I eyed the setup of the room. There was a musty mattress on a cot below the window and a washstand to its right. Nothing else.

I eyed the cot. I could probably jump from the mattress to the window ledge, but it would be a very tall jump, and the bars would make it tricky. Plus, I couldn't abandon Gavin. I needed to keep searching for the actual way out, not just an escape route that benefited me.

I glanced around. This wing seemed to be completely devoid of human activity, thankfully. Perhaps it wouldn't hurt to make some arrangements, just in case.

"Okay, little mouse, I want to thank you for your help so far. I really would like for you to stick around because I need to figure out how to spring my friend. Can you jump down for a moment, though?"

I waited until he crawled off my neck, landing gracefully by my side. He stared at me expectantly.

"I'm going to do something that will scare you. I'm about to change shape, and I won't be able to talk to you like this in my new form. But it will still be me, and I won't stay that way for long. So, I want you to stay near the duct and wait for me. Understand?"

He nervously rose to his hind legs.

I let out a little purr huff of appreciation. "Good mouse."

I trotted a couple of feet away from him and then shimmered up. I looked down at my tiny companion, who cowered against the wall, but he was brave for a mouse and did not run from me.

"Good mouse," I said again soothingly, and this time in human language. I did not expect him to understand, but hopefully he recognized the friendly tone.

As quietly as I could, I moved the cot away from the wall until there was a foot-wide gap. Then, I tilted the mattress, which was quite stiff, up against the wall to form a ramp to the window. The mattress top was now only an easy leap away from the window ledge. I had no idea what was on the other side, but I had to guess it was only a single-story drop to either the island or the lake below. I supposed if I needed to take this escape route, it would be a surprise for me.

As I stepped back to survey my handiwork, a crow cawed from a short distance away. I thought nothing of it at first, but as the sound increased, I realized I recognized it.

"Rupert," I breathed, disbelieving. I quickly transformed again and ran up my mattress ramp, leaping to the window in haste. At least I now knew that my escape plan worked.

"Cressida! Cressida!" the crow cawed, very close now.

"Rupert!" I called back urgently. I could now see him, a single black bird, making a beeline for my window. My heart leapt at the sight.

He landed on the ledge clumsily, as the bars did not leave much room. Flapping his wings to keep his balance, he exclaimed, "There you are!"

"Rupert! I've never been so happy to see you! How in Gaia did you find me?"

Rupert shook his head, nervously fluffing his neck feathers. "I—I've been flying for two and a half hours. Fleurette was so worried when you didn't come home! So she sent me to look for you."

"But how, Rupert? How did you find me?" I could not even imagine how a single crow could locate me when I was over one hundred miles from home. He always had a knack for finding me when I was out on a job, but I never really thought about how he managed it. After all, I usually didn't travel this far away.

He was generally a nervous bird around me, but his apprehension now took even greater heights. "Well, you see, Cressida, that is ..."

"Spit it out, Rupert!"

"Fleurette spelled me with a tracking device when you became a bounty hunter. It allows me to fly in a straight line directly to you at any time." He said this in a rush.

I was gobsmacked for a second. "She spelled you? With a tracking device?"

Rupert side-eyed me, unsure of my mood at this announcement.

"Rupert, that's the best news I've ever heard. Normally I'd think it stinks, but Fleurette's a genius. So, what happens next?"

Rupert straightened his beak, almost preening at the unexpected praise. "Now, I fly back and tell her where you are. I'm tired, but I can handle it. As soon as I am home, we'll get help your way!"

I deflated a bit. "How long will that take?"

He shook his head. "Three hours, as the crow flies? Not sure how long it will take to get over here after that, though. My job will be over."

"Good for you." I couldn't help being flippant with the crow. He brought it out in me. "Listen, tell Fleurette I'm okay, and that I'll try to stay safe until she can get here. It's the ACF that's captured me, but I don't think they know just who I am. Oh, and tell her Gavin is with me too."

Rupert flapped his wings and launched himself back into the air without a goodbye. He never stayed to chat long. But this was the first time I was genuinely glad he had found me.

I watched as the black bird flew off into the distance, staying at the window until he was just a small speck and wishing it was as easy for me to leave this dungeon.

I mean, I could have simply leapt out of the window and been on my merry way to safety if not for one little thing.

Gavin St. Cloud.

When had I developed a conscience and started caring for his well-being? It would have been so much easier for me if I had continued to see him as a woman-hating blowhard.

Sometimes having feelings for people could really blow up in one's face. Oh well.

I turned from the option of selfish freedom, jumping down onto the mattress. My mouse companion had stayed by the wall, watching me without much fear in his countenance. As I stared at him, I quickly did some mental work. I may have had a way to escape, but I still had to figure out a way to rescue Gavin. But how?

A key was clearly needed to open the cell door. I could track down the handful of humans that seemed to be working in the lower level and use some sort of subterfuge to obtain the keys ...

Before I could do more rumination, a sudden pulse of pure need obliterated my concentration. It called to every cell in my body, and I ceased thinking all together, reduced to an animal drive to find that need and answer it.

I did not question it but knew I had to find the source or die trying. It seemed to be coming from below me, so I instinctively fled into the duct to find my way back downstairs. The mouse let out a squeak of alarm at my sudden behavior, but I couldn't care less. I raced through the dark tunnel, chasing the pounding need. I leapt out of the duct and flew down the stairs, uncareful of staying hidden in the shadows, only mindful of the drive to find the source of the pervasive calling.

There. Through a door that stood before me. It was so close and yet I trembled with a desire to be closer. I just needed to open that door ...

As swiftly as the need had swamped me, it abruptly stopped. My mind cleared, and I could think again. I crouched, trembling in the hallway, completely at a loss of where I was or what to do now. What the hell was that siren song? Why had it called to me so?

Once I got over my shock, I realized I needed to get far away from the door. I made to slink back into the shadows.

A large, rough hand slapped down on my back, tightening around my scruff. I immediately froze as my kitten reflexes took over, even as my adrenaline kicked in.

"Whoops, little kitty. I'm not sure how you got out but let's get you back where you belong," a deep voice sounded above me. The hand lifted me by the scruff painfully. I curled my back legs up as I was lifted off the ground. My handler opened the door and with a swift movement, tossed me inside before quickly pulling the door shut again.

I was airborne for just a second. Within that time, I shot my tail out to stabilize my flight, and rotated my body upright for a smooth landing. Despite the perfect touchdown, I was still dazed from this turn of events, and I took a moment after impact to take in my surroundings.

The first thing that accosted my senses was the smell. Feces and ammonia and fear and stress. It was enough to momentarily blind me.

But once my nose paralysis ceased, I got my first good look at my new surroundings.

Those surroundings turned out to be cats. A whole room of them.

CHAPTER 26

It was amazing that I hadn't landed upon another cat after being carelessly flung into this room—there were so many. In fact, as I gathered my wits about me, I realized I was surrounded by a thick ring of my fellow felines.

This was not good.

I should have been consoled by seeing my own species, but instead, it only served to elevate my terror. After all, domesticated cats are a territorial bunch, prone to fighting amongst themselves if a threat is suspected and only accepting of cats they have a relationship with. Staring out at a sea of strange felines, I was in a bad position.

To add to the tension, some of the cats, who had seemed as shell-shocked as I was by my sudden appearance, had started to posture and hiss, raising the hair along their spines and arching their backs to appear bigger. My body responded to the threat, and my own fur stood at attention, although I actively denied my back to arch. Instead, I crouched low, tucking my puffed-up tail around my body to make myself smaller in an attempt to diffuse the situation.

Interestingly enough, many of the cats instantly lost interest in me at my meekness. These felines turned and wandered off, leaving only a handful of angry cats facing me. Still, any outraged cat was one too many, in my opinion. I needed to get out of this situation and fast.

Two of the hotheads decided they had given me enough warning and lunged simultaneously with twin screams. I flipped onto my back, all four feet fully clawed in anticipation. The first reached me and tackled my belly, but I was ready with a ferocious kick to its head, scratching near its eyes even as I took a claw to my chest. That cat backed off, apparently giving up the fight.

The other cat swiped near my head and managed to give me a good scratch on my left temple, near my ear. Before I could further defend myself, however, a newcomer barreled into it, yowling and flailing its arms like an angry tornado. The second attacker instantly retreated as my savior, a short-haired tortoise-shell, postured in front of me.

I stood, waiting for the tortie to make the next move. I couldn't be sure if she was a friend or foe.

Once it became clear that no other cats wanted to tackle either of us, she turned to assess me. She pointed her nose in my direction and sniffed the air.

"I thought so," she said to me.

Confused, I didn't communicate back. The feline boldly approached me. Still in defensive mode, I shrank back. She stopped and sat on her haunches, allowing me to get a good look at her before she approached any farther. Her body, an intricate patchwork of oranges, blacks, and browns, held no malice toward me. Only curiosity.

"You smell."

"Excuse me?" I could not ignore that comment.

"I've only ever smelled that smell on two other cats. You aren't like us. You're *other*. Which means only one thing." The tortoiseshell cat cocked her head to the side, studying me with green eyes. They reminded me of my mother's eyes.

"What's that?"

"You're in a load of danger."

I lashed my tail. "I could have told you that."

She pivoted her ears back in annoyance. "Not from us. Some cats, when brought here, decide that fighting is the best way to survive. They are soon proved wrong. No, you aren't safe from *her*."

"Her?" I did not like the sound of that.

"The cat killer. She is looking for you. Did you not feel the summons?"

I thought back to just minutes ago when I was called to this location, my mind hijacked by an intense need. "I did."

Her ears came forward. "There you have it. Only the *other* obey the summons, not us regular kin. Come, I will guide you to the ancient one."

She turned away from me and took a couple of languid steps. I did not immediately follow her, however. Now that I wasn't being harassed by an angry cat mob, I had a moment to take in my immediate surroundings.

It appeared to be a large room with two doors—one being the door I was thrown through and the other on the wall perpendicular to the first. Both were shut. Otherwise, all I could see were cats. Lounging on some dirty old blankets strewn on the floor. Using extremely dirty litter boxes shoved against one of the walls. Walking about, yowling. Posturing. Grooming in half-hearted defeat.

These cats were all prisoners, I realized with a sick feeling. Another thought occurred to me, which made me feel even worse. This was a whole shipment of cats, for sure, but there were more cats in this room than could fit in the boxes brought over with Gavin and me. That pointed to past shipments that hadn't involved me.

When she realized I had not followed her, the tortie turned

back to me and let out a small chirrup. The sound again reminded me of my mother, and here, surrounded by many strange cats
in an obvious place of death, I felt an intense pang of homesick-
ness. I shook it off. After just another small hesitation, I started
to follow her. After all, what other options did I have?

The many cats in the room gave us a wide berth, but I still
kept a wary eye on them. The array of felines was almost dizzy-
ing. Coats of all shades and patterns. Scruffy alley cats and sleek
well-fed house cats. Some older cats and some as young as kittens.

My sight caught on one particular cat that made my heart sink.
"Oh no," I sighed. "You?"

The young gray cat from the alley in Dogwood crouched in a
corner with a terrified expression on her face. She was still quite
large with her unborn kittens. She saw me and hissed, although it
was a feeble attempt at protecting herself. She decided to ignore
me and went back to trying to become one with the wall. Despite
her careful ways, she had fallen victim to the very thing she had
warned me about. The thought was terrible.

The room was old and not perfectly squared. The tortoiseshell
cat led me around a corner into a crumbled part of the facade.
Here, a large tabby cat sat stoically against the wall. At our approach, it stood up and walked to the side, revealing a hole in the
wall that its large body had been perfectly hiding. The hole was
just large enough for a cat to crawl through.

"Go on in," the tortie urged me. I hesitated but felt no animosity from the cats around me. *In for a penny, in for a dollar,* I
thought to myself as I crept into the crevasse.

The hole widened past the width of the wall, rounding out to a
cozy nook. Just enough light filtered in from the room to prevent
the den from being pitch black. Once my eyes adjusted, I saw I
wasn't alone.

In the far reaches of the tiny cave, there lay the oldest cat I had ever seen. She was skinny to the point of emaciation, her short black and white fur matted into clumps as if she had stopped grooming herself years ago. But her bright green eyes, sunken upon her skeletal face, caught mine, and a keen intelligence radiated in them.

My nostrils flared. She stunk horribly, another sign of her poor grooming skills, but beneath that I smelled a very familiar scent.

Like … me.

The old cat shuffled her limbs a bit as if to stand. The tortie pushed past me, approaching the wizened feline. She placed a gentle paw upon the shoulders of the old one, which stopped the almost frantic movements. Still, her ancient eyes never left me.

"Stay put, Serena," the tortoiseshell soothed at the emaciated cat.

The name jolted me. Where had I heard it before?

Serena, the elderly cat, let out a tiny sound that may have been an inquisitive chirp once upon a time. "You aren't Belinda, are you?"

The hairs along my spine stood up at the sound of my mother's name. "N-no," I finally replied. I hesitated a moment. "I'm her daughter."

"Her daughter," she mused. "Well, do you know what that makes me?"

It clicked where I had heard the name before. "That would make you Serena, who was Belinda's grandmother. Which makes you my great-grandmother." My mind reeled. I had found a living relative!

Serena's tail let out a little thump of approval. "You are correct, my dear. And what is your name?"

"Cressida."

"What a pretty name. Are you a Curtain?"

When worded in such a way, it always filled me with mirth,

even in dire circumstances such as this. "Yes, I am."

"Hmm. Just like your mother." She closed her eyes briefly. "Does that mean you are the last in line?"

"Yes."

"And you've been caught." Her green eyes shone with sorrow.

"Well, yes, I suppose. But not as a cat. As a human."

"Oh? So they don't know you are a cat?" She seemed to perk up a bit. "There's hope yet, then." She gazed at me, assessing. "Your markings are so unusual, dear. Very pretty. My Lottie was a tabby with a white muzzle and underbelly. And she tells me that your mother is a calico."

I did not have a reply right away because the present tense she had used in the last sentence threw me off. Lottie must have been her daughter Charlotte, my grandmother. To fill the time, I responded, "Er, yes, she's a calico, although she has tabby markings as well."

"Oh, how pretty!" cooed Serena. "It's been a very long time since Glivver's line has had a calico, and tabby calicos are incredibly rare. How I wish I could see your mother. Lottie was very proud of her daughter. She's told me so."

Serena's flip-flopping between past and present tense was confusing. I finally gathered the courage to ask, "Is she here also? Lottie, my grandmother?"

Serena looked puzzled momentarily. Then a shadow fell over her face. "No, I suppose not," she replied sadly. "But she was. It wasn't that long ago. I sometimes forget she's gone."

"Oh." Glivver had said she no longer felt the lifeforce of my grandmother, so it was not a big surprise to find out she was indeed deceased. However, it was still difficult to have been so close to meeting another family member of my very unusual family tree.

"Dearest, come closer and sit with me," my wizened relative

said, "and I'll tell you my tale."

I did as she asked, settling down in front of her. The tortie cat also crouched into a more comfortable position beside my great-grandmother. Serena looked pleased.

"Has your mother told you anything of your heritage?" she asked.

I let out the equivalent of a laugh. "Until a few days ago, I had never even heard of you or Lottie. Mom decided the less I knew of where I came from, the safer I'd be."

"Hmm, I can't agree with that, although I'm the one trapped in here, and she's the one free," mused Serena. "Well, when I was a young cat, I lived near Addelboro, and I met my husband Nathan there, so we settled down. We were happy. But while I was pregnant with Lottie, Nathan was killed in a botched robbery. There was nothing I could do to save him since I was stuck as a cat."

"How horrible!" I interjected.

"Well, it was a long time ago, and as you can see, my life has not exactly been on an upward trajectory for some time. In fact, I only had a good year after Lottie's birth before I was captured. What year is it now, dear?"

I told her.

She seemed lost in thought. "I've been a prisoner of the ACF for twenty-one years."

I gaped at her. That was longer than the average lifespan of a mundane cat. "Why on earth have you been stuck here for that long? Why are they collecting cats?"

She stared at me. "Tell me something, dear. What is it that all the cats in this cattery have in common, including you and me?"

I stopped to think. On the surface, the cats were a diverse bunch. Cats of all ages, all backgrounds. Angry cats and docile cats. Pregnant queens were not excluded either. That was a thought ...

I smelled deeply, ignoring the obvious bad smells and focusing on the pheromones emitted by the various cats. I opened my eyes, astonished. "They are all females!"

Serena looked pleased. "Exactly."

"But why?"

"Simple, dearest. They are looking for us."

When she spelled it out so plainly, I couldn't help but wonder why it didn't occur to me earlier. It was so obvious. "They think to stop the prophecy by wiping out our bloodline. By capturing all female cats in the hopes of snagging the right ones."

"Right on the nose!" She was strangely gleeful at my words. "But I won't give them the satisfaction of knowing they have me!"

"How? How have you survived here for so long?" My great-grandmother had been trapped in this room, or possibly this small den, for a very long time. It boggled my mind.

"I was lucky with the timing, I suppose. Back then, they simply caught cats and kept them in this room for a few months, thinking that any special cats would have to change into human occasionally. The cat killer, as we call her, had not yet figured out her calling spell, so I had time to find this lovely hidey hole and stay out of sight. That way, when she inevitably started randomly culling the cats, I was safe from her wrath." Serena looked at me with piercing eyes. "The call only speaks to us, my dear. It does not affect mundane cats. It's meant to force our kind into the open for easy pickings."

"How have you survived its call for so long?" I still shuddered when I thought of the urgent need the call had filled me with.

"Luck, dear. The first time she perfected the call, I very nearly answered. That was a couple of years into my imprisonment. It was only through the care and love of the mundane cats that

I was stopped." She turned and licked the ruff of the tortie beside her affectionately. "For my entire stay here, I've always recruited a small clowder of cats to be my aides, providing me with food, with companionship, and with protection. In return, I treat them like they were my adopted daughters. I have let many a pregnant queen kindle here in the safety of this den. It has given many kittens a fair start in life, for otherwise, the cat killer snatches them up immediately and does away with them."

My stomach soured at those words. I thought again of the frightened gray cat that had gotten caught, even after she had been made aware of the disappearing cats.

She continued, "My clowder has prevented me from revealing myself since the call started. They literally barricade me in this cave. It was harder when I was younger, but these days, well, I can hardly stand, so it's easier on them. In fact, Mitzi here is the only one I need these days. The perks of getting old, I guess."

"How old are you, Serena?"

"Pish, none of that!" she admonished me. "I'm Granny to you, you hear? I was robbed of that joy when they caught me." She paused. "And to answer your question, I'm twenty-seven."

My head reeled. Twenty-seven may have seemed old for a cat, but my kind could live much longer than that, even twice as many years, given the extraordinary fact that we only aged when we were in our cat form. Serena, however, looked to be so old that I doubted she had much time left.

"When was the last time you transformed? Granny?" I hastily added.

She closed her eyes in approval. "Not once since I got here. I've lived a full life as a cat, which has aged me quicker than not. This space is too small for a human, and it was too risky to leave this shelter for more than a few minutes. And even if I was exposed, I never knew if someone had eyes on me, so I never did try to change my shape. That human part of me died long ago. I was a beauty when I last saw my human face. I grimace to think of what I'd see now."

Twenty-one years as a cat, plus the added age of her time before imprisonment. It was no wonder Serena was aged beyond her years.

With this talk of her lost years and lost youth, she sunk into an air of pain and despair. The tortie, Mitzi, nuzzled against her cheek in an effort to buoy her spirits. Serena took comfort in the touch, even she changed the topic to another sad matter. "Now, Lottie, my daughter, was in much better shape than me, even though she was only five years younger than me."

"What happened to her?" I hated asking the question, even as the words left me, but my curiosity was too great.

My relative stared at me with her brilliant green eyes, assessing me, before she spoke again. "Lottie said she managed to evade the ACF for years, but they started canvassing the Dogwood area extensively, and eventually, they caught up to her. I was horrified when they brought her in." She seemed lost in thought. "That was, oh, four years ago? If I'm doing my calculations correctly."

"Mom said she became pregnant with me right after her mother disappeared, so about three and a half, yes."

"Close enough. Anyway, I managed to get Lottie sequestered in here as soon as I was able. Same as I did for you. My helpers at the time knew to be on the lookout for our unique scent. Time is of the essence, you see, because the cat killer makes her calls shortly after a new shipment wakes up. So, Lottie stayed tucked away with me. It was probably the happiest time I ever had in this place, being holed up here with my long-lost daughter. But for Lottie, being cooped up in here chafed her." Serena closed her eyes, sadness once again rolling off of her. "She never did want to stay in here, but I made her. In the end, though, she got out at the wrong time. Cat killer made the summons, and Lottie answered. She was snagged and carried through the wrong door."

"Wrong door?" I questioned.

"There's two doors into this place," Serena explained. "One leads to the hallway, which can mean the way to freedom. The other is where the cat killer comes and goes. If you go through that door, you don't come back."

"Oh."

"We could hear Lottie scream for days, both as a cat and as a human, as she was tortured for information. And then one day, the screams stopped, and that was that."

I shuddered at the implications of this.

"That wasn't that long ago. I measure time by the shipments of new cats, which happens about once every two months. I do believe three shipments have come in since then. And now you're here. I fear Lottie must have given up something worthwhile." Serena looked troubled.

I tried to organize my thoughts. Serena did not have a great grasp on time, living away from calendars and not being able to use her human brain for many long years, but based on her calculations, my grandmother must have met her demise around six months ago. Around, say, September of last year. Which coincided with the hiring of my father at Lightfoot Shipping Industries. An action that would lead to him being framed and wanted for questioning. What kind of questioning? If I had to bet money, it would be about the whereabouts of his wife.

The last known descendant of Glivver.

"I know what Lottie told them," I said to Serena. "It was about my father. Roger Curtain. Greg Elkins owns this place, and he is the silent partner of the company my father was employed by, for the last six months. I was hired to find my father after he was framed by Elkins but instead, I was trying to help clear his name.

They must have wanted him so they could find my mother and eliminate her. Elkins caught me snooping in his house and sent me here. But he doesn't know I'm exactly what he's been looking for. He thinks I'm a human." Except now he knew there was a link between Roger and me. "At least, he did when he sent me here."

"That's a mouthful if I ever heard one," responded my great-grandmother. "Is your mother safe?"

"Yes, I believe so." I tried to calm my racing thoughts. "She left my dad when she was pregnant and traveled far away from Dogwood. She's thrown them off her scent. And, until now, at least, my scent too. And even if Elkins had been successful in capturing my dad, he wouldn't know where she is. He'd only get killed in the end." I mentally grimaced at that thought. I was very glad I was able to get him to safety when I did. I may not have known my father well or for very long, but I already felt a connection to him. I wanted to keep him alive.

"It's a muddle, for sure. Child, there's one takeaway from this whole thing."

"And that is?" I prompted.

Her green eyes bored into me. "You need to get out of here alive, above all else. The future of our world depends upon it."

CHAPTER 27

I n the end, Serena convinced me to stay in the hole with her for at least another two hours. Her reasoning was that the cat killer lady always did the summoning spell twice on a day when a new shipment came in: once as the bulk of the cats awakened from their somnambulistic torpor and again about two hours later, in case any cats of my line were still passed out for the first one.

And as it turned out, my great-grandmother was right. I passed the first part of my confinement with a small nap. Once I awoke, feeling more refreshed, it was time to do something about my physical state. I'd been giving myself a very thorough washing, considering I had been a human for a long time and had gotten into a few scrapes in the process. I paid special attention to my face because the wearing of makeup had made me feel unclean once I was a cat. Plus, the scratch on my head stung, and a small amount of blood had trickled into my fur.

I was just finishing grooming the long fur on my tail when I felt it.

I needed to go. I needed to be where that call was. If I didn't, I might never be happy again. Why was that tortoiseshell cat suddenly barring my way? And that other cat behind her? They needed to move! That feeling of pure desire would destroy me if I didn't get through these cats.

But they stood their ground, standing tall and filling up the entrance. In my utter despondency, I hissed and looked menacing, but they didn't back down. Behind me, I barely noticed that Serena was desperately struggling to stand. Struggling and failing.

I wanted to scream at these felines, to claw their eyes out for standing in my way. I was too focused on pushing through to stop and fight, but the need to follow the pulsing summons was almost enough for me to become violent.

And then, it stopped.

I immediately crouched back, panting from my efforts. Serena, too, seemed exhausted beside me. Mitzi rushed to her side, purring and nuzzling her back into a state of calm. I simply stayed where I was, feeling confused at the fugue state I had temporarily found myself in and rather embarrassed by my actions.

"Don't be embarrassed," Serena said, as if reading my mind. "I've suffered through more of those than I can count, and still, it never gets easier. With my legs not working properly, it *has* gotten easier for my companions, though."

I nodded my head in a very human gesture. Her words helped me feel better, less like I was completely out of control.

Serena continued, "You should take the opportunity to get out now. She won't likely do the summons again today. Go to the door that leads to the hallway. You'll have to become human to work it. Mitzi will show you the way."

"Granny, I promise I'll get out of this. And if I can, I will save you too."

Serena let out a rusty purr, but she also didn't look like she believed me. "Be well, child," she told me as I exited. "And be safe."

Back in the cattery proper, I took in my surroundings. Many of the contained cats hugged the walls, some completely avoiding others, and some actively looking for fights to prove their place in the pecking order.

I turned my attention to Mitzi as a thought entered my mind. I had assumed most of these cats were strays, and feral cats did not give themselves proper names. If they had names at all, it was a nickname from their mother to denote a special attribute, such as fierceness, playfulness, or how well they hunted. "How did you get your name?" I asked her.

"I adopted a family when I was very young. I was barely out of kittenhood before I was captured and brought here. They had gifted me the name Mitzi."

"Ah," I said, at a loss for what to say. It was a tragedy that so many cats had been snatched over the years, disrupting and ending their lives and removing them from possible happy homes. Mitzi must have sensed my distress, for she took charge, exuding a sense of purpose as she hovered near me. No wonder my great-grandmother had chosen her for her clowder.

My eyes were drawn to the door across the way from Mitzi and me. The one Serena had called the wrong door.

"Careful," Mitzi murmured, "she sometimes makes unexpected visits to the cattery."

"But she won't know me from any other cat," I countered, and skulked over to the rather unassuming door. It was solid wood and painted a dismal gray, like everything else in this pit of a room. I could hear voices from the other side. I leaned in, perking my ear forward to amplify the sound.

"I just finished the second call. Tell Gregory there were no nibbles today," a soft, feminine voice said. The cat killer?

"Stock is getting low in Dogwood," a second voice, deep and manly, replied. It was a familiar tone, and I pictured the large, bald man as a possible owner. But then again, the woman sounded slightly familiar, too. I couldn't place why.

The man spoke again. "Are you sure we are hunting in the right location?"

The woman answered with a hint of anger lacing her voice, "No, of course I'm not. We are dealing with outdated information. If Curtain is single again, chances are good that Cat B has already queened. But if we don't know where Cat B is, we won't know where her daughter is either. Which is why we need Curtain to talk!"

I did some quick mental gymnastics. Cat B must be Belinda, my mother. Curtain was obviously my father, and the cat killer had accurately guessed that I existed. I was dangerously close to ending my line; I could feel it.

"Any news about our missing bounty hunter?" Cat killer asked. I perked up.

"No." The reply was succinct.

"She can't have gone far. I think it's time to get some answers out of her companion, though."

"I agree. I need more time with the other questioning, anyway." With that, I could hear the man Hobbs stomp over to the left, making his exit out of a door that apparently led to the hallway.

My heart pounded with fear. Not for myself, but for Gavin. I had left him alone too long, and now he was in danger. I needed to get back to him, but how? I was seemingly stuck in this room and a little turned around to boot. Finding Gavin would not be easy for me.

A commotion in a far corner caught my attention. Five cats seemed rather intent on pouncing at a corner of the room. It wasn't until I understood the excitement was over "Mouse!" that I sprinted over to investigate.

There he was, my little mouse, trying desperately to jump back into a hole in the wall but failing because of the many cat bodies swarming him. He wouldn't last much longer, given the intensity of the felines.

That simply wouldn't do. I had given my promise to my mouse that I would protect him.

I leapt over the fray, using my claws to bat away the intent predators, until I stood in the corner, my body blocking the little rodent from view.

"*Mine!*" I snarled at the interested felines. I hissed and lunged at a couple who did not want to take no for an immediate answer. "This mouse belongs to me! Any of you who say otherwise will have your soft spots ripped open!"

I was not a large cat compared to others near me, but apparently my vehemence was enough to convince the throng that this rodent was not worth the risk. It might have been my unusual scent, as well, that marked me as "other" that led the cats to back off. Whatever the reason was, I was left alone, allowing me to back away from the corner to inspect my tiny companion.

He quivered at his near demise but seemed otherwise unhurt.

"You okay, little friend?" I asked him with concern. He took a moment but rose shakily to his back legs. The dread in my gut lifted. "You are one lucky mouse, you know that?"

I flattened myself to the ground, and the mouse jumped into his spot behind my ears. Before I could start walking, though, he leaped off of me and into a small hole in the wall, large enough for him but much too small for a cat. But he made it clear that this was the way out.

"Through there?" I asked him. He replied in the affirmative. "But it's too small for me," I countered.

In response, he pawed at the edges of the hole. Tiny flakes of mortar broke off from his feeble attempts. The implication was clear enough, though. I raised my own paw and clawed at the hole's perimeter. The concrete easily crumbled into little bits at my digging, revealing more empty space just beyond.

My mouse squeaked like a tiny cheerleader as I continued scratching away the surface, enlarging the hole with efficiency. Within minutes, there was a sizable pile of crumbled mortar and concrete at my feet and an opening in the wall big enough to allow a cat through, about a foot off the ground.

Forget about eating this mouse. He was worth quadruple his weight in gold.

He scampered into this new cavity, glancing over his shoulder to beckon me to follow. I jumped in, keeping my legs bent to accommodate the low ceiling of the shaft. My diminutive guide led me along a straight path for a few feet before the tunnel opened into a larger hollow within the building.

From here, it was a matter of climbing into a defunct duct that took a sharp turn upward. Luckily, the inside of the duct was not smooth and allowed me to clear the vertical space in a series of jumps, with the mouse once again riding upon my neck. And once we were back on the horizontal part, I was delighted to see that we had connected with the same duct that led to the upper-level jail cell—and freedom—by taking a left or to the stairwell by taking a right.

As much as I wanted to heed Serena's advice and save my own skin, I couldn't. Not yet. "Okay, little mouse. I need to find my friend. How do we get back to the prison cells downstairs?"

The mouse bumped his nose against my right ear, guiding me to the stairwell. Once there, I cautiously crept down the stairs, feeling a sense of deja vu at my actions. This time, my senses were on high alert and not blinded by the urgent call of the cat killer's spell. I recognized these hallways, and sure enough, we passed right by the door that led to the cattery.

I was incredibly relieved to pass by that particular door without incident.

Minutes ticked by as my mouse continued to guide me. Before we got back to the cell that I had escaped from, though, I heard voices through the wall. I stopped, despite the mouse's urging to keep walking.

The voices were faint, but the timbre of one of them was definitely familiar. "Mouse, where is the door to this room?" I asked him.

He nudged me around a bend. There stood a door, metal like the others in this section of hallway, but this one had a small glass window upon it too. The voices were clearer from my new vantage. The deep baritone of Hobbs cut through the door, with Gavin's voice just a touch quieter.

I needed a visual on the situation. I needed my human body for the height advantage.

"Little Mouse, I'm going to turn into a human again. I'll probably stay that way for a while, so I want you to hide in my pocket. It will be safer there than wandering about on your own. Do you understand?"

My mouse raised up on his back feet immediately. He probably agreed with the safety bit, considering he had nearly been a snack for a bunch of cats just fifteen minutes ago.

I gave my surroundings one last sweep with my senses. Content with the knowledge we were alone in the hallway, I transformed.

The mouse was much less afraid of my change this time. In fact, as soon as I bent down and stretched out my hand for him he eagerly jumped on it and scampered up my arm. I held the left pocket of Gavin's jacket open for him, and he plopped inside. I could feel him turning about for a few seconds before he became comfortable and hunkered down.

With my tiny companion taken care of, I carefully approached the door. Keeping to one side, I slowly peered into a corner of the window.

Luck was on my side. I could clearly see both Gavin and Hobbs, but the massive man was turned slightly away from the door, and Gavin was placed perpendicular to it, so he would have had to turn his head to see me. He was too preoccupied to do that.

In fact, there wasn't much Gavin *could* do, given that he was seated in a wooden chair with ropes wrapped around his legs and torso. His arms were bound similarly with rope to the chair's arms. It was clear that Hobbs had already roughed Gavin up; his nose trickled blood, and the eye I could see looked puffy. A liberal smear of rusty red marred his white button-up shirt.

Hobbs still wore his customary black tee. His bulging muscles and bald head shone with sweat. He turned to Gavin, his forehead a mass of furrows from the menacing frown he wore.

"How did she get out?" he asked.

Despite his hazardous position, Gavin still wore his smug demeanor like a cloak. "Like I told you a million times already; I don't know. One minute she was there, and the next she was gone."

Hobbs grunted. "You really expect me to believe that? Stop lying to protect her!"

Gavin appeared to be frustrated. "Look. I'm not protecting her. It's her fault I'm here in the first place. She had no qualms leaving me behind to save her skin. She means nothing to me. I was only with her because I wanted to get in her pants. As far as I'm concerned, I hope you find the bitch."

His words stung like bees on my heart. Is that what he really thought of me? I should have left when I had the chance.

A faint vibration broke my sorry reverie. It was coming from the right pocket of Gavin's jacket. I reached my hand in, feeling around until my fingertips touched a smooth metal surface.

The pocket watch.

Gavin had been lying through his teeth. He was doing it to protect me. He really was a good guy.

Hobbs didn't buy it, though. "You sure about that story?" He placed one meaty hand upon Gavin's, swallowing it up with its bigger size. The gesture almost looked tender, like a lover caressing his beloved's hand. But Gavin's reaction was anything but romantic. He bucked in his bonds, trying to remove Hobbs' touch. He gasped in pain and then practically whimpered. Meanwhile, Hobbs stared at his captive with that same maniacal smile twisting his lips.

I didn't understand why a single touch could be so detrimental to Gavin until Hobbs straightened a few seconds later. Gavin's hand, where the bigger man had touched him, was bright red and looked like it was about to blister.

There was clearly magic at work. But what kind?

While Gavin breathed deeply, likely to recover from this latest bit of torture, Hobbs held up his right hand, turning his palm up. "Last chance, pretty boy," he threatened. As I watched, a small lick of blue flame formed above his palm and gained size until it was a whirling ball of orange fire. He inched this fireball closer to Gavin's face as Gavin tried to tilt his head back, alarm blooming upon his countenance.

Hobbs' face shone with the light of the fire. He enunciated every word clearly: "Where's the girl?"

CHAPTER 28

I sucked in a breath at the scene before me. Hobbs was a fire elemental, a rare breed of magic user that could create fire at will. Now I knew how the lid to our box was blown off. And I had a solid suspicion of who had actually burned the office building.

I also knew that Gavin was in for a world of pain unless I helped him. How I was going to help, I didn't know, but before I could give it any thought, I yanked the door open and marched inside.

Both men turned their heads and stared, not moving from their positions. My appearance was apparently the last thing either of them expected.

The door slammed shut behind me. It took all of my willpower not to jump at the sound.

"Hey!" I yelled forcefully. "Were you looking for me?"

Hobbs straightened, drawing the fireball away from Gavin's perspiring face. Gavin, while probably thrilled not to be burned, looked at me like I was an idiot. I began to think I was perhaps too hasty in my entry.

"As a matter of fact, yes," the large man replied. His ball of fire fizzled to nothing in his hand as he took a step back to survey me. "Lady, you've got a lot of nerve waltzing around the place like you own it."

"I'm the one with nerve?" I spat out. "I'm not the one framing innocent people and capturing cats like they're going out of style. And torture? How dare you!"

Hobbs seemed taken aback by my vehemence. He took a moment before giving me a smirk. "First of all, cats are vermin. We're doing the world a favor by taking them. You know what they're good for? About once a month, I get to round a bunch of them up in their room, and I use them for target practice." He mimed shooting fireballs from his hands. "They catch fire so easily. It's great entertainment to watch them run about like shooting stars."

I stared in horror as he smiled at his speech. This man was a monster.

"Also, have you looked around?" he continued. "This here room is where the prison guards used to take some of their prisoners for 'special questioning.' As in, punishment. Torture. And it's a tradition I've decided to keep. I enjoy the work, and I'm *very* good at it. So, little girl, I'd check your attitude at the door. What do you say to that?"

I felt ill at his words, but I did take a quick peek at my surroundings at his suggestion, never fully letting him out of my sight in case he decided to take me on while my attention was off him. The room was small, with a low bench behind Hobbs littered with archaic tools for torture, plus some larger weapons leaning up against a corner. My eye caught on a rather hefty steel club with a spike at the end. Perhaps I could stall for time and make a play for a weapon to knock Hobbs out. It was a crap plan, but it was better than nothing.

I pursed my lips in thought. "Let him go," I demanded, motioning my head to Gavin. "He's got nothing to do with any of this. I'm the one who put the pieces together."

"Cressida ..." Gavin muttered at me, not liking what I had to say. I ignored him.

Hobbs laughed as if I had made a funny joke. "It doesn't work like that. Your boyfriend knows too much. The only way he's leaving is in a box like the one he came here in. You too, girlie. If I'd had my druthers, I would have lit you both up back at the manor, but my boss is really particular about me burning his property. He seems to think you have something good to share, so he ordered me to keep you alive. So tell me, will you come forth with it politely, or do I need to mar that pretty face of yours? A part of me hopes you don't talk easily because I have a feeling you'd be fun to ruin."

I slowly took a step to the side, trying to make my way to the corner with the club as imperceptibly as possible. "You want to know what I know? I'll tell you. Roger Curtain was hired at Lightfoot Shipping on a ruse. He was paid legally, but the books didn't reflect that. Instead, the business has been funding this little hellhole of yours. ACF? I know what that actually stands for."

Hobbs crossed his arms as he listened. He grinned in that maniacal way again. "So you *are* on the inside track. Mr. Elkins seemed to think so."

I narrowed my eyes at him. "You could say that. I have no idea why you'd want to help bring Annie Coddle back, but I know that's your end game. And you thought Roger had a piece of the missing puzzle to do just that. All you needed was a reason to bring Roger here, so you decided to frame him." I looked at him speculatively. "By the way, I'm using the 'you' not for you personally, but for all of your seedy business partners and club members. I doubt *you* have the brains to cook up this whole scheme on your own."

Hobbs smiled cruelly, like he was tallying up all my barbs for later payment.

I continued: "So you framed Roger, but he personally gave *you* the slip at the office, didn't he? When that other worker walked into Roger's office, you thought it was him and grabbed him. When you realized your mistake, you had to clean up the mess. You're a fire elemental, so it would have been really easy to light up the place to cover your tracks and blame it on Roger.

"What you didn't expect was for Roger to go into hiding so well. Which is where I come in. But I'm curious—you had Roger served to you on a silver platter while he worked at Lightfoot Shipping. Why didn't you just snag him back then before he got suspicious?"

The bald man frowned. "That was not my choice to make. They wanted to make sure they had the right guy at first. They were waiting to hear him talk about his wife."

"Oh yes, the whole reason you wanted to bring him in for 'questioning,'" I sneered. "Roger's wife. She's the one you're actually looking for. Well, buddy, I have news for you. It would have done you no good to have Roger for that. He doesn't know where she is. Thank Freya he gave you goons the slip again."

At this point, I had managed to position myself between Hobbs and Gavin, with the weapons corner just a wall away. I had to keep rotating the bald man while we conversed.

Hobbs folded his arms with a smug look on his sweaty face. "You have it all figured out, don't you? It's too bad you got that last detail wrong."

This stopped me in my tracks. "What?"

He nodded. "We got Curtain in the end too. He was in one of those boxes, same as you. He just stayed asleep the whole time like he was supposed to."

I stared at him, hoping he was lying just to throw me off. My stomach tangled in knots.

"Don't believe me? Why don't you have a look for yourself? He's in that room." Hobbs nodded his head at a door to my right, opposite to which I had entered. It was nearly identical at first glance, with a viewing window. I stepped sideways toward the door, never taking my eye off the large man who would do me great harm if given the chance. Once I was close enough, I peered through the window.

This door led to a similar room as this one, but much smaller. There were two figures inside: an animal of some sort in a small cage and a man tied to a chair in a fashion similar to Gavin. Upon further inspection, the animal revealed itself to be a river otter, which turned and writhed within the tiny cage like an angry water current. And the man? He was blindfolded, but I recognized that sandy hair and the nose so similar to mine.

Roger hadn't gotten away after all.

"Oh no," I muttered to myself.

"So you see, girlie, we got everything we wanted in the end. And you get nothing."

A sudden rage churned my gut. How dare he put my father in jeopardy, after everything I'd done to keep him safe! I swiveled around, my face a mask of bitterness. Without another word, I raced over to the corner and grabbed the metal club. I swirled on one bare foot, raising it over my head to bash Hobbs with all my strength.

The downward motion of the club was halted by one of Hobbs' hands, which gripped it with vise-like brawn. Try as I might, I could not budge the club.

Hobbs smiled at me like a teacher might a wayward student. Any pleasantness on his face morphed into something much more wicked as the metal club warmed in my hands. The temperature continued to increase until I dropped it with a gasp, at which point I knew I had truly lost this small battle.

I sneaked a glance at my hands, which smarted terribly. The palms were reddened with minor burns.

Hobbs chuckled as he handled the club with ease, tossing it from hand to hand. "You see, girlie, a fire elemental can produce fire, but they can also create contact heat. Metal is a wonderful conductor of that."

I should have known.

"Now then," he continued, "I think you two have outlived your usefulness. Well, maybe not you, doll, since you seem to have an encyclopedic knowledge of the Curtain family. I'm going to enjoy getting more answers out of you. I think I'll bring your other friend out to play and see how much pain one of you can take before the other squeals. But time's up for your boyfriend. He obviously doesn't know anything. Say goodbye." He pulled a black sack out of his pocket and advanced on Gavin while I stayed behind him, mentally frozen.

"Time for a light-up," Hobbs sneered as he fit the sack over Gavin's flailing head.

No. This couldn't be how it ended. Not as long as I was still here.

I spun and grabbed the first thing I touched on the bench—a pair of iron forceps—and threw them at the back of Hobbs' head. My aim wasn't true, but I did manage to hit him in the shoulder.

He roared and turned, striking Gavin's chair with his body and knocking it over. I heard a small "Oomph!" escape from Gavin as he fell and hit the hard stone floor. But my attention had to stay on the very large, very angry man that was now fully facing me.

"You just don't know when to quit, do you?" he seethed.

"I really don't. It's a problem." As I mouthed off, I gripped the edge of my dress and ripped the side seam until my legs had free motion.

Hobbs raised both hands out from his sides, palms up. They

glowed with magic as he built a fireball in each hand. "Time to teach you a lesson."

I didn't wait for him to finish those fireballs. Instead, I ran at him.

Hobbs raised his left hand and threw the fireball at me.

I jumped toward him and shimmered. With all of my might, I stayed in that incorporeal form until my consciousness began to expand outside of myself.

The fireball passed through me and hit the bench with a heavy *wumph*.

As soon as the fireball was behind me, I lost hold of the shimmer, and emerged as a cat, still in my forward trajectory through the air. Hobbs' eyes grew wide at my sudden transformation, but I didn't have time to bask in the entertaining glory.

He began to raise his right hand, but I hit him squarely in the chest before he could fire off the other ball at me. Upon my impact, I screamed in victory and clawed my way up his chest to his neck and face, becoming a demon of teeth and razor-sharp claws. Hobbs bent backwards at my onslaught, yelling in pain as I carved multiple rivulets into his skin and tried my best to scratch his eyes out. He held the fireball in one hand, not daring to use it so close to his own head.

Likely disoriented from the pain and blinded by the blood running into his eyes, he lost his balance and toppled backward. I jumped off his face before he could crash to the ground. As soon as I leapt, he tried one last time to end me, shooting his remaining fireball straight up. The shot was much too wide, however. The fireball hurled up to the ceiling like a bullet and tore through the old masonry like it was paper.

I ran away from the downed man, afraid he would get his second wind and come after me, blood in his eyes or no blood. But before he could get back up off the ground, the ceiling rumbled ominously. Hobbs opened his eyes and looked up in alarm.

A chunk of stone and cement, the size of a hope chest, cracked away from the ceiling, loosened by the immense blast. It fell straight down.

Hobbs started to scream.

The chunk landed on his head and chest with a resolute, sickening crunch, ending his scream before it fully began. The man's body jittered for a moment, like a crazed puppet. A pool of blood seeped out from under the ceiling chunk as the movements stilled.

I stared at the scene in horror. Had I wanted to beat the man into a bloody pulp for what he was planning to do to us? Absolutely. Had I wanted to witness his messy death caused by his own magic? Absolutely not.

I reverted back to my human form. I felt funny in a way I couldn't pinpoint. Sure, my stomach was queasy from the gruesome death in front of me, but this sensation was different. I noticed an odd warmth under my skin. Could I be getting sick?

As much as I wanted to take a moment to come to terms with this development and ease the ill feeling in my stomach, now was not the time. Because not only did that large piece of ceiling cave in and kill Hobbs, but now there was a trickle of water leaking from the hole left behind.

From somewhere in the dungeon, an alarm sounded.

It was time to get us out of here.

CHAPTER 29

I rushed over to Gavin, who had been yelling in the background ever since the hood had gone over his head. I had filtered out this noise during my fight, but now I heard him loud and clear. It was mostly a mixture of threats toward the now-deceased Hobbs and pleas for my safety, whether it was begging the man not to hurt me or demanding I run and save myself.

He was still strapped to the chair firmly with the sack stuck on his head, despite his struggles and the chair being tipped over. I placed a hand softly on the arm facing upward to hopefully quiet him.

"Gavin?"

He stopped struggling. "Cressida, get this hood off me! What the hell is going on? What was that screaming demon? And why am I wet?"

The trickle of water from the ceiling was more of a steady stream now. I had a sinking feeling that the stream would continue to get heavier as the minutes passed and more of the ceiling buckled under the strain of the lake. For now, though, enough water had fallen to leave a spreading puddle on the floor of the small room.

I yanked the hood off Gavin. He blinked at the change in brightness but smiled in relief when he saw me. I examined the ropes binding him to the chair.

"Hobbs is dead," I said. "The ceiling collapsed on him. So there's that. But we have another issue. There's water leaking from the hole."

Gavin started and craned his neck to try to see the hole in the ceiling. "This section is completely under the lake. No upstairs. If there's a leak, we are in trouble. Get me out of these ropes!"

I crouched to my knees, tugging at the bindings earnestly, but they held fast. I didn't have a knife on me, nor did Gavin. Thinking fast, I rushed to the bench and grabbed the first item I spied with a blade: a hacksaw with pointed teeth. It was incredibly rusty, but it would have to do.

It was also rather dull I discovered as I hacked at the ropes on Gavin's arm. I was making a little headway, but the saw was not cutting fast enough for my taste. And to add to my anxiety, something in the ceiling must have given way, because the stream of water intensified, turning the pleasant trickling background noise into a scary splashing. My frustration increased.

The saw blade buckled and fell apart during my rough ministrations.

"Damn this thing!" I yelled as I angrily tossed it away. It hissed and steamed in the puddle where it landed.

I looked at it. How could it have gotten so hot as to evaporate water while I used it? The friction hadn't seemed that intense.

And then it hit me. My hands felt uncommonly warm. And that strange sensation, the hotness under my skin, was now located in the palm of my hand.

Could it be? I placed my palm on the ropes that had mocked the hacksaw. I focused on that strange energy, allowing it a means of escape.

The ropes I touched smoked. I gasped but kept my hand steady. Tiny embers ate away at the fibers, never fully catching on fire, but charring them at my discretion.

Gavin saw too and gaped. He wasted no time in ripping his arm out of the damaged ropes. I sat back at the marvel of my strange new power.

A power I seemingly stole from Hobbs.

"How?" he asked me, but I merely shook my head.

"No time to explain. C'mon, let's finish getting you free so that we can help the others."

He didn't argue, thankfully. Fully freeing him only took a matter of seconds with my new ability.

By now, the water level was a few inches deep, enough to cover the tops of my bare feet.

"I need to get Roger out. Help me!" I called to Gavin.

Together we forced the door open. Roger hadn't moved from his spot, bound as he was. The water on the floor had crept in here as well, under the door.

"Who's there?" Roger called in a timid voice. The otter stopped its writhing and let out a squeal at the sight of us, a rather joyous sound for conditions so dire.

"Roger, it's Cressida," I told him. Turning to Gavin, I said, "You free the otter while I work on Roger's ropes."

"Why is there an otter in here?" Gavin asked, perplexed. I didn't bother answering, as I had no clue. Instead, I turned my focus to Roger.

I lifted the blindfold off my father's eyes before laying a palm on each arm restraint. The stolen gift worked to eat through the ropes just as quickly as it had Gavin's. Roger smiled at me, seemingly not noticing the magic I was wielding.

"You *must* be my guardian angel," he commented. "You have a knack for showing up when I'm in need."

"Something like that," I muttered as I burned the last of the ropes off his legs.

He stood rather unsteadily. "How did you get around that large fellow?"

I glanced at the water on the floor, now licking at my ankles. "He met with an accident."

Roger did not seem taken aback by my statement. He wasn't cheerful about it either. All he said was, "How unfortunate." I couldn't tell if the comment was sarcastic or not. Frankly, I didn't care.

Instead, I focused on what was important. "We need to get out of here quickly. There's a hole in the ceiling, and the lake water is pouring in. Gavin, how is that cage coming?"

As an answer, Gavin managed to bend the wire bars enough to allow the otter to slip through. It did so immediately, running circles around Roger and splashing us with its gait.

"Time to go," I said. I marched out of the back room, entering the room with the corpse in the center. The water surrounding it took on a muddy red hue. I looked away, squeamish.

By the time we got to the door that led to the hallway, the water was past my ankles and dragging down my ripped dress. My feet were freezing, but I ignored it. Getting out of this flooding prison was a priority over worrying about painful feet.

The excess water on the ground made it difficult to open the door. Both Gavin and I pulled in unison, sending a small wave of water behind us. As the door begrudgingly opened, the hole in the ceiling let out a groan, followed by a sudden gush of lake water that seemed to be the alarming new rate.

"Move, move!" I yelled, ushering Roger through the door. The otter followed at his heels. Gavin pushed me forward, taking up the rear.

Out in the hallway, the sound of the alarm was louder. A man ran past us, splashing us with his steps, but he paid us no mind. Apparently, everyone was evacuating.

The water had been escaping under the door into the hallway this whole time, but now that the door was open, a steady puddle rippled along the floor ahead of us, growing in volume by the second. From the room we just left, the measure of water coming from the hole sounded torrential. We jogged as quickly as we could through the hallway, but by the time we reached the door that I recognized as the cattery, the water level was a good six inches deep and rising quickly. We were running out of time.

There was just one problem. Roger wasn't the only being I needed to save from this place.

I spun and grabbed Gavin's arm. "Listen, there's someone else I need to save from this prison. I want you to go ahead and make sure Roger gets out of here. Take this hallway. It will lead to a set of stairs. I'll catch up as soon as I can."

I should have anticipated that Gavin wouldn't simply listen and do what he was told. "No way. I can't leave you in here. You have to come with us."

I frowned at his concerned expression and shook my head. "Please, just help him. The only reason you're in this mess in the first place is because I dragged you into it. You owe it to yourself to save your hide at the first possible convenience. That's now. I'll be right behind you, I swear."

As sweet as it was that Gavin wanted to see me safely outside, I had a whole clowder of cats to get to safety, including my great-grandmother. And in order to successfully do that, I couldn't have Gavin breathing down my neck. Hopefully, he understood and let me be.

Instead, he grabbed my arm to pull me behind him, ignoring my words. I growled in frustration and punched him in the back of his shoulder as hard as I could.

"Ow!" he yelled, turning to look at me with pure irritation on his face. "What was that for?"

"For being an ass! I told you; I'll just be a minute or two behind you. I have no intention of drowning, but I just might drown *you* if you continue to ignore my wishes!" I took a deep breath. "Now, can you *please* get Roger to safety and stop worrying about me? I won't budge from this hall until you do. That means you're not only wasting your time to escape but mine too."

Gavin stared at me, his face devoid of emotion except for a small tick in his jaw. "You are without a doubt the most infuriating woman I know," he said. He picked up my hand again. I made to jerk it out of his grasp, but all he did was place a light kiss on my knuckles before releasing my hand. "Until we meet again, Cressida. It had better be soon."

With that, he turned and slogged away through the rising water with my father and the otter in front of him.

I breathed a sigh of relief as they turned the corner out of sight. Despite his shortcomings, Gavin was a good human. I could trust him to do everything in his power to see them out safely.

I marched to the cattery door and placed my hand on it. Before I could pull on the knob, a door just a few feet away opened, and a woman strode out. She stopped, startled at my presence. I froze as well, shocked.

She was a tall woman in her fifties, judging by the lines on her pale face. Her hair was loose, straight, and very long, a pale blonde cascade ending at her lower back. But this was not what caused me to stare.

It was her face.

She looked like Fleurette.

CHAPTER 30

Of course, this was not Fleurette, now that I had gotten a good look at the woman. Certainly, the rectangular shape of the face with the proud jaw was nearly the same, as was her mouth and the shape of her eyes. Fleurette's nose was not as narrow and pointed as this woman's, but the general shape still held true. The biggest difference between the women was their coloration; Fleurette was a study of warm browns in her eyes, hair, and skin complexion, while this new person was paler than even me.

Also, this woman appeared to be angry, an emotion I rarely saw in Fleurette.

She narrowed her eyes once she got over the shock of seeing me. "You!" she hissed. "You're the missing Curtain we've been searching for. I can't believe Greg didn't see the resemblance when he caught you. I suppose he didn't even know what Curtain looked like to *see* the resemblance."

I decided to play dumb. "I don't know what you're talking about."

Her eyes rolled. "You're the *heir*. To the legacy. I can't believe, after all this time of searching, you just waltzed in here."

She knew who I was, *what* I was. Time to go on the defensive. "I'm also the person who ruined your precious prison. And killed Hobbs."

Technically, I hadn't killed Hobbs; the falling debris had done that for me. But a little lie couldn't hurt at this moment.

She laughed maniacally. "Good for you. That prick deserved it. And I hate this place. But you"—she took a step toward me—"are still coming with me. You're my ticket out of here."

I widened my stance into a fighting position. "Over my dead body."

The woman cocked her head to the side. "That would be the ideal outcome, actually," she said. "After all, your presence is the only thing keeping her from returning."

And there it was. Just another affirmation that these nutjobs were indeed trying to bring Annie Coddle back. *Why* they wanted to allow her back into this world would have to wait to be answered. The woman raised her arms and began mumbling a spell under her breath.

I, too, raised my arms, summoning the fire magic for a fireball. I wouldn't go down without a fight.

The woman stopped mumbling, her eyes going wide with a look akin to fear. She seemed to be looking at my chest.

I took a millisecond to glance down. No, not my chest.

The necklace I wore. I could see it peeking out from behind the oversized tuxedo jacket I still wore.

"Where did you get that?" she asked in a breathy, almost-whisper.

"It was loaned to me." I refused to let my hands drop, even though the fireball wasn't very big. My stolen magic must have started to run out.

Her eyes stayed glued to the pendant resting between my clavicles. "No, it couldn't be," she murmured to herself. She looked stricken.

A male voice called out from beyond us, by the top of the stairs. "Thea, what's taking so long? We need to go!"

The woman broke from her self-induced trance and glanced at my quizzical face. "Stay away. Get out of here."

Before I could ask what was happening, she turned and ran, disappearing around the bend with much sloshing of water. I heard a heavy door slam not a minute later. If I had to guess, it was the door at the top of the stairs.

I only hoped she hadn't run into Gavin or my father as she left.

I took a deep breath to clear my mind from the odd encounter. I'd have to circle back to it later when my life and the life of the cats weren't in peril.

Before I could attempt to once again enter the cattery, a familiar sound echoed through the hall. A dog's deep bark.

I knew that bark from anywhere. "Grimm!" I yelled, barely believing my ears.

But suddenly, there he was, rounding the bend at a rapid speed. He saw me, let out a joyous bark, and launched his front legs onto my shoulders in a wet hug.

"Urgh!" His soaking wet legs trailed rivulets of frigid lake water down my bare skin. But I hugged him back anyway, ecstatic to see him. "Grimm! How in Gaia's greenery did you get here?"

"With me," replied a deep baritone voice from beyond Grimm.

I tensed, readying my stolen magic once again. But Grimm only lolled his tongue out and whimpered with pleasure at my presence as a man, tall and dark, stepped out of the shadows. He held his hands up placatingly.

"I'm sorry if I frightened you, Miss Curtain. My name is Melokuhle Ndou. I'm a GOG. It is a great honor to make your acquaintance."

Grimm retreated to four legs as I assessed the newcomer. I was understandably hesitant to trust anybody currently. A test was in order. "Mr. Ndou, what am I?"

He grinned, the white flash of his teeth almost jarring in the darkened hallway. "You are Cressida Curtain, of the line of Glivver, and currently, you are the last descendant. You are a cat."

I relaxed. "Thank you for humoring me. It's been a tough day already."

He nodded his head at my sentence. "Understandable, Miss Curtain. I am one of the regional GOGs for Eastern Oracune. Fleurette sent me to collect you from the prison. And your friend Grimm refused to stay behind. If you would follow me, please."

I caught the way he called Grimm my friend and not my dog; I liked this man. But I still had unfinished business. "Wait! I can't go yet; there are cats behind this door that I need to get to safety. And I need to make sure Gavin and Roger made it safely!"

Ndou pursed his lips. "Your friends are already out of the building and waiting in my boat. I met with them in the hallway and showed them the way we had come in. There were no guards or people in that direction, as they all seemed to have taken the stairs. But let me help you with your task, Miss Curtain."

I breathed a sigh of relief. They hadn't run into the Fleurette look-alike as I had dreaded. "Thank you. But please call me Cressida. What was your first name again?"

"I am called Melokuhle. If you think of me as being a 'mellow, cool guy,' it is easier to remember." He grinned at his mnemonic.

"That works. Help me open this door."

Together we pulled until the heavy door opened. I ushered Melokuhle through and then turned to Grimm. "I think it's best if you wait out here, partner. I think you might scare the cats too much. Sorry."

He whined but stayed put, wagging his tail slowly to show he held no hard feelings.

Inside the cattery, the water was about a foot deep. The sound of terrified yowling filled the room as I laid sight on an abundance of felines who looked completely hopeless at their predicament. The cats could still stand, but the level would soon be too high for them to do so. I needed to act fast.

"Melokuhle, I'm going to shift so I can talk to them," I said. He nodded in understanding. "But first, there's a severely elderly cat in that hole over there. I need you to fish her out and carry her to safety. She might have a tortoiseshell companion that may be freaked out by you handling her, but if you talk to the old cat and explain who you are and what you're doing, she can calm the tortie. Once you have her, leave the door open but get yourselves out. Grimm and I will be out shortly."

"This ancient cat, she is like you?"

I nodded. "My great-grandmother Serena."

Melokuhle's eyes grew wide at the name. "But she was my charge many years ago! I lost track of her after her daughter was born. This is fate!"

He immediately went to the hole, crouching down in the water to help Serena. I turned back to my task, shifting down into cat form. The size difference meant I was soaked within seconds, and I could barely keep my feet on the floor.

"Listen up, cats!" I yelled to the room at large. Multiple terrified eyes turned my way. "I'm getting you all out of here. Follow me!"

I half-walked, half-swam over to the hole in the wall I had escaped through earlier. It was still dry, being off the ground as it was. I turned around in front of it, pleased to note that the other felines had made their way over.

"Each of you needs to jump into this hole. Follow the tunnel until it opens into a bigger space, then take the duct up. You can use your nose to track my scent but make sure you turn to the west once you are out of the duct. From there, you can access a jail cell with a mattress leaning against the wall to the window.

Jump up to the window and jump down to freedom! I won't leave until every cat is out of this room."

One by one, the cats jumped into the hole. They moved incredibly efficiently, for which I was thankful, considering the water level was getting higher by the minute. I had to help the last few stragglers find purchase into the hole, since jumping out of neck-deep water was difficult. At last, though, every cat had made it out.

Melokuhle was long gone, but I double-checked that Serena was indeed missing from her hidey-hole. Mitzi was gone too. She must have stuck with Serena since I did not see her in the escape line.

That meant it was only me and Grimm that needed to get out.

I paddled my front legs while walking with my back legs to keep my head above water. With this strange locomotion, I made my way back to the hallway where Grimm patiently stood.

"Cressida, I am so happy to see you. Last night was the worst night of my life when you left." He nosed me lovingly on the head.

"Grimm, I am so sorry I left you behind. I never want to have to do that again. But can we discuss this when I'm not about to go underwater?"

"Oh. Of course. Here." Grimm crouched down, motioning me to climb onto his back, which was still well above the waterline.

I wasted little time in doing so. "Thanks. Now, how do we get out of here?"

Grimm turned direction and started wading down the hallway. "This way. We took a boat to the shore around back and found an old stairway that led down into the rocks. There was a door down there that the tall man surmised led to the basement level. It was locked, so he had to blast it open. The blast took the whole door and part of the wall with it."

A sudden boom from deeper in the dungeon startled us. The ceiling and walls groaned as if a great weight had been placed upon them. And the tell-tale noise of falling rocks boomed in front of us.

"That didn't sound good. Let's hurry," I urged my canine steed.

He complied, trotting through the water that was already up to his shoulders. We didn't get much farther, though. Instead of a doorway that led to our freedom, we were met by a collapsed pile of rubble, completely blocking the hallway in front of us.

CHAPTER 31

I suppressed the urge to panic. "Now what?" I asked. I hated asking the question, but seriously, I was at a loss. Our obvious escape route was completely compromised, and the water was rising much faster than before. To make matters worse, the cave-in had occurred before we had gotten to the stairs, leaving that means of departure void as well.

I could go back to the cattery and leave the same way the rest of the cats did, but Grimm's size meant that route was impassible for him; he'd be lucky to be able to stick his huge head in that hole. I refused to leave my friend behind to die in a watery grave.

"Are there any other ways we can get out of this?" Grimm asked.

"No. There are no windows down here, just solid walls. The only other hole is the one in the ceiling where the water is currently pouring in from."

"That's a way out, isn't it?"

My claws flexed of their own accord, digging into Grimm's wet backside. "You can't be serious."

He huffed and turned his head enough to give me a side-eye. "Do you have a better plan? Because the way I see it, it's either explore that option or give up and die right now."

I growled, a mix of irritation and terror. "Fine. I'll show you the way. But I can't guarantee it will be a viable option."

"That's my girl."

My heart pattered at his praise. The sensation was doused quickly once I realized what we were about to do. It was sheer madness, but what choice did we have? Grimm started wading in the direction I guided him.

"Cressida, if this doesn't work, I want you to take the exit you told the other cats to take. It's the only way you can make it out of here if my way isn't an option."

His words filled me with dread. "What will you do?"

"I will die, most likely. But I'll die with the knowledge that I had the best relationship with a cat any dog could hope for."

Fear seized me even as his words warmed my heart. "Then, partner, we had better hope your idea works. Because I'm not leaving you."

"Stubborn cat."

"Asinine dog."

Grimm was now paddling, as the water level surpassed his leg height. His back went under the surface as his legs left the floor, but I stayed attached to him, with only my underbelly and legs getting wet. I was light enough that I didn't pose a risk of dragging Grimm down.

He swam until we reached the door with the window. It was still open, propped by the force of the water. The last time I saw this room, the flow of water was probably about a foot in diameter. Now, it gushed from the ceiling with a volume easily three times that. The sound was intense, especially to my sensitive feline ears.

"Bring me to that bench!" I directed. The bench that held the torture tools was off to the side of the hole but still close enough that I could observe the ceiling to my satisfaction. Plus, the surface was just barely underwater, still allowing me to stand on it easily.

Grimm paddled over, skirting around the deluge of falling water. I jumped from his back to the bench, giving my body a little shake to dislodge some of the water from my fur. I eyed the hole.

It was hard to see through the raging waterfall, but based on the size of the downpour, I worried it still would not be sufficient to allow Grimm through. I needed to make it wider.

"Watch out!" I yelled at my companion. "I'm going to try to make the hole bigger!"

Grimm swam until he was against the wall near the bench. I shimmered up and gathered the stolen fire magic to my fists.

I only had enough oomph left to create one decent fireball. Having never thrown one before, I hoped it was enough to break the ceiling wider. With a breath and a quick prayer to the gods, I threw the molten ball, aiming for the section of ceiling next to the hole.

A loud *fwoom* rocked the masonry, and the ceiling let out a groan of defeat. Another large patch of the ceiling crumbled and fell, the chunks splashing me thoroughly. The volume of water pouring in more than doubled instantly.

I changed back into my cat form, noting that the water was already up to my belly and rising exponentially faster. Grimm swam closer to me, allowing me to regain my position on his back.

"Well, that seemed to do the trick," I said.

Grimm groaned in his throat. "How did you do that, Cress? You have fire magic now?"

"Had. I seemed to have stolen it from a bad guy. But I think it's all gone now."

As Grimm paddled in place, the ceiling loomed closer. The shrinking of our space triggered claustrophobia in me, a terrifying sensation I had never before experienced. My mouth opened in an involuntary pant. I tamped down on an instinct to panic.

The panic won out anyway. "Grimm, I don't think I can do this! I don't know how to swim! I can't—"

"You can do this, CC," Grimm replied, his voice calm. "You are the strongest cat I know. If anyone can swim out of a lakebed dungeon, it's you."

"But I can't swim! I wasn't meant for this type of thing."

"Do you remember our last job together? The swamp? You didn't think you could get in. Well, all you needed was a little push, and then you did great, even though you didn't enjoy it. So, here's your little push: we're going to go underwater, and you will hate it, but you will *do* it. Because you are tough, and you are brave, and most importantly, it's our only option now, love."

His words, soothing yet firm, helped me rein in the worst of my terror. He was right. What choice did I have? Dying wasn't an option.

I had one last complaint, though. "*Why* did it have to be water?"

It wasn't long before we were within touching distance of the ceiling.

"This is it, Cress," Grimm warned me. "As soon as this room fully fills, I'll swim up through the hole. I need you to climb closer to my head and dig in with your claws. Do not let go, do you understand?"

My head hit the ceiling. I gasped as my body became fully submerged. I crawled up Grimm's neck as he bade. Only our heads peeked out of the water now. "What if I hurt you with my claws?"

"The pain will be a good reminder that you're still there. Are you ready? Take a deep breath; our air is about to run out."

I clambered further up Grimm's head, sinking my claws into the fur and skin behind his eyes. Grimm flinched but stayed stoic through the pain. The water pushed our heads against the top of the ceiling.

Grimm sucked in a breath as his head went under. I did the same.

And then I was completely submerged.

I closed my eyes, keeping my claws extended and gripped tightly upon Grimm. Our bodies scraped against the ceiling as Grimm moved toward the hole.

And then, there was nothing scraping at my back. I felt almost weightless, my body trying to rise away from Grimm's head. Only my claws kept me tethered as we drifted up, up, up.

My lungs burned. Cats were not meant to be diving experts. I couldn't hold my breath much longer.

Grimm's sure strokes broke the surface, thrusting our heads into the air. I gasped a quick breath before shaking my head briskly to clear the water away from my nose. I breathed deeply, never so happy for my lungs to fill. Rapidly blinking my eyes to dislodge the moisture, I took in our new surroundings.

The bright morning light made me squint until my eyes adjusted. It was a major change to the dim interior of the basement level. The sunny weather, though crisp in temperature, was still exhilarating.

I carefully dislodged my claws from Grimm's skin and settled farther down on his back. "Grimm, I will never doubt you again."

He snorted. "Thanks, Cress. I'll hold you to that. Listen, I think we should head back to the prison's island. It's a closer swim than the mainland shore. Besides, Melokuhle may still have his boat there."

"Sounds good to me."

Grimm paddled efficiently in the direction of the island. Once on dry land, I jumped off of his back. I gave myself a thorough shake to dislodge as much lake water as possible. Grimm did the same. Once we both were satisfied with our level of dryness, Grimm bent his head to sniff at the ground, scenting for our party. After catching the scent, he led me around a bend, trotting with anticipation.

I spied a rut in the gravel by the edge of the water, which looked suspiciously like the track a boat would leave after being unmoored. Grimm confirmed my suspicion a second later, as he aimlessly circled the area where the boat had been.

"They left us," he said despondently.

Had they thought we had died? After all, we should have been emerging only a few minutes after Melokuhle did. Still, I found it staggering that they would give up so easily.

Grimm stiffened and perked his ears toward the building. "Listen."

I internally groaned. Now what? But I turned my ears forward, capturing the faint sound Grimm had heard. A grown man crying.

We raced toward the sound, Grimm beating me by a tail. The ground dipped here, showing a stairwell cut into the earth. At the top of the stairs sat Melokuhle, his back to us. He was hunched over, cradling something as he let out a keening cry. Beside him, Mitzi the tortoiseshell placed her feet on his arm to peer at the object in his arms.

My back hairs tingled as I pieced together this scene, causing a spike of dread to pierce my chest. "Oh no."

I transformed into a human and raced to his side. My great-grandmother lay peacefully in his arms like a baby, her head leaning over his arm as if she lounged in contentment. Her ancient eyes were open, but the unseeing stare could only mean one thing.

I placed a hand on Melokuhle's shoulder. He startled imperceptibly and turned to look at me before letting out another sob.

"Oh, Melokuhle," I soothed. "What happened?"

He used his free hand to wipe his eyes and turned his torso my way, showing more of Serena's body to me. "I got her out of the cattery and ran her to our exit point. Once I got outside and to the top of the stairs, she let out a gasping sound. I–I ..." he hitched his breath, losing the ability to speak.

"Shh, it's okay." I crouched down and rubbed both of his arms to help calm him. Mitzi purred and rubbed against his side.

He took another hitching breath and cleared his throat. "I looked at her. She was looking around but calm. She let out a big breath with a purring sound as she gazed at the sky." Melokuhle sniffled and took a second to regain his composure. "She didn't take another breath, Cressida." He broke down into sobs again.

I looked up at the sky, gazing at the last thing my great-grand-mother had seen. "She was trapped in that hole for the last twen-ty-odd years, Melokuhle," I said gently. "She was incredibly old and ready to die. I think she just wanted to see the outside world one last time. See the sun and feel the breeze on her fur. You gave her that. It was the best last wish you could have granted her. Thank you."

Melokuhle, openly sobbing, shifted Serena's body into a one-arm cradle. His free arm reached out, seeking solace in hu-man touch.

In any other circumstance, the thought of hugging a human, especially one I barely knew, would have been enough to make my spine crawl. I was demonstrably not touchy-feely, unless it was a family member. But Melokuhle, this tall man I had met just minutes before, had shown my great-grandmother more kindness in her last moments alive than she had received since being incarcerated. I would do anything for him to show him what a gift he had given her. I opened my arms wide and leaned into his one-armed hug, resting my damp head against his warm shoulder.

I allowed my own grief to find a passage out through some silent tears. Mitzi continued to purr and rub up against Melokuhle, a sign of her own understanding and acceptance. Even Grimm came over and leaned against my back, letting me know that he was there for me.

Together, we mourned Serena as the sun continued to shine with early spring warmth, one last gift to my great-grandmother.

CHAPTER 32

We left the island shortly, once Melokuhle's grief abated and his tears dried up. He reverently wrapped Serena's body in his jacket, choosing to continue to carry her.

Melokuhle explained that he had forced Gavin and Roger (and the otter) to take the boat back to the mainland where Fleurette waited, once he realized Serena had passed away. Incidentally, more than a few cats from the cattery had made their way to the party, and they also jumped into the boat before it rowed off. I could only imagine what Gavin had thought of *that*.

Melokuhle had no idea our lives had been endangered by the collapse of the hallway. He had assumed I was just taking an extra-long time evacuating the cats. I did not hold it against him to have not known. I doubted there would have been anything he could have done to rectify the situation.

With no boat, our options were to risk walking over the bridge at the front of the prison and hope no ACF members were skulking about, or swim to shore. I was drying out nicely and had no inclination to reverse that process. So, bridge it was.

As it turned out, we traversed the bridge with zero mishaps. I thanked whatever gods had made it so, because I was fed up with surprises for the day. We even found more cats that had stayed on the island, unsure what to do. Once they saw us braving the bridge, they scampered along too, joyous to be leaving the wretched place with its traumatic experiences.

We didn't see a single human. I surmised the destruction of Addelboro Correctional Facility—at least from the ground down—had been a blow to the operation, and they had evacuated and regrouped elsewhere. Still, I kept my human senses on high alert and told Grimm to do the same since his were currently sharper than mine.

Back on the mainland, we had a small trek to where Fleurette had stationed herself.

"She didn't want to meet too close to the train station and the bridge," Melokuhle explained as he skirted around the lake shore for half a mile. We walked a small hiking trail with amazing views of the lake. Even the prison, with its neo-gothic-inspired architecture, looked scenic in the middle.

The meeting spot was a larger clearing on the hike, safe and secure from prying eyes. As we approached the area, I heard raised voices. It was Gavin and Fleurette, from the sounds of it.

"... it's been too long. We should go back and look for her." Gavin sounded incredibly agitated.

"Go back and get who?" I asked as we reached the site.

Gavin and Fleurette were at the forefront of the scene, with Fal and Roger—and yep, the otter—at the other end of the clearing, sitting on a log together. And on the clearing floor beside Fal was Wren, fast asleep on her side with her hair fanned out under her. And here and there, a random cat could be found. It was a sight that quickened my heart with gratitude.

Both Fleurette and Gavin turned at the sound of my voice, their faces morphing from heavy concern to delight.

"Thank Hecate you're alright!" Fleurette rushed to my side, engulfing me in a crushing hug. "We were just about to send the boat back to find you."

"We were?" Gavin asked snidely. "As I recall, you shot that idea down when I suggested it." His face was still a mess, with dried blood on his upper lip and one eye nearly swelled shut. Still, he gazed at me with an obvious warmth, a reminder that Gavin was still unrequitedly smitten with me. I focused on my friend's hug to temporarily hide from the awkwardness of the situation.

Fleurette let go of me and waved her hand to dismiss his claim. "I was coming round to the idea," she replied. "You had barely made dry land before you wanted to turn around and go back for her. I had faith that Cressida would make it back."

"It was a bit hairier at the end than I care to admit," I replied with honesty. "But Fleurette, how in Freya's furs did you get here so fast? When Rupert told me he would return to you in three hours, I assumed it would be much longer before you came."

Fleurette glanced over at Gavin. "Now that Mr. Ndou has returned, will you please help him with his boat?"

"More secrets, ladies?" Gavin smirked. "I know, I know. I'd be happy to assist this fine fellow." He walked over to Melokuhle, who still held Serena in his arms. Together, the two men walked over to the boat, which was moored a short distance away.

Fleurette ushered me to the opposite side of the clearing, approaching the Ramberts and my father. Now that I was closer, I could see that Fal had placed a bandage on Roger's wrist. And Wren's head was lying atop an article of clothing that seemed very familiar.

"My vest!" I exclaimed with happiness.

Fleurette looked pleased. "I thought you might want it. You're never without it back home. Of course, now it's being used as a pillow. I should have grabbed other clothes for you too, but I wasn't thinking properly. I was a bit rushed."

I shrugged. "I'll make do. If I can just get this blasted corset off soon, I think I'll be more comfortable. But yes, now that we're back on the subject, how are you here so quickly?"

"As soon as Rupert returned and we knew of your location, I contacted Melokuhle, as he was the GOG closest to Addelboro. I told him to meet me here by the lake. And then Wren projected all of us over. It completely wiped her energy, poor girl." Fleurette spoke in hushed tones.

"She brought you, Fal, *and* Grimm? It's no wonder she's asleep." Wren's projectionism allowed her to project herself to other dimensions. Last summer, she learned she could also project others with her. She had amazing stamina, but performing these large projections took a lot of energy. She had just transported three people and a dog to a location she had never been to within a blink of an eye. That was no easy feat.

"How did you know she'd be able to get you here?"

"Honestly, I didn't," Fleurette admitted. "It was a calculated risk. But she was able to transport herself to other dimensions without first visiting them, so it made sense she'd be able to project to a new spot in the *same* dimension. Once I had the location from Rupert, I showed her on a map and hoped for the best."

"So, I understand why you brought Grimm, and Wren was needed, of course, but why Fal?" I asked.

Fleurette chuckled. "Because Fal refused to be left behind. Besides, I figured his healing magic might come in handy. He's a natural at it, unlike me."

As if realizing he had been under inspection, Fal looked up at us. "Cressida!" he shouted, jumping to his feet. He rushed over to me, giving me a hug.

Over his shoulder, I made eye contact with Roger, who gave me a friendly wave but stayed seated. He looked completely exhausted.

Fal let go of me and examined my face with the scrutiny of a mother hen. "How'd you get that scratch?"

I gave a small start and lifted my hand to my head, feeling around until I found the raised edges of a fresh scratch on my forehead. "Catfight," I said simply.

Fal tugged me over to the log, ushering me to sit next to my father. "Give me a minute, and I'll have that fixed right up."

"Oh, don't worry about it. You should really take care of Gavin next. His eye looks painful. He also has a bad burn on his hand."

Fal shrugged. "I tried, but he told me to help Roger first."

That was incredibly nice of Gavin. I would have said uncharacteristically so if I hadn't gotten to know him a little better over this adventure.

Roger stood up. "This young man is a standup individual. I really appreciate your help, Mr. Williams."

Fal blushed at the praise.

Roger scanned the lake, his faded blue eyes squinting at the sunny weather. "If you'll excuse me, I think I'll help those two with the boat." He walked away, the otter at his heels. I'd need to ask him about that soon, but there were more pressing matters.

Fal smoothed a tonic over my forehead, covering my wound. The mixture was slippery but soothing, dulling the pain immediately.

He smiled at his handiwork. "There. That should be healed within an hour. Any other injuries?"

I glanced at my hands. They had been burned by Hobbs, but ever since I had stolen his magic, they hadn't hurt. And the palms were a normal shade again. I must have been temporarily fireproof, and that alone had healed my burns.

I did have a cut on my ribs, but there was no way of getting to it short of disrobing. Besides, it was superficial. "No. That was it."

My jacket pocket gave an almost imperceptible vibration. Oh

right. The watch in the right-hand pocket.

Wasn't there something in the left-hand pocket too?

The realization hit me with complete alarm. "The mouse!"

Both Fleurette and Fal gave a start at my outcry. "What?" Fleurette asked in confusion.

I fished into the left pocket, my heart beating a rapid staccato. I couldn't believe I had forgotten about my mouse friend. I had shimmered with him on my person. Twice. I had never placed a living being in my interdimensional pocket before. I had no clue what that would do to an organism.

Please don't be dead, I chanted in my mind as I finally felt a small furry object with my fingertips. Ever so carefully, I wrapped my fingers around the listless body, bringing the tiny rodent out into my palm.

He was not moving and was very limp. My heart plummeted with the implication. I stroked his soft fur, mourning this tiny life. He would have died in the prison if not for me, drowning with his brethren, but it was an infinitesimal consolation that did little to remove the guilt.

My finger stroked over his ribcage. It moved.

I gasped and brought the mouse closer to my face to examine him. A shallow rise and fall shifted his little chest. I rubbed his side briskly, hoping to elicit further movement.

The mouse stretched and opened his beady eyes. He let out a squeak as he got to his feet, rather unsteadily. He acted as if he had been drugged but seemed otherwise fine.

"You're alive!" I cheered, petting his head. "I can't believe it. You really are one lucky mouse."

Fleurette peered at my mouse. "He was in your pocket the whole time?" She understood the implications as much as I did.

I nodded. "I wish he could tell me what it was like in my interdimensional pocket. It seems to have put him to sleep."

"It's nice to know that living things can transform with you," Fleurette mused. "I wonder what this might mean for the future."

My lucky mouse spun a tight circle in my palm, seemingly happy. There was no way I'd put him on the ground; the place was now teeming with random cats from the prison. I brought him up to my shoulder, allowing him to perch up there. He was more than content to stay there. I turned toward the lake, my heart feeling lighter than it had in a while.

Roger and the otter stood at the edge of the water, gazing out at the expanse. I approached him with more sound than I'd normally make so as not to startle him. He turned to me once we were side by side.

"It's odd," he said. "The last three years of my life have been nothing but heartache. Even when I landed that job, I wasn't feeling good about my lot in life. To have everything crumble so spectacularly should have me despairing right now. But instead, when I look out at this lake, with the sun shining and plants beginning to bloom, all I feel is at peace."

"You nearly died," I said, not sugarcoating it. "It puts a lot of things into perspective."

"You're very wise for one so young. I take it you've had a near brush with death as well?"

I shrugged. "Not counting today? Yes."

He nodded at my words. The otter nudged his leg.

"Oh yes," he said, as if the otter had reminded him. "What now? Will they come after us again?"

I pursed my lips. "As far as they know, we died down there. And you were already dead in the system, from what I could tell. But Roger, I wouldn't risk your safety on that assumption. They may not give up."

I tapped my chin in thought. I hadn't expected to be in this predicament. All I had wanted to do was clear his name so he could continue living his life. But Roger was a target of Annie Coddle, thanks to my mother and me. A normal life was not exactly attainable anymore.

"That guy over there, Melokuhle, and my friend Fleurette are part of a secret organization called GOGS. They are here to protect and help me, and they can offer you the same assurance."

"Why would they do that?"

"It's because of who was after you." *And because of who my family is.* The words to tell him I was his daughter were on the tip of my tongue. But looking at him, at the hell he had just gone through because of me, I lost the nerve. Instead, I said, "I'd like for you to accompany us back to Knobby Hill, where we can make sure you are safe. Will you do that?"

Roger stared out at the water. He turned to look at me with his kind eyes. "Miss Curtis, how could I refuse? You've truly been my guardian angel through this, and I'd be an idiot not to go with you. I accept."

A breath whooshed out of me. "Thank you, Roger."

The otter pushed on Roger's leg again to get his attention. He looked down and stared at the otter for a moment as it twirled in a little circle by his feet.

"Okay, I have to ask," I said. "What's with the otter?"

Roger gave a small grin. "Miss Curtis ... Cressida, this is my friend who helped me after I left my apartment rather suddenly. She took me in, and she helped me plan to get into the ball. She was waiting for me outside. When I left the mansion, I was unfortunately found out, and we were knocked unconscious rather suddenly. She's been like this ever since, I suspect, to keep her anonymity." He looked at her intently. "My dear, I know you are eager to leave and go home. I do believe I am in good hands with this company. Please, be well and may we meet again one day."

I was still trying to wrap my brain around the fact that the otter was also a person, a shifter, according to my father. I wasn't sure why it surprised me, given the fact that I was also masquerading in a body different to the one I was born in. Perhaps it was the fact I had never met another shifter before. The human shifters were a reclusive bunch, usually sticking to their own kind ever since the Shifter War tried to wipe them out over a century ago.

Still mulling this new information over, I watched as the otter tipped her head at my father with reverence before she slid smoothly into the lake. As she swam off into the distance, the sun shone on her wet head. I could swear it reflected a familiar violet hue as she cavorted in the water and finally swam out of sight.

Shaking my head, I turned to the goings-on on my other side. Melokuhle and Gavin had dragged the boat up onto the shore, the former having done so one-handed since he still cradled the body of Serena reverently in his arms. Once the vessel was sufficiently moored, Melokuhle reached into his pocket and produced a tiny bottle. Uncorking it with his teeth, he sprinkled the contents over the boat, muttering words of power under his breath. The boat shivered in place before it began to shrink. Within seconds, it was a mere four inches long. Melokuhle reached down and plucked the boat from the ground, placing it in the pocket of his shirt.

I gaped at the spectacle as I approached. "How did you do that?"

He smiled. "One of my special potions. It only works on objects, nothing living. It makes transportation much easier." He patted his pocket gently before his face turned somber. "I must get going, young one."

I glanced downward at Mitzi. She stayed by Melokuhle's feet, unsure of her place in the world now that she was free for the first time in her short life. She was plucky, that one, holding her own despite the drastic change of scenery and the strange humans and massive dog that now kept her company.

I also swept my gaze over to Gavin, who stood awkwardly nearby. I gave him a look. "Gavin, you need to get your face taken care of. Fal can help you now."

"Not pulling any punches, are you?" he shot back.

"No, and neither did Hobbs. Go get fixed up."

He laughed before screwing up his face in a grimace of pain. He did as I requested, leaving me alone with Melokuhle as I had hoped.

I spoke quietly. "What will you do with Serena? And her?" I motioned at Mitzi.

Melokuhle reverently stroked Serena's fur that peeked out of the jacket she was wrapped in. "I will honor Serena with a proper burial on my property. Her life will forever be cherished by me since I failed her long ago. She must have said something to this cat because she does not seem afraid of me. If she will let me, I will take her into my home and give her a wonderful life to make up for her imprisonment."

"You're a good man, Melokuhle."

He waved one-handedly. "I am just a man, Cressida Curtain. I have made errors. But I will make up for them with this one."

"Her name is Mitzi. Let me talk to her before you go and explain what is happening."

Melokuhle's eyes lit up. "It would be a great honor to see your true form if you would be so amendable."

I smiled at his reverence, as misplaced as I thought it to be. "Of course. Give me a second. Oh wait—here." I carefully scooped Lucky off my shoulder, placing him in Melokuhle's free hand. Fortunately, neither the mouse nor the man seemed to mind.

I trotted into the surrounding woods, Grimm by my side,

until I was sure of my privacy. Once I was changed into cat form, I bounded back, running up to Mitzi and ignoring the gasp of happiness from Melokuhle.

"Mitzi, are you well? I'm so sorry about Serena," I said.

She rubbed against my body, taking comfort from my company. She must have done this same maneuver with my great-grandmother hundreds of times during their captivity. "It's weird to be out again," she admitted. "But despite losing Serena, she's free too, and I can't be sad about that."

"This man, Melokuhle, was Serena's guardian years ago. He'd like to take you home and adopt you."

"Oh, I've already adopted *him*. Before she died, Serena told me to trust him, and I can already see he is a good human. I will happily live in his home. Thank you, Cressida."

My spirits lifted even higher. "Have a good life, Mitzi," I told her before dashing back to the woods to shift.

When I came back, Melokuhle was already straddling a mechanized bicycle with a large basket attached to the front. I had briefly noted its existence in the clearing but had not given it a moment's thought. Clearly, it belonged to Melokuhle, and it was how he had arrived on the scene.

He placed Serena in the basket with tender care. Having freed his arms finally, he motioned me over. He held out his hand to me, revealing my mouse in his palm.

"A friend for a friend," he said.

I let Lucky scamper from his palm to mine and then up to my shoulder. Once he was situated, I bent over and picked up Mitzi, placing her in the basket next to Serena.

"She's already chosen you. I know you'll take good care of her."

Melokuhle passed his hand down Mitzi's spine. She purred and settled into the basket, cuddling up against Serena one last time.

"This meeting was fortuitous. For me, for Serena, for you, and for Mitzi. May your days be filled with the breath of wind and the kiss of sun. Fate be with you, Cressida!" Melokuhle started the engine, which purred to life, and with a final wave, he rode away.

Gavin approached as I watched the tall GOG ride away. "That Fal is a wonder. How old is he again?"

I looked at Gavin, noting the swelling and contusions on his face already looked better. "He's sixteen. I'm glad you finally wised up and got some help. Your face was looking rather horrid."

"That would be a crime, wouldn't it?"

I chuckled as I turned to join Fleurette, who was sitting on the ground next to a stirring Wren. Gavin followed after me.

"Melokuhle took off?" she asked.

I nodded. "And how exactly are we to get home?"

Fleurette eyed Gavin with a steely look she usually reserved for misbehaving children or cats. "Mr. St. Cloud. You are being allowed a glimpse into a rather secret affair. Do not make me regret it."

Gavin gave a tiny bow. "I wouldn't dream of it. I swear with my life this won't leave the scene."

Fleurette scrutinized him for a heartbeat longer. "Very good." She turned to Fal. "As soon as your sister is fully awake, I want her to take you home."

"Can't we all go?" I asked, surprised.

She shook her head. "It was enough strain to bring over as many people as she did. Now there's more, and she's still depleted."

"But why do we need to go? Why can't we stay with you?" Fal's voice took on a pleading whine.

She smiled. "Because you and Wren have school tomorrow. Besides, I need you back at the house to take care of things. Someone needs to let my dad and Cressida's mom know what happened. We'll need to figure out a different means of transportation, and we might be gone for a few days."

"About that ..." Gavin interrupted. "I might be able to help with the transportation bit."

Fleurette and I exchanged glances. She smiled at me.

"We would be most grateful for your help, Mr. St. Cloud," she told him.

CHAPTER 33

G avin's help turned out to be very helpful, indeed.

Shortly after Melokuhle left, Wren roused herself enough to complain about being ordered back home with her brother. She relented in short order, however, after listening to the wisdom of her elders and receiving the "disapproving Flo look" from her guardian. She stuck around long enough to give me a crushing hug before grabbing Fal's arm and folding the two of them into nothingness. It was still a bizarre sight to behold, even after all these months had passed since the last time I witnessed it.

With the siblings taken care of, it was down to me, Roger, Fleurette, Gavin, and Grimm. I was more than happy to pass the reins to someone else for a change, because I was tired, dirty, and uncomfortable thanks to the once-fabulous dress I still wore. Not to mention, the eastern portion of the Oracune Region was a completely different climate than what I was used to—dry, dusty, and containing very few trees once we ventured away from the lakeside. It was a far cry from the forested greenery I was familiar with.

Gavin, though, knew exactly where we were and easily took charge. He breezily reminded me, "I told you, Cressida, I grew up near here. My father's house is just a couple of miles to the east."

What he failed to tell us was that his father's "house" was, in fact, a mansion that rivaled Elkin's.

"What is *this*?" I hissed as Gavin led us up a palatial driveway to a set of enormous front doors. I suddenly felt very grubby indeed with my ripped and water-stained dress, filthy bare feet, and an oversized tuxedo jacket that had definitely seen better days. In fact, the only member of our party who looked decent was Fleurette, and even she seemed out of place amongst this finery.

"I thought I had mentioned my father was rich," Gavin said in an attempt at an explanation.

"I assumed you meant he was well-off in terms of upper class, not that he *owned* the upper class."

I had no time for further argument, however. As we reached the massive doors, the right side creaked open, showing an older man in a fine uniform on the other side.

"Master Gavin!" he exclaimed.

"Ah, Darwin, good to see you!" Gavin greeted with true affection. He asked in a lower tone, "Is Rafferty here?"

Darwin seemed slightly ruffled by the question. "Your *father*, sir, is not currently residing at this home, you may be relieved to hear. He has temporarily taken up residence at the coast house."

Gavin visibly relaxed. "That is good news."

The butler continued, "Have you come to stay for a time, sir?"

Gavin turned to look us over before addressing the older man. "No, Darwin, sorry to disappoint you. I'm still not interested in making this my home." Gavin patted the man's arm. "But I think we will spend the night, and in the morning, I'll need to borrow one of the carriages in order to get back to Tinuka County. This was a bit of an unexpected visit for us."

Darwin bobbed his head at this. "Very good, sir. I will see to preparing rooms for you and your guests, and I will inform the groomsman of your traveling needs."

"Good man. Thanks, Dar."

I grinned at the nickname; it was evident that Gavin had a better relationship with his butler than he did with his father. I glanced over at Roger, wondering if we would have any sort of relationship. I had decided it was prudent to keep in the dark about the whole father-daughter thing for a bit longer, at least until we made it back to Knobby Hill. For his safety, of course.

It was entirely possible I was stalling. I chose not to examine that too closely.

Darwin was a marvel at his job; within no time he had us in guest rooms—Grimm naturally staying with me—with a promise of a filling meal to come. Each room had its own en suite bathroom, for which I was sure Gavin and Roger appreciated, but all I wanted to do was transform and give myself a good grooming. It would do nothing to fix this disaster of a dress, however.

A knock on my door broke me from my thoughts. I answered it, surprised to see Gavin on the other side. He held up a bundle for me.

"I figured you'd be more comfortable out of that dress. These are my old clothes, from when I was younger. They might be too big for you, but they'll feel better, at least."

I took the proffered bundle. "That's incredibly thoughtful of you. Thanks."

Gavin looked almost sheepish at my words. He pointed to his own thoroughly trashed button-up shirt. "I'm off to the shower and a change of clothes myself." His eyes twinkled mischievously. "You could join me, if you like."

I gave him a look but said nothing. I knew his offer was made in jest, and, in fact, was a cover for an unspoken conversation, one that hung in the air between us like over-ripened fruit.

Before I could address or dismiss the tacit heaviness, Grimm, who had snuck up behind me, growled menacingly.

Gavin only smiled. "I'll take that as a no." He sauntered off down the hallway.

I shut the door, shooting Grimm a look. "Was that really necessary?"

Grimm fixed me with amber eyes. He waved his tail back and forth, keeping it low to the ground. Clearly, he thought so.

I changed quickly, relishing the removal of the corset that bruised my ribs. Gavin's clothes were a bit too baggy, but their comfort was more important than their looks. And once I had donned my vest, it cinched up some of the looseness. Besides, I needed some cat time, which made the clothes a complete non-issue.

Grimm accosted me as soon as I was back in a communicative shape. "What on earth is going on between you and the clod?"

I stretched my back, trying to formulate an answer. "Grimm, you simply can't go through an experience like that with someone without having some of your perceptions changed. Gavin may have been an utter jerk to me once upon a time, but much of it is an act. I think some of my defensiveness has been an act, too. A means to protect my vulnerability."

Grimm snorted, clearly not convinced. "And the fact that you smelled like him?"

I glared at my partner. His jealousy was showing again. "We were trapped in a box together for hours while on the train. Things got real."

"How real are we talking?"

"Real enough that it turns out he's attracted to me. Has been from the start."

Grimm made an odd guttural sound in his throat. "And what

about you? Are you attracted to him?”

I flicked the tip of my white tail. “I suppose I am. We kissed.”

The great beast before me stumbled back a step at my revelation, the noise escaping his throat a pained moan. The sound made my heart lurch.

“Grimm, stop! My curse made it clear that my attraction was only that. It’s surface deep. I don’t love the guy, and I never will. I can’t. As soon as the curse flared, it killed any desire for Gavin.” I cautiously approached him. He would never hurt me, but he seemed in distress. I gently brushed up against his leg, rubbing my chin affectionately upon him. “Even if the curse hadn’t brought me to my senses, I still wouldn’t be with Gavin. We are too different. The fact that he reacted to meeting me with bullying as a means of flirting will never sit right with me. Any romantic entanglement would be unhealthy in the end. But even so, I can’t help that I feel differently for him, buddy. He showed me a side I had never seen before. I don’t hate him. But I don’t love him. That I can guarantee.”

Grimm relaxed, sinking onto his belly and nuzzling me with his snout. “*I* still don’t like him, Cressida.”

I purred placatingly, settling myself between Grimm’s front legs. “That is your decision to make. You don’t have to like him. But you have to respect my decision to be friendly with him.”

Grimm sighed through his nose, the air ruffling the fur on my back. “For you, Cressida, I’d do just about anything.”

That night, after a hearty meal in the much-too-grand dining hall, and after retiring to my room with Grimm, I stayed sleepless. My partner was not afflicted similarly, and his sonorous breaths made a steady backdrop to my insomnia.

Same with my mouse friend. Lucky had decided that Grimm was to be trusted, and he now slept curled up on the shaggy dog's neck.

I was more than tired; this day had been one of the worst in my short life, barring the day I had confronted Annie Coddle face to face. My mind would not quiet, though, as I was barraged by the mental images of the prison, of the cattery, of the countless felines who had been caught, tormented, and used as targets by the fire maniac Hobbs, of the death of my only other living relative ... The unsettling list went on.

To add to my mental unrest, there was a cat outside making a mournful caterwaul repeatedly. My feline brain interpreted the sound as one of immense longing and grief, of searching for something lost. It filled me with despair I was unaccustomed to.

I needed it to stop.

Extricating myself from Grimm's comforting warmth, I shimmered up. He stirred, but I placed my hand on his head.

"I'll be right back. Stay here," I whispered. He obeyed, repositioning himself carefully before closing his eyes again.

It was late, and the manor was dark and silent. I slowly made my way out of the room, down the hall, and to the grand entryway without meeting a soul. I turned the lock and opened one of the doors wide enough to allow myself out, thankful that the door wasn't magically alarmed. Once outside, I transformed.

I smelled her instantly. Feline, female, pregnant. I tracked her scent into the gardens.

She hissed when I came into view, but there was no menace behind it, simply an empty gesture. I approached her, my hackles raised slightly.

"How did you get here?" I asked her calmly.

The silver-gray tabby crouched down, making herself look

small in a submissive gesture. "I followed your scent. I–I didn't know where to go. What to do."

My heart went out to her. She was days away from queening, and she was scared.

She let out another low yowl of mourning. "I've only ever known the hardness under my paws, the noise of traffic, the smell of many bodies and of garbage. This place is all wrong. It's spongy and open, and the smells ... I don't want to stay here, but I don't know what to do. You are the only thing that is familiar to me, even though you smell weird too. So, I followed you."

I took this as an opportunity. I walked toward her, slowly as not to spook her. She shrank away at first but must have realized I meant no ill will. I purred as we sniffed noses. She relaxed once she knew I would not attack her.

I thought over options. "I know you do not trust humans, but I also know some wonderfully kind ones. They can help you."

"Are they the ones you travel with?"

"Yes. None will hurt you; I promise. We are leaving tomorrow to travel a distance away from here. At the end of the journey is a barn. You can live there and raise your kittens in safety. The man who owns the barn helps animals who are sick or injured. He would make sure your kittens find good homes. Come with us."

She waffled. "Are you sure no harm will come to me?"

"Completely sure. I would trust these humans with my life. Do you have a name?" I asked her.

"No. But my mother once called me Pouncer. I loved pouncing on my littermates and my mother."

"Come with me. I can take you into the house to sleep with me tonight. But I have a dog with me. He will not harm you, either."

She agreed, albeit reluctantly. She had no other options, and she knew it. I led her back to the manor, only transforming long enough to lock the doors behind me. In my guest room, I introduced her to Grimm, who politely offered his body warmth to the both of us. Pouncer was intimidated by the large dog, but comfort won out in the end. Together, the four of us cuddled, and at last, my exhausted mind gave in to sleep.

CHAPTER 34

The courtyard was a buzz of activity the next morning. I came downstairs with Grimm at my heels, Pouncer in my arms, and Lucky on my shoulder. The mouse was wary of the cat I carried, but I told both of them firmly that there was to be no eating of anyone that kept my company. Besides, the gray tabby was feeling off and assured me that she was in no condition to hunt.

I had expected a carriage with horses attached for our departure, but what instead greeted me was a mechanical carriage of larger proportions than I was used to encountering. A cab at the front was large enough to fit two people, the driver and a passenger; the body was a box with doors on either side, with comfortable bench seats positioned at the front and the back to face each other, like a stagecoach.

I sneered at the contraption. Gavin, who had been inspecting the engine compartment, caught my expression and smiled as he came over.

"I know, I know, you don't like MCs," he surmised. "But this will make the trip go much faster. We are over one hundred and fifty miles away from Knobby Hill, which would have taken three days of travel and a change of horses for each day to make the journey as quick as possible. This baby will get us there in just under twenty-four hours. Fleurette agreed with my reasoning and offered to take the first driving shift."

"Oh, she did, did she?" Fleurette was sometimes full of surprises.

"Yes, she did," Fleurette's voice startled me, sneaking up from behind. I turned to her. She carried a basket of food, which she passed to Gavin. Roger trailed behind her. "Gavin makes an excellent point, Cress. The sooner we get back, the sooner we can help Mr. Curtain with regaining his feet."

"And you can drive?" I clarified.

She laughed. "Of course! Dad does own an MC for his work. I learned to drive on it. It's a similar size to this one. You and I can take the first shift in the cab. Let the boys have some time in the carriage for a bit."

The implication was clear that she wanted a chance to speak with me alone. I glanced at the MC, worrying at my lower lip with my teeth. The cab was completely separated from the body, which meant two metal walls between us and the other passengers, which further meant it was safe from eavesdropping.

"Let's do it," I declared firmly.

"Excellent!" Gavin clapped his hands together with exuberance. "Ladies, enjoy. Roger, you're with me. Would you like forward or backward facing?"

"Don't forget Grimm!" I called out to the men as they positioned themselves. My partner grumbled but jumped into the body, claiming the floor between the seats. I marched over once Gavin was seated and held out Pouncer for him.

"What's this?" he asked, confused.

"This is called a cat." I placed her on his lap, despite his hands being held out in protest.

"I can see that, but why is it on my lap?"

"She is heavily pregnant and feeling uncomfortable today. She's also feral and has a distrust of humans. Since you have a distrust of cats, I thought you would make an excellent pairing, and maybe you two could learn to change some of your individual mindsets for the better if you got to know each other during the trip."

Before he could protest further, I extracted my head from the interior, shooting my father a quick wink when I saw the look of amusement grace his face at my words, and shut the door firmly.

As I had suspected, Fleurette wasted little time in asking for the story of our adventures during the ball and subsequent capture. I filled her in, detailing as much as possible, except when it came to the personal developments between myself and Gavin.

She listened intently, until I got to the part where we were discovered in the study. "So, Gregory Elkins, the same man that posed as the Ramberts' great-uncle *and* who put the bounty out on Fal when that failed, is the same man who framed your father? All to get information about your mother's whereabouts?"

"Yep. He was also behind the capturing of cats, for *decades*. I think his hope was to nab the latest of Glivver's line in order to put an end to the legacy. Elkins wants Annie Coddle to return, and he knows breaking the prophecy is the way to do it." I paused, thinking. "What's incredible is that he was nearly successful, considering he had caught not one, but two of my relatives. And the number of people willing to work for him! How can so many follow someone for such nefarious purposes?"

"Gregory Elkins is an influential leader, obviously. There will always be a section of a population willing to support someone no matter how corrupt their ideals seem to rational people. Elkins is no different. But it makes me wonder why he and his followers want Annie Coddle to return. What is their connection?"

I shrugged. "Beats me. But these people, these ACFers? I have the feeling they're not going to stop their plans over a single waterlogged building. I suspect more trouble down the road."

"ACFers?" Fleurette repeated with a wry smile. "Is that what we're calling them now?"

"Sure, why not? After what they just put me through, there's some less mild 'f' names that I could call them."

She shook her head at my flippancy. "Fair enough. Anyway, what happened after you were knocked out by Elkins?"

I continued my tale, explaining how Gavin and I had woken up in the wooden box together. I felt my face heat up as I recalled our steamy kiss, but I did not tell Fleurette about it. She was a step ahead of me, however.

"Something happened between you two, didn't it?"

I let out a small groan. "Yes. But the curse kicked in and stopped anything big from happening. At least I know how the curse works now. It killed any romantic ideas I had with Gavin very quickly."

"I knew it!" she crowed, too happily. "I'm sorry about your lust getting killed, but you knew he wasn't your true love anyway. But I could tell that you and Gavin had changed how you felt about each other. It was obvious in the way he was acting after his rescue. Do you trust him now?"

I pursed my lips to the side in thought. "I suppose I do. I let him know I had secrets I couldn't divulge, and he respected that. It was more than I would trust with any other outsider."

Fleurette nodded like she was expecting that answer. "I feel the same way after interacting with him. I'm going to keep an eye on him. He may be a candidate for a future GOG."

"Gavin?" I sputtered. "You can't be serious."

"Why not? You trust him, and we are down a couple of members. Fal and Wren won't be ready to take their parents' places for a few more years, at least. It's just an idea, but one I'm going to bookmark for the near future if this trend continues. We may need all the help we can get."

I hadn't thought about the hole the passing of the Ramberts had left in the society. Fleurette's idea made sense, although I couldn't imagine bringing Gavin into the fold just yet.

I continued my telling once Fleurette had finished her Gavin tangent. I described the horrors of the Addelboro Correctional Facility and my ultimate fight with Hobbs. I stalled as I described how I bested him.

"You were right," I admitted. "I held the shimmer for a couple of seconds longer, and it saved my life. But, Fleurette, something odd happened, too."

"What was it?"

"Hobbs threw a fireball through my shimmer state. When I transformed into my human form, I was able to use his fire magic for a bit. It ran out after using it a handful of times."

"Really? Well, dear, let's examine that. What are you when you are in the shimmer?"

I thought about that. "Glivver told me that when I transform, that in-between state is the closest thing to the true form of a familiar. She said that a familiar is a being of energy. When I was being attacked by Annie last summer, I was easily able to absorb the lightning spell she had placed on me because it was pure energy like myself. I took it in and shot it back out at the room until it had been used up. Do you think I did the same thing with the fire magic?"

Fleurette nodded, keeping her eyes on the road ahead. "It makes sense, doesn't it? If the fire passed through you, it could have left a trace of the energy behind, which you absorbed. Only instead of releasing it while you were still a being of energy, you kept it and became corporeal again. That allowed you to use the magic until it ran out." She glanced at me. "You're a real wonder, Cress dear. You have the ability to steal magic, however temporarily. This is something we must experiment with when we are back home."

I groaned. "More homework? Hold me back."

She chuckled, undeterred. "So what happened next?"

Her words resurfaced a memory I had not considered until now. "I went to rescue the cats as the place began to flood, and I ran into somebody who worked there."

"Okay, and?"

I took a deep breath. "Fleurette, I think ... it was your mother."

"What?" The MC swerved a little as Fleurette jerked the wheel in startlement. She corrected her steering before shooting me a glance. "What did you say?"

"She had blonde hair. Straight. Tall, like you. And her face ... I know you favored her looks over Lyle's. She looked just like you, except pale and older."

Fleurette was quiet, but her grip on the wheel blanched her knuckles.

I pressed on. "Was her name Thea?"

Fleurette's jaw flexed. "Althea."

She was clearly unsettled by this news. I didn't wish to upset her, but she needed to know. "Fleurette, she was working for ACF. She was there of her own volition. And she knew who I was as soon as she saw me. But in the end ... she let me go."

She stared ahead, her whole body tense. She swung her head in my direction. "You are *not* to say a word about this to my father, do you understand? It took him *years* to get over her departure. I will not put him through that again. Promise me, Cress. Promise that this stays between you and me."

The air in the small cabin grew heavy, constricting, intense. When I didn't immediately answer, Fleurette spoke once more, her voice taking on a commanding, echoing quality I had never heard from her before. "*Promise me!*"

"I–I promise." The pressure in the cabin faded.

Fleurette turned her head back to the road. "Good. Thank you. Let's not discuss this further. I need to wrap my head around it."

I sat there, still a little stunned at the odd sensation I thought I had felt. If I hadn't known any better, I would have guessed that Fleurette had cast a spell. But she would never have done that to me. Still, the only other time I had ever heard that echoey voice was from Annie Coddle, when I had been cursed.

It was best to appease her, since she was obviously upset. "I'm sorry, Fleurette."

She smiled, trying to regain her composure, although she still seemed on edge. I had never seen her this agitated before. "No need to be sorry," she said with forced cheer. "You've had your fill of problems recently, and now it's my turn, it seems. We all have issues. What's one more to add to the mix?"

What indeed, I thought to myself as we lapsed into silence, both of us mulling over the complexity of the implications our conversation had left us with. She was right, too. My trouble with my long-lost father, Gavin's obvious issue with his father, and now Fleurette's mother. It was all relative.

Nobody was perfect.

CHAPTER 35

The rest of our trip was uneventful, all except for about midday, when Pouncer went into labor right on Gavin's lap. He yelled for me from the back, causing Fleurette to stop the MC so that we could both investigate. He was disgusted at first, but once I explained that a cat would only give birth on a person if she truly trusted him, he softened and allowed her to stay.

After a couple of hours, the MC had five new passengers. We emptied the basket that had stored the food and lined it with a plush blanket for the new mother and her kittens. Gavin insisted on keeping the basket by his side, even when it was his turn to drive.

With Gavin, Roger, and the basket in the front for a leg, I managed to get a bit of a groom and nap in as a cat, much to my pleasure. It was bliss.

The delay we had encountered meant our journey took longer than anticipated, but by six in the morning, we rolled into Knobby Hill, having driven through the night. Fleurette was once again driving, and she parked the MC outside of the courthouse.

We all piled out, exhausted by the trip despite numerous breaks and bouts of napping. Stretching my arms, I yawned before turning to Fleurette.

"What is the plan?"

Gavin answered first. "I must go and look for Scarlet as soon as I'm able. I'll need to hire a driver to take this MC back to my father's estate as well."

I eyed the basket hanging from his arm. "I can take that if you wish."

"Actually ..." Gavin shied away from my proffered hand. "I'd like to keep Gin for now, at least until her kittens are older. She can keep me company in my room."

"Gin?"

He looked sheepish. "It means 'silver' in my mother's language. I thought it was fitting."

He had named the cat. My heart melted. "I suppose this means that cats have redeemed themselves to you?"

He shrugged his shoulders carefully so as not to jostle the basket. "I suppose it does."

I smiled. "Very well." I grew serious. "Gavin, I want to thank you. For everything. And I want you to know I'm going to have to take a hiatus from bounty hunting. That AFC organization knows who I am now and I'm not safe. I'll have to lay low, at least for a while. I suggest you do the same."

Gavin's forehead dipped in concern at my words. He carefully placed the basket down and took my hands in his own. "Concern for me? My, how you've fallen."

"I know. How could I sink this low?"

"I suppose it's a small consolation prize for the $15,000 I let slip from my fingers the moment I paired up with you."

"I would think the knowledge that you'll get well ahead of me in bounties collected would soften that blow too. We won't be neck and neck anymore."

Gavin grew serious. "But don't fret, Cressida. I'll be alright. They never got my name, but if they do put two and two together, I have a secret for you." He leaned in, the playful smile making a reappearance on his face. "St. Cloud is not my real last name."

I blinked. "It's not?"

Gavin shook his head. "I think it's no secret I don't like my father. After I left home, I decided to change my name to honor my mother. Her name was Moriko. She told me it meant 'cloud.' So, I took a snippet from my real last name and added the cloud part to it. *Voila*—St. Cloud."

"Well ... you learn something new every day."

Gavin sighed. "But please be careful. Let me know if you need anything."

I curved my lips into a sad smile. "I will. Thanks." And then he pulled me into a hug I was not expecting.

I had scarcely given his back a pat before Grimm let out a warning growl. Gavin let me go instantly. He looked at Grimm and bent down to one knee, placing his eyes at my partner's level. Grimm cocked his head in confusion.

"She's all yours again, Grimm," he told my partner with solemnity. "Thank you for letting me borrow her. Please take good care of her."

Gavin had never spoken to Grimm before, or even called him by his name. The respect shown with this simple gesture caught me off guard, making me like my fellow bounty hunter that much more. I could tell that Grimm was flummoxed by the change in demeanor too, for all he did was let out a little whine.

Gavin straightened. "I'm going to put Gin in my room, and then I'll need to search for my MC."

"Gavin, I know where your MC is. Let me help you get it back," Fleurette offered.

Gavin gave a little bow. "Thank you, Miss Williams."

Fleurette turned to me. "I'll take Gavin back to Deerhorn Manor. Before Rupert came back, I took an excursion there to see if I could find you. I saw his MC parked on the side of the road. I'll be a while. Why don't you take Roger to my father's?"

Her unspoken words were, *why don't you stop being a chicken and finally tell him who you are?* I gulped.

"Swell," I answered with a catch in my voice.

The early morning walk to Lyle's was fairly quiet. It had rained in Knobby Hill overnight, and the road beneath our feet was wet, but the smell was fresh and soothing after the high desert climate and stuffy MC ride. Grimm cavorted ahead of us, happy to be home and happy to have me back.

I was a bundle of nerves, however. The expiration date on keeping my hidden blood tie a secret was nearly past; it would not be prudent to wait any longer. Once we passed the town's boundary, I knew I had to say something. Time was running out; I could see Lyle's long driveway in the distance.

"Roger, there's something I need to tell you," I started nervously as we approached the turnoff.

"Yes, Miss Curtis?"

"Well, you see, Roger, I haven't completely been honest with you. My last name, it's not Curtis."

Roger glanced at me curiously. "What is it, then?"

I took a deep breath. "It's Curtain. My name is Cressida Curtain. I changed it because I didn't want to freak you out. You see, I have a very good reason to share the same last name as you."

Roger stopped walking, hanging on the words I was about to utter. I stopped too and turned to face him, my heart a galloping organ as I met his eyes. His expression was unreadable.

Before I lost my nerve, I blurted out, "I'm your daughter."

Roger did not move a muscle in his face. "Say again?"

I screwed my eyes shut for the briefest of moments. "I'm your daughter. You're my father."

He let out a nervous laugh. "I don't have any children."

I gestured at myself. "You do now."

"Who is your mother?" he asked, his voice a shade higher than usual. "Is it Andrea?"

I bristled. "Who is Andrea?"

Roger frowned. "An old flame from my college days. I'm sorry, Cressida. I haven't had many romantic partners. She was the only one I could think of to account for your age."

My breath whooshed out. "Yeah, no. Not Andrea. My mother is Belinda Curtain. Your wife."

Roger stared at me, cataloging my features with renewed interest. "That's not possible."

I smiled, though it was almost a grimace as I nodded in agreement. "It shouldn't be—you're right. But it's true." I fished into my vest pocket, finding the worn edges of my mother's letter. Pulling it out, I said, "She left this for you when she disappeared."

He looked shocked as he reached for it. "How did you know about this?"

I grimaced. "She told me about it. And I found it. After you ran away from Gavin and me that first time. I'm sorry to snoop, but I read it. I noticed she ended it without saying she loved you."

He looked down at the letter, trying to discreetly wipe his eyes. "I must have read this thing every day after I lost her. I couldn't understand what had changed. Why she left."

I nodded. I took a breath. "It was because of me. She left to protect me and in a roundabout way, to protect you. But she did love you, you know. She still does."

I took a shuffling step along the road, urging Roger to continue our trek. We were so close to the finish line. He continued to gaze at me in befuddlement before finally moving again, as if in a daze.

"I know it's hard to believe," I said to fill the silence.

He shook his head. "No, it's actually not all that hard to believe. I see her in you now that you've said it. The shape of your eyes, some of your mannerisms. And I can see myself too. It's a wonder I didn't catch on sooner."

"You did, on some level. It's the reason I seemed familiar to you."

"Of course. It makes sense, in a way. You seemed ... like you fit naturally with me. It's no wonder you wished to help me. You are everything a father wishes for in his children. I can't tell you how grateful I am to have found you, Cressida."

I ducked my head shyly, my eyes suddenly prickling with emotion. He accepted me as his daughter. He *liked* me.

My father wasn't finished speaking. "But the timing makes no sense. I can't wrap my head around how I could have a daughter in her twenties when I only married my wife seven years ago."

We had made it to the turnoff of Lyle's driveway. The path ahead of us was long enough that trees blocked the view of his house. I made a decision.

"Roger, you've just been framed for embezzlement and manslaughter, teamed up with an otter shifter, and escaped from a secret cult of worshipers wanting to bring Annie Coddle back to this world. Are you open to learning one more big secret?"

He looked flabbergasted before sputtering, "Well, yes, I suppose so."

"Excellent." I gave him a quick hug, one he didn't have time to reciprocate. "I'm going to run ahead and find someone you should meet. Grimm will lead you to the front porch, where we will be waiting for you."

Before he had time to respond, I ran down the driveway, rounded a small bend and disappeared from his view. As soon as I did, I transformed, sprinting the rest of the way until I screeched to a halt in front of the porch. My mother sat upon it, eyeing me like I was insane.

"Cressida, what on earth? Where did you come from?"

"Mom, I don't have much time to explain. If you had a second chance at true love, would you take it? Would you risk your great secret for the man you loved with all your heart?"

"Cressida, what are you on about?"

"*Would you?*" I practically yelled at her.

She arched her back ever so slightly at my tone. "I ... I don't know."

I sighed. My mother was obstinate to a fault. I supposed it ran in the family. "Well, now is your chance to find out."

Mom seemed poised with another question or a weak rebuttal, but she never got the chance. Grimm came into view, proudly trotting our way with Roger right behind him. My mother's eyes grew wide.

Roger approached, looking around for my human counterpart and a mystery person. But he only saw two cats, both staring at him.

"Roger," my mom breathed to herself.

My father seemed to take my disappearance in stride. "Oh, hello there," he said to us in a friendly manner. He did a double take at my mother. "I know you. You're the stray that I used to pet in the garden. How did you get here?"

This was the moment. With his attention on Mom, I shimmered, becoming human. Roger turned his head and blinked rapidly at my appearance. His mouth fell open.

"You know her because she was more than just a stray ... Dad." I tested the word out, finding it foreign yet to my liking. "Mom? This is your chance."

Roger turned his attention back to my cat mother. She looked up at me, fear in her expression, before meeting her husband's wide eyes. I saw the moment she resigned herself, as she closed her eyes and bent her head.

My heart plummeted as I thought she wouldn't transform.

But even the most stubborn of parents can surprise one, sometimes.

Her feline shape became amorphous as it shimmered prettily for just a fraction of a second. Then, before us sat my mother in her human form, clothed in her usual frumpy, brown housedress and a sharp look of distress upon her face.

"Belinda?" Roger said, his voice barely above a whisper.

"Roger," Mom answered. She looked like she was ready to bolt. She expected rejection to be next.

"All this time?" My father stepped closer to her, reaching a hand tentatively toward her face, wanting to touch her to make sure she wasn't an apparition. "Why didn't you tell me?"

Mom dropped her head, a teardrop leaking out and trailing down her nose. "I didn't know if you'd understand."

"I have spent the last three years barely alive, a shell of myself, because my reason for living had left me. This is why?"

My mother let out a sob. "I thought I had to. For her."

Roger—my dad— glanced at me. "For her? Our daughter, you mean?"

Mom straightened. "You know?"

Roger's hand cradled Mom's cheek lovingly. She leaned into the touch. "I know. Cressida told me. She's wonderful, Belinda. She's very much like you. And she's brought us back together. Forever, I hope. Because with you here, I finally feel like a whole man again."

At his words, Mom closed the gap between them, throwing herself into his arms. As their lips met in a passionate kiss, I turned away.

Nobody wants to see their parents make out, no matter how

happy the occasion.

"C'mon, Grimm. Let's let my parents reconnect in peace." I shimmered down, ready to bound through the wet grass by Grimm's side, my heart feeling lighter than it had in a while.

Love was still an elusive thing for me—I had learned this with certainty. But this truth did not weigh me down in the moment; I was too joyous that my parents were reunited and that I was the key to this happy outcome. Not only that, but my mother's fears were unfounded, and my father accepted both of us for who—and what—we were. It gave me a modicum of hope once more.

There was still a self-serving witch who would like nothing more than to destroy me, and she had a firmer grip on this world than any of us had previously suspected. But that was a worry for another day.

For now, I would rejoice in the little things that made this life so amazing. For now, all was right in my world.

It was enough.

ACKNOWLEDGMENTS

What an adventure a writer must go through to publish a book! I'm still disbelieving at times that I've written not one, but *two* novels now, with the third in the works. But Cressida's full story wants to be told, and I am happy to facilitate that for her. But, as always, I couldn't do it completely on my own.

First and foremost, I'd like to give a huge shoutout to my husband, Matt. Without him, *Unfamiliar Territory* and all subsequent books would likely have been dead in the water. He gives me encouragement when I need it, and works the "real job" so that I can pursue my dream. Thank you, Honey, for everything you do for me!

Thanks also go out to my parents for always believing in me, and to my kids, who proudly tell people that their mom is a published author. Also, to my amazing friends: Jennica, thank you for allowing me to vent when I need it, and to bounce questions off of you whenever I'm stuck; and Rachel, thanks for being my number-one fan, and for acting as a bit of a taskmaster for self-imposed deadlines. Ladies, I would not have gotten this far without you!

I am so very thankful to the professionals on my team as well. Many, many thanks go to my editor, Tina S. Beier. Tina, you have made this whole process so easy for this relative newbie, and I'm so happy to have found you. My cover artist, Angelee van Allman, continues to be a rockstar: Angelee, thanks for being able to read my mind to make your beautiful covers for me, and sorry for bugging you way more than I'd like to. And I'm so happy to have you on board as a beta reader too! Special appreciation goes to my proofreader, Cynthia Ley, for the last polish, as well as Nanci Remington, who gives the book one last set of eyeballs before it goes out to you.

I'd also like to mention NIWA (Northwest Independent Writer's Association) for being a great organization for questions and general support from fellow indie authors. I think my writing journey would look very different indeed without this great group.

But the last acknowledgements go to you, dear readers. Without your interest in my books, there would be no point. Your reviews, your newsletter signups, and your overall support all keep me going and let me know that this isn't all for naught. Thank you for believing in me! Together, we can tell the full story of The Familiar's Legacy. I can't wait!

ABOUT THE AUTHOR

R. Lindsay Carter wanted to be a zookeeper when she was a girl. Now, she is content to stick with her small menagerie at home, which includes her supportive husband and her two daughters. When she isn't in the throes of writing, you can find R. Lindsay creating art, reading, gardening, ignoring household chores, and otherwise lounging about, usually with her lap taken up by her dog and/or one of her three cats. Born and raised in the Pacific Northwest, R. Lindsay happily lives in Oregon.

BOOKS BY R. LINDSAY CARTER

The Familiar's Legacy:
Unfamiliar Territory
Relative Truths
Chasing Tails
Curtain Call

CONNECT

Follow R. Lindsay Carter for all the latest news!

Social Media:

https://www.rlindsaycarter.com

https://www.facebook.com/rlindsaycarter

https://www.instagram.com/author_rlindsaycarter

https://www.tiktok.com/@author_rlindsaycarter

Newsletter:

https://www.rlindsaycarter.com/newsletter/